"I could spend my whole life locked up in here," she whispered to the bird. "They keep me for my pretty colors and my song, and one day my youth will be withered and gone, like a flower pressed inside a book. But I will find a way out."

There was really only one way out, of course. And he was still at Rhodes, where they said he was building a new villa on Mount Philermus, overlooking the fortress. She was his, they told her, he possessed her; but she had not even seen him, and she had been in his dark and pretty prison for nearly two seasons.

Well, there had to be some way. She would not spend her days idly dreaming of some miracle that might bring her to his bed. She would wake the Devil himself and light all the fires of Hell under this Palace, but she would find some way to displace the Montenegran and find her way out.

They would regret the day they ever allowed this hell-cat into their cage of birds.

Until then she would wait.

So let him come.

She would wait.

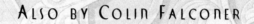

THE
SULTAN'S HAREM

A NOVEL

COLIN
FALCONER

CROWN PUBLISHERS • NEW YORK

For Anna Powell and Bill Massey,

with my thanks

Published by Crown Publishers, New York, New York.
Member of the Crown Publishing Group, a division of Random House, Inc.
New York, Toronto, London, Sydney, Auckland

Originally published in Great Britain by Hodder and Stoughton,
a division of Hodder Headline PLC, London, in 1992.

CROWN is a trademark and the Crown colophon is a registered trademark of
Random House, Inc.

Printed in the United States of America

Design by Lauren Dong

ISBN 0-609-61030-9

Acknowledgments

No book is written alone. I would like, as always, to thank my agents, Tim Curnow in Sydney and Anthea Morton-Saner in London, for their help and encouragement; Anne Mullarkey and her staff from the West Australian Library service for locating the vast number of books I needed for research; the staff of the British Museum Reading Room in London for their help in finding reference works; to my wife, Helen, for her endless encouragement and patience, even when I became a little difficult to live with, though I am sure my friends will find that hard to believe; to Anna Powell and Nick Sayers for their enthusiasm and their vision; and finally to Bill Massey, my editor, who sees the wood when I only see the trees. May the saints bless and guard him.

Foreword

Many of the background events in this novel can be found in histories of the Ottomans in this period. However, what can never be known is what happened behind the iron-studded doors of the Sublime Porte to give birth to so much violence and passion. In this respect, then, this is a work of fiction. Only the long dead could ever tell us how much is true.

The extract of poetry at the end of the book is from an actual work by Süleyman.

Pardedâri mikunad dar kasr-i-Káysar ankebût.

The spider spins her web in the
palace of the Caesars.

—A VERSE FROM SA'ADI

Contents

PROLOGUE

Topkapi Saraya, Istanbul, 1990

ONCE THERE WAS SILENCE.
Once a man would have had the flesh flayed from the soles of his feet for raising his voice above a whisper in this court of plane and chestnut trees, the sanctum of Allah's Deputy on Earth, the Lord of the Lords of this world, Possessor of Men's Necks, King of Believers and Unbelievers, Emperor of the East and West, Refuge of all the People in the Whole World, the Shadow of the Almighty Dispensing Quiet in the Earth.

Once, only the murmur of pages and viziers disturbed the grazing deer and parades of peacock, as the business of an empire that encompassed the Seven Wonders of the World was conducted in somber tones.

Once there was silence.

Now Mercedes buses rumble through the Sublime Porte, past the sleeping Church of St. Irene, and the fountain where the *bostanji-bashi* washed the blood from his sword after each execution. Now the gray-haired and superannuated executives from Frankfurt and Chicago and Osaka, Canons slung from their necks, their wives giggling like schoolgirls, are ushered through the crush at the Ortakapi by guides wearing Ray-Bans who do not even remark on the niches in the walls high above them, once the resting places for the heads of the Sultan's viziers.

Beyond the Ortakapi, a few yards from the Hall of the Divan, there is a sign on the stone wall that reads: "The Harem." Four elderly matrons from Ohio pose underneath while one of their husbands focuses a Minolta.

"Don't lean on the wall, Doris," he drawls. "I don't know if it can take the weight."

The great black doors swing open, and the tour is herded inside, into the cool and cobbled darkness. A young Turkish man in an open-necked shirt and unpressed trousers, his English distorted only a little by his lisp, stands to one side and addresses them over the whir and click of the cameras.

"*Harem* means 'Forbidden,' " he tells them. "Forbidden to men. Once the Sultan himself was the only man—complete man—who could have passed through that gate. And any woman who entered here might never walk out again."

Once there was silence here. It was broken not by the shouts of war and invasion, but by laughter. The laughter of a woman.

But first there was silence.

PART 1

THE SPIDER'S WEB

1

Rhodes, 1522

ILENCE, BUT FOR the steady rhythm of the rain, splashing into blood-stained pools, dripping from the eaves of the tents. Camels and men trudged through the mud; even the nostrils of the beasts of burden twitched at the stench of sick men and poor sanitation, but most of all at the reek of the moat.

The moat around the fortress was sixty feet deep and one hundred and forty feet wide, and in places it had been almost filled with the bloated bodies of the dead. The smell of putrefying corpses pervaded everything, seeping into clothes and hair and skin, pungent even in the silken sanctum of the Sultan's tent itself, despite the incense burners and the perfumed handkerchiefs that the assembled generals held to their noses.

The young man who sat with his legs astride the mother-of-pearl and tortoiseshell throne looked like a panther poised to spring. His lips were drawn back from his teeth in a snarl as he listened to the mumbled obeisance of his second vizier. His long artist's fingers curled and uncurled into claws, the face below the silken turban pale with rage.

"How many of your Sultan's men did you lose today?" he hissed, referring to himself, as he always did in public, as if he were some other person.

The second vizier's face was blackened with dried blood from a sword slash on his forehead. It had dried and crusted in his black beard, where it glowed, dully, like a thousand small rubies. Half a dozen times that day he had led the charge to the breach in the wall below the towers of St. Michael and St. John, while the grizzled old veterans of the Cross slashed down his *azabs* with their broadswords and their arrows. Women and children had torn up paving stones from the streets and hurled them down on their heads from the ramparts. He had even seen one of their pale priests take a turn at the walls to help upend the vats of boiling pitch. Some of his men had run, their nerve broken; Mustapha had cut them down with his sword, then rallied his soldiers again for a renewed effort.

And now, for the first time that day, he was afraid.

"How many men?" the young man on the throne repeated.

Mustapha dared to raise his head a little to stare into the Sultan's eyes. Oh, great God. "Twenty thousand, Lord," he whispered.

"Twenty thousand!" He leaped to his feet and every man in the room—except one—took a pace backward.

In the long silence that followed, several of the generals thought they could hear Mustapha try to swallow.

When Sultan Süleyman spoke again, his voice was soft and sibilant. Like the death rattle in a man's throat, Mustapha thought. "You advocated this expedition. For three centuries the infidels have taunted the Osmanlis from this fortress. Even the Fatih and my father Selim could not dislodge them. But you told your Sultan that this time it would be different!"

Mustapha was silent. He knew there could be no excuse for failure. Besides, he could not be sure his men would follow him to the walls again.

The silk of Süleyman's robes rippled in the light of the oil lamps as his body shook with the force of his rage. His hands were clenched into white fists at his side. A froth of spittle had formed in the corners of his mouth.

"Another twenty thousand of your Sultan's army lie in the mud at the foot of this accursed rock, the rest are afflicted with the pestilence, and still the walls stand! Winter is at hand; even now the storms are boiling on the horizon, ready to shatter the fleet and freeze the rest of your Sultan's army. Yet if Süleyman turns away now, it will be to drag the banner of the Osmanli, the banner of Islam, in the dirt! You brought your Sultan to Rhodes. What will you have him do now?"

Mustapha was silent.

"You advised this!" he screamed, and he stabbed his finger at the second vizier as if it were an iron spike. He turned to the bostanji waiting in the shadows, a sullen and malevolent presence. He made a quick motion with his hands to summon the deaf-mute and screamed, "Execute him!"

The negro strode forward and shoved Mustapha to his knees with one expert motion of his left leg and arm. The bands of muscle in the man's back tensed as he brought his *killiç* above his head to strike.

It was old Piri Pasha, the Grand Vizier, who moved first. He stepped forward, both hands held upward in supplication, momentarily distracting the bostanji. The blade of the killiç glittered in the light of the oil lamps.

"Great Lord, please! Spare him! Misguided he may be, but he has fought like a lion in front of the walls! I have seen him—"

"Quiet!" Süleyman screamed, and now there was saliva on his beard. "If you think he is so worthy, then you can join him in Paradise!"

It was as if an unseen hand had swept the room with a scythe. Piri Pasha! He was an old man, the Vizier who had survived Selim the Grim, and had been Süleyman's own tutor as a child. He himself had advised against the attack on Rhodes. The generals and counselors assembled in front of the young Sultan fell on their faces, each of them moaning forbearance.

It was only Ibrahim, the falconer, who dared approach him. "My Lord," he whispered, and took Süleyman's hand. He knelt, and kissed the ruby on the ring finger of his right hand.

Süleyman was about to summon his bostanji for a third commission when he recognized the young man at his feet.

"Ibrahim!"

"Great Lord, there is another way."

Süleyman seemed about to pull away from the young man, who still held his hand in both of his. Instead he said: "Tell it, then."

"The histories tell us that the Greeks besieged Troy for fourteen years for the sake of a woman. Will not the Turk, then, oppressed by piracies and invasions from this rock for over three centuries, endure one winter's siege?"

The bostanji shifted his weight. The killiç was growing heavy.

"What is your counsel, Ibrahim?"

"They say that when one of the Roman Caesars invaded an island, he would burn his fleet on the beach. Great Lord, perhaps if you were to build a villa on this hill, in full view of the castle, the defenders will know there is to be no reprieve until the fortress is ours. It will crush their spirit. And if our soldiers know your conviction also, it will give them heart."

Süleyman sighed, and eased himself back on to the great throne. With his forefinger he caressed one of the turquoise stones inlaid near the arm. "And what of them?" he said, nodding in the direction of the two men who still knelt, heads bowed, below the killiç. He looked at old Piri Pasha and winced. How could he have contemplated such a thing?

"There has been too much Turkish blood spilled today already," Ibrahim said.

What a diplomat you are! Süleyman thought. An almost imperceptible shake of the head and the bostanji vanished once more into the shadows.

"Very well," Süleyman told them. "The Sultan stays."

The Eski Saraya (the Old Palace), Stamboul

THE HAWK RODE the currents high above the city, its serrated wingtips dipping and tilting to each updraft and sheer. It floated two hundred feet above the great sea walls of Stamboul and its squalid, cobbled streets, where legless beggars pleaded for alms and flies hovered in black clouds over the melon rinds, even above the soaring domes and minarets of the mosques, now turning rose-gray in the settling dusk; its golden, unblinking eye focused on a young woman on the terrace of the Eski Saraya.

She was a striking figure, standing alone high on the walls of the Palace. Indeed, even among the three hundred women of the Harem, she was conspicuous for the two braids, tied with satin cord, that hung halfway down her back. Her hair was the color of fire, burnished yellows and golds and reds that shimmered in the sunlight, almost as if they might at any moment crackle like flame, a stunning contrast with her green eyes and pale Tartar complexion. She was tall and slim, still awkward with the echoed mannerisms of her youth.

Her face was turned to the northeast, beyond the distant hills of Rumelia, to a place far across the violet horizon; it was out of sight, yet she saw it. It was a place where the dry grass reached so high in summer that it almost touched a rider's girdle, a place where salt marshes gleamed in the moonlight, where a horseman could ride three days and nights and not encounter another living soul.

And as she thought of it, her lips parted slightly, and she let out a small cry that startled the nightingale that lived under the eaves of the terrace, trapped, like her, in an elaborate cage.

"I could spend my whole life locked up in here," she whispered to the bird. "They keep me for my pretty colors and my song, and one day my youth will be withered and gone, like a flower pressed inside a book. But I will find a way out."

There was really only one way out, of course. And he was still at Rhodes, where they said he was building a new villa on Mount Philermus, overlooking the fortress. She was his, they told her, he possessed her; but she had not even see him, and she had been in his dark and pretty prison for nearly two seasons.

They said he did not look at any of the women anyway. His favorite was Gülbehar, the Montenegran, the one they called "Rose of Spring." He ignored the other concubines, even though he owned three hundred of the most beautiful women in an empire that stretched from Babylon to Belgrade, each of them hand picked for him.

Well, there had to be some way. She would not spend her days idly dreaming of some miracle that might bring her to his bed. She would wake the Devil himself and light all the fires of Hell under this Palace, but she would find some way to displace the Montenegran and find her way out.

They would regret the day they ever allowed this hell-cat into their cage of birds.

Until then she would wait.

So let him come.

She would wait.

Rhodes

IT WAS THE day the Christians called the Feast of Saint Nicholas, when Süleyman entered the towns of St. Nicholas and St. Angelo, inside the crumbling walls of the fortress that had been the cherished prize of his father and even his great-grandfather, Fatih, the Conqueror. Already, at twenty-eight, he had achieved what they had only dreamed of. He had removed a thorn from the side of the Osmanli Empire; he had wrested Rhodes from the Knights of St. John.

"They say the Colossus once stood here. Now there is another."

Süleyman turned in the saddle. It was Ibrahim, grinning hugely, his Arab stallion prancing and fighting for its head, as if it had somehow absorbed some of its owner's ebullience through the saddle.

"It was your wise counsel that prevailed," Süleyman said simply.

"It's Christmas Day! Do you think they'll be celebrating now in St. Peter's Square?"

Süleyman looked across the square at a group of bearded knights praying on their knees outside their langue, their chivalric crest carved into the stone above the doorway. They were all scarred, one of them with a fresh pink cicatrix across his face, the skin smeared like mud around the place where his eye had been; another had a seeping bloodied bandage on an arm without a hand. They mumbled their prayers together, oblivious to the clanking of armor and steel and the smell of horse as the *yeniçeris* and his own *solak* bodyguard marched past them; they ignored the cannon booming in victory outside the gates and the fluttering of the green and white banners around them. It was not they who had surrendered; it was finally the burghers of Rhodes who had sued first for truce.

"They have nothing to celebrate," Süleyman said.

Ibrahim reined his horse closer, and dropped his voice to a whisper. "My Lord, you perplex me. You have won the greatest victory for the House of Osmanli since the Fatih took Constantinople. Do you not rejoice?"

"Those men fought bravely, Ibrahim. There is no bloodlust in me. It is our duty to Islam to conquer. We do not have to revel in it."

Ibrahim tried to keep his impatience from his face. But Süleyman knew what he was thinking, and allowed himself a tight smile.

"I amuse you, my Lord?"

"You always amuse me, Ibrahim. You know that."

Ibrahim looked at the ranks of white-plumed soldiers, with their long mustaches and harquebuses slung over their shoulders. They reminded him of rabid dogs on a leash. "You will let the yeniçeris have their day?"

"No, Ibrahim, I gave my word. Not this time."

"They only fight for the spoils you give them. They are like dogs feeding on scraps. You know what happens to a hungry dog."

"They will have to go hungry a while longer. There will be no looting here."

"We faced utter defeat here. You are extraordinarily compassionate, my Lord."

By Ibrahim's tone, Süleyman knew he did not think that at all. He thought he had forgotten the last four months. He would not have allowed any other man to dare speak to him that way. But Ibrahim, well . . .

Besides, Ibrahim was wrong. He had not forgotten; how could a man forget the reek of blood, the slightly sweet, nauseating smell of corpses rotting in the mud, or the screams of men dying in ditches, piled like hedgerows. How could he forget the sight of a once proud army dying by inches from pestilence in mud and freezing rain? But in the end God's Will had prevailed.

"So what now, my Lord?" Ibrahim said.

Süleyman thought of the Eski Saraya, and his favorite, Gülbehar. There he would find peace. There a woman's soothing touch could help a man forget such nightmares.

Perhaps she could help him forget also the terrible moment when he had discovered his own father in himself; if it were not for Ibrahim he would have executed his first and second viziers together. Even Selim had never done that.

He was shaken at this discovery of the Beast in his own soul. It had scarred him even more deeply than the carnage that had summoned it from the dark places inside him. He had never suspected that there lurked inside him such fury, such a spirit intransigent of spite. Without Ibrahim, he would have unleashed it. Without Ibrahim, the Beast might destroy him still.

He shuddered. "Let us go home," he said.

3

The Eski Saraya

W HEN A NEW slave girl was brought to the Harem, she immediately received instruction in the language of the Osmanli court and the Qur'ān; she was also assigned to one of the Harem functionaries for training in a specific duty.

Hürrem had been given to the Kiaya of the Silk Room, the Mistress of the Robes, an embittered Circassian with skin the color and consistency of leather who still clung to the memory of one fruitless night spent with Sultan Bayezid, Süleyman's grandfather. Now she lived out the remains of her life among the bolts of brocades and damask and satin, taffetas and velvet, the embroidered robes, chemises, and veils in various stages piled on the tables around her, her temper growing worse each day.

Hürrem enjoyed her position, or rather, she had decided to make the best of it. She had nimble fingers and a good eye, and her handkerchiefs had brought approving murmurs from the Sultan Valide, the Sultan's mother, the preeminent power in the Harem.

So she hummed a tune to herself as she worked, embroidering a square of green Diba satin—the best satin in the world, the Kiaya had told her, from Stamboul—with gold and silver thread, sewing an intricate pattern of leaves and flowers into the cloth.

She became engrossed in the work, and began to sing softly to herself, a song she had learned from her father, a Tartar song about the steppes and the north wind.

She did not hear the Kiaya enter the room behind her, but she felt the stinging slap on the ear. She started with shock, and dropped the silver needle onto the floor.

She jumped to her feet, ready to strike, and the Kiaya's eyes gleamed wickedly. "Go on! Hit me, you little minx! I'll have the Kapi Aga put you to the *bastinado!*"

Hürrem flushed beet red to the roots of her hair with fury, but lowered her hand.

"You do not sing here, little minx," the Kiaya told her. "I have told you before. This is the Harem. There is always silence."

"I like to sing."

"What you like does not matter. It is what the Great Lord wants."

"He isn't even here. We could discharge a cannon in the corridor and he would be none the wiser."

"Insolent little minx!" The Kiaya slapped her again, but this time Hürrem was ready for her and did not cry out. She took the blow, then shook her head like a puppy shaking water droplets from its fur. Her mouth twisted into a mocking smile, even though the Kiaya's open hand had left a pink imprint on her cheek.

"It is the Law!" the Kiaya shouted at her.

Hürrem leaned closer to her and whispered, "Keep your voice down. The Sultan might hear! He hates noise!"

The Kiaya turned away from her and picked up the handkerchief she had been embroidering and examined it critically, looking for fault. Finding none, she dropped it back on the bench with a practiced look of disgust. "Get on with your work!"

Hürrem shared the work with a raven-haired Jewish girl who had been bought from slave traders in Alexandria. "Market meat," the Kiaya called her. Her name was Meylissa and she had long legs and thin wrists and the quick, nervous movements of a sparrow. Out of the corner of her eye Hürrem could see her bent over the silk cushion cover she was embroidering, trying to make herself invisible. But she was too tempting a target for the Kiaya in her present mood.

"Let me see that," the Kiaya said, and snatched the piece of silk and brocade from Meylissa's fingers. Her lip curled into a snarl. "Look at this! The finest Bursa brocade and you've ruined it!" She slapped the younger girl smartly around the head. "What were you thinking of? Look at these stitches! A child could have done better!"

Meylissa bowed her head and said nothing. The Kiaya threw the material on the floor and slapped the girl again. "Undo all those stitches and start again! And don't expect any supper until it's finished. Do you hear?"

She turned and swept out of the room.

"Fat old hindbreath of a camel!" Hürrem said, tossing back her mane of hair. She sat down at the bench and started singing once more, louder than before. Silence is the Law! What nonsense!

She heard a tiny, muffled sound behind her and turned around. Meylissa was sobbing, her head on her arms, her thin body shuddering with the force of her despair.

"Meylissa, what's wrong? Meylissa . . . don't let her upset you! She's a hag! I've seen more intelligence excreted from the back end of a horse."

But Meylissa only shook her head, and the sobs came harder, her long fingers clawing at the rough benchtop, the nails rasping against the wood.

"Meylissa?"

Hürrem stood up, trying to curb her impatience. Really! Hadn't the girl ever been slapped before? She sat down at the bench next to her and put a hand on her shoulder, pulling her upright.

"Stop this!"

"It's not her . . ."

"What then? . . . Meylissa? Whatever's wrong?"

Suddenly Hürrem saw it, plain in the girl's huge brown eyes. She realized it was not the Kiaya who had done this to her. It was terror: naked, white eyed and desperate.

Merciful Heaven, what had she done? "Meylissa?"

Meylissa's eyes searched her face, the terror vying with a desperate need to confess, to trust.

"It's all right," Hürrem heard herself saying. "You can tell me."

"They'll kill me," Meylissa whispered.

"No one wants to kill you. Unless they mean to bore us to death with sewing . . ."

"You don't understand."

"Of course I don't. You haven't told me anything."

Meylissa clutched at the lap of her kaftan, bunching the material into a hard, brown ball. "I'm pregnant," she whispered.

At first, Hürrem thought she had misheard her. "What?"

"I'm pregnant. I know it. I've missed my bleed."

Hürrem wanted to laugh out loud. Pregnant! In this ladies' prison! And she thought this little Jewess was stupid! How on earth had she managed it?

"You've made a mistake."

Meylissa had stopped crying now. "It's not a mistake."

"How?"

Meylissa looked over Hürrem's shoulder. Hürrem could see the Adam's Apple bobbing in the brown girl's throat. In the dingy room the whites of her eyes glowed like enormous pearls. "The Kapi Aga."

The Kapi Aga! The Captain of the Guards, the Chief White Eunuch! Hürrem's mouth fell open in astonishment. Although he was in charge of the Harem Guard, he was never supposed to be alone with any of the girls, as he was not *rasé*—a complete eunuch—like the negroes. They said most of the white eunuchs had only been partly castrated, their testicles having been tied or crushed, like young lambs. Was it possible . . . ?

"He's supposed to be a eunuch."

"Of course he's a eunuch! Do you think I would have fucked a whole man? In here?"

Hürrem was shocked. Not only at the word—prim little Meylissa!—but at how in Meylissa's mind their roles were reversed. She thought Hürrem was the stupid one. And of course, the loner always thinks she is smarter than the rest, Hürrem thought. How naïve she had been! While she was still wrestling with the new language, thinking herself superior for her education and her upbringing, these farmers' daughters had already worked out how to smuggle in cucumbers and get themselves bedded.

But at least I am not pregnant, Hürrem thought.

"But if he's a eunuch . . ."

"They say sometimes a man . . . can regenerate. Even the black eunuchs, they have to check them every year to make sure nothing grows back."

"What nonsense! When you geld a horse, it stays gelded."

"But the white eunuchs, you know . . . they are not rasé—their things are not shaved off—like the black ones."

They were silent for a while. Meylissa was calmer now; talking had helped her. Hürrem continued to stare at her, appalled. Pregnant!

"But how?"

Meylissa glanced toward the door again and continued in a low whisper. "There's a courtyard at the northern end of the Palace. It's surrounded by high walls, and shaded with plane trees. There's a door in the wall, but it's always locked and there's never a guard."

"What were you doing there?"

"I was learning my Qur'ān, as we were instructed."

Hürrem almost smiled. Perhaps God had willed it! "Go on."

"He must have seen me. Perhaps from the northern tower. I heard a key in the lock. I was going to run away but . . ."

Hürrem cocked her head, waiting for this "but"; instead Meylissa only shrugged. "He said I was the most beautiful woman in the Harem. He said he would help me catch the Sultan's eye."

"How many times did it happen?"

"Five, perhaps six times."

"Six times! You know what they would have done to you if they had caught you?"

"They have caught me," Meylissa said, "haven't they?"

Hürrem was silent. She wondered what she would have done, if it had been her sitting in the shaded garden reading the Qur'ān. Probably the same thing. Anything, even mortal danger, was preferable to the stifling boredom in this dingy Palace. And the daily steam baths and massages they made you take, they had stirred something inside her. All this indolence and pampering worked on you like an aphrodisiac. But there was no man to take away the ache.

"What was it like?" Hürrem asked her.

"What was it like? What does it matter what it was like?" Meylissa hissed. "They are going to kill me. Do you know what they do to a Harem girl who gets pregnant without being bedded by the Sultan? They tie her in a sack and throw her in the Bosphorus!"

"I'll help you," Hürrem heard herself say.

"How can you help me? What could you do?"

"You'll see. I'll help you. You'll see!"

4

The Eski Saraya

THE ROOM WAS as he had remembered it. For the first time since he had entered Stamboul in triumph three days before, Süleyman felt he had come home. He threw himself on the wall couch. As he flung off his silk turban he tossed aside that other self, the Sultan of the Osmanlis, the man who was becoming more a stranger to himself day by day. He ran a hand across the smooth, shaved outline of his head to the scalplock at the crown of his skull. Ever since he had inherited the throne from his father three years before, he had had the feeling of looking out at the world from a darkened room and watching himself, like an actor in a shadow play. Even in his diaries he referred to himself in the third person.

He sighed, and his shoulders sagged. They called the Grand Vizier the "bearer of the burden." But the Grand Vizier was only a juggler, a balancing act of flattery, mathematics, and duplicity. It was the Sultan who truly carried the burden, the weight of Islam, and the needs of six million Turks; and that weight would be with him now until the day he died.

But here, in the silence of the Harem, there was respite. Here, there was scented wood burning in the tall copper hearth, the firelight rippling like the reflection from a fountain on the tiled walls. Here the silver incense burners hung smoldering from the ceiling, chasing away for a while the rank smell of blood that he had carried with him in his memory from Rhodes. Here there were no viziers, no generals, no protocols, no responsibilities. Here there was Gülbehar.

Süleyman heard the rustle of fabric as she entered through a rose damask curtain at the far end of the room. He looked up at her, feeling a mixture of relief, pleasure, and desire. Her long fair hair was tied in a single long braid down her back and the glow of the fire outlined the shape of her face in shades of ochre and pink. She wore a chemise—a *gömlek*—of almost transparent sky-blue silk, two diamond buttons shimmering and dancing against her flesh as she walked. Like sunlight rippling on water, he thought. Her waistcoat was of rich blue Bursa brocade, her long pantaloons falling in a white waterfall of silk to her ankles. There were pearls in her hair.

Gülbehar, Rose of Spring, he thought. How well they named you.

She fell on her knees and touched her forehead to the carpet. "Sala'am. Lord of my Life. Sultan of Sultans, Lord of the World. King of Kings."

He motioned to her impatiently. How many times had he told her there was no need? But she always greeted him this way, adhering to the formula. Right now he did not wish to be reminded who he was. He was a man come home; that was enough.

"Come here."

She almost ran the last few steps and buried her face in his neck. He felt the wetness of her tears on his neck and the scent of dried jasmine from her hair.

"When there was white on the minarets and you still had not returned, I thought perhaps you were never coming back. I am so frightened without you. There are so many whispers." She pulled away from him and stared into his face for the first time. "You were not hurt?"

"No scars that will ever show," Süleyman said, and for some reason he thought of Piri Pasha and how he had ordered the death of his boyhood mentor. If Ibrahim had not been there . . . ? Perhaps he was a tyrant like his father, after all. "How is Mustapha?"

"He is sleeping. He has missed you," she added. "He talks of you often."

He hardly knows me anymore, Süleyman thought. "Let me see him."

Gülbehar took his hand and led him through the apartment to the Prince's bedchamber. A candle burned in a long golden candlestick at one corner of the bed, attended by a turbaned page. Another page stood in the shadows at the other corner of the bed. If the boy turned in his sleep the candle would be extinguished and the other lit, so that there would never be a light shining directly on his face.

Süleyman leaned over the mattress. Mustapha had fair hair like his mother, and the same handsome, serene face. He was nine years old now, growing tall, as skilled at throwing a javelin as he was at learning the Qur'ān and reading mathematics. The next Osmanli Sultan, Süleyman thought. Enjoy your youth while you can. It is good you are growing broad shoulders.

He was struck again by the irony of having a son who looked so little like him, even less like one of the Turks whose ruler he would one day become. But every Sultan's wife was a slave and a Christian, since the Qur'ān decreed that no Muslim could be sold in slavery. So every Sultan was the son of a slave, the son of a Christian, yet divinely chosen as the Protector of the Great Faith. God's web was indeed a large one.

"He is well?" Süleyman said.

"He grows taller every day. He wants to be like his father."

Süleyman smiled in the darkness. Gülbehar, how transparent you are! Already you are courting my favor. It is terrible how all Osmanli sons learn to fear their fathers so much. But with good reason.

He touched Mustapha's forehead with his fingertips. The boy's jaw had fallen open in sleep. He looked like an infant again. "Bless you, my son," Süleyman whispered. Mustapha murmured in his sleep and rolled over.

Süleyman turned to Gülbehar. Her silhouette was outlined against the candle flame. Desire was like a physical blow, deep in the pit of his stomach. He wanted to take her now, pour his seed into her, like a flood, like a river, then sob on her breast like a baby. But that would not do.

Instead he said: "We should eat now."

Gülbehar brought the food herself, tiny squares of lamb cooked in aromatic herbs, pieces of chicken baked over a slow fire, eggplants stuffed with rice. Afterward there were figs in sour cream and sherbet from a cold gold goblet. Silent pages refilled their cups and bowls.

"What is the talk around the Harem?" Süleyman asked her. It always amused him to hear the gossip. And it was the barometer of his strength as Sultan also.

"They talk of you as a great hero," Gülbehar said, and he could see that she had assumed some of the glory as her own. "When the news came that you had conquered Rhodes, they said you would be remembered by history as another Fatih, a great Conqueror. That you are destined to be the greatest of all the Sultans."

"The price was high . . ."

"Our army will soon grow strong again."

What did she know of armies? Süleyman thought sourly. He tried again. "It was a terrible battle. If it were for a woman's ears, I could tell you things . . ." He finished the meal and dipped his fingers into a silver bowl. A page appeared instantly at his side to dry them.

"You must not think about that anymore."

"By day it is easy. But at night, in the darkness, it is hard not to remember."

He waited, but Gülbehar did not encourage him further. How can I tell her? He thought. I have to tell someone. Or perhaps that is just another burden I have to shoulder alone. He looked up at Gülbehar and smiled. So lovely. How wonderful of God to make such a thing as blue eyes. He let his gaze fall to the shadow of her breasts beneath the silk chemise and he thought he could feel the heat of her body across the table. But in every other way he felt so far away from her.

"When you were away," Gülbehar said, "I would take out your poems and read them. It always made me feel close to you again."

AFTER SO LONG feeling only hard things, the arm of a golden throne, the handle of a sword, the leather rein of a horse, it was a wonder to again touch something soft. Süleyman was hungry for it. His hands clutched at Gülbehar's body, squeezing her breast as if he wanted to take it for himself as a private treasure; it was only when she squealed with pain that he remembered himself and drew his hand away. The softness of her belly and thighs! He spread her legs apart, felt her wrap them around his hips, and he closed his eyes with pleasure. He wanted to fill her up, lose himself in softness, in warmth. He chased away the image of freezing rain, of a mailed arm protruding like a claw from the mud, the tower of St. Michael emerging from the dark clouds. Was it the smell of blood or the smell of defeat that had brought this terror to haunt him still? Gülbehar whispered her sweet magic in his ear and he pushed himself inside her, and with that one long urgent movement he felt his body spasm, the hot, sweet pleasure overtake him, the bitterness and sweetness pouring out of him.

Like a flood, like a river.

When he had finished he imagined they must be lying in a pool of his seed. Images tumbled over in his brain, future and past. Gülbehar with another son, the stinking moat at Rhodes, the executioner's sword sparkling like a diamond as it hung over Piri Pasha's head, Mustapha's sleeping face suddenly becoming his own, and then becoming his father's, a monster with its beard soaked in blood eating its own children. He groaned aloud and fell sideways, felt Gülbehar whisper soothing words in his ear. Her leg and arm snaked around him, and he felt the delicious sticky warmth on his own thigh. Then nothing.

When he woke again there was only the silence of the Harem, the blackness of the night, the mute slaves at their posts at the foot of the bed. A single candle glowed in the darkness. Gülbehar lay asleep beside him, hardly moving, silent in sleep as always. He opened his eyes and looked around the room, at the dark shadows in the niches in the walls where Gülbehar stored the manuscripts of his poetry.

This is my Harem, he told himself, my retreat, forbidden to all men but me. I have my favorite, my *gözde*, asleep under my arm, my seed still damp inside her; these are my poems around this wall, each a secret part of me enshrined in the rich language of Persian, my most personal and spiritual thoughts. Even within the protocols of the Harem, I have kept these rooms like a sanctuary.

Why, then, do I still feel so alone?

5

HÜRREM KNEW THAT she had been seduced when she began to anticipate the *hammam,* the morning baths. On the steppes bathing was frowned upon, even feared. Everyone knew washing led to chills, sickness, and death. The winter and the wind were their enemies, any luxury or indulgence impossible.

But here they insisted that the girls bathe twice a day, and shave every hair from their bodies. At first she had been terrified; but when she found she did not become sick, she was merely disgusted, not so much by the immodesty as by the indolence. She did not remember when she had begun to feel differently. She was getting soft, she realized. If her father could see her now, damn his barbarian soul to Hell! Well, she was still a Tartar. He would see.

There were three rooms; the *camekan,* or dressing chamber; the *sogukluk,* or warming room; and the largest, central room, the steam room or *hararet.* Hürrem quickly stripped off her clothes and one of the negresses—the *gediçli*—handed her a perfumed towel. She slipped a pair of rosewood *nalins* on her feet and went into the sogukluk, feeling the warmth of the steam on her gooseflesh. There was a large marble fountain in the center of the room with water that had been heated in the massive boiler below and a number of the girls were standing or sitting around it, scooping up the water in large copper bowls and pouring it over their heads. Hürrem joined them.

She looked around, while pretending to be occupied with her own toilet. She had never ceased to be amazed by the variety of flesh. Until she came here she had not realized that the world was so huge, and that human beings could be so different. Hair, nipples, skin, eyes. Such a rich profusion of shape and color. There were the gediçli with their tight black curls and mahogany skins; Greek girls with dark eyes and their hair in a thousand tight ringlets; golden-haired Circassians with blue eyes and pink buds of nipples; Egyptian girls with long, aristocratic profiles and nipples the color of bruised plum; Persian girls with hair the color of night and eyes as dark and deep as wells.

And so many shapes! As she scooped another bowlful of water over her body she pretended not to stare, silently comparing herself with the other girls. Some had full, pale, blue-veined breasts; like nursing mothers, Hürrem thought, except their bellies were tight and flat. There were breasts like teardrops, some mere buds; many of the Harem *houris* were young girls barely past puberty with hard, firm round breasts, impossibly tight and smooth. Hürrem looked down at her own body, slim and small like a boy, and wondered why they had chosen her for this place.

Well, perhaps I'm not as beautiful as some of these odalisques, she reminded herself. But I have golden hair like a fox. And cunning to match.

She picked up her towel and went into the hararet, her pattens clip-clopping on the marble.

It was like a scene from a milky hell. The steam seared the lungs, and clung to the skin in a scorching veil. She felt the perspiration ooze onto her skin, in a thousand tiny droplets. Naked silhouettes moved in and out of the mist like wraiths, the silence broken only by the click of a wooden nalin on the marble, the clank of a copper bowl, or the splash of a girl climbing in or out of a bath.

Light filtered down through the wraiths of steam from the windows in the domed ceiling, the vapor and the walls of gray-veined marble blending into one another so that it seemed there were no walls at all.

Hürrem lowered herself into one of the warm pools, and closed her eyes, enjoying the sensation of the water cleansing away the sweat, and lapping around her shoulders and breasts. She rested her head on the marble, scooped a handful of water over her face and pushed the damp hair from her eyes. Yes, it was a delicious sensation, she thought. Before I came here my body was attuned only to survival, to the movements of a horse, and the strength needed for manual work. Now these eunuchs and kiayas have woken something else in me.

But for what? All these women, their skins flushed and soft and tingling from the scalding of steam and hot water, flesh kneaded and massaged into suppleness by the gediçli, indolent and purring like kittens, primped and primed in silks and brocades, yet there is no man to appreciate or sate them. It was all a mystery, a bright, mythical, unattainable lure.

Hürrem felt movement in the water and she opened her eyes. A tall fair-haired woman was sitting on the edge of the bath just a few feet away, while two odalisques scooped water over her body and massaged the muscles on her neck and shoulders. The girl was leaning back on her arms, her head thrown back, her long fair hair almost touching the marble floor behind her. It was a pose of outrageous assurance and languorous pride. Gülbehar!

Hürrem felt her cheeks flush. Well, if there was any mystery, *she* knew. She felt an involuntary rush of envy and hatred, emotions she imagined she shared with every other woman in the hammam at that moment. Why you? she thought. With all of these women, why just you? Is it you who are so beguiling? Or is he just so easy to bewitch?

Gülbehar was aware of her stare and for a moment she lifted her head and opened her eyes. They appeared impossibly bright in the steamy mist of the hammam, like two sapphires embedded in ice. What was the expression on her face? Embarrassment? Curiosity? Pity?

Hürrem returned her stare for a moment then deliberately turned her back and eased herself out of the bath, leaving her bottom in full view a moment longer than was necessary. She immediately regretted the childish gesture.

She has no need to pity me, she thought as she snatched up her towel. Fear, perhaps. But not pity.

She disappeared through the mist, her nalins shattering the silence.

MARBLE COLUMNS AND arches led off the hararet into the *yeni kaplija*, smaller side chambers containing raised marble slabs where the gediçli tended to the odalisques, massaging their bodies, minutely examining their legs and arms, the pubis, vagina, and anus, even their noses and ears, ensuring no trace of body hair remained. Hürrem had long ago abandoned her protests against this indignity. She surrendered to the examination now without murmur. After all, they would do it anyway.

The black girl's name was Muomi, a sullen girl with tight jet curls and lips drawn continually downward into a pout. The other girls spoke about her in whispers. They said she was a witch and avoided her if they could. She had large, bony hands that seemed to pull joints and sinews apart when she worked, and some of the girls would come out after a session with

Muomi, their faces wet with tears. Hürrem enjoyed it. It shook her out of her indolence.

Hürrem flung herself face down on the cool marble. "Try to do it properly," Hürrem said. "I want it to hurt this time."

"I hurt you last time. I thought you were going to cry like a little baby."

"I'll give you two aspers if you can make me cry."

"You don't have two aspers." Muomi began the massage, her massive hands kneading the muscles at Hürrem's neck and shoulders until she thought her eyes would pop out of her head. She wanted to gasp aloud but instead she took a deep breath and waited. "They say you're a witch."

"Who says that?"

"The other girls."

"The other girls! When they bring them into this place they look for beauty, not brains."

"*Are* you a witch?"

Muomi's hands moved along Hürrem's spine. It was as if she were trying to drive the knuckles between each of the bones and squeeze them apart. Hürrem felt the wellsprings of tears flood her eyes and she buried her face in her arms to hide them.

"Well, are you?" she repeated.

"If I were a witch I would have wished myself out of this place a long time ago."

Muomi pressed her fingers into Hürrem's buttocks, her knuckles finding the joint of the hip and pelvis and Hürrem bit into the soft muscle of her forearm so Muomi should not know that she hurt her. "Your muscles are as hard as a boy's," Muomi conceded, grudgingly.

"A bit harder," Hürrem said. "I can hardly feel it."

Muomi chuckled. "Like that?" and Hürrem sobbed aloud.

When Meylissa entered, she found Hürrem lying on her back, while Muomi performed her depilatory. The gediçli had applied a paste of *rusma,* made with quicklime, and was expertly scraping away tiny hairs with the sharp edge of a mussel shell. Hürrem clasped her hands behind her head and watched her. Her breasts rose and fell tremulously with her breathing. Her cheeks were wet.

"Are you all right?"

"I owe this witch two aspers," Hürrem said.

"What for?"

"She wants the bostanji's job," Hürrem said. "From tomorrow she is going to be the Sultan's new Head Torturer." Muomi had pried her legs apart and was examining her perineum minutely for hairs.

Meylissa turned her back on the negress. "What's the point of all this?" she said. "Muomi is the only one who will ever care if we shave or not. The Sultan never will!"

Hürrem grinned. "We have to be ready. We can't let one golden opportunity be lost for one golden hair."

Meylissa perched on the edge of the marble and lowered her voice to a whisper. She put a hand on her slender brown stomach. "Soon I'll be starting to show!" As soon as she said the words her eyes filled with tears.

Muomi's head jerked up. "What's wrong with her?"

"She's remembering the last time you rubbed her back," Hürrem said. She clutched Meylissa's arm, her nails sinking deep into the flesh so that the other girl winced and tried to pull away. But Hürrem held her still.

"Not here!"

"What am I going to do?"

"It's all right. I have a plan."

"What are you going to do?"

"You'll see. Muomi here is going to help us too." And she grinned at them. The two girls looked at her, amazed, but Hürrem closed her eyes and gave herself up to the soft world of steam and Muomi's mussel shell.

6

FOR TWO MONTHS the Kapi Aga had known abject terror punctuated by periods of tremulous anticipation and delirious pleasure. He was a man with vivid imagination and in his mind he could see and hear what they would do to him if they ever discovered his secret. Yet he could not pull back now; even if one of God's messengers had handed him a guarantee, signed in gold by God Himself, that he would be caught, he knew he would still have come here today. The sexual pleasure—and she was a beautiful woman, made doubly so by the fact that she was forbidden—was only part of it. It was the confirmation of a manhood he thought he had lost, the rediscovery of potency that was at once irresistible and irreversible. He could endure any death, as long as he died a man.

Or so he told himself.

Each Thursday afternoon, an hour before dusk, she would come to the garden to read her Qur'ān. For the Kapi Aga, it was as if that whole week were precariously constructed around that dreadful, exquisite jumble of minutes when he could turn the key again in the rusted lock and enter the garden. Each time he pushed open the door he was never sure if he would find her or his own soldiers, their razor-edged killiç drawn. The garden had become the stuff of his every dream . . . and nightmare. Even as Head of the Palace Guard, and Keeper of the Girls, he could not call off his own dogs if he were discovered.

The iron-framed door creaked open—Merciful God, it sounded like a cannon shot in the silence of the Harem!—and he crept through, locking it once more behind him. He glanced up at the north tower. The only way they could be seen was from the rooms at the very top—it was from there that he had first seen Meylissa himself—and he had just locked the door to those two rooms himself.

Yet he still felt as if every member of the Divan was watching him now, the bostanji-bashi sharpening the hooks that would tear him apart.

The garden was shaded by high stone walls, the paths flanked by columns of white Paros marble and overhung with planes, cypress, and willow. It was always dusk here, though above the trees he could see the sun glinting on the minarets of the Harem mosque, turning them rose pink as it fell down the sky toward the dusty city.

He looked around for the familiar figure of Meylissa, bowed over her Qur'ān on a marble seat beneath the colonnades, or sitting under the overhanging branches of a willow; but there was no sign of her. He searched for movement in the shadows. The only sound was a lone nightingale chirruping sorrowfully in the branches above his head.

The Kapi Aga felt a mixture of disappointment and unreasoned terror. Why wasn't she here?

"She's not coming today."

The voice came from behind him. He jerked round in terror, instinctively drawing his killiç from its leather scabbard.

The girl crossed her arms and laughed at him.

She was a Harem girl, of course, but he did not recognize her. Why should he? There were so many. She was tall and slim with flaming golden hair and green eyes. She was wearing a yellow cotton kaftan with a gold brocade jacket, and a little green cap—a taplock—on her head. There was a single pearl tied at the cap's tassel. By her clothes he judged she had not been long at the Harem or risen very far.

He was shaking. His hands, his knees, his whole body. O mighty God. "Who are you?"

"Meylissa is not coming today."

"Where is she?"

"Here in the Harem. Where she is safe from the attentions of men."

"What are you laughing at?"

"You're as white as your turban. What's the matter? I'm not one of the Sultan's yeniçeris. I don't even have a sword. What are you frightened of? I'm just a sewing girl. Look I'm unarmed. I don't even have my needle."

The Kapi Aga attempted to compose himself. "Who do you think you're talking to? I'll have you put to the bastinado—"

He took a step forward and grabbed her by the arm, the edge of his sword held close to her face to intimidate her. But Hürrem smiled back at him. He gasped as he felt her fingers close around his groin.

"Meylissa says they still work. I'm only an innocent little sewing girl, but I thought they weren't supposed to."

"What are you talking about?"

"Meylissa is going to have a baby."

The Kapi Aga took a step backward, as if she had just told him she had the pestilence. She watched his face undergo a startling transformation. His cheeks turned a dirty, gray color like a corpse. The sword slipped from his fingers and clattered onto the marble.

The idiot! she thought. He'll bring the guards! Has he no self-control? For a moment she thought he was going to run.

"It's . . . not possible," he stammered.

"That's what she thought. I imagine that's what you thought too."

"Who are you? What do you want?"

"I'm Meylissa's friend." She looked at the killiç, lying on the marble. "Pick it up," she said, for no other reason than to test her advantage.

He bent to do as he was told. "What do you want?" he repeated.

"I want to help you."

"I remember you now," he said. "You're the Russian girl. We bought you from the Tartars." She watched him with amusement, each question, each calculation, illuminated on his face like a page from the Qur'ān. "Who else knows?" he said, finally.

"It would be so easy to toss us both in the Bosphorus in the middle of the night, and be done with the whole thing. That's what you're thinking, isn't it? That's why we have told one other. Someone whose name you will never know."

His lips curled in disappointment and distaste, as another avenue of escape closed to him. "I know you. The Kiaya calls you her little minx."

"With good reason."

"I can see that." He sheathed his sword with a gesture of finality. "So you want to help me?"

"Perhaps you do not need my help. Perhaps you will marry her and raise a family together."

"Do not mock me!" he hissed.

"I thought you would be pleased to know at least one of them still operates in the intended manner."

He took a step toward her angrily, then checked himself. "How do I know this is true?"

"You do not. You might never know for sure until it is too late. One night the Sultan Valide will come to you with orders to take Meylissa sailing on the Bosphorus. Then she'll give you two sacks. One for her, one for you."

The Kapi Aga frowned. "What do you want?"

"I'll eliminate your problem for you. Completely."

"Eliminate?"

"Completely."

"What do you mean?"

"I mean I know a way to get rid of the problem. In return you will do something that is within your power, but not in mine."

"A better position perhaps? One of the Valide's personal retinue? Clothes? Money?"

"I am surprised you value your life so cheaply."

The Kapi Aga glanced impatiently at the windows of the north tower, as if he expected to see the Sultan himself staring down at him. The sun was low in the sky now, and the minarets had turned blood-red.

"What then?"

"I want you to get me into the Sultan's bed."

"Impossible!"

"No, it is possible. As it is also possible that if the Sultan discovers what you have done he will have you hung on a hook and let you go black in the sun. You know the punishment."

The Kapi Aga rocked backward on his heels as if she had slapped him. His eyes were white and wide with astonishment. "The Sultan never sleeps with anyone but Gülbehar, you know that! What you are asking is not in my power!"

For the first time the slow, mocking smile that had played on Hürrem's lips vanished. "Enjoy your death. I believe the bostanji is creative enough to give you plenty of time to savor it."

And she walked away. The shadows crept across the garden, and the Kapi Aga stood watching them come, frozen with terror.

T HE HAREM DATED back to the time when the Osmanli Turks were no more than nomadic raiders living in the wild plains of Anatolia and Azerbaijan. The idea of the Harem had been borrowed from the Persians, as a convenience for warriors who were away from the tribe for a long period. When the Osmanlis gave up their nomadic lifestyle, creating a capital first at Bursa, then at Constantinople—now called Stamboul—the Harem had become an institution in itself and a rigid hierarchy had evolved, with its own protocols and government.

The Harem was governed not by the Sultan, but by the Sultan's mother—the Sultan Valide—and the Sultan was bound as much by the laws of the Harem as any of the girls. It was she who governed this reclusive community of eunuchs and virgins, with the help of the Kapi Aga, the Chief White Eunuch, who was both Captain of the Guards and intermediary between the Valide and the Sultan himself.

A girl first arriving at the Harem would be given a position in one of the many departments, with the Mistress of the Robes or with the Chief Kitchen Maker or in the kitchens. She might rise through the ranks to a position of some importance in the Harem administration through her own merits, but the only way she might attain real power was by becoming gözde—"in the eye"—in other words, if she caught the eye of the Sultan himself.

If he actually took her to his bed she became *iqbal,* and might be given apartments and an allowance of her own. She might have one night with the Lord of Life, or a hundred. But it all counted for nothing unless she bore him a son—and became one of his *kadins*. There were only ever four kadins, and no more; after that the abortionist was called in. These four kadins remained just a breath from real power, as each of them knew one of them must one day become the mother of the next Osmanli Sultan.

Süleyman had broken with tradition. Even though he was now almost thirty years old he still had only one kadin, Gülbehar, and just one son. It was a tenuous thread for such an exalted blood line as the Osmanlis to cling to, and Süleyman's mother was continually fretting over this oversight on her son's part.

Hafise Sultan, the Valide, was a Georgian, with long, lustrous black hair. She looked imposing and stately, sitting at court in the immense and echoing vault of gleaming onyx and veined marble that was her audience chamber. A misty yellow bolt of sunlight angled in from the glass-framed cupola high above and flashed on the mother-of-pearl and garnet that had been worked into a flower pattern in her hair. She looked entirely regal, except for her face, which had the soft lines and gentle gray eyes of a grandmother. She had the sort of face, the Kapi Aga thought, that one was always tempted to confide in. That was dangerous.

"You wanted to see me?" she asked him.

The Kapi Aga licked his lips, feeling suddenly as transparent as gossamer. He had practiced his speech long into the night, but now every word of it left him and he was filled with a sudden, black panic. "Crown of Veiled Heads . . . ," he mumbled, addressing her by her formal title.

"What's the matter? Are you unwell?"

"A slight chill . . ."

"A visit to the apothecary perhaps?"

"I shall do as your Highness suggests." Great God, get this over with!

"Something is troubling you."

He nodded. Troubling him! He had spent most of the morning contemplating taking a knife to his own throat. "I have heard word of unrest among some of the girls."

The Valide frowned. "Oh? And what is the cause of this . . . unrest?"

"Some of the girls . . . they are becoming a little . . . jealous."

"Harem girls are always jealous of something."

"It has become a little more serious than that."

The Valide gazed at him steadily, and the Kapi Aga had the uncomfortable feeling she was trying to look behind his eyes, like a stranger peering into a darkened room. "Go on," she said finally.

"It is Gülbehar. She is well loved by everyone, of course . . ."

"Except me," the Valide said, drily.

Well, I was counting on that, the Kapi Aga thought, ". . . but some of the girls feel it is not right that the Sultan ignores the rest of them this way. Some of them are becoming almost unmanageable."

"Well, that is your job, and that of the Kislar Aghasi, of course. To manage them."

"If there was just something I could tell them . . . to encourage them."

The Valide smiled, tapping a jeweled index finger on her cheek. "And what would you like to tell them?"

"That perhaps the Sultan would have use for them one day?"

"Who is to say?" The old lady's smile vanished. He had touched a nerve here, he knew. If anyone was truly unhappy about Süleyman's exclusive attachment to Gülbehar, it was his mother.

"They all cherish the opportunity to serve the Lord of Life."

"Of course they do!" She had been a slave girl once, before Selim had thrown his handkerchief across her shoulder. It was a long time ago, but she had not forgotten. "Are any of them a match for Gülbehar?"

"They all think they are," the Kapi Aga said, with a tight smile. Normally he would have allowed himself many such small jokes in the course of an audience. It was hard to relax this morning.

The Valide looked away, through the open window and across the gleaming cupolas of the Harem. She tapped the fingers of her left hand against her thumb, as if she was calculating something in her mind. "I shall talk to the Lord of Life," she said. "Thank you for bringing this subject to my attention."

The Kapi Aga wanted to scream: "Wait, I haven't said it all yet!" but instead he bowed and backed toward the door.

"One other thing."

"Yes, Highness?"

"Do you have any particular girl in mind?"

The Kapi Aga smiled. "Yes, Highness."

The Valide nodded. "What is her name?"

"Hürrem. Her name is Hürrem."

8

THE QUR'ĀN DECREED: "Virtue is at the feet of the mother." Whenever Süleyman came to the Eski Saraya, it was required by custom and by Allah that he visit his mother first. Süleyman had always enjoyed his mother's companionship, so this was one protocol that did not weigh too heavily.

This morning the wind was from the south, the first warm breath of spring. Hafise Sultan sat on the terrace on a divan, in a flowered brocade kaftan, the sun sparkling on the dusting of pearl and garnet in her hair. Süleyman smiled; she seemed to enjoy these useless baubles more than real gems. It was an endearing vanity.

"Mother." Süleyman kissed her hand and raised it to his forehead. He sat on the divan beside her, still holding her hand in both of his. One of her handmaids hurried to fetch sherbets and rosewater.

"You are well?"

"I feel the chill more than I once did. At my age you look forward to spring."

"You are not so old."

"I am a grandmother," she said. "At least I have one grandson. I suppose that is the same thing."

Süleyman threw back his head and laughed. "Mother, you are so transparent."

"I am saddened to see how lightly you treat an old woman's fears."

"You are not an old woman. Far from it."

Hafise pulled her hand away and chose a fig from the bowl of fruit in front of her. "And what of the conqueror of Rhodes?" she said, and there was unmistakable pride in her voice. "Where does the Divan urge you to strike now?"

"You will hear no war drum this year. All my generals are still licking their wounds after Rhodes. It will be a while before they are ready to stretch their claws again."

"And what about you?"

What was the use of pretending—with her? Süleyman thought. "The thought of another campaign sickens me to the soul."

"Any Sultan who will not carry the banner of Muhammad into battle may not remain Sultan for long. The yeniçeris will see to that."

"The one thing you do not have to remind me of is my duty. I would never forget that. But for this season at least I have had enough of war."

Hafise chose another fig with care, sifting through her own mind for the right words with equal delicacy. "A Sultan's duty is not only on the battlefield."

Süleyman sighed. Her first words that morning should have warned him. They were going to talk of Gülbehar again. "The Osmanlis have an heir," he said.

"And what if he sickens? A Sultan should have many sons."

"So they can murder each other when I am dead?" Süleyman thought about his father, Selim—Yavuz Selim, the Grim, they had called him. He had deposed his own father, Bayezid II, with the support of the yeniçeris, and then murdered his two brothers and eight nephews so his sultanate could not be challenged. There were even rumors that he had had Bayezid poisoned on his way to exile, so that the coup could never be reversed. Süleyman himself had never had a moment's ease until Selim's wasted and pain-racked body had finally succumbed to a stomach canker on the way to Adrianople.

"You have a duty."

"I have many duties."

"And you should not neglect a single one."

Süleyman stared at her. She was right, of course. She had been his conscience all his life. It was she, not Selim, who had taught him that duty took precedence above all else. Selim had loved power and bloodshed for its own sake.

"Gülbehar makes me happy."

"And that is good. But we are not talking about happiness. We are talking about heirs to the line of Osman."

Süleyman turned away, stared at the panorama of minarets and cupolas that punctuated the jumble of wooden houses clinging to the hillside above the Golden Horn. The Osmans had come a long way from their windswept tents on the Anatolian plain. For some reason he remembered his father's last words to him, before he sent him to Manisa as governor: "If a Turk dismounts from the saddle to sit on a carpet, he becomes nothing—nothing."

But then his father was a barbarian.

"At this moment the house of Osman has only two heartbeats," Hafise said. "It is not enough."

"What would you have me do?"

"I do not want you to give up your Gülbehar. It is only natural that you should have a favorite. But there are many girls in the Harem. Some of them are quite pleasing to the eye."

"So I should play the bull for the House of Osman?"

"Indelicately put, especially in front of an old woman, but yes, that is exactly what you should do. Perhaps it would be different if Gülbehar had given you more sons. But she has been your kadin now for nine years . . ."

"She pleases me."

"And another woman cannot?"

"I am comfortable with Gülbehar."

"It is not comfort you should look for from these other girls. Just a son."

Süleyman stood up suddenly. He noticed Fatim, one of his mother's handmaids, glance at him shyly from kohl-darkened eyelashes. He felt a wave of impatience, with her, and with himself. Well, what was wrong with him? Why was it so difficult to do as his mother asked? Perhaps it is my small rebellion against this burden, he thought, the one way I can demonstrate I am different from the beasts who came before me. These coquettish, hungry women made him feel shabby and degraded.

The girl saw the anger in his eyes and lowered her face, blushing and confused.

"I will do as you ask," he said, and kissed his mother's hand. I'll bull them all, one at a time, if that is what you want, he thought bitterly. I'll fill the palace with cradles.

And then perhaps you will leave me alone with Gülbehar.

THE KIAYA SNATCHED the cushion slip from Meylissa's hands and flung it on the floor. She stamped on it in the manner of a small child. "What is this? Are you deliberately trying to provoke me?"

Meylissa shook her head miserably, sobbing, unable to answer.

"Look at these stitches! I would not give such a thing to a peasant, never mind the Valide!"

"I'm sorry . . . ," Meylissa sobbed.

"What is the matter with you, girl? These last few weeks you have been quite impossible!" To add emphasis to her judgment, the Kiaya slapped

Meylissa hard on the ear. The girl's howls encouraged her, and she did it again.

Hürrem was contemptuous of Meylissa's surrender, but it was at least an opportunity to confront the Kiaya. She got up from her workbench and snatched up the silk cushion slip from the Kiaya's feet.

"It is not so bad. I can alter this easily."

The Kiaya twisted around. "Ah, the little red minx! You cannot keep still when you see fur flying, can you, my sweet?"

"Leave her alone. She is not feeling well."

"Perhaps we should send her to the infirmary, then. And if your stitching is so fine, you can do her work as well as your own!"

Hürrem flung the piece of material in her face. "Do it yourself, you old hag!"

The Kiaya slapped her hard on the cheek. Hürrem took one step back, then her own hand shot forward like a snake disturbed from its sleep. The sound of the slap was followed by complete silence. It was as if someone had discharged a harquebus in the tiny room. The Kiaya reeled backward, stunned.

Slowly, her face split into a slow, triumphant smile. "For that you get the bastinado," she whispered. "The Kapi Aga will have them strip the flesh from your soles with whips. It is spring now. If you are fortunate, you might take your first steps again in the winter. I will teach you to strike me!"

Two black guards had appeared in the doorway. The Kiaya grinned at Hürrem in triumph. But before she could speak, one of them stepped into the room and took Hürrem's arm. "You are to come with me," he said, in his curious high-pitched tremolo. "Bring your sewing things with you."

Hürrem hesitated, stunned by what she had done, by the miraculous appearance of the guards. What was happening? She picked up her needles, and the little bag of emery powder, and the green square of silk she had been embroidering into a handkerchief.

The Kiaya stared at them. "Where are you taking her?"

"The Kapi Aga has given us orders," the man said, and led Hürrem to the door.

"She is to be put to the bastinado!" the Kiaya shrieked, but there was no conviction in her voice, only bewilderment.

Hürrem let the guards hurry her away down the corridor. The words "Kapi Aga" had reassured her. There was to be no bastinado. She sensed immediately that the most crucial minutes of her life were about to take place.

9

THE COURTYARD WAS paved with almond-shaped cobblestones, surrounded by the somber high walls of the Palace, dominated by an ornate marble fountain. Windows looked down onto the courtyard from all four sides, and Hürrem had the sensation of eyes watching her everywhere.

Suddenly she realized where she was. This was the courtyard of the Sultan Valide. These were her apartments.

The guards hurried her to the center of the court, and released her. "The Kapi Aga says you are to wait here. And be sure to sing," one of them said.

"Why? What is happening?"

But the men had done as they had been ordered, and now they promptly turned and wheeled away, the sickle-bladed *yataghans* at their waists rattling in their scabbards. Hürrem watched them go. What was happening?

She stood, waiting, for long minutes, but no one came. Water murmured in the marble fountain, hypnotic, soothing. Perhaps, she finally decided, the Kapi Aga had arranged an interview with Hafise Sultan herself.

But if that was so, why had the guards left her here, in the courtyard? And why had they insisted she bring her work? And what else was it they had said? "The Kapi Aga says you are to wait here, and be sure to sing."

The Kapi Aga had ordered her to break the sacred silence of the Harem. Why?

She shrugged, and found herself a cool spot in the shade of the fountain and sat down, crossing her legs beneath her, Osmanli style, and spread the handkerchief on her lap. She took out her needle and took up her embroidery. Her heart was pounding wildly in her chest, and for the first time in her life she found it difficult to sing. She forced herself to hum a love song her mother had taught her, about a boy whose horse had fallen in the snow, trapping him; as he died by inches on the winter steppe, he told the wind how much he loved a certain girl, and how he had never had the courage to tell her. He asked the wind to carry his words with it across the plain, so that she would remember him. It was a stupid, sentimental song, Hürrem thought, but she had always liked the tune, and after a while the words came flooding back to her.

After a while she became so absorbed, she forgot her anxiety and did not even notice the tall, slender figure in the white turban until his shadow fell across her lap.

"The first law of the Harem is silence."

She looked up, startled, but the man was standing with the sun behind him and she had to shield her eyes against the glare. He did not speak like a eunuch, and his face was not black. There was only one other man who might walk freely here.

She was angry he had found her unprepared. "Perhaps we should cut out the nightingales' tongues, then," she heard herself saying. "And the bees. We should do something about them also. At this time of the year their incessant buzzing is enough to drive anyone to madness."

He seemed surprised by this answer. For a moment they stared at each other. Hürrem suddenly remembered that her first action should have been to lower her forehead to the ground and make her obeisance. She put down her embroidery and shifted her weight to her knees. She touched her forehead to the hot stone, realizing it was probably already too late. She realized she should also beg his forgiveness for breaking the silence. Well, she decided, there is no point to that now. He has spoken and I have answered him.

She suddenly became aware of the Kislar Aghasi—the old Chief Black Eunuch—standing behind Süleyman, his face beaded with perspiration, fanning himself with a silken handkerchief. He looked as if he were about to faint away.

"Do you know who I am?" Süleyman asked her.

"Yes, my Lord. Though I was a little slow to fathom it."

She squinted upward at him, and she saw the flash of white teeth. Perhaps he was smiling.

"What were you singing?"

"It was a song I learned from my mother, my Lord. A love song. About a stupid boy who let his horse fall on top of him."

"He was singing to the horse?"

My God, he was mocking her! "I think not. I dare to say the horse may have lost a lot of its charm by then."

She heard him laugh. There was a silence and she felt his eyes on her. "What is your name?"

"They call me Hürrem, my Lord."

"Hürrem? Laughing One? Who gave you that name?"

"The men who brought me here. It was because they could not pronounce my name. Though I suspect they were not intelligent enough to pronounce their own names either."

He laughed again. "Where are you from, Hürrem?"

She squinted up at him. The moment for which she had gambled so much, and all she could think about was the pain in her knees! How long would he make her squat here on these cobbles? "I am a Tartar," she told him. "A Krim."

"Do all you Tartars have hair of such amazing colors?"

"No, my Lord. I was the only one in my tribe so burdened."

"Burdened? It is quite beautiful." She felt him take a lock of her hair and run it through his fingers, as if he were examining a piece of material for quality and strength. "It is like burnished gold. Is it not, Ali?"

The Kislar Aghasi murmured his agreement. Liar! Hürrem thought. You have only ever spoken to me once, and that was to label me an undernourished carrot.

"Stand up, Hürrem."

She did as she was told. She tried to avert her eyes, as she had been taught to do, but curiosity got the better of her. So this was the Lord of Life, the Possessor of Men's Necks, the Lord of the Seven Worlds! He was handsome, she supposed, but not especially so. There was the shadow of a beard on his face, which lent a certain majesty to his long beaked nose. It could have been the face of a tyrant, but at that moment the lips and gray eyes were softened with amusement.

She felt him examining her minutely, the way his *spahis* had done the day her father had traded her. He did not seem displeased with what he saw, which was why she was dismayed by the way he sighed when he had finished his inspection.

"What is that you are embroidering?" he asked her.

"A handkerchief, my Lord," she answered. What did he think it was?

"Let me see it." She picked it up and handed it to him. "A fine piece of work. You have skillful hands. May I have it?"

"I have not finished . . ."

"Have it ready for me tonight," he said, and he placed it carefully over her left shoulder. Hürrem saw the old Kislar Aghasi's eyes widen in shock.

Placing a handkerchief over a girl's shoulder signified that she was now gözde, and that the Sultan wished to sleep with her. No girl had been so favored since the Sultan assumed the throne.

Süleyman turned and walked away, without another word. the Kislar Aghasi looked as if he would burst; then he remembered himself, and hurried after the Sultan to attend to his duties.

Hürrem watched them go, too stunned to move, her whole body shivering with triumph and excitement.

Gözde!

SÜLEYMAN HURRIED ALONG the cloister, feeling at once both angry and relieved. He was angry that he had once again been forced by his position into betraying his own conscience, but relieved he had acted so swiftly and decisively. After Hafise's lecture he had decided that he would choose the first of the odalisques that he came upon whose manner and appearance did not displease him too much. This . . . Hürrem . . . was appealing in an elfin sort of way, and she at least had an entertaining turn of mind. Harem girls were usually insufferably vain and empty beneath their pretty, pampered skins. At least this one might be different.

And if she got pregnant his mother should be satisfied for a while. And he could return to Gülbehar.

10

Topkapi Saraya

THE CRESCENT MOON seemed to tremble in the night sky, although Süleyman knew it was just a trick of the light. They had dined well on lobster, sturgeon, and swordfish, taken that morning in the Bosphorus, washed down with sherbets made with violets and honey. They had completed the meal with a bottle of Cyprus wine, though it was forbidden by the Qur'ān.

It was a small transgression, but one that gave him a measure of satis-

faction, for in all other ways each hour of his life was governed by protocol. Every morning, upon waking, he was immediately attended by the
Parer of the Nails, who attended to his manicure, and the Chief Barber,
who shaved his head. As the Master of the Wardrobe laid out his day's
clothes, each article scented with aloe wood, the Chief Turban Winder
curled yards of white linen around his *fez*.

From Saturday till Tuesday he arose at dawn to attend the Divan. Every
Friday he rode to prayers along the Divan Yolu to the Aya Sofia, in proces-
sion with his Grand Vizier, his astronomers, his Chief Huntsman, his Chief
Keeper of the Nightingales, the Master of the Keys, the Master of the
Stirrup, the Master of the Turbans, and four thousand of his yeniçeris and
Spahis of the Porte, his regular cavalry.

In the afternoon, custom required him to take a short nap, reclining on
two mattresses, one of silver brocade, the other of gold. He was attended
at all times by five guards, deaf-mute eunuchs with curved yataghans. Even
when he slept, he was not alone.

His whole life was circumscribed by the demands of state. Within the
confines of his duties, the small rebellions took on great significance for him.

Ibrahim, for example. They had become inseparable; during the siege of
Rhodes they had slept in the same pavilion, even worn each other's clothes.
He knew he had scandalized the court by showing such favor to a slave; but
then, for Süleyman, Ibrahim was much more than a slave. He was confidant, confessor, and counselor. If anyone helped shoulder the burden, it
was not Gülbehar or Hafise, nor even the Grand Vizier. It was Ibrahim.

Tonight he sat cross-legged beneath the window, strumming his viol. It
was their ritual on most nights to eat together at the Palace, and often,
when the hour was late and they had enjoyed a little too much of the
Cyprian wine, Süleyman's pages would roll out two mattresses from the
alcove in the wall and Ibrahim would sleep the night there also.

Ibrahim had been born in Parga, on the west coast of Greece, the son
of a fisherman. One day Turkish raiders came to his village and took the
young Ibrahim with them as plunder. They took him to the slave markets
in Stamboul, where he was bought by a widow from Manisa. She raised
him as a Muslim, and when she discovered the boy had a flair for music and
languages, she ensured that he received a good education. He learned to
play the viol, and could talk Persian, Turkish, Greek, and Italian fluently.
Later she sold him for a handsome profit into Süleyman's service when he
came to Manisa as the Governor of Kaffa province.

The slave-companion soon became a fixture at Süleyman's side. He was the same age as the Prince, *shahzade* Süleyman, though shorter and swarthier in stature, and less introspective. Indeed, it seemed sometimes to Süleyman that the young man would burst with the force of the energy that was contained in such a compact body.

When Süleyman became Sultan in 1520, he brought Ibrahim with him to the Porte and made him his Hasodabashi, the Head of his Household. In time he deferred more often to Ibrahim than he ever did to Piri Pasha, his old Grand Vizier, and after Rhodes he rewarded Ibrahim for his good counsel by making him a vizier. It was in itself a symbol of the egalitarian nature of the Ottoman system that a Christian slave could rise by his own merits to become almost preeminent in the greatest Islamic Empire the world had ever seen. What was it the Fatih had said? Süleyman thought . . .

"Our Empire is the home of Islam . . . from father to son the lamp of our Empire is kept burning with oil from the hearts of the infidels."

"So solemn, my Lord?" Ibrahim asked him.

Süleyman sighed. "Do you ever have regrets, Ibrahim?"

"Of course not. What is there to regret?"

"Do you not sometimes wish you were someone else? Do you ever wonder what might have happened to you if the pirates had not come to your village that day?"

"I know what would have happened to me. I would be eating fish for breakfast and supper and pulling them out of nets in between. Instead I sleep in a palace, drinking the best Cyprian wine, and am held in favor by the greatest Emperor on earth."

"Your life would have been simpler."

"My life would have been worthless."

Süleyman saw again that frown of irritation on Ibrahim's face. He thinks I think too much. Perhaps he is right.

"You enjoy it, don't you? You enjoy going to war, enjoy the endless politicking in the Divan."

Ibrahim's face grew animated. "We are at the hub of the world, my Lord. We are writing history here."

"We are serving Islam."

"Indeed, my Lord, I sometimes forget." Ibrahim returned his attention to the viol. "We are Islam's greatest servants."

Liar, Süleyman thought. You do all this for its own sake. Perhaps that is why I love and envy you so much. I wish I were more like you.

"I think sometimes you should have been Sultan, and I the son of a Greek fisherman. We might have been happier that way." He got to his feet, rubbing the tiredness from his face with the palms of his hands.

"Shall we sleep now, my Lord?" Ibrahim asked.

"You may sleep, Ibrahim. Your life is not as complicated as mine. I have yet one more duty to perform."

HÜRREM HAD BEEN taken first to the Keeper of the Baths to be bathed and massaged. Her nails were dyed, her hair perfumed with jasmine, her skin pommaded with henna to prevent sweating, her eyes blackened with kohl.

She was then returned to the Kiaya of the Robes, who dressed her in a rose-colored chemise and long purple velvet kaftan, and a robe of silver and apricot brocade over the top. The Kiaya of the Jewels had brought a diamond necklace that was as heavy as an iron collar, silver rings and bracelets, strings of fat pearls from the Arabian Sea to plait into her hair, and heavy ruby earrings that reached to her shoulders. She also gave her instructions to ensure that she returned all of them the next morning.

One of the gediçli held up a mirror for Hürrem to inspect her reflection. She studied the result with disbelief. "I look completely hideous."

The Kiaya of the Robes stood in front of her with her hands on her hips, examining her handiwork. "It is the way," she said.

"It is the way to make a man fall on the floor laughing."

"You ungrateful little minx," the Kiaya snarled. "Don't you realize the great honor that has fallen on you? Remember, it happened to me once, so don't think you are high and mighty. You could end up as Mistress of the Robes one day, and no more than that!"

"If you dressed like this for him, you are lucky he didn't make you Kiaya of the Royal Lavatory!"

The Kiaya hissed with outrage and sent the two gediçli out of the room. She turned to Hürrem. "Now listen here," she hissed, "I don't deny that you have never treated me as well as you could, but I'm still willing to help you. This is a once in a lifetime opportunity! I know what it's like. I was gözde once, when Bayezid was Sultan. Let me tell you what you should do to please him . . ."

"I do not need advice from a failure. I know what to do! I have to get pregnant!"

And she swept from the room.

11

THERE WERE TWO guards, the same ones who had led her to the courtyard earlier that day. They escorted her along a maze of gloomy, cold
cloisters and down a narrow staircase. Her brocade gown and the trailing sleeves of her silk kaftan were continually catching and tearing on the
splintered wood. Finally she felt a chill draft of air on her cheek and she
was pushed forward into the night through a heavy iron door, into a boxlike
carriage. She caught a whiff of horse and moldering leather and then a soft,
fleshy hand pulled her inside.

The carriage jerked forward and she heard the clatter of the horses'
hoofs on the cobblestones. As her eyes adjusted to the light she made out
the bulky silhouette of the Kislar Aghasi sitting opposite her.

"Where are we going?" Hürrem said.

"To the Sultan," the Kislar Aghasi said. "He awaits you in the Topkapi
Saraya."

The curtains on the carriage were drawn. Hürrem tried to draw them
aside to look outside, but he snatched her hand away.

"Is it far?"

"Not far," the old eunuch told her and she could feel his eyes watching
her, huge and white in the darkness, like a cat. "The Kapi Aga arranged this
for you." It was a statement, not a question.

"Why would he do that?"

"A question I have been asking myself."

She could not see his face in the darkness of the carriage. She had the
eerie sensation of conversing with a pair of eyes. "And what answer did you
give yourself?"

"I have none. As I also have no answer for why he looks so pale. Like a
man waiting to be executed." He paused. "Or perhaps he is just unwell."

"Perhaps."

"Do not misunderstand me. Should the Kapi Aga fall into disfavor I
would not weep too many tears. Remember that."

"I will," Hürrem said.

Soon afterward, the coach clattered to a halt, and the door was thrown open. Hürrem looked around quickly as she got out. So this was the Topkapi! The great tower of the Divan loomed above her in the darkness, and torches dotted around the gardens glimmered through the overhanging branches of the plane trees.

Two halberdiers, the heavy tressed plumes on their helmets covering their eyes, led her through a great iron-studded door and across the cobblestones into the heart of the Seraglio, the Kislar Aghasi wheezing and puffing as he waddled along behind. Hürrem was struck by how orderly and spacious it all seemed, after the drab and gloomy confines of the Eski Saraya. The walls were of stone, not wood, and there were wide courtyards and she could hear the sound of a thousand trees whispering to the night wind.

They finally reached two great wooden doors, inlaid with mother-of-pearl and tortoiseshell, that led to the Sultan's private chambers. Two of the Sultan's personal bodyguards, the solaks, stood on guard at either side of the doors, their yataghans drawn.

Hürrem took a deep breath. This was the moment she had schemed and gambled for. Well, she told herself, there is no need for nerves. You do not have to beguile him. Just accept his seed, take it gratefully, and let it flower into freedom.

The Kislar Aghasi threw open the doors and led her inside.

Hürrem looked around the room in awe.

The walls of the bedroom were decorated with a faïence of Iznik tiles, peacock blue, orange, and viridian in rich patterns of flowers and fruit. The ceiling rose to a great dome and below it censers on long golden chains glittered with turquoises and rubies. A fireplace, like a great copper pyramid, dominated one wall. Oil lamps glimmered in niches in the walls.

The bed itself was on a raised platform in one corner of the room, hung with a canopy of gold and green Bursa brocade, supported on columns of fluted silver. The quilts and cushions were made of crimson velvet, laced with pearls. Tapers burned in platinum candlesticks at the four corners.

Süleyman himself sat on a divan of shimmering gold velvet. He wore a robe of apple-green brocade and a turban of pure-white silk, with a clasp of heron's feathers and an emerald, as large as a child's fist, rippling in the folds. He had one arm stretched languorously along the back of the divan. He looked faintly bored.

Hürrem heard the door shut gently behind her as the Kislar Aghasi crept from the room. They were alone.

He looked at her for a long time in silence. She could almost hear him thinking, "What have they done to you?"

She tried to choke the sob of despair in her throat. She should have trusted her judgment in the first place. Instead she had allowed the Kiaya to humiliate her once more.

She quickly untied the brocade robe and let it slip to the floor, then unfastened the diamond buttons of the kaftan and pulled it over her head. She ripped off the diamond necklace, and flung it on top of the robe with the earrings. Finally she loosened the pearls from her hair and shook her hair free.

When she had finished, she had on only her chemise and harem trousers. She indicated the rich pile of garments at her feet. "The Mistress of the Robes chose my wardrobe herself," she said. "Of course, these days she is half-blind."

He had not moved. Why doesn't he do something, say something? she thought. Then the realization struck her. He is as much at a loss as I am!

She had to shake him from his torpor. She knew only one way to do that. She fell to her knees and covered her face in her hands. She began to weep.

"What is wrong?"

"Lord of my Life, why did you choose me? There are so many beautiful girls in the Harem. I am not good enough for you. I know nothing about love or men."

She heard him rise from the divan and come toward her. She resisted the impulse to try and glimpse his expression. She felt him touch her shoulder.

"Please. Get up."

"I am too ashamed. You think I am ugly."

"I think you are . . . delightful. It is just when you first entered . . . you are right, the Kiaya must be half-blind."

She groped for his hand and allowed him to lift her to her feet. She looked up into his eyes, searching his face for some clue to what he was thinking. "I never wanted this," she whispered. "I am frightened." Well, it was half the truth, at least, she thought. I am frightened.

"Any girl in the Harem would willingly change places with you right now, I suspect." He seemed amused, even intrigued. That was good.

"Then let them. They are all far more beautiful than I."

"Come and sit down." He led her to the divan and sat her down beside him. He still held her hand. "I think you are quite exceptional," he said, and his fingers toyed with a strand of her hair.

She moved her head slightly, trapping his hand between her cheek and her shoulder. "What should I do?"

He hesitated. "There is no . . . protocol for this."

He leaned forward and took her face in his hands, almost shyly. He brought her face toward him, very slowly, and kissed her. She sniffed the sour aroma of wine. I have learned your first secret! she thought.

His hands were on her shoulders. He pulled her toward him with sudden urgency. He pressed her face roughly against his own and she felt the sharp stubble of his beard against her mouth and her cheek. This is my moment, Hürrem thought.

She groaned aloud and felt his fingers tighten their grip on her shoulders, bruising the soft flesh. Yes, you like that, don't you? she thought. As she suspected, the Lord of the Lords of this World wanted proof that he was indeed greater than other men. Here is the Shadow of God upon the Earth. Tonight I shall do all I can to make him suspect that he truly is.

He pushed her back on the divan. She felt his fingers tearing at the pearl buttons of the chemise. She surrendered to him, lips slightly open, eyes slightly closed. She murmured softly, almost as if having a man love her could somehow give her pleasure.

IT WAS STILL night when she woke him from his sleep. "Please do it again," she whispered. "It may never happen to me again. Please, just one more time. It is so wonderful with you."

Süleyman wanted only to sleep, but this was a new discovery: a woman who enjoyed this as much as any man! He was sure she must be a harlot by birth if not by profession, but he did not care. This was one case he would not bring before the judges of the *ulema*. A woman's soul, the judges of Law had decreed, was not as great as a man's, more on a par with a dog or a cat's. But her soul must still be brought to salvation in time.

But not yet.

Not yet.

12

The Eski Saraya

AS AN IQBAL, Hürrem was given an allowance of two hundred aspers
and her own apartment, together with enough organza, silk, taffeta,
brocade and satin for the Mistress of the Robes to outfit a complete
wardrobe. She even had her own bath, carved from rose-veined marble,
with cascading fountains of scented rosewater. Nightingales twittered in
cedar cages on the terrace.

She was also allowed her own gediçli. Hürrem asked to see Muomi.

The young negress seemed neither pleased nor surprised at Hürrem's
summons. She stood sullenly on the terrace, shuffling her big, splayed feet,
her face a sullen mask of indifference.

Hürrem studied her, sitting with her legs drawn under her on the divan.
"Are you happy working every day in the hammam?" she asked her.

Muomi shrugged by way of answer.

"As iqbal, I am to be allowed to choose a handmaid. The work will be
far easier than what you are used to."

Muomi shrugged again.

Hürrem got to her feet and walked slowly toward her, until their faces
were just inches apart. "I want you to help me. Tell me what you want in
return."

Muomi sniffed, as if something foul had offended her nostrils. "When I
was seven years old, the magic man in our tribe came to my family's hut
with a stinging nettle. He parted my legs and rubbed the nettle into my
cleft. That was to make it swell. The next day he came back and washed
between my legs with butter and honey, then cut away everything that gives
a woman pleasure, and cauterized the wound with a red-hot ember. My
mother pretended to cry with joy to cover my screams. When I married,
my husband opened me with a knife to take me. Then he had me sewn up
again, until the next time. It was the same when the baby came. Then when
the traders came, they took me and my baby, but my baby was a boy so they
took him away from me. I don't know if he's dead or alive. If he's alive, they

will castrate him, the way they castrated me. Now, whatever happens, I will spend the rest of my life in this place, a slave. If not to you, then to someone else. So tell me—what could you possibly offer me?"

Hürrem stared at her for a long time. "Revenge," she said finally.

THE OKMEYDAN, THE Place of Arrows, looked down through groves of plane trees and rosebushes the size of apricot trees, to the dark waters of the Golden Horn. It was nearly summer, the time of year when the war drum beat in the court of the yeniçeris, when the Grande Turke would set out again from Stamboul to raid the Lands of War.

But this year there was to be no war, and soon Süleyman would remove the court to Adrianople for the hunting. He and Ibrahim now went regularly to the *meydan* with their arrows and spears for target practice, where Ibrahim had set up the statues they had plundered from Belgrade along the slopes. The notion of using Greek gods as targets seemed somehow to amuse him.

Now he bounded through the grass like a small boy, running to fetch those arrows that had missed their mark, crowing with delight when his aim was good and his arrow split itself apart on its marble victim.

Finally they rested in the broad shade of a fig, and pages brought them olives and cheese and sherbets.

"If only our marble statues had been Charles or Frederick, I should have pierced their hearts a thousand times!"

"Your aim is excellent, Ibrahim. If I were a boar, I should start running toward Russia now."

"Your eye is good also," Ibrahim lied.

"No, no. My mind is on other things today."

Ibrahim drained his silver goblet, then carefully selected an olive, chewing it slowly while he placed the chalice an arm's length away. Then, with great theatrics, he spat the stone into the cup. It rattled as it reached its target and Ibrahim grinned in satisfaction.

"You are like a child sometimes."

"But it amuses you?"

Süleyman smiled. "You always amuse me, Ibrahim."

"So what is troubling my Lord?"

Süleyman sighed. With Ibrahim he could always say or ask whatever he pleased. "When we came from Manisa, you were able to establish your own harem?"

Ibrahim grinned again. "It is not as extensive as yours, my Lord."

"But you have a favorite?"

"Of course. Whenever I am with a woman, she is my favorite."

It was not the answer Süleyman had hoped for. How could he explain his problem to someone like Ibrahim? Ever since he had bedded Hürrem, he had been unable to chase the image of her from his mind. The next night he had chosen another of the Harem girls—his duty, after all, was to the Osmanli line, not himself. The girl had been a simpering, grinning Georgian girl, with the most startling, deep-black eyes; which may have extended right through her head, Süleyman decided, for all the sense she made when she opened her mouth. When he took her to his bed she had lain there pliantly, crying out only once, when he entered her, and that a cry of pain, not pleasure.

She was classically, faultlessly beautiful, but that, he decided was not enough. Not for him, anyway.

And what of Gülbehar? She had been his favorite for nearly ten years. She had been a slight, shy girl of fifteen when he had first lain with her. She had been a virgin, and so had he. Until Hürrem, he thought she had satisfied all his needs. But now?

The whole experience had left him with a feeling of inner contradiction, as if his soul had been split asunder, and the two parts of himself were at war. One Süleyman wanted to summon Hürrem once more, wash the memory and the scent of her from his mind with repetition.

But the other part of him was afraid. It was not good for a woman to find as much pleasure as a man. Her soul was tainted by the sins of Rachel. If he encouraged her in her vice, was he not tainted by it too? And what of Gülbehar? He felt the first sour gnawing of an emotion he had never expected to feel in connection with a woman.

Guilt.

"Does a woman have a soul, Ibrahim?"

"Does it matter, my Lord?"

Süleyman did not answer. For the first time he decided Ibrahim could not help him. In politics he was a diplomat and a statesman. But in the matter of women he was a barbarian like the Muslims he secretly despised.

Ibrahim leaned closer, and for a moment the grin fell away. "Is it Gülbehar who troubles you, my Lord?"

"No, it is another."

Ibrahim raised an eyebrow. "May I inquire her name?"

"Her name is Hürrem," Süleyman said.

"Hürrem?" Ibrahim said. Another woman in Süleyman's bed? Of course, Süleyman had taken other women before. Indeed, Ibrahim had often encouraged him to choose from his Harem more often. Then why did he suddenly feel this gnawing of unease? It was nothing, it meant nothing. Süleyman often fell into these strange moods for no reason.

He aimed another olive stone at the goblet, but this time it landed softly in the grass, a man's footstep wide of its mark.

13

MEYLISSA'S FACE WAS gaunt, her eyes hollowed by fear. In the milk-colored mist of the hammam her head floated on the rippled surface of the bath as if disembodied, like some terrible ghoul glaring its accusation at Hürrem. The eyes followed her on her way to the pool. Hürrem stopped beside the pool, allowed Muomi to remove the clinging shift of gauze and lowered herself naked into the water.

The head came toward her through the water.

"You look ill," Hürrem whispered.

"I am sick every morning. The Kiaya wants to send me to the infirmary."

"Don't let her."

"Do you think I'm stupid?" Meylissa came closer. Hürrem imagined she could smell the desperation on the girl, a sour, rank scent, like sweat. "Every day my waistline gets thicker. I cannot pretend forever that it is the sweetbreads. You said you would help me!"

"Why do you think I came here?"

Meylissa's brown eyes flashed with anger. "I forgot. You have your own hammam now. Does the Sultan visit you every night?"

"I will help you."

Fear had made her spiteful. "How? Will you plead for me with the Sultan? You are gözde, but you are not the Valide. Not yet, Hürrem."

"There is a better way."

"Tell me."

"Muomi."

Meylissa shifted her gaze to the black girl. Her voice was laced with both suspicion and hope. "Your gediçli?"

"She is a witch," Hürrem whispered.

"That's nonsense," Meylissa said, but without much conviction, Hürrem thought.

"She is going to make you a potion. An abortive."

Hürrem saw Meylissa's bottom lip begin to quiver. Hürrem realized that this perpetual terror had driven the girl close to the point of hysteria.

"Be brave, Meylissa," she whispered.

"It is too late . . ."

Hürrem grabbed her arm, Meylissa tried to pull away. "Don't be such a milksop! Of course it's not too late! Do you think this is any easier for me? What if the Kislar Aghasi finds out what I'm doing? They'll kill me too!"

Meylissa nodded, all the spite gone from her face now. "When?"

"I will send Muomi to you tomorrow. But you must not tell anyone about this!"

"Of course I won't."

Hürrem released her. "Everything will be all right."

Meylissa moved away through the mist of steam. Hürrem heard the splash of water as she climbed out of the pool, saw her silhouette outlined against the wall. Great Heaven, she was getting big, Hürrem thought. Soon, she would have no waist at all.

But before then she would have nothing to worry about.

GÜLBEHAR LAY NAKED beside him. Süleyman stared down at her, feeling his excitement grow. It was not just that she was beautiful it was the familiarity of her beauty that he loved. Perhaps this protocol that I hate has molded me into its creature after all, he thought. I love order and repetition too much.

He touched her breast, almost reverently. It was white and rounded, and he followed the passage of a blue vein on the white flesh, from the nipple and up toward her shoulder. He watched the nipple tighten and constrict, another small miracle of the flesh.

Gülbehar looked up at him and smiled with simple pleasure.

He felt another stirring of doubt. She likes this because it pleases me, he thought, and that is the proper way. With Hürrem, it pleases her also, and that is sinful. Why then, do I feel so empty now?

He studied the rest of Gülbehar's body, the ivory muscles of her stomach and thighs, the stimulating triangle of vermilion where she had painted her pubis with henna, as was the fashion. She moved her legs apart, in readiness for him.

Süleyman eased himself on top of her, and began to push himself inside her. Gülbehar bit her lip, and winced at the pain, but smiled again to reassure him. He pushed again, watching her face intently for evidence of what she was feeling.

She is so eager to please me. She has never asked any more than to sate all my hungers. Why should it ever be any different?

He was inside her now and he began to move more urgently. He closed his eyes and the image of Gülbehar's face disappeared, as if a stone had been thrown into a pool of clear water. Instead he thought of Hürrem, her head thrown back into the pillow, her mouth open in a silent scream, her body arched under him as if she were in the grip of some great torment, the mane of golden red splayed across the pillow. He felt his orgasm come swiftly then, every muscle in his body trembling as the spasm passed through him.

He groaned aloud, and then the strength left him, and he felt Gülbehar's arms enfold him and pull him down on top of her.

He opened his eyes, still gasping for breath, and looked into her face. Gülbehar was still smiling.

"It was good, my Lord?" she whispered.

"Yes," he lied, "it was good."

His hunger was gone. So what more could he want?

The answer was simple. He wanted Hürrem.

HÜRREM SAT ON the terrace, watching the dawn break over the city, the silver sliver of the crescent moon fading into the seeping blue of morning. The calls of the *muezzins* broke the crystal silence. Another night had passed without him. Another night he had spent with Gülbehar. Another night had driven her further into exile.

It had been almost a week now, and Süleyman had not asked for her again. The moment was a passing one. One could not remain an iqbal for ever. If she did not become pregnant, and the Sultan continued to ignore her, she would return to the sewing room and the taunts and lashes of the Kiaya of the Robes.

She would never allow that to happen.

Never.

14

THE KAPI AGA had died a thousand deaths in the week since he had first spoken to Hürrem. Every moment was an unholy terror, waiting for the summons to the Sultan's presence that would be the harbinger of the Sultan's long, slow revenge. There was not a moment that he was free of the dull ache of remorse, no night that he could find any sanctuary in sleep, no day went by that he didn't wonder if there might not be some way to escape. But where could he hide that the Sultan's claws could not reach him, in an empire that spanned three continents?

It was a warm, scented evening, there was nightingale song from the leafy branches of the plane trees. It was soothing, it was treacherous, for there was no safety, no warmth here. Every stone of this accursed place was dangerous.

He turned the key in the lock of the ancient iron door and inched it open. He crept through into the garden.

She was here.

"I DID AS you asked," he said.

Hürrem knelt on the grass beside the marble fountain, a Qur'ān illuminated in green and gold lying open on the wooden stool in front of her. She was wearing a taplock of green satin, a chemise of matching emerald damask, and white silk pantaloons that were so sheer he could make out the color and shape of her flesh beneath them.

He would have found her desirable, if he were not so terrified of her.

Hürrem looked up, the intimation of a smile on her lips. She studied him curiously, with her piercing green eyes, then returned her attention to her Qur'ān. He was not a bad-looking fellow, she thought. Eyes as dull and savage as an animal, but you would expect that in a Serb. They dressed him well: a pelisse of green velvet, yellow slippers, a white sugarloaf turban. The effect was not too unpleasant.

"I said I did as you asked," he repeated.

"I know."

"And now?"

"Now?"

"You must fulfill your part of the bargain."

She turned a page of her Qur'ān. The Kapi Aga tried to control the rage building inside him. How pleasant it would be, he thought, to slice off her head. Be done with this little minx right now. Watch her life's blood spurt over the word of Muhammad and up the gray stone wall. He could almost hear it pulsing out of her neck. If only it would solve the problem.

"When does the Sultan return to the Eski Saraya?"

"Our bargain—"

"When?"

"He goes north to Adrianople tomorrow for the hunting. He will not be back until the leaves fall."

The Kapi Aga noted with satisfaction how the blood drained from her face. Well, that stopped her smiling. How much longer do you think you will remain gözde, little minx?

"We had a bargain," he said.

"There is one more condition."

The Kapi Aga took a step forward, his fists clenched. "I have done as you asked," he hissed, "You can make no more demands of me!"

Hürrem did not even look up. "While I keep your secret for you, I can do as I please."

He looked at her helplessly. Impotent, he thought. Yes, once more, I am impotent. All because of this little witch. "You said you would help me."

Hürrem closed the book, the heavy pages slamming shut with finality, the sound echoing around the tiny court. She got to her feet and came toward him. To his amazement, she ran a fingernail down the length of his arm and took his hand.

"I will help you. After tonight, you will no longer have a problem. You will no longer have to live in fear."

His mouth was suddenly dry. Hürrem moved closer. He could feel the heat of her body and the softness of her thigh against his groin. He felt the murmur of her breath on his cheek. "What do you want?" he said, but his voice did not sound like his own.

"I want some of your juice," she whispered.

MEYLISSA WAS EMBROIDERING a kaftan the color of burnished gold, for the young shahzade, Mustapha, and had taken her handiwork to the window to examine in the fading afternoon light. She heard someone enter the room behind her and her whole body tensed. The Kiaya!

"Did I frighten you?" Muomi said.

"Oh, it's you." Muomi stared at her. Meylissa fidgeted. Muomi's hypnotic, hooded eyes always made her feel uncomfortable. "What do you want?"

"I have what you wanted."

Muomi stretched out a hand and placed a small blue and white jar on the bench. It had a rounded cork stopper. Meylissa snatched it up, removed the stopper, and sniffed.

"It's foul."

"Swallow it all. It will make you sick and kill the baby."

Meylissa replaced the stopper. Suddenly her hands were shaking. "Thank you."

Muomi gave her a pitying look. "It's nothing to do with me," she said, and shuffled out.

15

THE KISLAR AGHASI woke to the sound of a woman screaming. At first he thought it might be just one of the girls howling in her sleep—some of the new ones did that, and he generally organized a beating for them the next day to encourage them to stop. But as he came awake he realized this was no young girl's nightmare. He had heard screams like this before, coming from the bostanji's torture chamber. He felt a cold, sticky sweat erupt all over his body. He swung his legs off the cot, and reached for his wooden pattens, his hands trembling.

The candle had not burned down very far, so he guessed he could not have been asleep more than an hour. He took the candle and hurried out into the corridor, his great belly shivering like jelly inside the nightshirt.

The screams were coming from the dormitory on the floor above. He summoned two of his guards and hurried up the wooden stairs.

MEYLISSA ROLLED NAKED on the floor, tearing at the bare wooden boards with her fingernails, as if desperately searching for some physical escape from the agony in her body. Another spasm shook her body and she curled her knees into her body like a fetus, vomiting blood. Blood and saliva were smeared across her pretty dark face and chest, and her lips were drawn back from her teeth in a snarl, like a dog caught in a trap.

The girls gathered around her, staring, frightened and fascinated by the details of death. Some of them had their legs sprayed with a fine pattern of blood, and when Meylissa writhed again they screamed and jumped back as if she might infect them with this terrible thing also.

Meylissa stared back at them through the angry black mists of her pain and tried to scream: "I'm not sick. It's poison!" But the ugly sawing noises in her throat did not sound like her own voice, nor like anything human. Pain coursed through her again, and she doubled over and screamed.

She felt arms clutching at her, trying to hold her, but she snarled at them and kicked frantically at the air, trying to be free of the agony that was slashing its way through her stomach. She opened her eyes once and stared into the frightened, hairless face of the Kislar Aghasi and at his shoulder she saw Hürrem. She tried to fathom her expression. She wanted to point her finger at her in final damnation, but the eunuchs were holding her arms and she could not talk because her mouth was full of warm blood. She started to choke and the blackness closed across her eyes like a curtain.

Maritza River, near Adrianople

THE HUNTING DOGS flushed the partridge from its lair in the sagebrush, and it exploded into the air, its short wings beating frantically at the air. Ibrahim laughed with excitement and raised the heavy leather gauntlet on his left wrist. The female peregrine falcon was quivering, sensing the closeness of the prey.

Ibrahim removed the leather eye hood from the bird, the huge golden eyes blinking at the overcast. Almost at once the peregrine rose into the air, its huge wings sending the bird soaring to its pitch in just a few seconds.

Ibrahim and Süleyman spurred their horses and set off to chase.

The falcon dipped its wings and stooped. One moment it was riding the air currents, as weightless as the air itself; the next it fell from the sky, like a rock. The partridge flapped at the air in its panic, slow and fat and heavy, with no chance to escape. The falcon hit it from above in an explosion of feathers, the long talons finding purchase in its spine, the blow so violent that the bird died in flight.

For an instant, victim and prey fell together toward the ground. Then the falcon released its death grip and wheeled away, triumphantly, and allowed the partridge to fall, dead, into the swamp.

Ibrahim gave a whoop of delight and galloped hard to the edge of the black water, while the dogs splashed in ahead of the hoofs, vying with each other to retrieve the prize.

Ibrahim looked up and stretched out his gloved arm for the falcon, still wheeling high above his head.

The boar watched the intruder from its sanctuary in a grove of wild rose, its small, yellow eyes bright with fear and confusion. It was panting, as it backed farther into the gorse and thorns. From one side came the yapping of the hunting dogs, from the other the thunder of hoofs and the shouts of the archers. It could not retreat farther into the swamp.

It had only one choice.

Snorting with rage, it charged from the brambles.

Süleyman saw it come, and shouted a warning to Ibrahim. He saw it strike Ibrahim's Arab high on the flank, one yellowed tusk piercing the stallion's side, tearing a bloodied hole in its stomach. The beast bellowed with surprise and agony, and reared back, viscera trailing from the wound. The boar charged again and Ibrahim was thrown on to the ground.

Süleyman was still fifty yards away. He spurred his horse on, pulling the bow from the leather scabbard on his saddle, aiming quickly. His first arrow thudded into the boar's shoulder, throwing it on to its side. It staggered to its feet, squealing, turning to face this new torment.

Süleyman reined in his mount, pulled another arrow from the jeweled quiver that hung from the saddle, and took careful aim. The second arrow hit the boar behind the shoulder, angled in toward the heart, burying itself almost to the flight.

The boar staggered back, its hindlegs giving way under its weight.

Suddenly it was as if the air itself was being rent apart by giant hands, as arrow after arrow thudded into the boar's gray body. It sagged back, blood pouring from two dozen wounds. Moments later it was dead.

The yeniçeri archers cheered and ran forward, and almost immediately Süleyman's horse was surrounded by solak horsemen. Süleyman ignored the captain's shouted apologies and jumped from his horse.

"Ibrahim?"

Ibrahim's Arab was still on its feet, wheeling and bellowing, as the hunting dogs yapped and span around its legs, attracted by the blood, licking and jumping at the viscera trailing from its flanks. Several of the yeniçeris milled among them, one of them trying to catch the horse's reins, while the others swore and slashed at the dogs with their killiç.

The wounded stallion, streaming froth from its mouth, its eyes bulging in its head from pain and terror, wheeled toward him. Süleyman staggered back. But then the dogs were on to it again and the horse wheeled once more and galloped away through the quince trees and was gone.

Süleyman looked around, dazed. Where was Ibrahim? Was he dead?

Suddenly he saw him, knee deep in the swamp, his white kaftan stained with bracken and mud. His turban was askew, lending an air of madness to the broad, wicked grin on his face. In his right hand he held the partridge by its bloodied neck.

"We have our prize!" he shouted to Süleyman.

"I thought you were dead!" Süleyman hissed.

"While I have my Sultan to protect me, how could I die?"

There was such boyish innocence about him, almost as if it had not occurred to him that he might have been injured. In fact, he looked so pleased with himself, and with his trophy, that Süleyman threw back his head and laughed too.

They were in Süleyman's pavilion, the music of Ibrahim's viol all but drowned out by the croaking of the frogs from the swamp. The light from the candles rippled on the billowing scarlet folds of the tent.

Süleyman was still elated from the excitement of the hunt, and could not sleep. He sat cross-legged on the divan while Ibrahim finished the tune he was playing, but his mind was not on music. He had come to a decision, resolving a matter that had troubled him for some weeks. He had weighed his own choice against the demands of tradition and court protocol, his indecision only prolonged by his need to justify himself to his own conscience.

"I am replacing Achmed Pasha as Grand Vizier," he said suddenly, while the last notes of Ibrahim's melody still hung in the air.

"He has been derelict in his duty?" Ibrahim said. Even he looks surprised, Süleyman thought.

"No. But he does not have the ability."

"But he has served in the Divan for many years . . ."

"Yes, yes. But he is not suitable. I intend for him to become my governor in Egypt. I do not intend to humiliate him." Süleyman frowned at Ibrahim's objections. When did Ibrahim himself ever worry about what was proper?

"Who will you replace him with?"

Süleyman felt like a father about to give a treasured gift to his son. He experienced a thrill of pleasure. "You, Ibrahim."

Ibrahim looked away. "Me?"

"Yes. You will be my new Grand Vizier."

Süleyman waited, but the expected gush of gratitude, the familiar boyish grin, did not appear. Instead Ibrahim cradled the viol in his arms and stared gloomily at his hands.

Süleyman felt a prickle of irritation. "What's the matter?"

"Some of the Divan will question why you have given me this post ahead of Achmed Pasha."

"It is not for the Divan to question my judgment on anything."

"It is only what they will say privately that concerns me."

"What they say privately cannot harm you!"

"But it will seem that I have been appointed in the Pasha's place because of our friendship."

Süleyman stared at Ibrahim in astonishment. This was not what he had expected at all. Ibrahim had always accepted the positions he had given him before with relish, even triumph. Süleyman did not believe that Ibrahim was at all concerned with the opinion of his peers in the Divan, or for Osmanli protocol.

"You wish me to reverse my decision?"

Ibrahim was silent for a long time. A night breeze ruffled the folds of the tent, like a long, drawn-out sigh. The exasperation of God? Süleyman wondered. "I am afraid," Ibrahim said.

"Afraid?" Süleyman thought of Ibrahim emerging from the swamp with the partridge, the awe he had felt just then. It had almost seemed that Ibrahim's belief in himself had completely subsumed all fear. "You are obviously not afraid of being gored by a wild boar or trampled by your own horse. So what is it you are afraid of?"

"You, my Lord."

Süleyman stared at him in amazement. "Me?"

"The Grand Vizier's neck is always under the sword, my Lord. Though I would deem it the greatest honor a man could have, yet I confess I am still a little afraid."

Süleyman suddenly understood. He remembered his own father, who had disposed of eight of his own viziers in as many years. Indeed, a common curse among the Turks had been: "May you become the vizier of Selim the Grim!" He remembered how, blinded by his own rage, he himself had almost executed poor old Piri Pasha.

"You have nothing to fear from me, my friend."

Ibrahim looked up, the eager, black eyes pleading. "I always thought I wanted this. Until now. You should not raise me so high that when I fall, it will be fatal."

Süleyman stood up and walked over to Ibrahim, and placed his hands on his shoulders. "I give you my word. While I live, I shall see that you never come to harm. May God be my judge."

Ibrahim took Süleyman's hand and kissed the ruby ring. "You have brought me fame beyond my wildest dreams," Ibrahim whispered. "I pledge myself to serve you till the day I die."

16

The Eski Saraya

WHERE WAS SHE?

The Kapi Aga stared around the shadowed court, torn between the panicked desire to run, and the urgent need to stay and find her. The shadows mocked him.

She is not here. She has betrayed you.

The body is the real traitor, he thought; the burning of the senses that draws you toward pleasure and pain like a moth to a flame. This same flesh that could bring him ecstasy could lure him also to all the torments that Satan—or the chief bostanji, which was the same thing—could devise.

What was he doing here? She was one of the Devil's spawn too, he knew that now; she had proved it to him. He should find a way to be rid of her, take the risk that there was no third conspirator.

Ah, but then he would lose the warmth of that body also, the feel of her warm breasts pressed against him, the hunger of her mouth, the impossible, forbidden ecstasy she brought him to. There was no pleasure he could ever imagine that compared to what he had found in this shadowed court, with its whispering fountain and marble walk and long-fingered planes. Here he was no longer a eunuch, and the terrible, excruciating razor's edge of danger brought him to such a pitch of excitement that even the love of life itself paled in comparison.

But what if Hürrem became pregnant also? There seemed to be no end to this dark tunnel of flesh and its consequence; at the very moment of the last spasm of his climax the black terror would descend on him again, filling his gut with cold, dreadful panic. He would rush from this shadowed garden of his torment, vowing never to return, promising himself he would find a way to be rid of her.

But his body had enslaved him. Within days, sometimes hours, he could think of nothing else but the next time. The image of her body—of his own, as a complete man again—blotted out everything else. These few minutes each week in this shadowed court had become his life.

He tried to pretend they might never be caught. That it would never end.

He heard the rustle of fabric behind him, and he spun round. "Hürrem!"

"Did I frighten you?"

The Kapi Aga felt as if his heart were about to lurch out of his chest. It was beating so hard it almost hurt. "Where did you come from?"

"I was watching you. From behind the pillar."

He stared at her. She was wearing pantaloons of white silk and a gömlek of sheer emerald silk, open to the waist, exposing the gentle swell of her breasts. It rose and fell with her breathing. The Kapi Aga could not take his eyes away.

Hürrem took a step toward him. "Let's do it. Quickly."

She was wearing a gauze veil, attached to the little green taplock she wore on her head. She removed it with a swift, practiced motion of her right hand. The Kapi Aga stared at her. She looked so composed, so controlled. Was she never frightened?

He looked up at the north tower. The windows there stared down at him like two terrible black eyes, watching. The doors were locked, he reminded himself, but nevertheless he pulled Hürrem farther into the shadows below the wall.

Hürrem lifted up his robe and felt for him. "How does it feel to be a man again?" she said.

Was she mocking him? he asked himself. He wondered, as he had wondered a hundred times, why she was doing this. Was it just lust? Did she feel nothing at all for him?

"You killed her," he said.

"It was Muomi's fault. The abortive was too strong."

"You did it deliberately."

"What if I had? Do you think I am worse than you? You would have killed us both if you thought it would save your neck."

The pantaloons lay on the marble. She unfastened the three diamond clasps of the gömlek. He tried to tear his eyes away from the hard little body, concentrate on the lies and truths that her face might betray. "She was your friend."

"While you were practically strangers. You made her pregnant as she passed you in the cloister."

She leaned back against the wall. The Kapi Aga felt his mouth go dry. She was watching him, with that tight little smile on her face, knowing he had no power over her at all.

Her nipples were hard. With desire, or from the cold? He thought he knew the answer to that. It did not matter. He was so swollen he was almost upright. How many complete men could boast that? He took her roughly by the wrists, pressing her against the wall.

"Perhaps one day I will introduce you to the Bosphorus." He put his right hand at her throat. It was a small neck, and his hand could have enclosed it easily. He moved it down to her shoulder and to her breast, squeezing as hard as he could, trying to make her cry out. But her eyes stared back at him, hard and green.

"They say it's rough this time of the year. You should be careful you don't fall in yourself." She lifted his robes and wrapped her thighs around his hips, guiding him toward her. She took a fold of his robe and stuffed it into her mouth to prevent him from crying out as he entered her. The fountain could not disguise such a sound.

The Kapi Aga could not breathe. The intensity of sensation overpowered him, and he bit down on the silk in his mouth, felt all control leaving him. The hatred boiled up inside him; hatred at her for this power she had over him, hatred to all women, and hatred at himself for his weakness. He began to shake.

Hürrem wrapped her arms around his neck and moved her hips so that the silken parts of her gripped and stroked the whole length of his erection. "Give me your juice," she whispered in his ear. "I want it all."

He felt his climax take him over the precipice into shuddering, blinding bliss. For a few scarlet seconds he was free of her, free of his servitude to women, and he gave himself up to it. He did not want to come back. It was like death, and if he were able he would have lost himself in it. That this orgasm could shudder on for always. But when it ended only the cold evening and the fear remained.

Life was a trap. There was no way out. You looked for escape and you were led by the nose to slaughter.

THE KAPI AGA did not hear of his success from Hürrem herself. One day he awoke and found the Palace alive with rumor: the iqbal was with child!

Relief quickly transformed itself to a fresh terror. What should he do now? He could not go to the garden again. To make love to the Sultan's kadin was an offense too terrible to contemplate. Yet, if he did not, what would Hürrem do? Would she betray him? But how could she, without betraying herself?

Then another thought struck him. What if the child was his?

He realized he had no way of reading her mind. He was a pawn in a game he no longer understood. From the moment he had opened that gate for the first time to seduce one of the Sultan's odalisques, he had lost the power over his own life.

He was helpless. There was nothing to do but wait.

17

HAFISE SURVEYED HER son's new iqbal with the practiced eye of a woman who has spent almost all her adult life in the treacherous world of the Harem. She could tell at once that this one was a different proposition to Gülbehar. It was in the way she walked, the way she held herself. Her eyes were a little too knowing, her tongue—or so she had heard—a little too quick.

But that was perhaps not such a bad thing. She had not survived so many years herself in Selim's Harem without a certain wit. And, yes, a little steel.

"Hürrem," she said warmly, extending her hand, "I am delighted with your news. Come and sit here beside me."

Hürrem smiled and seated herself at the other end of the divan. It was a warm afternoon, and they were sitting on a terrace over the shaded, eastern court of the Palace. Finches twittered in ornate cedar cages hanging from the eaves, and there were sherbets and melon and *rahat lokum* laid out on the low table in front of them. Behind them the city shimmered in the afternoon haze, the cupolas of the mosques shining like diamonds among the dust.

"Süleyman is away hunting at Adrianople. I have sent a courier today with a message for him. I am sure he will be as overjoyed with your news as I am."

Hürrem put a hand on her stomach. "We will have to wait many months to gauge the extent of his pleasure."

A good answer, Hafise thought. If it's a girl, we are all back at the beginning. "If God wills it," she said. Hafise reached out and took a strand of Hürrem's hair, held it to the light.

They all touch me this way, Hürrem thought. As if to remind me that I am Osmanli property.

"You have beautiful hair," Hafise said. "Not red, yet not gold. Where are you from?"

"My father was a Khan of the Krim Tartars, Crown of Veiled Heads," she said, trying to conceal the depth of pride in her voice. It would not do to let the Sultan's mother know she felt superior. Hafise was, after all, only the daughter of a Georgian peasant.

"And how did you come to us?"

"My father saw an opportunity."

Hafise smiled. "For you? Or for himself?"

"The spahis had to tie him to the ground and force the guns and the money into his pockets. He struggled and screamed. It was terrible."

Hafise did not smile. "You laugh when you say these things, but there is no laughter in your eyes."

Hürrem felt the Valide's scrutiny. She needed this allegiance, she decided. Yet she should not underestimate this woman, peasant stock or not. This plump and pleasant little chicken had the eyes of a hawk. "Why should I cry? He still lives in a tent, I live in a palace. In the end I did better from the trade."

"So you are happy here?"

"I will be happier when my Lord returns."

"I was married to Sultan Selim for many years. I can count the number of weeks we spent together on my fingers. It is a lonely life, Hürrem."

Hürrem nodded. "I shall take your advice, then, Highness. I will go back to my father. Can you arrange a horse for me?"

Hafise laughed, in spite of herself. The girl was mocking her a little, but there was truth behind what she said. Why be miserable over things you do not have the power to change? "I am afraid even I cannot do that. Now you have the Sultan's child, this Harem will be your home for the rest of your life."

"Then I shall have to arrange for larger rooms."

Hafise smiled and indicated her own apartment. "Like mine, perhaps."

Hürrem smiled back. "If God wills it."

"I would not be surprised if that is His design." Hafise selected a piece of lokum, flavored with pistachio nut, and bit into it. "If there is anything you need, you must tell me. In Islam, the mother is sacred, and never more so than now. Everything will be done to ensure your comfort."

"There is one thing, Highness."

"Yes?"

"I want a bodyguard."

Hafise looked up at her, startled. "A bodyguard? Here?"

"I am frightened."

"Of what?"

"I have heard rumors. That I will not live to see my baby born."

"Who dares threaten you . . . and the Sultan's child?"

Hürrem averted her eyes. "I don't know. It might be just talk."

She's lying, Hafise thought. She knows who it is, but dares not say. There is only one person who would wish her dead. Gülbehar! She shook her head. No, that was impossible. Gülbehar was not capable of *that*. But the girl did seem frightened.

"If you think these rumors are true, you should have your servant girl taste all your food, even try on any new clothes before you wear them, in case the fabric has been poisoned. As a precaution I will have the Kislar Aghasi assign one of his eunuchs to you."

"Thank you, Highness."

"We must ensure that nothing happens to the Sultan's son."

Hürrem smiled her understanding. They are all so sure it is a boy, she thought. But that is the one thing over which I have no control.

THE KAPI AGA watched from the north tower, saw her move out of the long shadows in the court and come to sit on the marble bench beside the fountain, then open the Qur'ān on her lap. His fist closed in an agony of indecision. She had come again. Why, why? What was she trying to do? Soon she might be Süleyman's kadin, what more did she want? They could not continue now, the risks were too great. But if he did not go . . . what would she do?

He had to talk to her, had to end this torture. Even his desire was gone now; when he had discovered that she was pregnant, it had seemed to evaporate and the vacuum inside him was quickly replaced by a longing to survive. This must stop.

What did she want? What would she do if he did not go to meet her? Would she—could she—somehow betray him over the death of Meylissa?

He made up his mind and hurried from the room, locking the door behind him. He hurried down the wooden steps to the courtyard.

He hesitated for long minutes at the iron gate, the big metal key resting in the lock. The key and the lock, he thought. Men and women. You put the key in the lock and you open the gate to dreams and to nightmares. There was nothing as compelling as a locked door.

He had to discover what she wanted.

He turned the key, and slipped inside. Hürrem looked up, and her eyes widened in surprise. Then she dropped the Qur'an, stood up, and screamed.

The Kapi Aga stared at her, the astonishment on her face—faked, he knew—mirrored his own. What was she doing? He heard someone moaning, and recognized the sound of his own voice. He wanted to run, but his muscles would not respond.

He knew what she had done.

He looked to his right and found himself staring into the startled face of one of his own black guards.

"You little whore!" he whispered. He drew the jeweled dagger from his pelisse and slashed at her. Hürrem screamed again and fell backward, the stroke scything the air inches from her face.

The Kapi Aga did not see the guard rush at him. He was aware of the sudden flash of the blade, and he heard its deadly whisper. Then the dagger was gone and with it, his right hand. He gasped and clutched at his wrist. There was no pain, not then, but he screamed in horror, and stared at the stump, gagging, and the spurt of bright blood.

Then he fell to his knees and tried to wrench the dagger from the fingers of his severed hand. If he could kill her now, it would be all right. They could do what they wanted with him. As long as the little witch was dead.

But then the guards were dragging him away, and he screamed again, this time at the sudden white hot pain in his wrist and he saw the dark stains soaking the cobbles, the trail of blood leading away from the little harlot in the green taplock. He tried to scream his curses at her again, but then one of the guards struck him with the heavy steel handle of his yataghan and he groaned and his head fell back.

THE HAWK SOARED on the updraft from the baked cobblestones of the city, then wheeled and dived toward the Bosphorus, hovering again over the walls of the Topkapi Saraya. Its golden eye picked out the twin towers of the Gate of Felicity, where the head of the Kapi Aga was turning black and wrinkled as an olive in its niche high in the wall. Outside the walls his decapitated body still hung from the huge hook where it had been tormented for three days, the steel point penetrating the ribs and the thigh, a rope lashed from the scaffold to the wrists holding it upright. It would be there till the carrion crows had finished their work and the sinews and ligaments rotted from the bones.

The hawk wheeled again, out toward the Golden Horn and the old wooden palace high on the hill beside the great mosque of Bayezit. On a balcony among the brass domes, a woman stood with her hand over her swelling belly. She was conspicuous for the two braids, tied with satin cord, that hung halfway down her back. Her hair was the color of fire, and on her lips there was a smile.

The months would pass quickly. She touched her belly. So let him come. Let him come.

THE DAY OF the birthing there was white on the roofs of the Harem.

A birth chair and swaddling bandages were brought to Hürrem's apartment, incense was burned, rose petals were strewn over the marble floors, amulets and blue beads were hung around the room to ward off the evil eye.

Hürrem had never experienced such pain. When the baby would not come, the Harem midwife, a terrible Nubian who perhaps weighed as much as three odalisques, sat on her stomach to force the child from her womb.

Hürrem screamed. A stick of ivory was jammed between her teeth to silence her.

"Bite down!" the midwife hissed. "Bite down and be silent!"

Finally it happened. Crouched over the chair, supported on each side by the midwives, she delivered up the child, the Nubian receiving the infant in a cloth of linen, while she recited the declaration of Faith.

Allahu Akbar . . . God is Great . . .

The Kislar Aghasi stood watching, ensuring there was no substitution of the precious child. He took the child himself to the white marble fountain and gave it the customary three washes. Sugared oil was placed in its mouth to ensure a sweet and amiable tongue; kohl was smeared round its eyes to guarantee a profound gaze. A diamond-encrusted Qur'ān was touched to its forehead.

Hürrem clutched at the midwife's shoulders, blinking the perspiration from her eyes. "What is it?" she begged her. "Just tell me what it is!"

It was the Kislar Aghasi who answered her. "You are delivered of a son, my Lady," he told her.

"A son," Hürrem repeated. She smiled at him, then fainted dead away.

PART 2

DARK ANGEL

18

Venice, 1528

SHE WAS A vision in black velvet, a dark angel with hair as black and lustrous as coal, eyes like two chips of turquoise. She had high patrician cheekbones, and full lips, moist and red, as if they were bruised. The bodice of the *vestura* was fashionably low-cut, the skin at her shoulders and breasts was smooth as ivory, and the small gold cross at her throat—he could imagine the warm pulse—seemed to taunt him.

Twice forbidden.

The *piazza* was crowded and noisy, ringing to the cries of the hawkers, the oaths of sailors gambling and singing in the arcades, the harsh staccato of the Armenians and Dalmatians, and the harmonious melody of the Venetians. An Albanian pushed past in his baggy trousers, chewing a nub of garlic like a sweet; a *togato* in the purple robes of a senator replied with a wave of the hand and an "addio caro vecchio" to the respectful salute of other citizens.

It was as if none of them were there. Abbas watched her ascend the steps to the portal of the church. She walked with almost exaggerated grace, her gaze to the ground, but just once she looked up and Abbas felt as if he had been punched hard in the chest. Her lips parted just slightly, enough for him to know that she had seen him, that his presence had affected her in some manner. God alone knew how.

He could not breathe. She was the most perfect woman he had ever seen in his life. He wanted to run forward and grab her arm, run with her from the piazza.

The old hag who was escorting her gave him a contemptuous and dismissive glance as they climbed the steps of the church of Santa Maria dei Miracoli. Then they disappeared inside.

"Did you see her?" he whispered.

"Of course I saw her," Ludovici answered. "That's Julia Gonzaga."

"You know her?"

"My step-sister knows her. She's her cousin."

"Her cousin?" Abbas grabbed Ludovici's *saion*—the fashionable waist-length scarlet smock he wore over his shirt—and pulled him toward the steps.

"What are you doing?"

"I want to see her."

"Tu sei pazzo—you're mad!"

"Come on!"

Ludovici grabbed his friend's arm. "Do you know who her father is? Antonio Gonzaga—he's a *consigliatore!*"

"I don't care!"

"You don't care?" Ludovici was alarmed, but not surprised. Abbas was one of the most passionate, headstrong young men he had ever known. Reckless, his father called him. If it was his fault, it was also his charm. Perhaps it was in his blood, Ludovici had decided. A Moor is a Moor. But this time he would not allow him to make a fool of himself. Besides, there was real danger in this.

"I just want to look."

"You are not meant to look! She's a Gonzaga!"

"Stay here, then," Abbas said, and he pulled away and sprinted up the steps. Ludovici hesitated. To hell with him! *Corpo di Dio!* It was his funeral. He turned and started to walk away, but then changed his mind and ran up the steps after him.

THE GAUNT, DISAPPROVING faces of saints peered down from the richly gilt ceiling. A bust of the Vergine della Santa Clara frowned at the pews from her balustrade on the cold gray and coral marble walls. *Putti* and sea monsters cavorted on the pilasters of the arched columns.

It was dark inside the church, and cold after the warmth of the piazza. Light angled in from the stained glass above the apse, like two giant fingers; they seemed to point out for him the two figures kneeling at the prie-dieu before the altar. Abbas felt a prickle of apprehension. The marble images of Francis and the Archangel Gabriel glared down at him from their niches in accusation at his trespass. He felt that at any moment they would suddenly groan into life and jump down from the walls to confront this intruder.

They are just pieces of marble, he told himself. They have no power. But the sanctity of these images reinforced Ludovici's warning. He was stepping into another world now, a world he did not fully understand.

He felt a hand on his right shoulder and almost cried aloud.

"Ludovici!"

"Did you think it was Gonzaga?"

Abbas glanced at the half figure of the Archangel behind him on the wall. "Someone a little more celebrated than that," he said, and grinned at his friend's confusion. He turned back to the two shadowy figures at the altar. "She is the loveliest thing I have ever seen."

"She is not for you, Abbas."

"Perhaps."

"Perhaps! You might as well reach for the moon, Abbas!"

The old woman with Julia heard their voices and raised her head from her prayers. Abbas and Ludovici ducked behind the shelter of the pillar. Abbas put his finger to his lips. They waited.

But when he looked again, they were gone. He turned toward the nave, and saw the old woman hurrying the girl down the aisle. The girl looked back once, her face framed for a moment by a pool of yellow light flooding in through the great doors. Then the *duenna* pulled her away.

"Tu sei pazzo!" Ludovici hissed.

"I was raised a Moor and a Muslim, in the desert. Yet I am forced to live here in a Christian republic, on the water!" Abbas grinned at him. "If you were me, perhaps you would go a little mad too!"

MAHMUD STOOD ON the balcony of the *palazzo,* both broad hands on the balustrade, watching the sunset through a veil of pink over the snow-topped peaks of the Cadore and the backdrop of blossoming clouds to the west. The gondolas and galleys and distant islands faded into dark relief against the pearl gray of the lagoon. It was a sight that never failed to stir him, a harbor befitting the greatest naval republic of the Mediterranean. Sometimes he even forgot that this was not his heritage, that he was merely a paid mercenary. But that was the reality of the matter; it was a lesson his son must learn.

"It is quite impossible!" he growled.

"I have to meet her," Abbas said.

"How long have we lived among these people? Six years? And still you do not seem to understand the first thing about them!"

"We can protect their lives but not marry their daughters."

Mahmud rounded on his son, his body taut with rage, and Abbas felt his resolution falter. It had not been an easy thing to confront his father. The Captain General of the Republic was a bear of a man, his shoulders bulging the silken fabric of his doublet, the great frizzled beard adding to his size and ferocity. When he was angry, as he was now, his eyes shone in his dark face like lamps.

"There are reasons for our presence here," he said. "There is a reason for everything." The reason, of course, was that the Doge never trusted his army to the command of his own nobles, as each of them feared—with good reason—that it might be turned against him. In fact, the Captain General was rarely an Italian and often, as now, not even a Christian.

For myself, Mahmud thought, I have a brother prince in Barbary who would sleep more soundly if I were dead. Yes, there is a reason for everything.

"They treat us like dirt," Abbas said.

"The *magnifici* treat everyone like dirt. They mean nothing by it. It is habit."

"But we have royal blood."

"What royal blood?" Mahmud crashed both fists onto the walnut table that stood between them. "The royal house of a Muslim prince? What does that mean to them? I will tell you what we are . . . we are mercenaries. Do not pretend to yourself that we belong here. You may live in a palazzo and dress like the son of a togati, but you are not one of them. Remember that."

"Then what am I to do? Who am I to marry?"

Mahmud turned away. "Do as the other young bloods do, and find your fun on the Ponte delle Tette—the Bridge of the Teats!" Abbas knew the place. It had earned its name from the women who stood stripped to the waist in the doorways, leering at the young men. "Anyway," Mahmud added, "you are too young to think about a wife."

Abbas took a deep breath. He had never defied his father before. "I want to meet Julia Gonzaga."

Mahmud sighed. He was not angry anymore. What was the point? It was like a small child petulantly demanding his own castle. It was unattainable, and that was an end to it. Even if Gonzaga were the kind of man who could entertain the thought of his daughter marrying a blackamoor—and Gonzaga was certainly not that kind of man—there was a statute in the Republic forbidding any Venetian noble to marry outside his peers. A *magnifico* of the Council of Ten could not even speak with a foreigner in private, even the Captain General of the Army.

Especially the Captain General of the Army.

"It is just your youth, Abbas. Tomorrow you will have forgotten all about it."

"You judge me poorly," Abbas said and left the room.

FROM THE BALCONY of her father's palazzo, behind the latticed screen of the *loggia,* Julia Gonzaga watched the theater of the Venetian night. The lanterns hanging from the stern of the gondolas left rippling tracks on the surface of the canal. Voices whispered along the *fondamenta*, and a young couple vanished arm in arm through a dark *sottoportico.* Julia pushed aside a stab of envy.

She thought again about what had happened to her that afternoon in the church of Santa Maria dei Miracoli. Why had the boy stared at her like that? And who was he? He was black, a negro perhaps, like some of the *gondolieri*, yet he did not dress like one. He wore a jeweled *bareta* on his head, and his linen *camicia* was open at the front, as the more fashionable young noblemen wore their shirts.

So who was he?

Yet another mystery to add to mystery on top of mystery. It was like living in a great house where all the rooms had been locked to her. There was the mystery of her father, a strict, somber presence who moved in and out of the shadows of his palazzo like . . . like, she thought blushing, the shadow of God Himself. There was the mystery of her mother, who had died in childbirth, never known, never spoken of.

But most of all there was the mystery of men.

Her father had intimated to her that one day she might marry one. The notion provoked two sentiments in her: dread and relief. A man was somehow different, she knew that, but in ways she could only guess at. According to the Bible and her duenna—her governess, Signora Cavalcanti—young men were the Devil's work, and would put her very soul in jeopardy. Yet there was part of her that wondered if damnation might not be better than this. She was already buried alive. What could be worse?

Lately she had begun to think about men continually. Against her intention, she was sure, Signora Cavalcanti had awakened a terrible fascination in her, invoking the sort of compelling curiosity of a locked cellar door. Despite her trepidation, Julia was hungry to find out what lay beyond.

But how?

19

T HE GIRL STANK of wine and sweat. She collapsed, laughing, onto Ludovici's lap. He put his hand inside her dress, laughing too, and popped out her breast, weighing it in his hand as if it were a fine vase he was displaying to a guest. It was white and heavy, and the nipple, he noticed, had been rouged.

"Now look, Abbas! What are you getting so upset about? See, they're all the same underneath!"

The woman shrieked and cuffed Ludovici playfully round the head. She pulled up the bodice in a feigned attempt at modesty.

"She's like a whale drawn up onto the beach," Abbas said with disgust. "All that is missing are the gaffer's hooks."

The prostitute's laughter died in her throat. She stared at Abbas with a look of outrage and pain. "*Bastardo!*" she swore at him. "Heathen! I suppose you'd rather hump a camel!"

She flounced away. Ludovici was still laughing. He picked up the goblet in front of him and drained some more of the thick *rosso* down his throat, some of it spilling onto his white *camicia*, where it spread like a bloodstain across his chest.

Abbas looked around. The *taverna* was crowded, mostly with the young sons of togati and their whores. The place was a riot of color; in the tightly controlled society of La Serenissima, as Venice was known to its inhabitants, it was only the working classes and prostitutes who could wear what they liked; the wives and daughters of the patricians always dressed in black. The young noblemen meanwhile had hair to their shoulders, their shirts wide open at the front, their baretas glittering with gemstones.

The place reeked of sour wine and perfume. From the rear came the even less appetizing aroma of urine.

"Don't take life so seriously," Ludovici was saying. "A man just needs a hole to wiggle around in. Who cares who it belongs to?"

Abbas shook his head. His friend was drunk. "If it matters to Gonzaga, it matters to me."

"You were never so fussy before." Ludovici grinned at him. The red wine had stained his teeth. He looked ridiculously young. Yet he's older than me, Abbas reminded himself.

"Perhaps I know better now," Abbas said. It was true. He had paid these doxies for their favors and feigned endearments, and it was never like the love the troubadours sang about. Some of them made him pay more because he was a Moor; others charged him less because they were curious. They were all very drunk, or very coarse, or God forgive him, very old.

"A man needs it," Ludovici had said to him once, "like having a good shit. Only it's a lot more expensive."

Abbas stood up, disgusted with the memories, impatient with the noise and the smells and Ludovici's laughter. He pulled him to his feet. "Let's go!"

Ludovici shouted a protest as Abbas dragged him outside. The goblet clattered onto the wooden floor as the door slammed shut behind them.

Abbas stood his friend against the wall of the taverna, holding him up by his shirt. It was sodden with wine. "Listen to me," he whispered. "You have to help me."

Ludovici tried to focus, startled by the sudden urgency in his friend's voice. "What's the matter?"

"Julia. Can you get a letter to her?"

"Tu sei pazzo!"

"Maybe I am. Will you do it?"

"Please, Abbas . . ."

"Will you do it?"

"Gonzaga will kill you!"

"I don't care about Gonzaga. I want to meet her. Just once."

"For God's sake . . ."

"You said she is Lucia's cousin . . ."

"It makes no difference . . ."

"She can take a letter for me."

Ludovici's shoulders sagged in defeat. It was useless to argue with Abbas when his mind was made up. "I will ask her."

Abbas beamed and clapped him on the shoulder. "It will work, Ludovici, you will see!"

Ludovici felt suddenly sober. He shivered. "It's dangerous, Abbas."

"Danger gives meaning to life."

"It can also end it. Don't do this. If you do meet with her—and that is impossible, Abbas, for she goes nowhere unescorted—you will be in grave danger. You cannot lightly toy with such a man's honor."

Abbas turned, his face half in shadow, the light of the moon lending an eerie intensity to his eyes. "And I have my honor, Ludovici! My father may be happy to be the Doge's dog of war, but I intend to be my own man!"

Oh my God, Ludovici thought. Love and rebellion. A potent mixture. Enough to blind him to common sense.

"Don't do this," Ludovici whispered.

"I will write the letter tonight!" Abbas put a hand around Ludovici's shoulder and led him down the *ruga* toward the Piazza San Marco. All the way Ludovici cursed himself for a fool for ever having mentioned Lucia's relationship with Julia.

No good would come of this. He knew it.

A LINE TAGGED with clothes danced in front of a dove-gray plaster wall. On the other side of the canal an old duenna leaned out of a window to haul up a basket of provisions from a gondola moored beside the *riva*. Sunlight reflecting from the canal threw dappled shadows on the façades of the palazzi, even penetrating the gloom of the *loggie*.

Julia had draped her lacework across her knees, enjoying the warmth of the yellow sun on her skin as she worked. Lucia sat with her, murmuring the petty gossips she had heard from her brother. Lucia visited her often during the summer—escorted by her duenna, naturally—to gossip and sew. It was a welcome relief for both of them from the monastic solitude of their daily lives.

"I hear you are to be married," Lucia said. She was a dark, thickset girl with the beginnings of a faint mustache on her upper lip. Her older brother, Ludovici, was fair and did not yet even have a man's beard. Life was not fair, Julia thought.

Julia glanced up at Signora Cavalcanti. She scowled back at her in triumph. "Yes," Julia said. "In the autumn."

"Is he handsome?"

"I have only heard my father speak of him." Julia pretended to study her lacework. "He is a member of the Consiglio di Dieci also. His wife died three summers ago."

From the corner of her eye she could see the disappointment—or was it horror?—on Lucia's face. She leaned closer. "How old is he?"

"He is in his sixtieth year. But he may yet be handsome." She fought to keep the tremor out of her voice. What a match her father had made for her! Her lip quivered in anger and self-pity. Well, at least he seemed content with it.

"What is his name?"

"Serena. Don't ask me his first name, I don't remember."

Signora Cavalcanti looked up sharply, hearing the petulance in her voice. Julia lowered her eyes.

"I have seen him," Lucia said. "He is very . . . very important."

He's like a dead leaf, Lucia thought. How appropriate they would be married in the autumn. If he lived that long. Already he looked as if all the juice had been squeezed out of him. She stifled a giggle. Poor Julia!

They lapsed into silence. Signora Cavalcanti put down her embroidery and rubbed her eyes. "I think I shall rest," she said and went inside. Julia heard her pull the drapes at her bedroom window on the *terrazzo* above them.

Lucia waited until her own duenna had left them for a moment, then reached into the folds of her vestura and produced a letter, sealed with red wax. She almost threw it into Julia's lap, as if it were aflame.

Julia gaped at her, astonished. "What is this?"

"It's a letter," Lucia whispered, glancing toward the open doorway that led from the balcony, "Quickly, open it!"

"Who is it from?"

"You have an admirer!"

Julia imagined that this was how she might feel if she fell in the canal. Complete surprise, embarrassment, very cold. She held up the envelope. There was one word written in black ink: Julia. She tried to swallow.

"Well, open it!"

Lucia's face betrayed the enthusiasm and curiosity of a child. Julia quickly tore it open.

I love you. You are the most beautiful woman I have ever seen in my life. I must meet you. I will face any danger. Just tell me what I must do.

Julia read the words over and over, and her hands began to shake uncontrollably.

"What does it say?" Lucia whispered urgently.

"Who is this from?" Julia asked her.

"I don't know. A friend of my brother's."

"Who?"

"He would not say. He just asked me to give it to you. Show me!"

Lucia tried to read the letter but Julia snatched it away angrily, folded it, and slipped it down the front of her vestura. At least it would be safe there from the eyes of Signora Cavalcanti. She tore the envelope into small pieces and dropped them over the balcony into the canal.

They floated and fell like snow.

"Why does this friend of your brother's send me letters? Does he wish to disgrace me?"

"Ludovici said that it was the only way."

"The only way for what?"

"I don't know. The only way you might ever meet, I suppose." She gripped Julia's arm. "What is it all about?" she asked her, now thoroughly enjoying this intrigue.

Julia tried to compose herself. Her cheeks felt hot. She was at once terrified and elated: terrified of the consequences if her father should ever find out; elated at the sudden and unexpected entry of romance into her life.

She was also startled by her own reaction; almost at once she had begun to form a plan. A part of her was screaming inside: This is madness! You are bound to be discovered! You will disgrace the family name, and your soul will be condemned to torment!

Another part of her wondered which punishment might be considered worse by her father.

But it was impossible. To meet a complete stranger, without introduction, without escort. No, she would burn the letter. As soon as Lucia left, she must burn it immediately.

If the author of the letter were a suitable companion—husband even—for her, then he would have arranged a meeting through her father. Whoever it was, he was obviously not a togati, or the member of any noble family of any note.

And yet.

"What are you going to do?" Lucia asked her.

And yet.

"My duenna sleeps every afternoon between three o'clock and five. I study the Bible in my bedroom. Tell your brother . . ." She forced herself to swallow. ". . . Tell your brother that his friend should have a gondola waiting by the canal at that time. If he is any earlier, or any later, I will not come down, and he is not to bother me again."

Lucia started at her in awe and surprise. "You are going to meet him . . . without your duenna? Without your father's knowledge?"

"Yes, I am," Julia told her. "I don't care if I'm damned." She thought about her marriage to a sixty-year-old consigliatore. "I'm damned anyway . . . aren't I?"

20

JULIA WRAPPED THE long *mantello* cape more closely around her shoulders, pulling the hood low over her forehead, throwing her face in shadow. It was not too late to turn back, she reminded herself. She looked back up the stairs. It was dark and cool, and she could hear Signora Cavalcanti's snores from her bedroom. Pig.

She opened the heavy wooden door a few inches and peered down the gray stone steps. The light hurt her eyes and she squinted against the glare. Mary, Mother of God, forgive me, she murmured. It was there! The gondola was moored on the iron rung at the foot of the steps. The gondolier was a tall negro with a scarlet satin camicia with slashed sleeves, his broad-rimmed hat trimmed with more scarlet. He was leaning on his *punta,* with arrogant ease, almost as if he were mocking her fright.

She inched the door shut once more and took a deep breath, closing her eyes.

It's not too late to go back.

Go back to what?

Go back to her room and open the great black Bible on her bureau. To take her needlework to the window to catch the light and ease the strain on her eyes. To watch the gondoliers grin and bow their heads, to peer at the curtained canopies and wonder . . .

To go back to her room and wait for a sixty-year-old senator called Serena.

She made some final adjustments to her hood and opened the door. She ran down the steps, pulled the curtains aside, and jumped into the gondola.

She stifled a sob of surprise—and horror.

He was black.

Not as black as the gondolier, but a Moor certainly. She remembered him immediately; he was the boy who had been staring at her at the church of Santa Maria dei Miracoli. This was why he could not approach her father. He was not only not a son of a magnifico, he was not even Venetian!

The hood still hid her face, but it was as if he could read the expression on her face. "They tell me I have all the trappings of a fine gondolier," he said, grinning, "but my father would not permit it. He thinks the son of the Defender of the Republic should aspire to greater things."

"Your father—?"

"—is the Captain General of the Army."

Mahmud, the Moor! She had heard of him. It made sense to her now.

"If you find my appearance too shocking, my Lady, you may leave the gondola and you will never hear from me again. Because I will throw myself in the river." He grinned again, and she found her initial outrage evaporating.

"I may only be away for a few minutes," she said, but her voice sounded barely like her own. He nodded to the gondolier and pulled the curtains behind them. She heard the clank of the iron rung and then the gentle splash of water as the gondolier steered them toward the center of the canal.

"Where are we going?"

"Nowhere. Where can we talk more anonymously than in here?"

There were heavy blue velvet curtains on all sides so they had total privacy inside the tiny cabin. She noticed a not unpleasant must of mildew and walnut. All she could see outside the cabin was the gaily colored hose of the gondolier as he stood at his position on the *punta piede*.

Julia turned her attention to her companion. He was young, she realized, almost as young as herself. His skin was the color of walnut, his hair tightly curled, though not like the jet-colored wool of the negro gondolier. His features were smooth and rounded, like a statue cast from bronze. He was wearing a white linen camicia and a doublet of rich blue silk, and a ruby glinted in his left ear.

He was quite the most exotic thing she had ever seen in her life.

"What's your name?" she said.

"Abbas."

"Abbas . . ." she repeated, testing the sound of it on her own tongue.

"It is not a Venetian name, but as you can see, I am not quite Venetian myself."

She reached inside the folds of her mantello. "Here is your letter."

He seemed confused. "I do not want it back . . ."

"It is dangerous. If you like I will burn it . . ."

"I do not want you to burn it." He took it from her. "I meant what I said."

She felt her cheeks grow hot. What was it he wanted from her? "You know Ludovici Gambetto?" she said.

"His father is a general and adviser to my father. We are both renegades, I suppose."

"Both?"

He seemed surprised that he needed to explain. "We are both out-siders, after a fashion."

"The Gambetti are one of the noble families of Venice."

Abbas looked embarrassed. "You don't know?"

"Don't know?"

"Ludovici came from outside the marriage. Signor Gambetto had a mis-tress. When she died, Ludovici was still an infant. Signor Gambetto assumed responsibility for him but . . . but he's still an outsider."

Julia stared at him. Mistress? What was that? And how could a child be born outside a marriage?

"Perhaps I should not have told you," Abbas said. "I assumed you knew."

Why would she know? No one ever told her anything. "It was never mentioned."

"I am sorry for . . ." He spread his hands and looked around the little velvet canopy ". . . for this. I wanted my father to speak for me, but he said it was impossible. But I had to talk to you, I had to. You are the most beau-tiful woman I have ever seen in my life." He reached up and pulled back her hood. She froze, thinking he meant to touch her. But as the hood fell away he just stared at her, studying her face with frightening intensity.

"You are magnificent," he whispered.

For a moment she wanted to laugh; it was the most glorious thing any-one had ever said to her. She had suspected her own beauty for a long time, but suddenly the risks of the afternoon all seemed worthwhile. She would have run the gauntlet of a thousand knives for this sort of adoration.

She felt the blood rush to her head. She had no idea what she was meant to do or say. She pulled the hood back over her eyes. "I should be going back."

"Not yet."

"If my duenna discovers this . . ."

"Just a few minutes more." A shadow passed over the canopy as the gon-dola glided under a bridge. She heard the shouts of urchins playing on the cobbles. "Am I too offensive to gaze at?"

"Oh no," she whispered, "it's not that."

"I have to see you again."

"I cannot."

"You must. I have never felt like this before in my life. It is like being on fire."

"I am to be married," Julia stammered.

He seemed angered rather than dismayed. "When?"

"October. My husband is to return from Cyprus . . ."

"I cannot let it happen."

"You must stop talking like this. You're frightening me. We must go back."

He lowered his voice to a whisper. "Could you love a Moor like I love an infidel?"

"Take me back," she said, but her voice cracked and betrayed her.

A few minutes later she heard the clang of iron as the gondola moored again at the foot of the steps outside the palazzo. Julia stood up and the gondola swayed. She fell and Abbas caught her arm.

"Let me see your face once more."

She pulled away from him, and slowly drew back her hood. She watched his lips part in a smile of pleasure. It transformed his face. For some reason she saw in her mind the image of a rosebud, clenched tight as a fist against the frost, bursting into blossom with the first warmth of spring.

Him? she wondered. Or me?

"I will not think of anything else until I see you again," he said.

"I cannot see you again," she lied, and she scrambled out of the gondola and ran up the steps. She did not stop running until she had reached the sanctuary of her own room, where she knelt before the wooden crucifix on the wall and prayed for forgiveness, and then for another chance to sin.

21

ANTONIO GONZAGA HAD noticed a subtle and worrying change in his daughter. He worried over the rose-pink flush in her cheeks and the suppressed ripple of excitement in her manner. It was not commensurate with a young lady whose thoughts should have been fully occupied with religious instruction and lacework.

The maid set two plates of *squazzetto,* a rich broth made with rice and chicken, in front of them. Gonzaga watched his daughter take up her spoon.

"Put your shoulders back."

Julia did as she was commanded.

Gonzaga could not conceal a frown of irritation. The sooner she was married and off his hands, the better.

"A young lady of breeding should not slouch at table."

"Yes, Father."

"Soon you will be the wife of a member of the Consiglio di Dieci. He will expect proper manners from you."

"Yes, Father."

What could be wrong with the girl? he thought. He had seen that cow-look on a woman before: his wife, on their wedding night; and his mistress, whenever she was pregnant. Something that happened with all too frequent regularity.

He swallowed a draft of thick, red wine and drummed his fingers on the table as he pondered the change. Surely the thought of marrying Serena had not raised this blush in her cheeks? If it had, she had sorely misjudged her man. That, after all, was not the purpose of marriage. The suspicion of such sluttish thoughts in his own daughter made him flush with anger.

He pushed his plate away and stood up.

Julia looked up, alarmed. "Father?"

"I feel unwell. I shall rest. You will have to excuse me." He left, leaving her to finish her supper alone.

GONZAGA SAT AT his desk in his private study, staring gloomily into the candle. The room was consistent with a man of Gonzaga's influence and gravity. A painting of the *Death of the Virgin* by Carpaccio dominated the room; two smaller paintings, a Virgin and Child by Bellini and a portrait of himself, for which he had commissioned Palma Vecchio five years ago, hung on either side of the door. Persian and Syrian silk carpets hung among the tapestries on the walls and two bronzes by Il Riccio stood above the fireplace.

There was a timid knock on the door.

"Chi Xiè?" he snapped. "Who is it?"

"Signora Cavalcanti, Excellency."

"Enter."

Signora Cavalcanti entered softly, and bent to kiss the sleeve of his black velvet gown.

"Excellency," she murmured. "You wished to see me?"

"I am troubled, Signora Cavalcanti."

"No failing on my part, I hope, Excellency."

Gonzaga inspected her minutely. "I do not know, Signora."

The duenna wrung her hands. She was terrified of Gonzaga. In his long black gown with its sumptuous *alto e basso* velvet weave, his bareta and stole, also of black velvet, the silver buckles and plates at his girdle, and the somber gray eyes staring at her from beneath the long, beetle-black eyebrows, it was how she imagined it would be to stand before God at the Judgment. "I assure your Excellency I have been most diligent in my duties."

"Have you?"

Mistress Julia! But what could be wrong?

"I believe she may be concealing something from you."

Signora Cavalcanti thought hard, trying to fathom some error in her performance. This was an old trick of his, she knew, eliciting a full confession out of merest suspicion. "I do not think so, Excellency."

The silence hung in the air. Finally Gonzaga said: "Has she spoken much to you about the joyous occasion of her wedding?"

"Very little, Excellency."

"The anticipation of it gives her pleasure?"

If she were a grateful child, perhaps, Signora Cavalcanti thought. But she does not possess a grateful bone in her surly little frame. But she could not repeat this thought to Gonzaga, so she said: "I am sure she is most overjoyed."

Gonzaga's fingers beat a tattoo on the arm of his chair. "She is never left unattended?"

Signora Cavalcanti thought guiltily of the *siesta* she had become accustomed to taking each afternoon. "No, Excellency."

Gonzaga seemed to sigh and relent. "Keep an eye on her, a very close eye. I have my position to think of."

"Yes, Excellency," the duenna said and turned gratefully for the door. Yes, she would keep a much closer eye from now on. She had no idea what might have disturbed her master, but whatever it was, she would find out. And she would take her discovery to him as an offering, and his gratitude and renewed faith in her would be her just reward.

THEY WERE ON the terrazza, their lacework resting on their knees, the late afternoon sun dipping below the roofs of the palazzi. It was silent in the house. The duenna had left them but Julia had not yet heard her draw the heavy drapes at the window above.

Lucia leaned toward Julia and whispered: "Did you meet him?"

"Who?" Julia said.

Lucia glared at her. "You know what I'm talking about! Tell me!"

Julia shrugged. "Perhaps."

"Well?"

Julia smiled and said nothing.

Signora Cavalcanti suddenly appeared on the terrazza. "What are you two girls whispering about?"

"Nothing, Signora," Julia said.

The duenna sat down and picked up her lacework. She looked at Julia, then at Lucia, her face pinched into a scowl of suspicion.

The rest of the afternoon passed in silence. Julia could feel two pairs of eyes fixed on her, both questioning, but she did not look up, and said not another word.

22

JULIA DREW BACK the hood of her cloak, slowly and deliberately, enjoying the thrill of power it always gave her. She was enthralled by the emotions her appearance seemed to stir in him. It was vanity, she knew. The vice of the Devil.

Mary, forgive me, she thought, but I love this.

She had never meant there to be a second time. But each afternoon, after that first meeting, the gondola had appeared at the steps below the palazzo and finally the temptation had been too great. She just wanted to see that look in his eyes once more, even wanted to feel that same thrill of fear. Just wanted to feel alive.

The second time made it easier to do it again. Now how many times had they met in tryst like this? Half a dozen, more? It was her only, precious secret. For the first time in her life she had power. Her father, and Signora Cavalcanti, no longer controlled her totally.

Vanity, fear, power. Perhaps these were the things that made life worth living.

Mary, forgive me.

"Julia," Abbas whispered.

"Just for a few minutes," she said. It was the words she spoke every time, like a ritual, a bargaining chip to Fate. Who will ever condemn me for just a few minutes? The other hours of the day my Confessor will find me faultless.

He reached toward her, his palm upward. On the last two occasions she had allowed him to touch her. This was their signal. She put out her hand and allowed him to hold it. He cradled it in his palm like a small, wounded bird.

"I love you, Julia."

"It's impossible . . . we have to stop."

"I cannot stop now. If they consign me to all the fires of Hell I cannot be in worse torment than I am now."

"Stop," she murmured, but she did not want him to stop. She wondered if she could live without this now; Abbas's passion, the way he made her feel as if she were the most beautiful and important woman in the world. How could she go back to watching the world through her window?

"I will stop when they put me in the earth."

"Abbas, I am to be married . . ."

"Come with me."

"What?"

"Come with me. I can arrange passage on a ship."

Julia stared at him, at once horrified and fascinated. "No."

"We can go to Spain. We will be safe from your father there. My father will give us money . . ."

"No . . ."

He was squeezing her hand so hard it hurt her. "What else is there?"

"Take me back."

"What else is there for either of us?"

He was right. It was so easy to pretend she could play this game forever. But with the autumn she would be condemned to another palazzo, another window. An old man, somber and gray like her father. She shuddered at the thought. But to run away, to leave Venice . . . her cool, dark world was as much sanctuary as prison. It was as if he had invited her to leap with him into a chasm. Her mind raced, and one thought jumbled into another and she knew she could not trust herself anymore.

"Take me back."

"Please, Julia. Ever since I saw you in the church, I knew I would marry you. I will do anything, anything. I would rather die than give you up."

He means it, Julia thought. For the first time she realized this was no game. Abbas was as dangerous as her father. He meant what he said. He would stop at nothing now. She was terrified, she was exhilarated.

He means it.

"Please take me back." She was pleading now.

"Tell me you will come with me."

"I cannot."

"You must." He leaned toward her. He is going to kiss me, she thought, and she started to tremble. *You must not do this!* she wanted to scream at him. *God will punish us for this! This is going too far!* Instead, she closed her eyes and kept perfectly still, became aware of the curious aroma of another body close to hers, the soft scent on his clothes. His lips brushed hers gently, and then he pulled away.

"Come with me," he repeated. She opened her eyes. He was staring at her in that curious, intense way of his. As if her answer were written in miniature, somewhere on her face. What if no one ever looked at me like this again? she thought. The notion was intolerable.

"I must go back."

When they reached the palazzo she climbed the steps in a trance. She was scarcely aware of the gondolier's grinning face, the door creaking open on its hinge. The blackness yawed in front of her, escape more terrifying than sanctuary.

"So, you have deceived me."

Mary, Mother of God! She looked up. As her eyes adjusted to the gloom she saw two bright, malevolent eyes watching her from the top of the stairs.

"Signora Cavalcanti!" Fright was almost immediately replaced by an unexpected surge of anger. This was no sanctuary. She was a prisoner. They might just as well chain her to a wall.

The duenna's eyes were alight with triumph as she descended the stairwell. "What have you been doing?"

Julia turned and threw the door open. She heard Signora Cavalcanti howl in outrage; her scream was cut short by the slamming of the heavy oak and iron door. Julia ran back to the canal, but the gondola was already gliding away from the steps. Julia was about to scream a warning but then she heard the duenna's footsteps on the stone flags behind her. To call his name would be to betray him.

The old woman's hands were on her shoulders, wrestling her back toward the doorway, and she screamed once in anger and frustration, and she saw a movement of the curtains on the gondola, but she could not be certain that Abbas had seen her or heard what had happened.

ANTONIO GONZAGA was dressed in the scarlet robes that denoted him as a man of rank, a Consigliatore. He stood by the window, his hands clenched into fists against the shutters, staring over the roofs of the palazzi to the campanile of San Marco. Behind it, he knew, was the Ducal Palace. What would they say about him there if word of this scandal ever leaked out? What would happen to his alliance with the Serene?

His rage was like a closed fist in his belly, squeezing tighter and tighter . . . his daughter! Behaving like a common prostitute! He wanted to cut her throat.

"Who is this boy?" he growled.

Julia lowered her eyes and tried to stop her knees from trembling. She could not have answered him even if she wanted to. She had never witnessed such fury anywhere. She was afraid she would lose all control of her bladder and disgrace herself. But how can I disgrace myself further, she thought, in my father's eyes at least?

"I said, WHO IS THIS BOY?" he roared at her.

Julia could feel Signora Cavalcanti watching her, her eyes glittering with sadistic amusement. Julia said nothing. She would not betray Abbas. That much could be salvaged from this.

The blow took her completely by surprise. It sent her crashing to the floor, and for a few moments she could neither hear nor see. When her senses finally returned, the Consigliatore was standing over her, his legs braced, both fists clenched.

"You will tell me who it is."

"Never," she heard herself saying.

This unexpected steel in his daughter only infuriated him further. He roared aloud and grabbed a fistful of her hair and shook her, like a dog, then dragged her around the marble tiles. He screamed curses at her, using the sort of language she sometimes heard in the markets, but had never expected to hear from him. When he finally released her, there were long tufts of blue-black hair curling between the fingers of his fist.

Julia put her hands over her head to protect herself from further abuse, and curled into a ball on the floor, sobbing.

When she opened her eyes she saw that even old Cavalcanti looked shocked.

"You will tell me his name."

Julia could not answer him. The defiance caught in her throat. She screamed again as Gonzaga pulled her to her feet, his fingers locking around the puffed sleeves of her vestura, ripping it apart. He cuffed her again and again round the head with his open hand while she twisted and writhed to try and escape the blows. Just as suddenly, he released her, and she fell heavily to the floor.

He would get no sense out of her tonight, he realized.

"Cover yourself up, whore," he said. He had torn off the shoulder of the vestura, exposing her breast. Julia made a fumbled attempt to replace the torn scraps of material over herself. But her hands were shaking so violently she could not do it.

"Take her to her room," Gonzaga said to the duenna. "Then come back here. I want to talk to you."

Signora Cavalcanti had never been so frightened in all her life. She had always revered His Excellency as a stern man, but the scene she had just witnessed had shaken her. It was one thing for a righteous judge to pronounce sentence, quite another for him to take a turn himself at the wheel of the rack.

But when she reentered the study, Gonzaga had composed himself once more. He was seated at his desk, his hands folded on his lap, his face set into a mask of stern deliberation. Only his hair, awry under his bareta, evidenced the violence that had taken place a few minutes before.

"My daughter is shamefully stubborn," he said.

Signora Cavalcanti did not know what to say. She looked into the desperate face of Carpaccio's Virgin and was ashamed.

"Is it possible she does not realize the extent of the injury she has done me?" Gonzaga said.

"I have instructed her faithfully in her duties to the Republic and to God," the duenna was quick to reply.

"Perhaps." Gonzaga let the word hang in the air like a threat. "But if this is true, then why does she defy me in this way?"

The duenna realized she was on trial. But what was she to say in her defense? Perhaps she should have kept her discovery to herself after all. Well, it was too late now.

"Many questions arise from this," he was saying, "for instance, how were these meetings arranged?"

Signora Cavalcanti swallowed the urge to say, *I don't know*. It would be tantamount to expressing her failure. She should have thought this through, she realized now.

"I will find out," she said.

"I hope so, Signora Cavalcanti. In fact, I rely on it."

He smiled. The duenna never liked it when the Excellency smiled at her. The effect was not pleasant.

23

A BBAS FOLLOWED THE coach on foot from the palazzo. He lost them along the narrow *calles*, but caught up again in the bustle of the *mercato* around the Campo Santa Maria Nuova. He pushed aside the fruit vendors and peddlers who were too slow to get out of his way, vaulting a handcart loaded down with bolts of silk.

The church of Santa Maria dei Miracoli dominated the piazza. It was one of the city's most beautiful churches, its façade constructed of rich yellow, gray, and white antique marble. The coach was pulled up below the steps of the front portal, in the shade of the great dome.

Abbas stopped on the far side of the piazza, and watched the two figures descend from the coach, one of them short and stocky, the other tall, lean and graceful. The women of Venice might perhaps look the same to a casual bystander, he thought, dressed all in black with their ample skirts, puffed sleeves, and dark veils, but if you knew *her* you could pick her from a thousand other women just by the way she moves.

Julia!

"This is madness!" Ludovici breathed in his ear.

"Have you never been in love, Ludovici?"

"This is not love, this is suicide! Come to your senses, Abbas!" Ludovici put his hand on his shoulder and tried to pull him away.

Abbas shrugged free. "I cannot live without her."

"You breathe, you eat, you drink. That's all there is to living! You can manage that without a woman, can't you?"

"That's not life, Ludovici! There is no life without passion!"

"They know about this now! You saw the duenna on the quay! If Julia tells Gonzaga your name there will be hell to pay!"

"She will not tell him."

Abbas started to walk toward the steps of the church. Ludovici ran after him. "What are you doing?"

"I have to see her."

"You cannot . . ."

"They will not see me! I just have to . . . look . . ."

Ludovici shrugged in resignation. What was the point? He would not listen to his counsel. At the very least Gonzaga would ruin Mahmud, and he and Abbas would be expelled from the Republic—if he did not end up in prison.

He watched him bound up the steps of the Santa Maria dei Miracoli, blind to everything but his own desires. Like a child, Ludovici thought. A headstrong, passionate, willful child.

THE CHURCH WAS empty. Saint Francis seemed to be pointing his long marble finger at Abbas in cold mockery. The frieze of naked putti, dancing and kicking, over the main arch, grinned back at him. Abbas stopped and looked around, confused.

They moved past him swiftly, shadows among shadows; by the time he was aware of what had happened they had already reached the doorway, and he saw them for only an instant. He realized the duenna had been waiting for him to come. Ludovici was right. He was a fool. It had been a baited trap.

"Julia!"

She turned, stumbling, dragged along by the old crone in front of her. She threw back her veil for a moment and he saw the anguish written there. *Corpo di Dio!*

He started to run after, and stopped. What was the point? What could he do now?

He stood at the top of the steps. Ludovici looked up at him, his face drawn into lines of frustration and pity. A coach rattled away down the Via delle Botteghe, the horses' hoofs ringing on the cobbles.

"ABBAS MAHSOUF? THE *Moor's* son?"

Signora Cavalcanti nodded eagerly, reveling in her own mendacity. She had lured the young man out so easily. She was sure Gonzaga would reward her handsomely for this.

Gonzaga stood up, and the oaken chair crashed onto the marble tiles behind him. "A *Moor?*"

"I saw him with my own eyes. He called her name as we left the church of Santa Maria dei Miracoli!"

Gonzaga raised one thick eyebrow like a question mark. "And how did you know he would be there?"

Signora Cavalcanti flinched. "He was there once before. I remembered."

" 'Once before'? You said nothing of this to me."

"It seemed like a trifle."

"I see," Gonzaga said, heavily. "A trifle! How could this trifle occur?"

"I saw someone else there."

"Who?"

"Ludovici Gambetto."

He stared at her, appalled. "You think she has had commerce with both of them?"

Signora Cavalcanti shook her head vehemently. Heaven forbid! "He was just looking on. I saw his face as we left the piazza. I believe the Moor is friendly with him."

Gonzaga went to the window and stood with his back toward her, looking out over the Great Canal. She could not fathom his expression. "My brother-in-law's bastard!"

The duenna studied the floor and waited her turn to speak.

"You think this is how messages were passed?"

"She and Lucia visit each other often."

Gonzaga was silent for a long time. Finally he said: "I congratulate you on your discoveries. You shall have your reward, Signora Cavalcanti. You may leave me now."

The door closed softly behind her. Gonzaga pounded the palm of his hand against the wall. What was he to do? If he brought the matter before the courts he would be the laughing stock of all Venice. His daughter and a blackamoor! He would almost certainly be forced from his position on the Consiglio di Dieci.

He could bring the matter to the attention of Ludovici's father, but even that was fraught with danger. His wife had been a long time dead, and now old Gambetto was maneuvering for position as the next Doge, rival to Gonzaga himself, and he might welcome such an opportunity to create a scandal.

No, the matter called for greater subtlety and patience. Ludovici could be punished over time. Abbas must be taken care of now.

What was it that Signora Cavalcanti had said? "She and Lucia visit each other often." He smiled. There was the answer! Lucia was the conduit. If water could flow one way, it could flow the other.

But this time he would use it to his own advantage.

WHEN LUCIA ARRIVED that afternoon, her duenna was dismissed, and instead of being taken to the drawing room overlooking the Great Canal, Signora Cavalcanti ushered her into the private study. She was astonished to find Signore Gonzaga himself awaiting her.

He rose to greet her, his black gown flapping like the wings of some great bird of carrion. "Ah, Lucia. How pleasant to see you again."

"Excellency," Lucia said, suddenly alarmed. She bent to one knee, and kissed the hem of his sleeve.

"Come and sit down here with me." He glanced up at Signora Cavalcanti, dismissing her with a glance. The door closed behind them.

Gonzaga sat down again and studied her in silence, his face frozen in the travesty of a smile. The seconds stretched to a minute and the silence became intolerable.

Lucia felt herself beginning to panic. He must know, he must. Why else would he want to talk with her—alone? How much had Julia already told him? If he caught her in a lie it would be worse for her. What if he told her father?

"Now then, I believe you have something to tell me," he said at last.

"I . . . I did nothing wrong," she stammered.

"It's all right. Julia has told me everything."

"You are not angry?"

"With her, yes. With you . . . yes, I am angry with you, too, my dear." He fixed his executioner's eyes upon her, and, still smiling, he said: "But you may yet find pardon in my eyes. You were, after all, only a messenger."

"I did not know what was in the letter. My brother asked me to give it to Julia. That is all."

"You think, all in all, that it excuses you?" he asked gently. "That there is no fault in doing what you did, as you were innocent of the contents of the letter?"

Lucia stared at him. What was he driving at? What did he expect her to say? "Yes, Excellency."

He beamed, but for some reason Lucia did not feel like smiling with him. "That is good," he said. "Because I wish you to play your role once more."

"Excellency?"

"Tell me, did you ever deliver letters from Julia?"

"No, Excellency."

Gonzaga smiled. "Good. Because that is what you are about to do now." He unlocked the drawer of his desk and produced an envelope with a heavy wax seal. He passed it to her.

"This is for Abbas."

Lucia stared at it. "Who is it from, Excellency?"

"From Julia, of course."

He smiled again. He was lying.

"Pick it up."

Lucia hesitated. "Excellency . . ."

Gonzaga leaned across the table. His smile suddenly vanished. "Understand me well, child. You will give your brother this letter to hand to Abbas, and you will tell no one—no one—of our conversation. *Capisci?* If you fail me in this I shall inform your father of the part you and your brother played in this infamous episode. Furthermore, I shall bring down such calumny on both your heads that neither of you shall be able to show your faces in La Serenissima ever again. Do I make myself quite clear?"

Lucia nodded and picked up the envelope with trembling fingers. She felt as if she were going to faint. Gonzaga did not need to elaborate on his threat. As a member of the Consiglio di Dieci he was more powerful than the Doge himself.

"May I see Julia now, Excellency?"

"She is unwell and unable to receive visitors," Gonzaga said. He stood up and opened the door. "Signora Cavalcanti will show you the way out." He put a hand on her shoulder as she passed him. His fingers were as cold as death. "Be sure that Abbas gets his message. I shall know if he does not."

Lucia nodded her head but could not find her voice. As the door closed shut behind her she shuddered with relief. All she wanted now was to pass on this final errand and be done with this business forever.

24

My Dearest Abbas,

I am to be sent to the convent at Brescia until my marriage. Time is short. If you truly love me, as you say, I put my trust in you. I can get away but once more. The great door that leads to the Canal is now forever locked, but there may be another way. If you will wait for me at midnight tomorrow on the Ponte Vecchio I will come to you there. I will go wherever you choose to take me. My life is now in your hands.

This last week has been torment. How am I to live without you? I would rather die than lose your love. May the hours pass swiftly till tomorrow night!

A thousand caresses.

Julia

Abbas read the letter twice more. A gnawing of doubt was quickly washed away by the tide of excitement that rushed over him. She wanted to come with him!

Ludovici watched, his impatience growing. "What does she say?" he hissed.

Abbas carefully tore the parchment in half and held the pieces over the candle. The yellow flame consumed them, a thick skein of black smoke spiraling upward. Abbas did not speak until the flames had licked around his fingers and the missive was no more than a few wispy black leaves on the table.

"Nothing," he said.

ABBAS WAS USHERED to his father's council chamber at the Ministry of War, the Savio alla Scrittura. His father looked up from the chart that lay open on the table in front of him, and sent the two Provveditori Generali delle Armi from the room. He continued to study the chart—a map of the Peninsula and the surrounding Ottoman possessions—glancing up only briefly from beneath the thick beetling eyebrows.

"What is so urgent that you disturb me here?"

"I am sorry, Father."

"Well?"

"I need money."

"Is your commission as an officer in my army not enough?"

Abbas took a deep breath. All his life he had been afraid of his father. He imagined the Prophet must have been a little like his father, stern and courageous and proud, awesome in both his physical and mental presence. He did not remember his mother—she had been a concubine in Mahmud's harem before Venice—and so his father had become all things to him, father and teacher, master and confidant, mentor and confessor. Now he was confronting not only Mahmud the man, but his whole upbringing. It was the first time he had ever gone against his father's wishes.

"I have to go away."

Mahmud turned his attention from the chart to his son. "And why would you need to leave Venice?"

"I intend to marry Julia Gonzaga."

Mahmud straightened, tucking his thumbs into the broad silver buckled belt at his waist. He walked around the great oak table toward Abbas. The way he moved reminded Abbas of a great brown bear he had seen once in the forests near Belluno: slow, powerful, and menacing. On that occasion Abbas had had ten archers at his back. He wished they were there again now.

Mahmud studied him. "I have told you. It is impossible."

"Nothing is impossible."

"What do you mean by that?"

"I have been meeting secretly with her. We plan to elope."

Mahmud put out a hand to steady himself on the great table. He puffed the air out through his cheeks in a great sigh. "You little fool," he gasped.

"I love her."

"What has love to do with it? You have put both our necks on the block!"

"I will go to Ferrara. I have fought in two campaigns against the Ottoman already and your name is known across the Peninsula. I will find myself a commission in any army. Once it is done, Gonzaga will have to accept it. A year, perhaps two, and I will be back in Venice."

Mahmud shook his head. "Your resource far outweighs your understanding. How you have managed to deceive Gonzaga for so long I do not know, but do not think he will ever forgive you for it. Or me."

"Once we are married, what can he do?"

"Does anyone else know of this?"

Abbas shook his head. No, not even Ludovici. Especially Ludovici. He had done so much, he would not endanger his friend further. "No one."

"Good." The blow was so sudden, so unexpected, that it lifted Abbas off his feet. He suddenly found himself on his back, staring at the vaulted ceiling, his head feeling heavy as stone. There was buzzing in his ears, like a thousand bees, and he tasted his own blood in his mouth.

Mahmud lifted him easily from the floor and pushed him against the wall. "Now listen to me! I love you, and I will not let you ruin your life— and mine—by one rush of youthful lust! Buy yourself a mistress if you wish, but leave Julia Gonzaga alone! Do you understand me?"

Abbas sank forward, resting his head on his father's shoulder. He closed his eyes against the wave of nausea that threatened to overwhelm him. As the effect of the blow subsided, he felt his father's hold on him relax.

"Goodbye," he whispered, and wrenched himself free. Before Mahmud could stop him he rushed from the chamber and was gone.

No MAGNIFICO WAS allowed, by law, to speak with the Captain General of the Army alone. The threat of conspiracy was constant, and the Consiglio di Dieci was vigilant against any nobleman who might try to use the army for his own purposes, as Sforza had done at Milan. So Mahmud was accompanied everywhere by two senators, the Provveditori Generali delle Armi. They were with Mahmud now as he burst into the private chambers of Antonio Gonzaga.

Gonzaga sat at the far end of the room, the lead-paned windows at his back. The dome of the San Giovanni Grisostomo loomed behind him against a mauve sky.

"Most reverend Signore," Mahmud murmured, and bent to kiss the sleeve of Gonzaga's robe.

"I am told you wish to see me on a matter of some urgency," Gonzaga said, with a glance at the two Provveditori. "A matter of private and not national importance, I am to assume?"

Mahmud straightened, but he could not meet Gonzaga's eyes. He fidgeted with embarrassment. He would rather have discussed this with Gonzaga alone, but that could have been even more dangerous than the predicament in which he now found himself.

"A matter of the utmost delicacy, Signore."

"Is it to do with my daughter?"

Relief—and yes, a touch of fear too, Gonzaga was delighted to witness—betrayed itself on the Moor's face. "Yes, Signore. You have some knowledge of what I am about to tell you?"

Gonzaga knew that caution was paramount now. He must guard the Moor's tongue and his own. The two Provveditori were almost licking their lips with anticipation of scandal.

"All I know is that Lucia Gambetto has been foolish enough to pass letters between my daughter and her stepbrother Ludovici." Mahmud was about to protest but the expression on Gonzaga's face halted him. He saw him glance toward the two senators and immediately understood.

"I was led to believe that a certain . . . meeting . . . was planned," Mahmud said.

"I have heard that also," Gonzaga said. "Of course, such an indiscretion would never be allowed to eventuate." Damn the boy, Gonzaga thought. I did not believe he would confide in his father. Now I will have to find some other way. Unless . . .

"I am most relieved to find you so informed," Mahmud said. "I felt it my duty to warn you."

"You have my thanks, General. May I ask where you came by this information. Your son, perhaps?"

Mahmud hesitated. Now that there was a way to contain this scandal, it was not necessary to reveal to Gonzaga—or the Provveditori—that he had not seen his son since the evening of the previous day. "His duty is to Venice. As is mine, Signore."

"You will convey my thanks, then, General. Be assured, I will allow no taint on the name of Gonzaga."

Mahmud bowed and made his leave. As he made his way from the palazzo he tried to settle the gnawing of doubt that assailed him. What was it that made him feel that he had somehow been manipulated? Well, it was enough that Gonzaga had been warned. At least now there was no possibility that his son's life—and his own—would be ruined by something that could be easily bought for a few *zecchini* anywhere in the Republic.

25

THE SHADOWS HAD become Abbas's friends. All the previous night and this long day he had hidden; planning, anticipating. With the little money he had, he had paid passage to Pescati, on a merchant galley that would sail with the morning tide. He had no idea how they would reach Naples from there, but Abbas was not concerned with the future. All that was important now was to get out of Venice.

Ludovici had a mistress—the daughter of a poor baker who had been happy to exchange a hungry mouth for a bag of gold zecchini—and Abbas had hidden all that day in the apartment Ludovici kept for her at Guidecca. When Ludovici returned that evening he told him Mahmud's soldiery had been out looking for him all that day in the city, turning out all the inns and tavernas in their search.

"What have you done?" Ludovici had asked, his eyes wide with horror.

"I cannot tell you. I have already involved you too much."

Ludovici shook his head. "The game is becoming deadly serious, Abbas. I warned you of this."

"I have always been deadly serious, Ludovici. You construed my purpose too lightly." He grinned and nodded his head toward the somber dark-haired girl who watched them from the other corner of the room. "I think the poor girl thought you intended to share her with me. Do not worry. Tonight I shall leave, your house and your mistress intact."

Ludovici did not smile. "Where will you go?"

"I cannot even tell you that." The grin fell away and he embraced him. "Thank you. You are the greatest friend a man could ever have."

Despite Abbas's protests Ludovici had pressed a purse in his palm. Abbas did not protest too much. Without it, he would have barely enough money to buy a loaf of bread when they reached Pescati.

HE HEARD THE great clock in the Piazza San Marco chime the twelfth hour. He pulled his mantello more tightly around his shoulders against the night chill and searched the shadows. Would she come?

The gondola was moored on an iron rung on the steps below the bridge. Abbas could hear the water lapping gently against the hull. He heard a footfall on the cobbles, saw a dark shadow in a hooded cloak darting from the calle on the far side of the bridge. Abbas felt his heart lurch in his chest.

Julia!

He ran on to the bridge. She saw him too and started to run toward him. "Julia!" he whispered.

He stretched out his arms.

He suddenly became aware of other sounds. There were footsteps behind him on the bridge, and from the calle on the far side. The *milizia di notte!* The night police!

"Julia, be careful!"

He reached for her, and the hood fell back. In the flood of the moon he glimpsed the crooked, bearded grin of a total stranger.

"Aren't I the beauty you were expecting?" the man said. Abbas saw the flash of a blade, felt the point of it jabbed hard between his ribs. "I may not be your Julia, but I know the way to a man's heart."

Abbas brought his knee up suddenly. The man squealed like a butchered pig and doubled over, collapsing in the shadows at his feet. Abbas gasped. As he fell, the man had lunged forward with his dagger, slicing into his side.

He leaped away, and drew his own sword, trying to distinguish harmless shadows from his enemy. How many were there? From the sounds of the footfalls there must be another three, perhaps four.

In his terror he raised his sword and slashed down at the figure at his feet, felt the blade crunch against bone. The man shrieked, his scream breaking the silence like the wail of a banshee.

The shadows suddenly came alive. Abbas backed away until he felt the solid stone of the bridge against the small of his back. He heard the gondolier—curse his yellow soul—paddle the gondola away from the bridge. At the same time two more shadows rushed on to the bridge and were transformed into the shapes of men by the light of the three-quarter moon.

To his dismay he realized they were not as amateur as their colleague, who was still sobbing his life away somewhere near his feet. They moved in unison, coming at him from right and left simultaneously. Abbas struck out with sword, chest high so they could not duck away, but they had not made the mistake of moving in too close. To his horror he realized they were waiting for something.

He turned to his left.

He saw another movement, this time above the level of his eyes and there was a shadow on the moon. Something heavy fell over his head and shoulders and he instinctively threw up a hand to protect himself. A net! As his two assailants moved in he tried to shuffle away. He tripped over the dying man, enveloping them both in the mesh. He felt something warm and sticky on his free hand, heard the man thrash and scream underneath him.

He tried to stand up, but only succeeded in wrapping the net even tighter around himself in his panic. The man beneath him writhed again. He still had the knife! He felt a searing agony in his cheek and nose and he twisted away, and now there were new screams.

This time they were his own.

HE DID NOT remember how long he had been awake. It was pitch black in the hold so it was impossible to tell when the fug of dazed stupor had ended and when the burning fire in his face had brought him fully conscious once more. All he was aware of was the stench of the bilges, the slow slap of waves, and the nervous scampering of the rats.

And there was something else, some other taint that he remembered only too well from his early experiences on the battlefield. The smell of corpses.

Whoever his assailants were, it seemed they had not meant to kill him. Why had they brought him to this stinking ship's hold? He remembered the net and the agony of the dagger slicing into his face. They must have cudgeled him then. All he remembered after that was a fiery, panicky blackness.

He tried to move but they had bound his hands and his ankles. He sobbed aloud against the pain in his face and tried to reason out his predicament.

It was all too plain what had happened. Julia had written no letter. It had all been a carefully baited trap.

Gonzaga!

He heard footsteps outside and men's voices. The door was thrown open and torchlight flooded the room.

He turned his face from the intrusion of the sudden light and instead found himself staring at the face of the bearded stranger from the bridge. His eyes stared back at him in cold surprise, like a dead fish. Beside him lay another corpse, this one an old woman, dressed in black. Her throat had been cut and her face was black with dried gore.

A man laughed. Abbas turned to face his captors. They were bearded, shoeless sailors, the kind who could be bought at the Marghero wharf any day of the week for a few zecchini. One of them—Abbas was immediately aware of the smell of cheap wine and the stifling odor of his body—bent down and brought the flaming torch a few inches from his face.

"Well, you don't look as pretty now," he grinned. "Bartolomeo stuck you with his knife before he died. Sliced away half your face. Not that it will matter much to you anymore."

The two men behind him laughed.

He leaned closer. Abbas tried to shrink away from him, terror so overwhelming him that he could not think or speak. He thought he was going to faint. "See that other one next to Bartolomeo? She was Gonzaga's duenna. Put up a fight she did. Not that it did her much good. Ever seen anyone slaughter a pig? It was like that." He grinned with satisfaction at the memory. "But she was luckier than you, that's a fact. You'll wish you were her before the night's out."

Abbas felt one of the men tugging at the breeches at his waist, while the other sliced apart the bonds at his ankles. They gripped his knees and began to pry his legs apart.

He shrieked in panic and tried to kick himself free. But they were too strong.

The first man drew his knife. Abbas shrieked. Consciousness ebbed away into cameos of minor detail, like shattered pieces of glass . . . the man's rotten teeth . . . the boils on his chest and back . . . the dead duenna's gray hair floating on the pool of bilge in the corner.

He shrieked again, every muscle in his body straining against the cords at his wrist and the hands and bodies that held his legs. He knew what they were going to do now. He knew why they had not killed him on the Ponte Vecchio.

"So you wanted to let Signore Gonzaga's daughter play with these little toys, huh? Well perhaps we'll give them to Signore Gonzaga and he can give them to her."

"NOOOOOOOOOOO!"

He felt himself urinating and the men laughed.

"Say goodbye to them, Moor," the man sneered. The blade flashed in the torchlight and the world twisted and sheered into a hot and infernal place.

A MILK AND marble dawn. A funeral procession of gondolas, draped with black velvet, emerged from beneath the Ponte Molino, and glided silently across the Sacca della Misericordia and across the lagoon toward the cemetery island of San Michele. Julia watched them until they disappeared into the gauze curtain of mist. It was as if they carried her spirit with them.

Today she was to be taken to the convent at Brescia, to await the arrival of Serena and what her father referred to as "the joyous occasion of her wedding."

It was more like being buried alive.

Abbas, Abbas.

Where was he now?

PART 3

ROSE OF SPRING

26

The Sweet Waters of Europe, near Eyüp

CLUMPS OF SUNFLOWERS dazzled the eye, bright splotches of gold on the hillside. In the distance the city rippled in dusty amber behind the gray land walls. The whole Harem had been brought in canopied *caïques* along the Bosphorus, a welcome respite from the oppressive monotony of the Eski Saraya.

The girls reclined and gossiped on blue and crimson Persian carpets in the shade of the cypress trees, while the gediçli fed them peaches and grapes and sweetbreads on silver salvers. Negro musicians entertained them with flutes and viols; piles of silk cushions kept their pampered bottoms from the hard ground; dancing bears and monkeys performed listlessly on the grass.

Gülbehar sat apart from the others. One of her gediçli produced a mirror and held it up for her inspection. The handle was encrusted with sapphires—a gift from Süleyman after the birth of Mustapha. She examined her reflection and brushed an errant hair back into place.

"And where is Hürrem?" one of the girls whispered, watching her.

"The Kislar Aghasi says she is with Süleyman," another girl said. "Now he spends all his days with her, as well as his nights."

Sirhane, a raven-haired Persian girl, popped a grape into her mouth. "In the bazaars they say she is a witch, that she has cast a spell over the Lord of the Earth. How else could she have removed the Rose of Spring from his affections so quickly and to the exclusion of all else?"

"Look at her," another girl whispered, watching Gülbehar's gediçli combing out the long, silky hair. "If the Lord of Life will not look at her anymore, what chance do the rest of us have?"

"They say even the Grand Vizier fears her," the one called Sirhane said. "The Kislar Aghasi whispered to me that the Lord of Life even goes to her to discuss politics and that she advises him on military campaigns."

"The Kislar Aghasi has a fertile imagination."

"He swears it is true!"

"The Grand Vizier would have her drowned in the Bosphorus!"

"Perhaps he cannot," Sirhane said, and suddenly all the other girls were watching her, their faces displaying both speculation and scorn. No one was more powerful than the Grand Vizier! Sirhane enjoyed their attention. "Anyway, I feel sorry for Gülbehar. The Lord of Life has disgraced her."

"Gülbehar is still first kadin," another girl said. "And one day she will be the Sultan Valide. Her day will come."

"They say God is punishing the Lord of Life for making a witch his kadin. That is why his last son died in his cradle."

Sirhane shrugged. "But Hürrem has two sons still living. And she carries another child now."

"None of them will ever rival Mustapha!" another girl shouted, and there the conversation ended. The girls' attention wandered in indolence to the dancing bear, and Sirhane dared not voice the other whisper she had heard from the Kislar Aghasi: that Hürrem was plotting to get rid of Mustapha also.

Besides, it was only a rumor. And rumors such as that were dangerous.

Topkapi Saraya

THERE WAS SILENCE here, among the kiosks and the ornamental ponds. There was only the sigh of the wind through the plane and chestnut trees and the gentle murmur of water in the ornamental fountains to disturb the gazelles grazing among the leaves.

Süleyman liked to walk here, to compose his thoughts and find respite from the endless demands and requests and entreaties of the Divan and the Harem. Once he would always come here alone, but now he brought a companion to share the reflective silence. He brought Hürrem.

The last five years had been many times blessed, he thought. When he had returned from hunting at Adrianople, shortly after their first union, he had found her already plump with new life. Early the following year she had delivered up a boy. At the Valide's insistence they called him Selim.

He had not shared his mother's excitement. She saw the consolidation of the Osmanli line; he saw only conflict. While she rejoiced in the blood, he gloomily contemplated the spilling of it some time in the future. The memories of what his father had done to his own bloodline in order to secure his throne would never leave him.

But the result was that Hürrem was now his second kadin. He could not ignore her now, and he did not want to. While he had always been comfortable with Gülbehar, he had never been able to share the burdens of his position with her.

When Achmed Pasha rose in revolt in Egypt in the autumn following Selim's birth, he sent Ibrahim to crush him. While he was gone, Süleyman found himself bringing his problems to Hürrem. He found to his surprise that she had a shrewd mind with a natural grasp for the intricacies of court politics, and he began to confide in her more and more, even after Ibrahim's return. Her caution was a counterfoil to Ibrahim's instinctive aggression.

She had opened a new world to him. While Gülbehar was pliant and predictable, Hürrem continually surprised him. On one visit she might be sullen and passionate; on another, effusive and playful. She might soothe him with her singing and her viol or excite him with her dancing. She might dress like a slim boy in military *dolman,* or a dancing houri in gossamer. He never knew what to expect from her, though she seemed to have an uncanny ability to anticipate his own moods.

Her delight in lovemaking was unholy and he knew her soul was in constant danger, and that he must one day send her to the *mufti* for education. But for now her infidel soul afforded him an infinity of pleasure. Her gasps and cries of ecstasy gave him greater feelings of power than all the ceremony of the Divan and the groveling of ambassadors with their gifts.

Hürrem was his pleasure. Everything else was his duty. He was sure God would be patient a little longer.

If the little Russian girl—he even called her, affectionately, "little *russelana*"—showed an instinctive talent for politics, she had ample opportunity to put her skill into use in the Eski Saraya. She had carefully cultivated her friendship with his mother, the Valide, and Nature had helped her cement the relationship by providing her with another son, Bayezid. She had failed in the labor chamber only once, when one of the twins she had produced was a girl. The boy, Abdullah, had died just last year; but Mihrmah was now three years old.

She was not the devoted mother that Gülbehar had been, but that did not disappoint him; he wanted her for himself. Besides, Gülbehar was the mother of the shahzade, the next Sultan.

"I wanted to talk to you," he said as they walked.

"Yes, my Lord," she said, eagerly.

"It is the Hungarian question again."

She nodded her head. Here, in the garden, she wore no veil and let the wind blow freely through her long red hair, like a banner. Süleyman felt a rush of pride in her. Sometimes he thought of her as his own creation.

"Frederick is sending an envoy to treat with us. He does not know that the *voivoide*, Zapolya, has sent his man also. He has already met in secret with Ibrahim."

Hürrem, he knew, understood the situation. Two years before, Süleyman's army, marshaled by Ibrahim, had annihilated the Hungarian forces on the plain of Mohaçs. Their own king had been swallowed up in the massacre, drowning in a swamp after his horse fell on top of him during the retreat. Since Hungary was too far from Stamboul to be permanently occupied by the army, it had now become a wasteland of warring bands, coveted by noblemen such as Zapolya, and the Hapsburg family, under Frederick, brother of the Holy Roman Emperor.

"What would you do, my Lord?"

"We have slain the King of Hungary. The horses of the Osmanlis have set their hoofs in Buda, so it has become the dominion of Islam. There is no other King of Hungary but I."

"So every summer you must send your army to regain what it has conquered the year before."

Süleyman brooded on this. "The dogs are always at the door when there are scraps to be had."

"You must guard every entrance to the house. If you become too preoccupied with one, the real danger may be waiting elsewhere."

"I will not treat with Frederick, even if he were willing. Then I have exchanged a dog for a rabid wolf."

"What about Zapolya?"

"Zapolya is an upstart. He is no king."

"What is a king? It is not the crown that makes a king, it is the sword. Make Zapolya your gatekeeper and let him have his piece of iron for his head. In return demand his tribute and free passage for your armies. Let him call himself king if that is his pleasure. While there is no border to you, you remain his master."

"He cannot hold back Frederick's armies."

"He can keep the borders until a real army is assembled. One that is worthy of your attention. One that may lure Frederick himself into contest. Or perhaps even Charles."

Süleyman looked down at the black waters of the Bosphorus, white foam streaked across the surface by the wind. On one side lay Asia, on the other Europe. Here, from Seraglio Point, he was always reminded of the microcosm of his Empire; one could not look too long to one side and forget the other. Hürrem was right.

"Zapolya, then."

"If my Lord considers my counsel wise. In all things I defer to your greater wisdom."

Süleyman nodded, pleased with Hürrem's diplomacy. Ah, she was a rare treasure indeed!

The Eski Saraya

THEY ATE *KEBABS* of lamb on silver skewers with pine kernels, drank perfumed rosewater from goblets of Iznik glass. After the gediçli had removed the bowls they sat for a long time in silence.

"Have I offended you, my Lord?" Gülbehar said at last.

"You have not," Süleyman answered.

"You have not asked for me for many months. When you come here, it is to see Mustapha."

"Do not deem to question me."

Gülbehar hung her head. Süleyman felt sorry for her; she had been a good wife. All she had ever demanded until now was some Venetian satin or Baghdad silk or a tortoiseshell comb. And she had given him Mustapha.

He had not meant to hurt her this way. But each moment he spent with her, he compared her with Hürrem and his impatience grew. He could not be at ease with her; pity and frustration inexorably turned to anger.

He got to his feet. Gülbehar looked up at him, startled. "You are leaving, my Lord?"

"I have other matters to attend to."

Gülbehar looked miserable. "Hürrem . . ."

It was an unpardonable breach of protocol, but Süleyman decided to ignore it. "My Lady," he said, and took his leave of her.

IT WAS ALWAYS dusk in the Eski Saraya. Even on a summer midday, the sun could not chase the shadows from the endless dim corridors and the warren of tiny rooms and hidden courtyards. Concubines, their hair tressed with dark rubies, sloe eyes darkened with kohl, appeared fleetingly on the shadowy staircases like ghosts, ungratified and forgotten. A world of dusty lanterns and baroque mirrors and beauty creased with ancient grime.

It had infected Hürrem's mood. This is my inheritance, she thought. I am a heartbeat from living death. This is my legacy from Süleyman should he die now.

She had come so far. She had given him sons, and she had woven her web around him, helping him forget this dusty storehouse of beauty. None of it had been easy. The strain of her childbearing had sapped her, but after each confinement she had surrendered to Muomi's massages, to starvation and to innumerable vials of the gediçli's foul-tasting potions in order to restore her figure. She had had wet nurses for the children so her infants would not suckle her breasts dry.

Yet it might all be for nothing, it could all be snatched away from her in an instant. Only one woman had it all, had power over her own life; not the wife of the Sultan, but the mother.

"Muomi! Muomi!"

The gediçli appeared instantly, hovering at her post just outside the door. "My Lady?"

"Come," Hürrem said, and summoned her into the room.

Muomi sank to her knees on the carpet at the side of Hürrem's divan. "My Lady?" Muomi repeated sulkily. The whites of her eyes appeared luminescent in the gloom of the chamber.

"There is something I want you to do."

"Another potion, my Lady?"

Hürrem nodded slowly. "I want you to kill Mustapha for me."

27

The Eski Saraya

THE VAULTED STONE kitchens below the Old Palace were cramped and hot, thick with a miasma of spice, sweat, and steam; heat rose in waves from the open oven furnaces. The clatter of pans and the shouts of the cooks and the scurrying of veiled gediçli through the fug of heat and noise formed the daily backdrop to the confusion and travail.

No one paid attention to the tall black girl carrying the tray of oranges, as she drifted through the hurrying pages and servants and cooks. No one had cause to notice her as she left; even if they had, the most observant of spies would not have realized that the platter of oranges she carried was different from the one she had brought with her.

AT FOURTEEN, MUSTAPHA had grown into everything that Süleyman had hoped for in a son. Like every prince he was trained at the Enderun, the Palace school, with the cream of the boys recruited in the *devshirme*. He was an outstanding swordsman and horseman, an outgoing and popular boy, already a favorite among the yeniçeri who often came to cheer him at the *çerit*—a horseback game using wooden javelins—in the Hippodrome.

He was also a talented scholar. He had learned his Qur'ān, Persian, and mathematics quickly and expertly. But his other qualities—he was a natural leader with an almost reckless courage and easy charm—overshadowed these achievements. Süleyman knew the Osmanlis could have no better shahzade than this.

Today Mustapha sported a pulpy plum-colored bruise above his right eye, which was almost swollen shut. Süleyman shook his head in feigned horror as his son knelt to kiss the ruby ring on his right hand.

"What has happened to you?"

"It happens all the time," Gülbehar said behind him. "He was hit by a javelin in the çerit. Nothing I say to him seems to make any difference."

"Should I be more careful, Father?" Mustapha grinned.

"You should be careful not to be hit so often."

"He would spend all day on his horse, if he could," Gülbehar said.

"There is nothing wrong with that. There was a time when the *ghazis* did not have fine palaces to sit in, or laws to make. It is good that the next Sultan knows what it is like to have a horse under him."

Mustapha grinned in conspiracy with Süleyman's mild reproach. He knew he had an ally here.

"He knows nothing else."

"A boy can have too much schooling," Süleyman answered.

He studied his son. He was already just a few fingers shorter than Süleyman himself, with a broad white grin and the first sproutings of beard on his chin. And the eyes! They were brimming with the zest and energy of youth. When Süleyman had been his age his eyes had been clouded with doubt and terror, wondering when the shadow of his father might fall across his own face. Thank God Mustapha would never have to experience that horror.

Gülbehar sat on the divan, her hands folded carefully on her lap, her face drawn into a mask of disapproval. "Leave us now, Mustapha. I wish to talk with the Lord of Life alone."

Mustapha grinned again and sala'amed to his father. He kissed Gülbehar on the cheek and left the room.

Süleyman sat beside her on the divan. "You are too severe with him," Süleyman said.

Gülbehar's dark eyes flashed briefly. "He is all I have."

"A young man needs to enjoy youthful pleasures while he can. He will have responsibilities soon enough, as God shall be my witness."

"But every day he brings home from the Hippodrome some fresh injury. Last week he was thrown from his horse three times! What if he dies, Süleyman? I have no son, and no master. My life is over."

Süleyman stared at her, angry that she had articulated the truth to him so bluntly. "As God wills," he said. Only the softness of his voice betrayed his fury.

"You only ever come here to see Mustapha."

"That is my right."

"Do I no longer have rights?" Ah, that much at least is true, he thought. He had ignored the *nobet geçesi,* the "night turn" that was the prerogative of every kadin. He should by custom sleep with her at least once every week. Gülbehar had not dared to raise that question before now.

Süleyman stood up, angry at her for raising it even now. She had never questioned him before. Perhaps that had been the trouble all along. Guilt made his rage all the more potent. "You may be first kadin, but you are still just one of my *kullar,* my family of slaves. You will do as I command, and you will not presume to question me."

Gülbehar wilted before his anger. She hung her head. "She has bewitched you."

"Who?"

"Hürrem! The little red-haired minx! She has bedeviled you and now she wants dominion over the Harem—even over you!"

"And what do you want?"

Gülbehar looked up at him miserably. "Only to serve you."

"Then keep your silence," Süleyman said. "Serve me by keeping your silence."

And he turned his back, the embroidered white silk of his kaftan flapping about his heels. Like a great bird taking flight, Gülbehar thought. Taking flight forever.

Then he was gone, the impassive black mutes at the door staring fixedly like statues, dumb to all meaning.

THAT NIGHT AFTER the final prayer the *killerji-bashi* came to Mustapha's chamber and asked him if he would like to eat. Silent pages brought him his meal on a gold tray. There were tiny squares of meat broiled in herbs, squash stuffed with rice, figs in sour cream, and fresh, plump oranges.

The meal was served in tiny blue and white Iznik porcelain bowls, each bowl hand painted in cobalt and olive with *rumi* and *hatayi* scrollwork. The killerji-bashi tasted each dish for poison, as he did at every meal, then bowed and left the room. Mustapha sat cross-legged on the carpet and ate in silence. Occasionally he would raise the index finger of his right hand and one of the pages would step forward to refill the golden goblet with sherbet.

When he had finished, Mustapha studied the oranges. He picked one up, peeled the skin off one side, and tasted it. It was dry, and slightly sour. He dropped it on the tray and pushed it away; instantly, another page stepped forward with a bowl of perfumed water. Mustapha dipped his fingers into the bowl and then allowed them to be dried. He got up and went into the bedchamber. It was customary for the pages to take whatever he had left and as he left the chamber he saw them fall on the tray like starving street dogs. The sight always disgusted him.

His pages had already unrolled the mattress in his bedchamber, but he did not feel tired. He sat cross-legged at the Qur'ān stand, and read two more *suras* by the light of the candle before the first spasm gripped his stomach.

BY THE TIME Gülbehar arrived, the pages who had served the prince's meal were already dead, their eyes bulging with their death agony, their bodies contorted by the spasms that had racked them. Mustapha was pale and shaking, but still alive. The Palace physician had administered an emetic, and Mustapha groaned as his now-empty stomach rebelled once more.

Gülbehar fell on her knees, sobbing, and cradled her son in her arms, feeling his body tremble. "Who has done this?" she screamed at the terrified faces of the pages and guards. "Who has done this to my son?"

"We will find whoever is guilty of this," the new Kapi Aga promised. By the Prophet's Holy Beard, if Mustapha had died his own neck would have found its way on to the Gate of Felicity . . .

But Gülbehar was not listening to his terrified promises. She began to rock the boy in her arms like a baby, sobbing with grief and fear and rage. "Who has done this?"

The killerji-bashi, the shahzade's food taster, was delivered to the bostanji, who awaited him below the Ba'ab-i-Sa'adet, in his torture chamber. He was examined closely, insistent on his innocence between his screams. Despite his protests, he was finally able to tell them at least which food had contained the poison, by the simple expedient of force-feeding him each morsel that remained on the shahzade's tray.

"It was the oranges," the bostanji finally reported. "Somehow they had poisoned the oranges."

Süleyman ordered that everyone involved in the preparation of the prince's meal be examined also; the two cooks, the page who had brought the tray from the kitchen.

All died screaming, begging their innocence, pleading for mercy that never came.

28

GOLD SPIGOTS DRIPPED warm water into the marble bath. Naked bodies, alabaster, coffee, and ebony, beaded with water, moved in and out of the mists. Black gediçli in gauzy bath chemises, scooped water from the baths into gold-plated bowls and poured it over the heads of the girls. The slap of flesh on warm marble echoed from the cavernous dome.

Hürrem perched on the edge of the navel-stone, a huge hexagonal slab heated from beneath by an unseen furnace. She allowed Muomi to soap her back with thick lather, then dowse her head and shoulders with warm water. The other girls passed her, their eyes averted, perhaps out of jealousy, Hürrem thought, more likely out of fear.

Hürrem surrendered to Muomi's hard knuckles working the muscles in her back. Later she would have her work on her stomach and thighs. She would not allow herself to grow old and fat in here. A girl could not afford to be without fangs in this snakepit.

She closed her eyes, tried not to brood on how closely she had come to resolving her problems. The oranges had been her idea. She knew the killerji-bashi would not suspect a whole fruit. She had pierced the oranges with needles and Muomi had poured her hemlock into the tiny pinpricks. It was pure chance that had saved the shahzade. Never mind. She would find some other way.

Then she saw her. The gauzy bath chemise clung to her heavy breasts. Hürrem noted with pleasure that her belly was growing thicker. The reason was plain; one of the slave girls hurrying behind her was carrying a silver platter of candied fruit.

"You will need a whole procession of slaves soon," Hürrem whispered as she passed.

Gülbehar had not seen her but she recognized Hürrem's voice immediately. She wheeled around, identified Hürrem through the mist of steam. "What did you say?"

Hürrem noted with pleasure that Gülbehar's eyes were immediately bright with passion.

"I said you will need more than just two slave girls soon, or your breasts will be dragging on the ground. Perhaps two to carry each one on a silver platter. Like the fruit."

Gülbehar gaped at her in fury. This little minx was goading her. Actually goading her!

"How dare you speak to me like that . . ." Gülbehar could barely catch her breath. "I know it was you! You tried to murder my son!"

"You are getting old. Your mind is playing tricks."

"It was you, little witch!"

"Then run to your Sultan and tell him your suspicions. If you dare!"

Gülbehar felt the hot tears brimming in her eyes. Hürrem was so certain of her hold over him! The worst of it was that she was right. Süleyman would never believe her.

"If you hurt my son, I will kill you!"

Hürrem smiled. "I do not think my Süleyman will allow that." Hürrem put both her hands on her own stomach. "How many more Sultans do you think I might yet grow in here?"

"Mustapha is . . ."

"Mustapha is all you have. I have three, and I may have many more, since the Sultan no longer comes to your bed. Why is it you cannot keep him from me, Rose of Spring? Because you are stupid, or because you are dull?"

"Leave my son alone!"

Hürrem lowered her voice to a whisper. "Say goodbye to your little bud, Rose of Spring!"

Gülbehar lashed out with her right hand. The slap stung Hürrem's cheek. She struck back, but at the last moment she weighted the blow, so that it caught Gülbehar only a glancing blow on the side of the head. Gülbehar struck out again, this time with her nails. Hürrem grabbed her shoulders and pulled her toward her, and they fell to the floor. The gediçli jumped back, screaming. The silver tray clattered onto the marble.

MUOMI HELPED HÜRREM stagger back to her private chambers, the pain in her stomach leaving her doubled over and gasping. She was still dripping wet, the thin bath chemise wrapped lightly around her. Her hair hung in wet tangles around her face and there were streaks of thin watery blood on her forehead and cheek.

Muomi helped her to a divan, and stood back, staring. She was puzzled more than frightened. She sensed that Hürrem had anticipated this, that it was part of some elaborate plan. If that were true, she was impressed.

"Shall I ask for the physician?" Muomi said.

Hürrem laughed, despite the pain. She had landed heavily when she had tussled Gülbehar to the floor. Well, if she lost the baby, that would still suit her plans. Two sons was enough anyway. "How could the physician help me?" All he would be able to examine was her hand, and that from behind three rows of armed eunuchs.

"You are badly hurt."

"Bring me the mirror."

Muomi fetched the jeweled mirror and handed it to Hürrem. She held it up and examined her reflection. There were some small scratches on her cheek, two deeper ones on her forehead. Damn the little bitch. She didn't even know how to fight properly!

"Scratch me," Hürrem said.

"My Lady?"

"Scratch me!" Hürrem grabbed Muomi's wrist and drew her nails down her cheek. "Harder!"

With elaborate care, Muomi brought her fingernails to Hürrem's face and began to rake deep scratches down her cheeks. She did it again, and again, and again. She grinned, suddenly. So pleasant to take away; so pleasant not to be the victim.

"Enough!"

"Once more, my Lady."

Hürrem screamed and twisted Muomi's hands away from her face. She groped for the mirror. Her face was a bloody mask, unrecognizable.

"Are you satisfied, my Lady?" Muomi said. She sounded breathless, as if she had just made love.

"Yes, I am satisfied, Muomi."

"Now will your Sultan love you more, looking like that?"

"No, Muomi. But he will love Gülbehar less," Hürrem said, and tears of pain mixed with the blood that trickled down her cheeks.

29

THE ESKI SARAYA trembled.

Süleyman strode through the darkened cloisters, the Kislar Aghasi shuffling behind, his face streaming with tiny rivulets of perspiration, babbling with fright. It was as much as he could do to keep pace with the Lord of Life.

Like a great white eagle, he thought, watching the tall figure striding ahead of him, the robes of the white kaftan fluttering behind him. And its talons are bared.

The Lord of Life had heard of the terrible incident in the hammam through his mother, the Valide. News traveled quickly in the Harem. There was so little else to talk about but gossip. Even the smallest thing, an imagined slight or a hard look, would be conveyed to the Hafise Sultan within the day.

And this terrible episode in the hammam was no small thing.

The Kislar Aghasi saw the Lord of Life halt before the doors of Hürrem's apartment. The two eunuch guards appeared to quiver at his approach, but continued to stare resolutely ahead.

The Kislar Aghasi waited, his breath racking painfully in his chest.

"Tell her I am here," Süleyman said.

The old eunuch nodded and went inside but it was Muomi, not Hürrem, who waited inside the door to greet him. She sala'amed, and remained on her knees.

"The Lord of Life wishes to see your mistress," he said. He had already sent a messenger ahead to warn Hürrem to be ready.

"She cannot see him," Muomi said.

The Kislar Aghasi stared at her, stunned, as if she had answered in a foreign language. "What did you say?"

"My mistress is distressed beyond words that she cannot accept the honor he does her by visiting her here. But she cannot see him. It is not fitting that the Lord of Life gaze on her face while it is so disfigured."

"Disfigured?"

"She hopes that time will heal her wounds and she will regain what former beauty she possessed. But she cannot let the Lord of Life gaze on her in her present condition."

The Kislar Aghasi stood there, helplessly, the pain in his chest growing worse. He was growing old, too old for the tribulations this little Russian had brought to his Harem. It had been so easy once, when there was just Gülbehar. How did the Chief Black Eunuch tell the Sultan that his second wife would not see him? There was no precedent for it in the protocol.

"She must see him," he said.

Muomi stared back at him and said nothing.

He hurried past her into the private sitting room. Hürrem was there, seated on a divan of green brocade, a heavy veil drawn over her face. She made no movement as he entered.

"My Lady," he said.

Still she said nothing. This was just intolerable, he thought, dabbing at the perspiration on his face with a silk handkerchief. They were toying with him, Muomi and this little red-haired witch.

"The Sultan wishes to see you," he said.

Hürrem slowly lifted the veil from her face and the old eunuch gasped. There were ugly red scabs over her nose, her cheeks, even across her eyes. It looked as if she had been attacked by a feral cat. Well, this was not the way he had heard it. The rumors had it that although it had been unseemly, neither girl had been badly hurt.

He uttered a sound a little like the sob of a small animal and hurried from the room.

❖

"TOO DISFIGURED TO see me?" Süleyman repeated slowly. He stared at his Chief Black Eunuch. The poor old man looked as if he were going to faint.

"It is what she says, my Lord."

"Gülbehar!" Süleyman whispered.

"My Lord?"

GÜLBEHAR WAS EAGER with excitement. The Kislar Aghasi's messenger had informed her that the Lord of Life was in the Eski Saraya, as she had anticipated. She was sure he would come to her now, convinced that he would hear of the outrage the Russian minx had inflicted on her in the hammam. The snake had shown itself at last. Süleyman would see her now for what she was. She would tell him how she had tried to murder his beloved Mustapha. He would put her and the black sorceress to the bostanji and the truth would come out.

And Süleyman would come back to her. Everything would be all right.

She prepared the table herself, set out sweetmeats and rahat lokum and sherbet, and settled herself on the divan. Her hair had been braided and brushed, her body freshly bathed and perfumed. There were pearls braided into her hair and a livid-red ruby at the hollow of her throat.

She tried to settle patiently to wait on the divan, but it was impossible. She could not wait to tell Süleyman what the woman had said to her, how she had provoked her so, her whispered threat against Mustapha. He would understand. At last she could make him see. She was, after all, his first kadin, the mother of the next Sultan.

She went to the window, staring through the grille at the glittering water of the Horn, and beyond, the red-roofed palaces climbing the hill of Galata. A bright, glittering world that belonged to her son. But in here it was dark, and cold. It had been dark and cold for too long.

It would change now.

The door crashed open.

There was no sweating old negro to usher the Lord of Life into her chamber. No time to settle herself. No time to prepare.

Süleyman stood in the doorway, his face ugly with rage. He slammed the great door shut behind him and advanced to the center of the room.

Gülbehar dropped to her knees in front of him. "Sala'am, Lord of my Life, Sultan of Sult—"

He grabbed her arms and forced her to stand. Gülbehar sobbed in pain—his fingers bit into the soft flesh of her upper arm like steel pincers—and surprise.

"Take off your veil."

Gülbehar shook. What was the matter with him? What could have incensed him like this? She pulled back the veil, and watched his face twist into a scowl of contempt.

"Not one scratch . . ."

"I do not understand, my Lord . . ."

He drew back his hand and slapped her hard across the face. He did it twice more. After the fourth blow she fell to the floor.

She lay there, sobbing. What was wrong? What was happening? When Süleyman spoke again, his voice was so soft she could barely discern the words. "If you take from me the pleasure of looking on her face, I swear . . . I will kill you."

"Please . . . my Lord . . ."

"Your jealousy poisons the whole Harem!"

"What is wrong? What have I done?"

"Enough! Do you hear me? You are mother of Mustapha. You will one day be the Valide. Be content with that!"

"What has that little minx said to you? It was not I that—"

He raised his hand again and struck her, grabbed her by the hair and dragged her to her feet, struck her again and again while she screamed at him to stop. The rage roared in his head, deafening him to her screams. It was only when he saw the blood smeared on her white chemise that he finally stopped. He let her fall, limp as a rag doll, his hands held away from himself, staring at the smears of blood.

For a long time she lay at his feet, sobbing. He stood over her, panting, suddenly appalled at what he had done. When she finally raised her face, her lips and eyes were swelling, and there was blood welling from her mouth and her nose, livid against her marble-white skin.

"My Lord . . ."

"Silence!" His breath was ragged in his chest and he struggled to control it. "Never deem to keep me from her ever again." His anger spent now, he reached down and took her arm to pull her to her feet but she twisted away from him.

Süleyman felt a pang of remorse. I might have killed her, he thought. I was so close to the edge. If there had been a dagger in my fist, I would have bled the life from her. She had been his kadin for so many years, since he was a boy, and yet in his anger he might have killed her.

"You must leave here," he whispered. "It is best for you."

He walked from the room, leaving her to her bitter tears.

30

The Hippodrome

GüZüL WAS A Jewess; once a month she was allowed inside the Harem to sell gems and trinkets to the odalisques. But that was not her true function; in the closed world of the Harem, Güzül was that rarest of creatures, a go-between. Over the course of the years, she had become Gülbehar's voice to the outside world.

She was no longer youthful. Her skin was the color of tobacco, and wrinkled; her eyes glittered in her head like small sapphires in a leather pouch. To compensate for her fading youth, she dyed her hair with henna, and tied it with bright ribbons, the remembrance of vanity. Ibrahim decided that once she must have been very beautiful.

For her errand she had chosen a cloak of rich scarlet silk, and there was a small round cap of satin, also scarlet, on her head. She had a waistcoat of gold damask and white kid leather shoes. There were silver bracelets on her ankles and wrists, and pearls in her hair. Her hands and feet had been dyed with henna and there was rich, dark kohl on her eyes. She looked like a brigand's queen.

At sunset the stone of Ibrahim's palace turned to the color of rose. The imposing walls and wooden shuttered windows echoed the splendor of the great Topkapi that stood less than half a mile away on the other side of the Atmeydani. It was a reminder to everyone, from the horsemen playing çerit below, to the faithful filing into the Aya Sofia, to the cobblers and bakers in the city, and to the yeniçeris beyond the Sublime Porte of the Ba'ab-i-Hümayun, that the Greek was the greatest and wealthiest and most trusted Vizier the Osmanli Empire had ever known.

The size of the Audience Hall recalled to Güzül her true insignificance.

The great carpet on which she knelt, fully ten paces by five, the ivory and tortoiseshell throne, the copper and turquoise censers, the silver candle holders, were all fit for a Sultan. Ibrahim himself, in his great white turban and satin robes, appeared as she imagined the Lord of Life himself might look.

He has succeeded in creating the illusion that he is much taller than he is, Güzül thought. Probably it is the turban, fully twenty inches high, with its thick band of gold at its base. It would be hard not to be impressed by him, or by the great ruby he wears on his finger, the size of a bird's egg.

Difficult not to be impressed; difficult not to be afraid.

Life had gone well for Ibrahim. After Süleyman had made him his Grand Vizier, he had built him a palace on the other side of the Hippodrome out of the public purse. Süleyman had even given him his sister, Hatise Sultan, in marriage.

The rising star had carried another satellite in its orbit. He sat cross-legged, at the foot of the marble steps that ascended to Ibrahim's throne, facing away from her, so that she could not see his face. But she knew who he was.

They said Rüstem Defterdar had been born a Bulgarian, and had been brought to Stamboul many years ago by the devshirme. He had been educated in the Enderun, the Palace school, and had excelled in mathematics. He had risen quickly through the ranks of the Treasury department, thanks, it was said, to Ibrahim's patronage. One could guess, Güzül thought, how useful it might be for Ibrahim to have one of his own manipulating the purse strings. Rumors of abuses and *baksheesh* were rife, though no one, of course, would dare raise their voices against Ibrahim. Not unless they wanted to make a closer inspection of the spikes on the walls of the Ba'ab-i'-Sa'adet.

She wondered what Rüstem was doing here. Perhaps Ibrahim is seeking his advice on other matters now, she thought.

The great man was watching her. He saw her glance in Rüstem's direction but he addressed her as if they were alone. "Well, Güzül, tell me, what brings you to my humble *seraglio?*"

"My mistress, the Rose of Spring, sends her felicitations. May your house always increase in health and prosperity."

"I thank her for good wishes. May God always protect her and may her beauty never fade."

"*Inshallah.* As God wills."

"I have heard whispers, Güzül."

"What whispers, my Lord?"

"That your mistress quarrels with the Lady Hürrem in the Eski Saraya. One may only pray that the conflict will be resolved to the satisfaction of all."

Güzül decided to abandon the polite language of the court. "She is to be exiled, my Lord."

Ibrahim paused, but allowed no reaction to show on his face. "Another rumor, Güzül?"

"My mistress begs for your intercession with the Lord of Life, my Lord."

"I do not have such power, Güzül."

That is not what they say in the bazaars, Güzül thought. There they say that you are Sultan in all but name. But I dare not say that, even here. "My mistress asks only that you speak for her with the Lord of Life."

"This is business of the Harem, and no affair of mine. You know I would like to help your mistress if I could, but this is beyond any small power that I have. She should perhaps plead her case with the Kislar Aghasi."

"My Lord, my mistress only asks that you examine the consequences of her departure."

Ibrahim leaned forward, one arm resting on the throne. His face betrayed the dawning of unease. "Yes, Güzül?"

"You have always been a friend to Mustapha. One day he will be the Sultan. His mother would like to remember you kindly."

"Is that a threat, Güzül?"

"No, my Lord. But my mistress would like you only to know that she has a long memory for her friends."

"Her great virtues are well known and boundless."

"My mistress would like you also to remember that she has never sought to challenge the power of the Grand Vizier."

Ibrahim laughed, surprised. "Of course not."

"Yet Hürrem is perhaps ready to challenge you now."

The words echoed in the silence like a horseshoe dropped on the marble floor. For a long time Ibrahim stared at her, his fist clenched on the arm of the throne. Finally he said: "You think so, Güzül?"

"In the bazaars they say she has bewitched him, my Lord."

"The Empire is not ruled by carpet salesmen."

"My mistress wants only to remind you that he spends long days and nights with her, my Lord. He talks to her of politics."

"More Harem talk!"

"My mistress only asks that you speak for her with the Lord of Life. You are a wise and faithful counselor. She wishes only for your continued well-being, my Lord."

"You have made your point, Güzül."

"My Lord," Güzül crept forward and kissed the carpet at the foot of the throne and crept out. Ibrahim watched her leave, his face knitted into a frown of indecision. Hürrem, a threat! Impossible! And yet . . .

Ibrahim looked at the man still kneeling silently, patiently, at the foot of the throne. "Well, Defterdar, what do you think?"

"It is always wise not to make more enemies than is absolutely necessary."

"He indulges this little Russian girl of his. But . . . challenge the office of Vizier?"

"That is a question only you may answer, my Lord," Rüstem said.

Ibrahim watched his face. Can you see what I am thinking, Defterdar? If you have discerned my real problem here—that the Harem is the one part of the Empire where I have no control—then you have not allowed your doubts to show on your face. But then, you allow no emotion to the surface. I sometimes wonder if you ever feel anything at all; and that is why I have chosen you above the others. Sometimes I allow the rush of my blood to cloud my judgment.

"The Rose of Spring is the mother of the shahzade," Ibrahim said. "One day she will be the Valide. I will do what I can to help her."

"It may also help you gauge the extent of this Harem girl's influence," Rüstem said.

Ibrahim looked at him sharply. He had not even considered that. But of course Süleyman would be led by his counsel. Had he ever overruled him before?

Well?

31

Topkapi Saraya

TONIGHT IBRAHIM'S VIOL pleased him not at all. Süleyman stared gloomily at his hands, while the pages removed the last of the dishes of rahat lokum—the sweet, pistachio-flavored "rest for the throat" with which he finished all his meals. Ibrahim finished his ballad and laid down the instrument, his head cocked to one side.

"Something is troubling you, my Lord?"

Süleyman nodded, slowly. "Yes, Ibrahim."

"You are troubled by the envoy, Haberdansky?"

Süleyman scowled. Haberdansky! The Hapsburg ambassador. Frederick had had the temerity to dispatch him to his court with no tribute and no terms, other than to claim Hungary was part of Frederick's empire by royal birth and demand its return. It had given him great pleasure to accede to Ibrahim's suggestion that he was shown true Osmanli hospitality in the dungeons at Yedikule.

"No, it is not politics that wearies me, Ibrahim."

"Yet it is something that must be resolved."

"Yes, yes."

"Perhaps, my Lord, you will let your Grand Vizier know of your decision when you have made it."

Süleyman smiled in spite of himself. There was no reproach in Ibrahim's voice, and the corners of his mouth were drawn up in a self-mocking smile. He is right, Süleyman thought. He came to me for a final decision on this days ago.

He sighed. "What do you think of this Zapolya?"

"He is never a king but I think he will make a fine vassal."

Süleyman nodded. It was the same reasoning Hürrem had suggested to him. "I had reached a similar conclusion," he said. "We can make him our gatekeeper. While he may wear the crown, as long as he gives us tribute, in gold and in slaves for the devshirme, the kingdom remains ours."

"It is settled, then?"

"Yes," Süleyman said. "Give his envoy your decision."

Ibrahim picked up the viol once more, and gently plucked at the strings. Süleyman felt a prickle of irritation. He could not find rest, even here. All he could think of was the war of nerves taking place in his own Harem.

"There is something I must discuss with you," he said, finally.

"Yes, my Lord?"

"It is about Mustapha."

"My Lord?"

"He shows great promise, both as a leader and a warrior. He is fourteen years old now. Perhaps it is time he was given a governorship, to test his mettle for the great burden he must one day accept."

Ibrahim put down the viol. So it was true! Süleyman planned to exile Gülbehar from the Harem under the guise of Mustapha's first governorship.

"He is still young," he said.

"Only a year younger than I, when my father sent me to Manisa."

"A year is a long time in one so young."

"Still, I think it is time. But I accept what you say. We should have his mother accompany him, to guide him. They are very close. Do you agree?"

"I would counsel against it, my Lord."

"I have made up my mind."

Ibrahim blinked in surprise. Süleyman had never taken up a decision before without his blessing. "There is danger in blooding him too soon. We should weigh this carefully."

"Not this time, Ibrahim. There is nothing further we need trouble ourselves with."

"I would counsel forbearance, my Lord. We should wait at least a year."

"He is my son. I know him best."

"But to give him a governorship so soon—"

"Will you give me peace, Ibrahim! I have said that I have made up my mind! You are a fine Vizier but you are not the Sultan!"

Ibrahim stared at him. Süleyman's eyes were blazing with a sudden heat. He is dry powder, ready to explode, he thought. Someone else has primed him for this. He will not listen to me because he has been warned against it. Now who could have done that?

Ibrahim knew it was dangerous to provoke him further. "As you say, my Lord, I defer to your greater wisdom."

"I shall go to bed. I am tired," Süleyman said.

Süleyman undressed and eased himself under the coverlet of the sleeping mattresses the pages had laid out on the floor. While they stood guard by the two candles at the foot of the bed, Ibrahim continued to sit cross-legged on the carpet, strumming a melancholy tune on the viol.

As he played, Ibrahim closed his eyes and saw the strings of the viol extend beyond the gray walls of the Palace, beyond the seven hills of Stamboul, across the Black Sea and the Mediterranean and the Aegean, across the drifting sands of Egypt and Algeria, the mountains of Persia and Greece, the broad rivers of the Euphrates and the Danube, the plains of Hungary, and the steppes of the Ukraine, the holy cities of Jerusalem, Babylon, Mekka, and Medina. At the end of the strings danced princes and *pashas, shahs,* and *sheikhs,* and he and Süleyman had played the tune. But now new and sticky strands were uncoiling like tentacles from the great city, and he could feel them entwined around his own body and that of his beloved *padishah.* And the hands that held the web were soft and white and feminine, and the nails were painted scarlet.

He shivered against the chill of the room and for the first time in his life he was a little afraid.

SÜLEYMAN SAT ASTRIDE a white horse in the cobbled courtyard, the topaz like a dark heart on his turban, the heron's plume bending to the breeze. His white robes billowed with the unseasonal north wind. His face was drawn into a tight, stern mask. It was impossible to fathom his expression, even if the pages and guards that stood near by had had the temerity to look at him openly. And, on pain of death, none of them would.

He saw Mustapha climb easily astride his own horse—the boy looked more at home in the saddle than he did on his own long, still-growing limbs—and wait, staring hopefully toward the shadows beneath the east tower.

Süleyman made the slightest movement of his knees and his stallion trod slowly forward, its ears pricked for the slightest command from its rider.

Süleyman reined him in alongside Mustapha's mount. He reached across and put a hand on the boy's forearm. "May God bless your journey and keep you safe," he said.

"Thank you, Father." There was a flush to the boy's cheeks, his youthful enthusiasm straining against his self-imposed dignity.

"Do well."

"I shall do all I can to serve you."

"It is not me you serve, Mustapha, it is Islam. Remember that. Even Sultans and their princes are only servants. Islam is our master. Go in peace."

"Yes, Father."

Süleyman felt a great weight in his chest. How strange it would be to come to the Harem and not find Mustapha there! He heard movement behind him and saw three veiled figures cross the courtyard and hurry inside the waiting coach, Gülbehar and her two handmaidens.

One of the figures waited, staring at him from behind her veil, waiting for some sign that he might come and speak to her, but Süleyman turned away.

When he looked back she was gone.

Süleyman waited until the tiny procession had left the court and the great doors of the Eski Saraya had slammed shut behind them. When they were gone, he felt a curious sense of elation, as if, at last, he were somehow free from part of his burden.

PART 4

THE CUSTODIAN OF FELICITY

32

The Ionian Sea, 1532

A BEWILDERING CONTRADICTION OF the senses. The colors and pageantry of Heaven, the nauseating stench of the Beast.

The galley looked like some giant water beetle, the twenty-seven sets of oars on each of its flanks like spindly legs pushing it across the tensile surface of the glittering blue water. Pennants and banners stirred listless at the mast and stern, the golden lion of Venice asleep in the sun. The poop, elaborately carved and gilded, was covered with an awning of purple and gold under which the officers and gentle cargo reclined at ease, on rugs and low divans, perfumed handkerchiefs held to their noses to filter out the appalling smells that wafted from below and surrounded the great ship like an invisible and malignant vapor.

The sails were braided along two great curving yards above the fore and main masts. Out of sight in the semidarkness in the bowels of the galley, twenty-seven rows of naked slaves pushed her across the ocean. They sat chained to wooden benches, their own urine and feces swirling in the bilge around their ankles. They had been rowing now for eighteen hours without a break. One of the under-officers moved down the rows of benches with bread soaked in wine to stuff into the gasping mouths of those who seemed close to exhaustion. Several men had already passed out in their chains. They had been flogged back to consciousness with a rope dipped in brine. Two who had not recovered promptly enough were unshackled and tossed over the side.

Julia Gonzaga saw nothing of this from her chair under the purple and gold tabernacle. Brocaded curtains spared the passengers from such unpleasantness, although she had caught glimpses of the wretches at the oars several times during the journey, and the sight of it had seared itself into her memory like a brand. She had never seen such utter despair and filth, and the image had haunted her for every second of the ten days they had been at sea. The captain had explained to her that they were only heathen, captured Turkish sailors and Arab pirates, and so no better than animals. But she was unable to drive the deep sense of shame from her spirit. She closed her eyes to the bright glare of the Mediterranean and fingered her rosary, and tried to focus her thoughts on more Christian sentiments.

It was the first time she had ever left Venice, La Serenissima, and she was both exhilarated and afraid. Pietro, her husband, had been visiting his estates in Cyprus when he had been taken ill, two months before. From her latest news it seemed the illness might be a long one, and he now demanded her presence at his side. Julia guessed that he wanted her as a nurse and not as wife; he had shown little passion for her as a woman, and any secrets he might have unlocked for her had remained a mystery. On their wedding night he had kissed her on the cheek at the door to her bed-chamber and slept in his own room, a ritual he had maintained every night since.

The only time she had entered his bedchamber had been to nurse him when he was overcome with another bout of illness, a situation that had become increasingly frequent over the last two years. He would have her sit by his side day and night and read to him from Plato. It was the only thing she did that ever seemed to please him. She had decided long ago that he was an irritable and irascible old man, too full of his own impor-tance, and she cursed her father every day for making the match for her.

Politics. It was all he cared about.

She should have enjoyed the voyage, the fresh salt air, the glittering ocean, and the bright spring flowers blooming on the islands. She wel-comed the relief from the cloistered atmosphere of the palazzo, the gloomy corridors, the must of damp, the monotony of her lacework and daily matins. It would have been wonderful, if it were not for the smell. The stench rising from the slave benches reminded her of the ugliness below, and the ugliness awaiting her at her destination. The smell of an ancient and decaying husband.

For no reason at all, she wondered what had happened to Abbas. Abbas . . . no man had spoken to her as he had done, before or since. Abbas! He glowed like an icon in her past. For a few glorious days she had felt alive.

"Pleasant thoughts, my Lady?"

Julia looked up, startled. It was the captain, Bellini, a plump young man with florid cheeks and quick, furtive eyes. "I beg your pardon?" Had he seen her smiling through the heavy black lace of her *mantilla?*

"One has so much time to reflect on these long voyages."

"I was thinking of my husband."

"Ah." Bellini looked away and pointed toward the horizon. "Another ten days and I am sure you will be reunited. It might be less given a good wind. The oars are a poor substitute."

"Indeed."

Bellini held his handkerchief up to his nose for a moment and breathed deeply. "How long since you have seen your husband?"

"It must be nearly six months."

"A long time. You must miss him."

Julia recognized the gently mocking tone in his voice, and felt a flush of anger, despite herself. "More than you will ever know," she replied, and was pleased at the blush of embarrassment she excited in the young man's face.

If only I knew, she thought bitterly.

Bellini sought refuge in his own esteem. "With a fair wind . . ." he began, but the sentence caught in his throat. "*Corpo di Dio!*" he swore and rushed across the deck to fetch his telescope. But a cry from the sailors furling the sails on the yards of the foremast confirmed Bellini's fears.

The triangular lateen sails of the galleot appeared suddenly from behind the cliffs of an island less than a mile distant. The blades of the oars hovered and dipped, hovered and dipped again as she came on.

"Turks!" Bellini shouted, his voice high-pitched with panic. He ran down the steps that led from the poop on to the bridge across the slave decks. "Row!" Julia heard him scream. "Row!"

There was a blast of whistles and the heavy slap of whips. She heard men shrieking protest at this new punishment. The galley lurched as the helmsman on the platform above the poop leaned on the long tiller, swinging the galley hard to starboard, away from the oncoming Turkish pirate. Already it seemed twice as large on the horizon. She could see its oars clearly; dip-pause-sweep, dip-pause-sweep.

Suddenly the decks were a swarming mass of men, clambering down the yards to their positions in the prow and poop, soldiers scrambling for their harquebuses and crossbows. Fear erupted in perspiration from their bodies, stared from their eyes, and broke in tumbled curses from their mouths.

The long beaked prow of the Turkish galleot was clearly visible now, perhaps no more than a half mile from their stern.

Dip-sweep-pause.

Julia gripped Bellini's arm. "What's going to happen?"

The captain stared at her without really seeing her, his eyes white and wide. "I don't think we can outrun them. *Corpo di Dio*, where's our consort?" He searched the horizon desperately for the warship that he had allowed to slip from his vision in his complacency.

"Can't we outrun them?"

"They're lighter and faster. Besides, their oarsmen are all freemen, and rested. They've been lying in wait for us."

"What's going to happen?" Julia said, and a cold fist gripped her insides and began to squeeze.

But Bellini pushed her aside without answering and ran to the bridge over the slave deck. "Row! Row!" she heard him scream, and the screams and the slap of the whip and the clanking of the irons redoubled.

She looked to the stern and gasped. The galleot was less than a quarter of a mile away.

THERE WAS AN unearthly, primitive sound drifting up from the slave deck, above the cries of the pilot and captain and soldiers, over the steady "Thrum! Thrum!" of the war drum. The men at the oars were defying their officers, their curses and their whips, their voices raised in a strange, gutteral chant:

"La illaha ilallah Muhammadu rasul allah . . . La illaha ilallah Muhammadu rasul allah . . ."

God is great and Muhammad is his prophet.

Julia turned and watched the galleot, the green flag of Islam fluttering at the mast, just two hundred yards astern. So this was the heathen she had heard so much of. This was the Devil Islam.

Their *rais* stood at the poop, urging even greater effort from the men at the oars below, while a huge Arab, bald and bare chested, gave the stroke on the tambour. The oar blades rose and fell in perfect unison. She could see the white puffs drift from the prow as several of the Turks opened fire with their harquebuses. One of the soldiers on the bridge above the slave deck screamed, clutching his face, and disappeared over the side. She heard a muffled thud as his body struck the lower deck, out of sight.

Several of the galley slaves cheered.

"La illaha ilallah Muhammadu rasul allah . . ."

The galleot was sweeping toward them now from the stern on the starboard side, safe from the Venetian's bow chasers, the forr'ard guns. Julia heard a roar as the Turks fired their own guns. The water in front of them churned to foam and then part of the rigging in the main mast collapsed in a scream of cracking timber.

Julia watched, paralyzed with terror. She heard another sound now, the *chamade,* the cry the Turkish rowers made to frighten their enemy. *"Allahu Akbar! Allaaaah!"* One of Bellini's officers saw her and started to push her toward the hold.

"For the love of God," he screamed, "get below! Get below!"

She ran.

She reached the ship's ladder and stopped. From here she could see the oarsmen hunched at their benches, their backs striped from the blows of the galley masters, straining half-heartedly at their oars, faces creased with pain and hope. She could also see the Turkish galleot's iron-tipped fighting prow, the *rambade,* scything through the water toward them.

As she watched, it crashed through the oars on the starboard side as if they were twigs, and the splintering of wood was drowned by the screams of the oarsmen as the looms of the oars snapped back into their chests and faces. The bilge turned red, as men clawed at the shattered remains of their faces. She saw one man trying to push his own viscera back into his torn stomach.

Then the rambade crashed through the starboard bulwark and the galleot lurched again and Julia toppled forward into the darkness.

WHEN SHE OPENED her eyes she found herself lying on her back at the foot of the ship's ladder. The hatchway was empty, but a filmy mist of white smoke drifted across the deck. She could hear men's voices, angry voices shouting orders, others screaming in pain or begging quarter. The grating of steel and the discharge of the harquebuses faded quickly, replaced by a terrible howling and rattling, like a thousand demons.

She slowly realized what it was. It was the galley slaves, begging for their freedom.

She lay quite still. There was nowhere to run to now. She dragged herself to the bulwark and hugged her knees to her breasts, waiting. She groped for her rosary and started to whisper her prayers.

"Holy Mary, full of grace . . ."

She heard footsteps on the decking over her head and three dark shadows blotted out the sunlight in the hatchway. The men all wore turbans, and carried curved swords.

They stopped halfway down the ladder and stared at her. Then one of the men shouted something she did not understand and the others laughed. Then she was being pulled to her feet and dragged roughly back up the companionway.

33

Algiers

AFRICA ROSE OUT of the horizon unexpectedly, the little village of Sidi Bou Said stark and white against the scorched red earth. Behind it rose the steel-gray silhouette of Djebel Ressas.

As the galleot sailed past the headland, the lateens filled with the breeze that might have once saved the shuffling and miserable huddle of humanity on the deck below. They emerged one by one, blinking in the sunlight, from the dark hold.

The fortress of Algiers loomed from the sea. Below it, whitewashed buildings piled up the hillside like blinding white cubes, under the mouths of the Osmanli cannon and the flapping green banner of Muhammad.

The harbor was teeming with ships, all flying the green crescent flag of Islam. As the galleot slipped past the rock at the harbor mouth, the prisoners fell silent, their heads bowed, resigning themselves to their fate.

Julia, being a woman, was kept separate from the other prisoners. She dared a glance at them now from behind the black lace of her mantilla, and gasped. They had been stripped naked, except for thin strips of material round their groins, and their hands and feet were chained. They all stared at the deck, bowed and humiliated. None of them looked toward her, not even Bellini. She barely recognized him. Without his uniform, he looked much smaller and much fatter, his stomach livid white like goose fat.

Julia felt her cheeks flush hot, and she looked away. She fingered her rosary and concentrated on her prayers.

The galleot was moored at the quay below the harbor mosque and the *souk,* and a crowd soon gathered along the waterfront to gawk at them. The men were led off first, the Turkish pirates pushing back the mob of brown-skinned Arabs in their burnooses and flapping gowns. They hawked and spat at the Venetians, screaming at them in a strange guttural tongue, their faces almost white with hate.

Julia felt her whole body begin to shake.

Then one of the Turks—she took him to be their rais, their captain—gripped her arm and led her off behind them, pushing her ahead of him through the crowds.

Julia had not given up hope. Humiliation, anger, terror, contempt, all competed for attention inside her. Her husband and her father were mag-nifici, after all, both prominent members of the Consiglio di Dieci. Venice was at peace with the Osmanlis, her husband traded with them, had even entertained members of Süleyman's court at his table. The worst that could happen, she told herself, is that I will be ransomed. The nightmare cannot last.

She glanced at the spitting, cursing faces in the crowd around her and bit her lip in anger. Heathen! *Heathen!*

The rais hurried her along.

The crowd followed them through the Kasbah, along narrow alleys piled with filth. Rats scurried away amid the garbage as they approached. They stumbled farther into the maze of streets, the men herded along ahead of her. Julia kept her eyes down, too ashamed to look at the naked, shambling men. Ventians all of them, now looking no better than . . . than their own galley slaves . . .

The Bey's Palace loomed ahead of them. They were ushered through the great gate, past the black slave corrals where the caravans from the Sahara brought the Nubians and Sudanese and the Guineans. The black men, women, and children had been herded in together; some of the women still had babies at their breasts, which they suckled unashamedly, and the men were quite naked . . .

Corpo di Dio!

They were led into a courtyard, a vast esplanade of white sand enclosed on all four sides by arched colonnades. Hundreds of sweating bodies created a miasma of stink; there was a din of voices, a score of different languages, some shouting orders, some babbling in fear, others haggling furiously. Julia hesitated, her senses overwhelmed. The rais cursed her and pushed her ahead of him.

Julia suddenly realized she had lost sight of the others and for some reason she felt abandoned. Desperate and helpless as they were, they were her last link with the world she knew.

They moved into another courtyard and the babble of voices became muted. The courtyard was empty, though there were many footprints in the bleached sand. Julia looked up.

A fat, swarthy man sat in the shade on a pile of cushions. A young negro boy stood behind him, cooling him with a fan of ostrich feathers. His white kaftan was trimmed with gold thread, and there was a large turquoise in his white muslin turban. The rais spoke to the man quickly. Julia heard one word repeated over and over: Gaiour.

The fat man was staring at her, a soft smile on his lips. He lifted an arm as a signal that he was about to rise. The negro boy dropped the fan and helped the man to his feet.

"What is your name?" the man said.

"You speak Italian?"

The man smiled again. "Of course. What do you think I am? A barbarian?" He came closer. "Do you speak Turkish?"

"Of course not."

He smiled again and lifted her mantilla. Julia froze. No Venetian gentleman would have ever dared to lift a woman's veil. Only her husband could do that. But equally, she dared not snatch his hand away. She had done that to the rais, on the day she had been captured, and he had slapped her round the face for her trouble. She could still feel the sting of it.

The fat man glanced at the rais. "He is right. You are beautiful. What is your name?"

"Julia Gonzaga. My father and my husband are both members of the Consiglio. They will reward you well for my return."

The fat man smiled again. "My Sultan will reward me more," he said. "Allow me to introduce myself. My name is Mehmet Ali-Osman. I am Bey of Algiers, in the service of Sultan Süleyman, King of Kings, Lord of Lords, Emperor of the Seven Worlds." He effected a mock bow. "I am his lifelong servant. As you are now also."

"I am no one's servant."

"You are too proud. Pride and beauty often accompany each other, but that is no matter."

He walked around her, and Julia felt him inspecting her minutely with his eyes. She endured this new humiliation, staring intently at the white sand. He faced her again and then put out one pudgy hand and gently squeezed her breast, as if examining a piece of fruit. Julia screamed and stepped back, shaking.

The rais growled at her but the Bey shook his head, roaring with laughter. "Your modesty will not be worth much to you now, *bellissima!*"

He turned to the rais, and for five minutes a heated argument raged around her. Julia could understand none of it, but from the expression on the face of the pirate, and the way he spoke, she dared to hope that he was about to draw his sword and pin the Bey to the wall. She had never hated anyone as much as she hated this fat little man who had dared impugn her modesty.

But then the Bey reached into the folds of his robe and produced a leather pouch. He opened it, and poured a number of gold coins into his palm and handed them to the rais, who laughed, and slapped the Bey on the shoulder as if they were lifelong friends. The enmity of a few moments before had suddenly vanished.

Then he was gone, and she was left with Mehmet Ali-Osman.

"Julia, my bellissima, you are now a member of the Sultan Süleyman's kullar, his slave family. Bless the day!"

"My father . . ."

"Your father no longer exists, nor your husband. The Kislar Aghasi will pay me well for beauty such as yours! I shall make a tenfold profit from you." He clapped his hands and two turbanned soldiers appeared from the shadows. "Take her inside and guard her well. Make sure she is given something to eat and drink. Who knows, one day she may be mother of the next Sultan!"

As she was led away she heard Mehmet Ali-Osman settle himself again on his cushions, his laughter echoing around the empty court.

AN ENDLESS GLITTERING blue ocean that hurt the eyes; sudden, violent summer storms that left her groaning and weak with nausea, with no escape from the vile stench of the bilge and the taint of vomit. Week after week they sailed across the Osmanli Empire, now and then glimpsing the inverted mirages of islands or a distant coast.

Julia felt sick the whole time, seasick, lonely, and terrified. The Turks watched her, their eyes bright and hungry and hard, but none of them dared offend her or touch her. She was the Sultan's meat now.

They brought her food, barely edible, but she noticed it was the same mess of rice and dried meat they ate themselves. They gave her a cabin below decks, guarded every night by two of the crew. But although she felt their eyes on her every time she stepped on to the deck, none of them spoke or tried to communicate with her in any way.

Once Julia stared into the waters and considered throwing herself over the side of the boat. But a part of her still clung to hope. Her father would have her released. She was not the Sultan's whore yet. By the time she arrived in Stamboul he would have heard of her kidnapping and a legation from the Venetian ambassador would be waiting on the dock to negotiate the ransom.

Sunrise, sunset on an endless blue ocean.

One morning she came up on deck and there, in front of her, were the mountains of Anatolia, rising purple from the horizon, shrouded in mist. A few hours later they put in at Smyrna, and Julia experienced a thrill of relief and terror. At last. The waiting was almost over.

A few days later, at sunset, they sailed past Troy, and through the narrow neck of the Dardanelles into the milky blue of the Marmara Deniz, weighing anchor, waiting for the dawn.

THE SURFACE OF the sea was as still and shiny and gray as the blade of a sword. Stamboul rose from the dawn like a hand rising from the mist, the pointed minarets of the Aya Sofia like fingers pointing toward the sky. The sun reflected on the golden domes of the mosques that were ranged on the sides of the seven hills, and chased away the mist that clustered at the foot of the sea walls, and the jutting arm of Seraglio Point. The waters swarmed with Greek *caramusalis* and fast caïques. She even saw the golden lion of Venice hoisted on a flag on one of the galleys, just a hundred yards away, and she felt an almost physical pain. So close.

Then they were round the point and inside the curving arm of the Golden Horn. But there was no legation from La Serenissima waiting for her, and Julia's fingers tightened on the rail. She closed her eyes, knowing that everything she had once remembered was now left behind.

34

Manisa

GÜLBEHAR WATCHED THE riders from the latticed windows of the palace. The iron on the horses' hoofs rang on the smooth stones of the Roman road and echoed along the valley walls. The sound reminded her of the bells that were rung every hour in the cloisters of the Eski Saraya in Stamboul. Another world from here, she thought. She did not miss the dusty stairwells or the drafty rooms, but she missed being close to *him*. When she was his kadin, she had felt his warmth. Now, for all the freedom of her new life, her bed was always cold.

Now, without Mustapha, she would have nothing.

The evening sun had dipped below the hills, and the fields of barely and wheat were filtered through sepia. The breeze carried with it the smell of woodsmoke.

The riders drew closer. She could see them clearly now. There were a dozen of them; one rode ahead of the rest, his voice booming up the valley even from this distance. He was dark, with a sparse beard, and wore a loose-fitting robe and turban. A stag, its throat pierced by an arrow, lay across his saddle. Blood had seeped from the wound and stained his horse's flank.

Mustapha.

"So. We shall be dining on venison," Gülbehar murmured to herself. Her son looked pleased with himself. No doubt they would be regaled with the story of the hunt all evening.

He rides like a true shahzade, she thought, watching him. His youth and lack of experience does not intimidate him. He shouted something, lost on the wind, and the other spahis shouted with laughter. What a son! Gülbehar thought. A fine horseman and hunter, he had also excelled in his mathematics and languages, as well as the Qur'ān. Already he could speak Persian and Italian as well as he could speak Turkish. He was popular with the yeniçeris and the spahis, and at only eighteen, he had been governor at Manisa for four years already.

Already they said he would be the finest of all the Osmanli Sultans, greater even than his father. So many talents, so few flaws. Ah, Gülbehar thought, but they do not know you like I do. You have a flaw, and you are blind to it. And it will kill you, if I do not save you.

The riders entered the great oak and iron gate and dismounted in the courtyard. Mustapha swung down from his horse, looked up at the latticed window and waved, still laughing. He could not see her, of course. But he knew she would be there, watching.

Such a fine young son. Such a lion.

Such a lamb.

THE YEARS OF exile had changed her. Not physically—although a close observer would have noticed the tiny lines that bitterness had etched into her eyes and the corners of her mouth—but the heart of the Rose of Spring had grown thorns. Her beauty had once made her passive, for it had given her everything; and her nature may have even accepted the loss of Süleyman.

But she would not let them take Mustapha; she would not let that witch harm her cub.

They ate in silence. Mustapha had returned buoyant from the hunt, had described the chase of the stag for her three times before he had caught her mood and allowed it to infect him. Elated with his own success, he resented his mother's dark mood.

"The venison is good, isn't it?" he said stubbornly, choosing another square of the broiled, rich game from a dish.

"Delicious," Gülbehar murmured. "Tell me again about the hunt."

"You are not really interested, Mother. Let us not play games with each other."

Gülbehar looked up at him. Even on his haunches he towered over her. At eighteen he stood well over six feet tall, with a silky bronze-gold beard and an intimidating physical presence. His eyes were bright and quick, constantly on the move, mirroring his passion and restless energy. He reminded her of her own father, a Montenegran mountain bandit.

"What is wrong?" he said at last.

"We must think about your future," Gülbehar said.

"My future?" He laughed. "I have the simplest future of any man. For now I am Governor of Kütahya. One day I will be Sultan of the Osmanlis."

"Will you?"

The smile disappeared. "Mother, please."

"It is four years now. Your father asks to see you less and less. Meanwhile the witch insinuates herself further into his court . . ."

"He is my father. That is enough. How he conducts his Harem is no business of mine."

"You are blind."

"You see conspiracy everywhere."

"She tried to have you poisoned!"

"There is no proof of that."

"Who else would want you dead?"

"The Osmanlis have many enemies."

Gülbehar clenched her hands together in her lap. The knuckles were white. "It was her. You stand between her and the throne for her brood."

"My father would never betray me."

"He does not even know what is happening under his very nose."

"What would you have me do?"

Gülbehar lowered her eyes. "You have many friends at the Porte. Perhaps it is time you thought to use them."

"For what purpose?"

"Your grandfather would have taught you that."

Mustapha paled. "I will not raise my hand against my father. It is a sin before God."

"There are greater sins. They are being committed right now in the Palace at Stamboul."

Mustapha raised a finger and one of the deaf-mutes hurried forward with the scented fingerbowl. He washed his fingers and held them out to be dried. "The throne will come to me as God wills. I will not raise my hand against my own father." He reached across and took Gülbehar's hands in his own. "I love you, Mother. But you see phantoms everywhere." He smiled suddenly. "If Hürrem is my enemy she will answer for it in time. But I will not harm him."

After he had left, Gülbehar clapped her hands and waited while the pages removed the dishes from the room. She sat for a long time, brooding in silence. Then she had one of her maidservants fetch Güzül.

The Eski Saraya

JULIA HAD NEVER seen anything quite so ugly in her life.

The Kislar Aghasi was young, perhaps not much older than herself. He was dressed in a kaftan of flowered silk, with a broad sash at his waist, over which he wore a *pelisse* of emerald green, lined with ermine, the long sleeves sweeping the ground. There were thick rubies on the plump little fingers that drummed impatiently on the edge of the throne. A white cat purred and dozed on his lap.

None of these refinements could disguise the fact that he was obscenely fat. Great rolls of it lolled inside the folds of his garments. Then there was his face; it looked as if a sculptor had fashioned it from putty, then sliced off the most prominent features with a wipe of disgust, leaving the face smeared and distorted.

Julia had learned some Turkish on the long trip from Algiers, and she heard him speak abruptly to one of the guards who had brought her. She heard familiar words: "Gaiour," "Bey of Algiers," "woman."

He pointed to her. "Take off her veil."

Julia had also learned during the long sea journey that she could avoid further humiliation by performing their commands herself, rather than have them touch her with their filthy hands. As he spoke the words, she reached up and drew back the black mantilla lace.

She watched the Kislar Aghasi's face undergo an astonishing transformation. He seemed to jerk in his seat, as if he had been stabbed in the back. His mouth fell open.

He leaped to his feet, the heavy throne slamming onto the marble behind him. He pointed at her and bellowed: "Get her out of my sight!"

The guards only stared, stunned by his reaction.

"GET HER OUT OF MY SIGHT!" he screamed again, and then he was gone, another door crashing behind him. The guards gripped her arms and led her away.

Topkapi Saraya

THE KUBBEALTI, THE Hall of the Divan, was the hub of the Empire, and around it the great wheel of command revolved, the spokes reaching out to Algiers, Greece, and Hungary, to the Crimea and Persia and to Egypt.

For eighty years, in the small chamber under the watch tower of the Second Court, Osmanli Sultans had held court for four days in every week, from Saturday until Tuesday, receiving petitions, resolving legal matters, receiving foreign envoys, deciding all business of foreign policy and of state. Every matter, from the most humble dispute between merchants to the declaration of war, was made here.

On the morning of Divan, a long line would extend in absolute silence across the gardens of the Second Court as petitioners would wait for their right to bring their case before the Sultan. Süleyman, in a turban of snow-white muslin and a kaftan of white satin, would sit on a cushioned dais opposite the door, the Grand Vizier on his right, the Kaziaskers of Rumelia and Anatolia, the European and Asian provinces of the Empire, sitting directly behind him. Agas, pashas, and mufti would sit in their proper order of rank to either side, secretaries and notaries on the ground, their quills and parchment ready to record the imperial decrees and judgments.

Only the Sultan had the right to speak. Others could offer their opinion only as requested, or when sought on a particular point of secular or religious law that was their speciality. The Sultan's decree was final.

But it seemed that Süleyman had grown tired with the tedious perquisites of his power. He had abrogated his duties to Ibrahim, who now presided over the Divan in his place, and would report his decisions twice a week to the Sultan for him to ratify. A small latticed window had been cut in the wall high above Ibrahim's divan so that Süleyman might watch the proceedings whenever he chose, but Ibrahim knew he was seldom there.

Meanwhile Ibrahim was consumed with the changes he had witnessed in Süleyman. Perhaps they had come too far, too quickly. They had conquered Rhodes and Belgrade, and crushed the Hungarians and their king at Mohacs. Süleyman had achieved what his father, even the legendary Mehmet Fatih had failed to do, and his greatness was established. Since their last expedition to Vienna he had appeared withdrawn, disinterested.

It is the witch, Ibrahim thought.

ON THIS PARTICULAR morning the petitioners were made to wait as the Sultan debated with his generals the object of that summer's campaign in the Lands of War. Ibrahim allowed the mufti to speak first.

"Sooner or later the Sultan must deal with the Persian Shah, Tamasp, who dares shelter the Shi'a heretics and raid with his horsemen against our own borders. He offends against Islam. It is the Sultan's duty to bring him to heel!"

Ibrahim bowed his head in deference to the Islamic judge, although for himself, he would rather have placed the charlatan's head on a spike above the Gate of Felicity. He addressed the other generals. "Indeed, I agree with the mufti. The shah is indeed an offense against God and the Sultan. But should we fetch a cannon to quash a mosquito? Though Shah Tamasp has indeed offended Islam, the greatest prize to present before God is the capture of the Green Apple." It was a reference to Rome. Indeed every Sultan, before ascending to the throne of the Osmanlis, was traditionally asked the question by the Aga of the yeniçeris: "Can you bite from the Green Apple?" meaning, "Can you deliver us Rome?"

Ibrahim paused, to let his words take effect. "Surely, our greatest threat must be the man who calls himself Holy Roman Emperor? At the moment he is troubled on his southern flank by Francis; the Christian heretic Luther is inciting rebellion against the Pope in Germany; Charles's own nobles are engaged in feuds between themselves. The time to strike is when our enemy is weakest. Vienna's walls are ready to crumble and then the whole of Christendom will tremble at our approach!"

He turned to the Aga of the yeniçeris. "What say you, Achmed?"

The Aga weighed carefully. Remember Rhodes. "As long as our kettle is full, my Lord, we will eat. My men are restless for another chance to blood their swords."

Ibrahim turned to his other generals. Mahmut, Aga of the Spahis, and Çehangir, Kaziasker of Rumelia, both spoke for Vienna.

"We can deal with the heretic Tamasp at our leisure," Çehangir added. "But Frederick is at his weakest now. Let us strike and lay Vienna at the feet of our padishah!"

Ibrahim smiled. It had been six years since their last great victory. No empire could stand still. The ghazis knew that; as soon as a man stepped down from his horse, his muscles began to grow soft. Perhaps too, on the long road to Vienna, Süleyman would find himself again, and forget this Harem girl who was making him weak.

"Then it is decided," Ibrahim said. "The Sultan goes to Vienna."

35

The Eski Saraya

THE FIRST TIME she had come here, she had been almost paralyzed with horror, and with embarrassment. She could never have conceived of such a place in a thousand years. Julia could never remember being naked anywhere except in her own private bath, and even then she had felt sinful without clothes. But here, in the Palace of the heathen, the women seemed to rejoice in it.

They had taken her clothes, forced her to bathe—the Keeper of the Baths had scowled with disgust at the stench of her clothes—and then she had been required to undergo the most humiliating operation she could ever imagine any Christian woman being subjected to. They had shaved her, completely, under her arms, her nostrils, her ears, and then . . . even now she closed her eyes when she thought of it. There were no words for what she felt. They had outraged her completely, and she knew that she could never go back now. She could never return to La Serenissima and look her father and her husband in the eye. They would know. God would know. She was defiled and she was ashamed.

She felt completely numb. She could not imagine there was anything worse that they could do to her.

The ritual of the baths renewed the agony. Every day she was forced to come here, to undress in front of the other women, to bathe and to submit to the attentions of the black gediçli. She tried to avoid the eyes of the other women, tried to imagine she was not there and did not understand the laughter and the whispered taunts behind her back, though she was surprised to find she understood them very well. In the last few weeks she had learned their language very quickly.

She quickly removed her bath chemise and slipped into the water. At the lip of the bath two girls, one with a hawklike nose and skin the color of a hazelnut, the other white as alabaster with startling blue-black hair, were examining each other for hair. The search became more intimate, and Julia knew she should turn away, but a terrible fascination made her watch.

The hazel-skinned girl parted the other girl's legs, casually, her fingers tracing a line around the other girl's groin, then to the lips of her *kouss,* parting them gently. Julia heard the other girl gasp, and whisper some endearment she did not understand. The Egyptian moved closer and began to move her middle finger very slowly and Julia realized that her finger was inside the other girl now.

Corpo di Dio! Another outrage, another image from Hell! The two girls heard her gasp and the little Egyptian turned around and smiled at her, mocking her. The white-skinned girl had thrown back her head and her long braided hair brushed the edge of the marble bath. She groaned and lifted her buttocks from the marble, moving her groin closer to the other girl's fingers.

Julia looked away, stunned, and found herself staring into a pair of the blackest, deepest eyes she had ever seen.

"You are the Gaiour," the woman said.

Julia nodded. Gaiour, she had learned, meant Christian. Julia felt as if her cheeks were on fire, and she splashed some of the water on them. It was like a nightmare, a recurring, terrible, endless nightmare.

"Don't be frightened," the girl said.

There was a kindness in her voice that Julia found reassuring. "What are they doing?" Julia whispered.

The girl shrugged. "They are easing the tensions of boredom. Why not? There is no man to do it for them."

Julia looked at the negro guards and wondered, but she said nothing. She felt so stupid already.

"What is your name?" the girl asked her.

"Julia."

"I am Sirhane," the girl said. "I am from Syria. My father sold me to the devshirme."

"The devshirme?"

"It is like a tax. The Sultan's men come every few years and take away the best boys and girls for royal service."

"I am sorry."

Sirhane grinned. "What for? I wanted to come. Do you know what I would be doing right now if I were not lying here in this bath? Picking cotton! What would you rather do?"

Julia did not answer. "Tell me something," she said: "Do all of these women belong to the Sultan? They are all his wives?"

Sirhane laughed delightedly. "Of course not! He has only two kadins, and one of them is far away, in Manisa. That just leaves Hürrem and she is getting old, so there is hope for the rest of us."

"I do not understand. Speak slower."

Sirhane came closer and to Julia's horror, she put her arm around her. "You will need someone to take care of you. Don't you know anything, Gaiour?"

"I just want to go home," Julia mumbled.

"You have a husband?"

"Yes."

"Is he a good lover?"

Julia did not understand the word for lover, and would not have known what it meant if she had. So she said: "He's an old man."

"Then why weep any more tears, Gaiour? Perhaps, if *kismet* is kind with you, you will find yourself the best husband in the world. Sultan Süleyman himself!"

"I am already married."

Sirhane laughed again. "Oh, Gaiour, you have so much to learn!"

Julia knew instinctively that she had found a friend, and her body began to shake uncontrollably. All she wanted was someone to take care of her again, to explain what was happening, to help her, to comfort her. She put her head on Sirhane's shoulder. Sirhane embraced her, and Julia felt the warmth and softness of her body through the water and the smell of her reminded her of her mother, an ancient, arcane scent. She put a tentative arm around Sirhane's neck, and wept, but all she could think of was her Confessor in the Campo Santa Maria dei Miracoli and she knew she was slipping further from Venice, and from God.

THE KISLAR AGHASI stood at the latticed window that overlooked the hammam and wept.

Rather they break me on a rack than this, he thought. Rather they had pierced me with hot irons, scourged me with iron-tipped whips, than put me through this. If I had the courage I would have ended my life long ago. What devil in all the hells would ever have thought of a torture so exquisite as to rob a man of all means of loving a woman, but leave him yet the desire, as fierce and strong as it was when he was a youth?

Light poured down through the hundreds of small rounded windows in the high vaulted cupola. The hararet was misty with diffused yellow sunlight and steam vapor and the breath of hundreds of women. They sprawled on the warmed marble sofas, or on the edges of the baths, braiding each other's hair, naked except for their gauzy bath chemises; or slipped naked into the pools to pour water over their breasts, to lie languorously in the warm clear water, laughing and gossiping or singing.

He saw Julia's milky silhouette through the rising clouds of steam slip into the baths, saw another girl move toward her through the waters and embrace her.

His fingers wound themselves tightly around the steel latticework of the window in an agony of frustration.

He would rather be dead.

And now the Venetian.

Now this.

Süleyman studied the infant in the flickering light of the candle. So thin, so pale. He reached out tentatively, and touched the child's back, felt the grotesque lump on the spine, ran his finger along his legs, as thin as the muzzle of a harquebus.

Hürrem watched him, surprised. He had never paid the slightest attention to her other children as infants. Yet he came often to lavish attention on the grotesque and deformed son she had now delivered him.

"He eats?" he asked her.

"The wet nurses say he has little appetite, he will not thrive. They do not think he will survive."

Süleyman nodded and returned his attention to little Çehangir. "You must pick him up every day and croon to him. It will help."

Hürrem gaped at him. "Yes, my Lord." She wanted nothing to do with the little monster. The delivery had almost killed her. She did not think she would ever forget the terrible pain.

Süleyman straightened and reached into his pockets for a handful of golden coins. He gave them to the wet nurse. "Look after my son well," he said. He led Hürrem from the chamber.

When they were alone, Hürrem helped him remove his turban and brought his head to her breast. He nuzzled her, hungrily, and started to tear at the pearl buttons of her chemise. She let him take her, and spend himself in her. Afterward they lay on the divan, her thighs still wrapped around his body, his head between her breasts.

"You make love like a lion," she whispered.

"What would I do without your lies, little russelana?"

"My Lord is troubled?"

"Matters of the Divan," he said.

"You wish to talk?"

It was always this way. First, the physical solace of her body; then he would unburden his mind also. At first, it had amused her to concentrate her mind on the problems of politics and power that he brought her. It was enjoyable to exercise her wits on something other than the gossip of the Harem and the small problems raised by the daily routine of the hamman and the depilatory. Süleyman always seemed delighted with the answers she gave him, and over time she came to realize that her mind was quicker than his—though of course, she kept this thought to herself. But now the game had become something else; it was an instrument of power. Because Süleyman brought his problems to her in trust, it gave her power over him—and over Ibrahim also.

Süleyman sighed. "It is spring. Every spring it is always the same. My agas press for another campaign. They wish to go north again, against Vienna."

"And what of Ibrahim, my Lord?"

"Ibrahim clamors louder than any of them."

"He longs for glory. For Islam, of course."

Süleyman smiled. "Yes, little russelana, of course."

"Yet I wonder if it is wise."

"Tell me your thoughts."

"It is a long road to Vienna. Perhaps too far to take an army, even the army of the Osmanlis. If you should go through a door, you must know how to get out again."

"The real prize is Frederick. Or even the Emperor himself."

"Charles will not come! Why risk everything in battle against the greatest army in the world? He will find an excuse to delay. You will not find him at Vienna. When you withdraw for the winter, Frederick will come and take the city back again, and everything will be as before. You will have nothing to show but a long trek through the mud."

"I cannot stay the hungers of the yeniçeris another summer."

"You have told me the Persians have been raiding the eastern borders, and murdering our mufti. Send them to Asia, then. Perhaps we serve God better by preserving his judges."

"The Persians! They are no more than flies nipping at the rump of a lion. We have only to swat them with our tail to remove them."

"Perhaps God wishes us to be His swatter of flies, though of course, there is little glory in it."

Süleyman laughed aloud. "What I would not give to put you into debate with Ibrahim!"

Hürrem held his head in her hands, felt the tiny pulse of blood at the temple. This is all I have, she thought. When this pulse stops, life stops for me also. Until I can find some way to rid myself of the curse of Mustapha, I must try and keep you from harm.

"Do not go, my Lord."

"Do not go?"

"Let Ibrahim shoulder the burden. Let him chase Frederick through the Austrian mud!"

"Impossible! If my army goes into battle I must be at their head. It is the way. The yeniçeris expect it."

"The way! If it is not your way, then what does it matter?"

"I cannot."

"Do you love war so much?"

"You know I do not."

"Then why?"

"It is my duty, Hürrem."

"Duty has made the King of Kings a slave!"

Süleyman jerked his head away, his face suddenly flushed with anger. "Enough!"

Hürrem cradled his cheeks in her hands, and bit her lip, contrite. She cursed herself, silently. She should know better than to make him angry. A wasp was trapped with honey, not vinegar. "My Lord, I did not mean to offend you."

"The place of the Sultan of the Osmanlis has always been with his army."

"It is just that I love you so much, my Lord. The summers are endless without you. And I am so afraid that one winter you will not return . . . do not be angry with me."

Süleyman moved his hand from her waist to her breast. "Enough of politics," he whispered. "I will think on it at my leisure. Now I want you again."

She put her arms around his neck and smiled. "You are truly a lion," she whispered.

He felt her warm thighs wrap around his waist, drawing him in. Fortunate Son of Selim! he thought. To have found so much in just one woman!

Tomorrow perhaps he would decide where he must strike next. Tonight his weapon would find a more friendly target.

Yes, a lion! O Fortunate Son of Selim!

The Eski Saraya

THE GIRLS OF the Harem were housed in a long dormitory next to a stone courtyard. The mattresses were kept in wall cupboards during the day, and unrolled on raised platforms at night for the girls to sleep. Only the iqbals had their own apartments.

Julia lay on her mattress in the darkness, and tried to force the memories of the day from her mind, but sleep eluded her. If the dormitory had been at the top of the walls, she would happily have flung herself from the window. These animals had degraded her totally. She was no more than a beast to them.

It was not that they had enslaved her to one man; her own people did that also, she supposed, in their way. But she had expected that it would be done privately, that even if she were to be one of many wives, she would not be paraded naked before other men.

She curled her knees up to her chest, against the anguish in her mind. She had never imagined the Harem might be like this; a thousand nightmares could never have been like this.

She lay awake through the night, too angry to weep, too bruised to sleep. So much for her priest and his Christian God. They were no help to her in this place.

36

Pera

THE QUARTER WHERE the Venetian ambassador—the *bailo*—and the rest of the Venetian traders built their palaces overlooked the Horn, looking directly south toward the city and the Topkapi Saraya. The suburb was known, with typical Venetian modesty, as the Comunità Magnifica.

Ludovici had built a small palace there, with a marble terrace opening pleasantly onto the water. From here he could watch his own ships sail

Any man would tremble with pleasure at this spectacle, Süleyman thought. So why do I only feel this cold terror? Why is my Harem the most difficult place for me to be?

The great door slammed behind him. Süleyman dismounted. How long since he had performed this ritual? Before he became Sultan, certainly, before Gülbehar. He felt a hundred pairs of eyes watching him, in curiosity, in supplication, though none of them dared look at him directly. The choice he made in the next few minutes would change one of these girls' lives forever and irrevocably.

Or so they believed.

The Kislar Aghasi touched his forehead to the stone. "Great Lord."

"You are to be complimented," Süleyman told him, adhering to protocol. "They are all quite exquisite."

"Thank you, my Lord."

The Kislar Aghasi moved into step behind him as he passed along the line of girls. A blur of faces, eyes demurely lowered, cheeks blushing pink, courting him. He bowed and greeted each one, and the Kislar Aghasi whispered her name to him.

Why is it that I don't drink from this fountain until I burst? Süleyman thought. Other men would. They say Ibrahim has a harem almost as great as mine, and that his appetite is insatiable. He continued along the line of women, wondering which one he would finally choose. They are all so beautiful that beauty itself becomes meaningless, he thought. This one, for instance. She is like a porcelain doll. It is as if she might break if she were handled too roughly. She might have been fashioned by a master craftsman from a single piece of alabaster. Such perfection was intimidating.

"What is your name?" he said.

The girl whispered something, but it was so soft he could not hear. He turned to the Kislar Aghasi.

"What did she say?"

The Kislar Aga seemed to hesitate. "Julia," he mumbled at last.

"Julia," Süleyman repeated. He returned his attention to the girl. Perfection indeed. He took the green handkerchief from the sleeve of his robe and draped it over her shoulder to indicate he had made his choice. The handkerchief was one Hürrem had embroidered for him herself. He knew she would be watching, and he knew he had made his point.

"I shall walk in the gardens now," he said to the Kislar Aghasi, who was staring at the girl with an expression he could not fathom. These eunuchs were strange creatures.

He walked on, out of the courtyard, to stroll among the peacocks and ostriches, and sniff the scent of jasmine and orange.

HÜRREM TURNED AWAY from the window, and her fingers closed around the long silver candlestick that stood on the low table by the divan. She flung it across the room, splintering the faïence of blue Iznik tile that lined the apartment. Muomi ducked away, out of range.

Hürrem's face was pale with rage. For a long time she stood bolt still in the middle of the room, the only movement the flaring of her nostrils and the working of the muscles in her jaw. If Süleyman could see you now, Muomi thought. Then he might not think you so pretty.

"I have to stop this."

"He is Sultan," Muomi said, carefully. "How can you stop him?"

There was a silver salver of pastries by the divan. Hürrem picked it up and hurled it across the room. "Who is this little kouss?"

"I don't know her name. She was brought here from Algiers. They say she was captured from a Venetian galley by corsairs."

"How do I stop it?"

For the first time since she had been with her, Muomi was afraid. "My Lady . . ."

Hürrem grabbed the large gold ring that hung from Muomi's right ear and pulled hard. Muomi screamed and fell on to her knees.

"How can I stop this . . . ?"

". . . you're hurting . . ."

". . . I want you to go to the apothecary . . . one of your potions . . ."

". . . don't . . . !"

Hürrem released her, and clutched her fists to her sides, trembling. I must not lose control, not now, she thought. Lose control and you lose everything.

Muomi was panting, her hands held to her ear. "If you kill her he will only choose another. And the Kislar Aghasi will know what you have done."

"What then?"

Muomi looked up at her, her face sullen, her eyes glistening with hatred. "Don't ever hurt me again."

". . . Tell me what to do, Muomi."

The black girl shrugged. "There is another way."

"What? Tell me . . ."

"Can you sup with him tonight?"

"With Süleyman? He will not come to me now."

"Then find a way."

"It will be difficult."

"For you?"

"What can I do?"

"There is a mixture . . . it can take away a man's passion. You can ensure he does not fall in love with her."

The tension seemed to drain from Hürrem's body. She allowed herself a smile. "You can get what you need?"

"Any apothecary in the city will have the herbs."

"Then I will send one of the pages to get them for you." Hürrem settled herself back on the divan. "Now send a message to the Kislar Aghasi. Tell him I need to talk with him urgently. I dare say he is expecting it."

JULIA WAS TAKEN first to the Keeper of the Baths to be prepared. She was carefully shaved, every part of her examined minutely for hair, then bathed in water that had been perfumed with jasmine and orange, and her hair shampooed with henna. Afterward she lay on a warmed marble slab, while black gediçli massaged her shoulders, her back, her thighs and calves with a mixture of warm rice flour and oil. Heated water steamed in pots beside her to keep the mud pack warm and supple.

When the Kislar Aghasi entered the baths, he found her sitting naked on the edge of the marble, while the gediçli fussed around her, each silently focused on a small part of her, the only sound the rustling of their linen chemises.

He clenched his jaw tightly to stifle the sob of pain that bubbled in his throat.

Julia stared into the distance, as if none of them existed, her eyes blank and dazed. A gediçli worked on each of her limbs, painting the nails of her hands and toes, another slipped aloe under her tongue to sweeten her breath, then set to work lining the lids of her eyes with kohl. Yet another knelt to dye her pubis with henna, in the traditional manner. Julia did not cooperate, nor did she resist. She let them manipulate her body, as if she weren't there, as if it were not a part of her at all.

I wonder what she is thinking, Abbas asked himself. Is she back in Venice, with her lacework, watching the gondoliers on the Grand Canal? Is she in the canopied gondola with me, or is that just my vanity wishing it were so?

Somewhere behind him the Mistress of the Robes was arguing with an assistant over the right choice of wardrobe.

How many sleepless nights did I dream of this? Abbas thought. How many times did I imagine what it would be like to be with you, to see you quite naked? In all my imaginings, you never sat there like this, looking straight through me, quite untouchable and untouched. I am not here, none of these others are here for you. You are alone, and as unreachable as you always were.

But so beautiful. Even though they have dyed your hair with henna, and blackened your eyes and reddened your lips, like one of the prostitutes Ludovici was so fond of, they cannot paint over your dignity and your grace.

And your body is as perfect as I knew it would be. The curves and hollows, pulses and shadows, all as perfectly proportioned as if they were fashioned by a master sculptor. The nipples were like small rosebuds, every muscle in her thighs and shoulders and stomach defined clearly against the skin, as if carved from marble.

How can I feel this way? Abbas wondered. How can I desire what I cannot possess? Why do you still torment me when you have nothing left to offer me?

Perhaps this is the purest form of desire; and the purest form of agony.

As he watched another of the girls began to smooth a silky dust of golden powder on to Julia's arms, her back, and her breasts. It made her skin shimmer like beaten gold, the candlelight reflecting off it like thousands of miniature diamond chips.

Julia . . .

He turned reluctantly away. Hürrem wanted to see him. Well, of course. He imagined she would.

HÜRREM SAT HUNCHED on the divan, a silk handkerchief bunched in her fists, twisting it around and around her fingers in her anxiety. Her eyes were red from tears. Abbas almost felt sorry for her.

He executed a *temennah,* his right hand touching his heart, his lips, his forehead. "My Lady. You wished to see me?"

Hürrem sniffed, dabbing at her eyes with her handkerchief. "What am I to do, Abbas?"

"My Lady?"

"I hear the Lord of Life has chosen to spend the night with one of the houris."

"It is his right, my Lady. You should not upset yourself. You are still second kadin. Nothing can change that."

Hürrem dabbed at her eyes again. "What is her name?"

Abbas hesitated, suddenly alarmed. He became aware that there might be danger here. "Julia," he said, warily. "She is a Venetian."

"A cultured lady of court."

"As you say."

Hürrem seemed to consider. "I wish to see the Lord of Life. Could he perhaps sup with me tonight?"

"I do not think it is possible, my Lady. When the Sultan chooses a girl . . ."

"I did not ask you your opinion!" Her voice was like the crack of a whip. It silenced him, immediately. He studied her more closely. Perhaps she had not been crying, after all.

"My Lady?"

"I wish to see the Lord of Life . . . tonight. He is still in the saraya, visiting the Valide. Is that not correct?"

"As you say, my Lady . . ."

"Ask him to sup with me. Tell him I am contrite and I wish to make my peace."

"It may not be possible to—"

"Abbas, do you remember what happened to the last Kiaya of the Robes? Perhaps you were not a part of the Harem then?"

Abbas felt his mouth go dry. The minx had not lost her teeth, after all. "I am not sure I follow you, my Lady."

Hürrem stood up and came toward him. She stood so close he could smell her perfume. She looked up at him, smiling. "Yes, you do, Abbas. Everyone here knows what happened to the last Kiaya. And she did not dare offend me the way you offend me now."

"I mean no offense, my Lady. It is just th—"

"I do not want to hear your contrition, Abbas. Tonight the Sultan may sleep with another woman, but do you know in whose bed he may lie tomorrow night? When a woman has a man between her legs, Abbas, she has his undivided attention. So unless you are sure what will happen tomorrow, remember the Kiaya—and do as I ask."

"Yes, my Lady."

Abbas left the room, hating himself for his weakness. Why was life so important to him, that he should do anything to preserve it? This instinct for survival had betrayed him yet again.

All right, he would be her puppet. But let her harm Julia, and the worm would turn.

45

PREPARED THE MEAL myself," Hürrem said.

There were vine leaves stuffed with milk-fed lamb, small pieces of spit-roasted chicken, *shish ketabi, revani* cakes, halva, and sherbets. Süleyman sat down and regarded her warily. He felt like a stranger with her now. As if he had betrayed her somehow.

She watched him eat in silence.

"You are not hungry?" Süleyman asked her.

She shook her head.

He picked at the food. "It is good," he murmured. "You have used new spices?"

"Muomi has a thousand recipes, my Lord."

He chewed another mouthful of food. He studied her face. She had been crying, he was sure of it, though she gave no outward sign. But her eyes were pink and the lids swollen.

"Shall I make shadow play?" she asked. She was like a small child sometimes, he thought. Always so eager to please me.

"Not now," he said.

She lapsed into silence, watching him with a half smile that seemed as fragile as shadows. "Shall I fetch my viol?"

He shook his head. The food was good, but he had no appetite for it. He pushed his plate away.

"Please eat, my Lord."

"I am not hungry."

"Have I given you offense, my Sultan?" she whispered.

"No, there is no offense."

"But there are times I have been presumptuous in your presence. In my passion for you, I have forgotten my place. If you are angry, then I know it is my fault."

Hürrem looked thoroughly miserable. Süleyman wanted to reach out and comfort her. But that would not do. He could not let her see that his pain was as great as hers. She had to understand that as much as he loved her, he had a duty to Islam and the Osmanlis, and she had a duty to him. Duty was a hard lesson to learn, God knew, and it was as well that she learned it now.

"You are my sanctuary, my little russelana. But I am still seigneur. You must remember that."

"Yes, my Lord."

He got to his feet. Hürrem did not raise her eyes. Instead she suddenly leaned forward and kissed his feet.

Süleyman was shocked. He had never meant to humiliate her so.

"Hürrem," he whispered gently, "we are bound by duty. I cannot be as other men."

He must go, he thought, before his resolve weakened. Poor Hürrem. She did not understand. Yes, it was true, she had bewitched him. But she was no witch. She had entranced him with her innocence, and her devotion.

AFTER HE HAD left, Muomi entered the room and knelt by the half-empty dishes on the table.

"He has hardly touched his food," Hürrem said. "Will it be enough?"

"Yes," Muomi whispered. "It is enough."

ABBAS BARELY RECOGNIZED her.

They had dressed her in a rose-pink silk chemise with blue harem pantaloons, a *dhuma*—a heavy kaftan with pearl buttons and gold threaded buttonholes—and a headdress glittering with emeralds, diamonds, and opals. Her eyes were ringed with kohl, and the rest of her face was concealed beneath the bead-fringed *yashmak*.

There were silver chains, as thin as threads, at her wrists and ankles, a thick gold necklace with a pearl droplet, another gold amulet hanging from the headdress.

As she rose, one of the gediçli helped her on with the heavily brocaded ferijde cloak, the broad hood and long sleeves covering her so that not even a finger was visible.

My Julia.

He escorted her through the dark corridors of the Palace to the waiting coach.

When they set off, he stared at the still, cloaked figure opposite him and wondered what she might say if she knew that the fat, scarred eunuch opposite her had once courted her on the canals of Venice.

"Are you frightened?" he said.

"Yes."

"You must not be frightened. The Sultan is a gentle man. He means you no harm."

After a long time he heard her say: "What must I do?" There was a tremor in her voice. She was on the edge of panic, he realized.

"Have you ever lain with a man?"

"No, never."

"Never?" *Corpo di Dio!* Never! There was no God! If there was, he was a sadist and a tyrant! How else could Fate bring together a virgin and the eunuch who loved her unless it was for sport?

What could he say to her? How could he help her now? "You must simply do as he asks. He will show you."

"Why did he choose me?"

"Because you are the most beautiful woman in the world," he heard himself say, but after that he kept his silence, or he knew he would give himself away. *I will lead you to my master's bed*, he thought. *Let the gods have their joke. There is nothing I can do about it now. Let us be done with this, for I have plumbed the depths of all human despair now. If you are lucky, your fate will be better than mine.*

Topkapi Saraya

WHEN ABBAS ENTERED the bedchamber, Süleyman was waiting. He lay on the bed in a simple white robe edged in ermine, the plume of a white egret fastened to his turban with a cluster of white diamonds and rubies. The room was fragrant with the aroma of the brass censers that hung from the high, vaulted ceiling.

Abbas touched his head to the carpet three times. "Great Lord."

Süleyman watched him, reminding himself of the protocol. "Kislar Aghasi, I have mislaid my handkerchief. Do you know who has it?"

"Yes, my Lord. I will have her bring it to you."

Abbas eased his great bulk from the floor. Süleyman watched him. There was something wrong with Abbas, he decided. He had looked ill recently. Tonight his face was wreathed with sweat—it was not a hot night—and his eyes had that terrible frozen look he had seen often enough in battle. He hoped he was not sickening.

Abbas went to the great door and ushered in a small, cloaked figure. He removed the ferijde and whispered something to her, pushing her forward. He hovered at the door, longer than he should.

"Go," Süleyman said.

The door shut softly and they were alone.

The girl was trembling. She took out the green handkerchief he had placed across her shoulder that morning, fell to her knees, and crawled on all fours toward the bed. She lifted the coverlet, raised it to her forehead and lips, and crept up the bed.

Süleyman waited, wishing with all his soul that he were with Hürrem.

SÜLEYMAN ROSE NAKED from the bed, stared accusingly at the girl who lay curled on the mattress below him. The candlelight cast long shadows over the hills and valleys of her body, put a passion in her eyes that was not there.

He threw on a silk robe and went to the open window. The full moon sat fat and low over the Asian shore at Üsküdar, burning phosphorus onto the black mountains of the clouds. A full moon, a witching moon. Perhaps that was the reason, he thought.

Perhaps she really has bewitched me.

She was beautiful, this Venetian girl. Her body was like silk, a paradise for the eyes and the touch. Yet he had been unable to raise his passion for her. He had no appetite at all. He might as well have been . . . Abbas!

Something . . . someone . . . has made a eunuch of me! The Sultan of the Osmanlis, as impotent as his own Kislar Aghasi!

Fear and rage and confusion tumbled over inside him. He felt his own cheeks burn hot with his humiliation. The girl watched him from the bed, doe-eyed and frightened, saying nothing. She had uttered not a word since Abbas had brought her here, damn her.

But would her silence hold when she returned to the Harem?

She was not like his Hürrem, this girl. She had no new tricks to excite him, no soft moans to urge him to play the stallion. She simply lay there and offered her beauty, a small currency in the Harem. Perhaps it was simply that. Perhaps there was no witchery. Perhaps no woman could ever stir him again, once he had lain with Hürrem.

But in the Harem they would not understand. In the streets and the bazaars, the rumors would redouble, and they would shout again that he was bewitched, no longer a real man, no longer a real king.

He turned and looked at her. She had drawn her knees up to her chest, and she was watching him, her only movement the slow blinking of her eyes.

He walked swiftly to the door and threw it open. "Abbas!"

The halbediers on guard outside the door jerked with fright. "Where is Abbas?"

One of them ran to find the Kislar Aghasi.

Süleyman slammed the door behind him and went to the bed. He picked up the girl's clothes and flung them at her. "Get dressed!"

A few moments later, Abbas appeared in the doorway, clutching a candle. His eyes were wide with fright. "My Lord?"

Süleyman pointed to the girl. "Get her out of here!"

"She does not please you, my Lord?"

"Get her out!" He grabbed Julia by the arm—she had only the harem trousers and the silk chemise—and dragged her into the corridor. He left her sobbing on the carpet.

He drew the yataghan from the belt of one of the halbediers and went back into the bedchamber, slamming the door behind him. He held the point of the blade to the Kislar Aghasi's chin. A thin trickle of blood oozed down the line of his neck and stained the collar of his pelisse.

Abbas gasped, and almost dropped the candle.

"She is to speak to no one tonight! And if she is alive tomorrow morning, your head will be feeding the crows on the Gate of Felicity by sunset. Do you understand me?"

"Yes, my Lord . . ."

"Get out!"

ABBAS HURRIED THROUGH the cobbled cloister of the Topkapi Saraya, the sealed parchment clutched in his right hand. He made his way to the cell of the Aga of the Messengers. He had to get his message across the Bosphorus to Ludovici. Now. Tonight.

Julia was locked away in a cell below the Ortakapi. It was nearly midnight, which meant that by the time he received the message Ludovici would have perhaps less than five hours to make his preparations.

"Julia," he murmured, as he ran, "Julia, what have you done?"

46

DAWN.

Abbas led Julia through the great gate at the Bosphorus wall of the Palace, and down to the water's edge. He paused a moment to look up at the water-blue sky, saw the birds the Stamboulis called the Damned Souls wheeling above them. The flock of white wild birds never made any sound; even the beat of their wings was silent. They were never seen feeding or resting; they seemed to drift perpetually over the black waters of the Bosphorus, watching. The Stamboulis said they were the souls of the houris who had been drowned in the waters below.

It was the traditional way for a Sultan to be rid of a brother's wives when he assumed the throne, or to punish a girl who had somehow found herself pregnant by one of the white eunuchs. They said the mud at the bottom of the Bosphorous was thick with the whitening bones of former concubines.

Now you, Julia.

Abbas shuddered when he looked at her. She had been crying and the kohl had stained her cheeks, and her braided hair hung in a rich tangle round her face. She was wearing only the pink chemise and blue *salwar*. He saw the two bostanji study her body speculatively through the thin silk.

"What's happening?" she murmured.

Abbas saw the assassins watching him. He would give them no reason to speculate. "You are not to return to the Eski Saraya," he said. He took her arm and led her down the bank to the waiting caïque.

"Where are we going?"

"Just do as you are told," Abbas said.

"Please, tell me what is happening."

"*Silenzio!*" he hissed at her, and the sound of her own language stunned her into silence.

There was a large sack spread on the floorboards of the boat. When they reached the water's edge, Abbas turned and lifted her easily on to the caïque, with her feet resting on the sack. He took a silver cord from the folds of his pelisse, then grabbed her hands and tied them behind her.

"What are you doing?"

Abbas did not answer her. There was a pile of large smooth stones in the stern of the caïque, and he placed them on the sack one by one. Then he lifted the sides of the bag around her and pulled it over her head, knotting it with rope.

"Remember I love you," he whispered in Italian, and pushed her onto the decking. Then he stepped out of the caïque, and joined the two bostanji in the other boat.

A FRESH BREEZE ruffled the surface of the Bosphorus. The cries of the muezzin calling the faithful to prayer echoed across the water from the European and Asian sides of the city. The tower of the Divan rose through the mist, sunlight glinting off the spire.

A beautiful morning to die, Abbas thought.

They rowed past the promontory of Seraglio Point, and the somber sea walls of the Palace, towing the other caïque to a point midway between the peninsula and the Asian side. Abbas stood at the bow and searched the water, saw a Greek fishing boat, a caramusali, appear for a moment on the dappled water, before being swallowed again by the swirling curtain of mist.

He ordered the bostanji to deck their oars and they drifted for a moment in silence. Abbas looked to the stern, at the tiny boat drifting behind them on the end of the rope. The shapeless bundle was still struggling in the sack, so that it rocked gently in the water.

"Take the lines," Abbas shouted, a little louder than he needed to.

The bostanji grabbed the ropes that led from the stern of the caïque and began to pull on them, so that the other boat began to roll and take water. Finally it listed to starboard and capsized. There was a soft splash as the sack tumbled into the water. A rash of bubbles floated on the surface for a moment and then was gone.

Abbas searched the mists again for the caramusali, but saw nothing. He indicated to the bostanji that they should cut the ropes and then he sat slumped in the bow while they rowed back to the point.

JULIA GASPED AS she hit the water, felt the stones dragging her feet first to the bottom. She had known, as soon as the Kislar Aghasi had tied her hands, what was to happen, and she knew it was pointless to struggle. She had resolved to suck in the water straight away, to get it over with quickly, but some primordial instinct for survival weakened her resolution and when the caïque capsized she had taken a lungful of air and tried to hold it, struggling against the bonds behind her back, trying to free her hands.

To her astonishment, they fell away.

As she fell through the water she felt as if someone had pierced her ears with two hot needles. She tried not to scream against the pain and lose her last breath of air. She scrabbled and tore frantically at the mouth of the sack and suddenly felt it come free.

The Kislar Aghasi! she thought. He meant me to escape!

The sack fell away from her and she struck out blindly at the murky green of the water, saw the silvery surface far, far above, felt her own chest pumping in agony for another breath.

So far away.

She paddled desperately with her arms, bobbed suddenly and unexpectedly to the surface, tried to gulp in more air but only swallowed in more water, and started to choke.

She fought the water with her arms and legs, but her mouth filled with water and red panic overwhelmed her and she knew she was going to die.

Something touched at her arm and she clawed for it, desperately. Then nothing.

ABBAS LOOKED BACK once, saw the caramusali glide silently between the caïque and the Asian shore, saw two figures on the deck struggling to pull something on board. He looked away quickly in case the bostanji followed his gaze but by then the mist had closed around them again and the morning kept her secrets.

THERE WAS SNOW on the great gate of Ba'ab-I-Hümayun when Süleyman returned from the Lands of War. He sat sullen on the great Arab stallion, deaf to the cheers of the yeniçeris and the crowds who had lined the Divan Yolu to welcome him back. This time they had not even reached Vienna. Ibrahim had been stalled for over a month by a tiny garrison of soldiers at Güns, and the campaign had petered out into a series of raids by his *akinji* horsemen and retribution between his generals over which direction to strike.

He returned in mourning. Hafise Sultan, his mother, was dead. Though he mourned her, a part of himself felt strangely liberated. He said his prayers for her, and felt the weight of the burden lifting from his shoulders. Each day the voice that had constantly reminded him of duty, duty, duty, receded in his memory.

The European campaign had been an exercise in futility. The interlude with the Venetian girl had been a disaster. It was abundantly clear to him now who was his wisest counselor, both on the battlefield and in bed.

He had been away too long.

Hürrem, bewitch me again.

PART 5

THE PASSAGE OF DUST

47

The Eski Saraya, 1535

A GEDIÇLI USHERED HER through the apartment. Güzül was impressed, despite herself. Hürrem had her own garden with a marble fountain and an aviary with nightingales, canaries, and some birds she had never seen before, large, hook-beaked creatures with feathers of red, green, and royal blue. It was whispered in the bedesten that she had even been presented with a bed from Amoy in China, made from ivory, and inlaid with aloes and sandalwood and large pieces of pink coral. It was supposed to have cost more than 90,000 *scudi,* a fortune in itself.

Hürrem lay face down on a slab of marble, warmed from below by the palace boilers, while Muomi massaged her neck and shoulders. Her private hammam, Güzül noticed, was as large as Ibrahim's audience chamber.

She executed a ceremonial sala'am on the floor, waiting on her knees for Hürrem to acknowledge her presence.

Hürrem blinked open one eye and a soft smile lit her face.

"Ah, Güzül."

"Would my Lady honor me so as to examine my poor wares?"

With a slight movement of her head Hürrem assented. Güzül bent down and unknotted the green silk handkerchief that she carried in her arms and spread the assortment of ribbons and lace and trinkets in front of her, repositioning each one so that it might catch the sun to better advantage.

Muomi continued to work the long, powerful fingers into the muscles of Hürrem's shoulders. She still retains her slim body, Güzül thought. She was reminded of a cat, sleek and satisfied, stretched on its favorite divan. The eyes were half-closed in dreamy torpor, the limbs stretched in languorous ease. You would not think she has had five babies, she thought. Yet, by all accounts, she has had a wet nurse for all of them, and has paid them little enough attention after the cord was cut. Her brood will have to fend for themselves if they want to grow.

The moist, thick strands of red-golden hair clung to her face and cheeks. It was as if the green eyes were watching her through long stalks of dry grass, a predator in wait. Güzül shuddered.

"So how is your mistress?" Hürrem said, suddenly.

Güzül felt the blood drain from her face. "My mistress, my Lady?"

"Rose of Spring."

Güzül suddenly found it hard to breathe. She did not dare look up into those terrible green eyes. She concentrated on the baubles on the carpet before her. "My Lady is mistaken."

"My Lady is never mistaken," Hürrem said, and she yawned. "You are Gülbehar's creature. You come to Stamboul to bring messages for her and spy on the Harem."

Güzül said nothing. She waited.

"Do not be afraid. All I want is a little information from you. That is the only merchandise you have that I am interested in."

Hürrem scratched slowly at the calf of her right leg with the big toe of her other foot. Güzül watched the muscles of her buttocks tense. They were still small and hard. Like a boy, Güzül thought. While Gülbehar grows fat and lazy on sweetmeats in Manisa, Hürrem starves herself and drinks from some secret fountain of eternal youth. Or perhaps it is the potions this Muomi gives her to drink.

Witch.

"I am only a messenger, my Lady."

"Exactly. But who is it, I wonder, who receives you here in Stamboul. Who is my Lady Gülbehar's friend in the court?"

Güzül was silent. She felt her knees begin to tremble beneath her. It was impossible to stop the tremor. Her own body was betraying her.

"You are right to be afraid, Güzül. It is true that you serve the woman who might one day become the mother of the next Sultan. But that is tomorrow and you may not live that long. Today it is I who whisper to the Sultan in the quiet moments, and if I choose, I might whisper to him that a certain gypsy peddler came to his Harem and called his favorite kadin a witch to her face and insulted her beyond her imaginings."

Güzül put out a hand to steady herself. "My Lady."

"The choice is yours. Think about it for a moment."

Hürrem closed her eyes again, and surrendered to Muomi's attentions. Güzül felt faint. She knew she had played a dangerous game, but it had never seemed real. Now she was faced with the certainty of death, and her bowels turned liquid.

"Ibrahim . . . my Lady," she managed, finally.

Hürrem's eyes flickered open. "Ibrahim," she murmured. Her features seemed rested from the massage, but her eyes were suddenly cold and empty. "So. I should not be surprised. He is like a jealous lover, is that not so, Güzül?"

Güzül could not find her voice.

"You have a choice to make, old woman. You cannot serve two mistresses. And yet you have only one life. Life is cruel, isn't it?"

"My Lady, I will do anything . . ."

"You do not yet know the bargain, Güzül. Over there, on the table, is a small stoppered bottle. There is a small amount of liquid inside it. I want you to put it inside your robe and take it with you to Manisa. Then I would like you to find a way to pour the contents into Mustapha's drink. Do you think you could do that, Güzül?"

Güzül groaned aloud.

"A difficult choice, I understand. But before you rise from your knees, you will have made it. You or Mustapha. Which of you is going to die?"

"It is impossible, my Lady. The food tasters sample everything . . ."

"Perhaps you are thinking that Ibrahim might save you. It is true he has the Sultan's ear. But there are other parts that are more desirable to possess. And far more persuasive. So what do you decide, Güzül?"

"My Lady, please. Anything else . . ."

"What do you decide?"

She means what she says, Güzül thought. If I do not agree, she will have me killed without a second thought.

God, help me in my sorrow!

"I will do what I can," she said.

"If you fail, do not look forward to my compassion."

"But, my Lady . . ."

"It is a simple bargain, Güzül. There are no rewards for failure."

Güzül stared at her, her eyes blank with dread.

"Thank you for showing me these trinkets," Hürrem said, "but I am adequately provided for."

Güzül gathered up her jewelry with trembling fingers and wrapped it inside the large handkerchief, carefully knotting the corners. She crawled on her knees to the marble table and picked up the pretty blue and white Iznik bottle as if it were her own death warrant. Which it might yet prove to be, Hürrem thought. She crept from the room, a much older woman than when she had entered.

When she was gone Hürrem closed her eyes and groaned as Muomi worked her knuckles into the muscles of her buttocks, almost as if she was trying to squeeze apart the joints of her hips. I will have to settle with you, Ibrahim, she thought. It was inevitable, though I have tried to avoid it. You have wanted to possess Süleyman.

But he is mine.

THE DIVAN WAS a long rectangular room, with low sofas round the walls. A wickerwork grilled window bulged from the end wall, hung with a curtain of black taffeta. The courtiers called it the "dangerous window," for this was where Süleyman might come to stand at any time, to listen to the proceedings of the Divan. It meant that when the pashas came to report to him at the end of the day, they could hold back nothing, for they could not know whether he had come to the dangerous window that day or not.

But today he was there. He watched as Ibrahim listened attentively to an Armenian trader's long complaint of some minor usury against a Jewish merchant. He wondered at his Vizier's endless capacity for detail, his tireless love of the manipulation of even the smallest instruments of power. Süleyman had returned briefly to the Divan on his return from Vienna, but had soon passed over the irksome duty once again to Ibrahim. Thank God for men like him, he thought. He experienced a warm glow of pride, the same paternal rush of affection he felt sometimes for Mustapha.

How far the ghazis have come, he thought, since they warred and raided on the great plains of Anatolia, their life and their culture carried with them in their black goat-hide tents. Now the sons of Osmanli lived in great palaces, prayed in the great Christian cathedral of the Aya Sofia, the masterwork of the Byzantine Emperor Justinian; now he, Süleyman, administered the rebuilding of this great city that stood at the gateway of Europe and Asia, and allowed former Christians to attend to the running of this great Empire while he formalized the kanuns that would establish a great Muslim civilization for centuries to come.

It was the task God had meant for him, he was sure. Fifteen years now he had been Sultan, and he was tired. Tired of the *jihad,* and the endless campaigns demanded by his Agas and the yeniçeris, tired of the smell of blood and the bodies piled like windrows in the moats of great fortresses that would fall to the infidel once more as soon as he withdrew his army for the winter.

It was no longer a time to destroy. Let Ibrahim guard the Empire. He would give these ghazis and their Christian slaves a civilization that would last a thousand years. He would rebuild the city to the glory of all Islam, give them kanuns that would guarantee peace and government, and bring these restless nomads home.

He sighed. From now on he must build, not destroy.

48

Topkapi Saraya

TO DINE WITH Süleyman in his private apartments was a privilege that had been granted to no other man, but Ibrahim no longer anticipated the honor as he once did. He had been a regular visitor to Süleyman's seraglio, but now the invitations to dine were less and less frequent. When he did come, he found Süleyman had become a tiresome companion at meals, brooding on administrative matters, or talking endlessly about the plans he had made with the builder, Sinan, for some new mosque complex. It seemed to Ibrahim that he had forgotten the lifeblood of the Empire, of any empire. He had made what seemed to Ibrahim the cardinal error. He had grown tired of conquest.

After the killerji-bashi had removed the plates, Ibrahim refilled two crystal goblets with Cyprian wine, and began to read aloud from the history of Alexander. He recited the march into Persia, the defeat of the Persian Emperor Darius at Guagamela, and the capture of Babylon.

Ibrahim paused in his reading and looked at Süleyman. "We must go there too, my Lord."

Süleyman nodded. They had received the news in the Divan that day; the Persian Shah Tamasp had recaptured Babylon. As Defender of the Faith Süleyman could not ignore such a dire challenge to his authority. It could not go unchecked.

The Shah nurtured the heretic mullahs, allowing them to spread their heretical doctrine in Mesopotamia and even into Azerbaijan and Armenia. They were a vile canker that must be sliced from the flesh of Islam. They dared preach of the infallibility of their *imams,* of mortal human beings, even claiming mystical interpretation of the Qur'ān. They offended him as no Gaiour, whose sin was after all only ignorance, ever could.

To have them preaching their evil in the holy city of Baghdad was not to be borne.

"Yes, Ibrahim," Süleyman agreed. "We cannot turn our backs on the Sufavids any longer."

"Why so solemn, my Lord?"

Süleyman sighed. "Must we always be rushing to the gates, Ibrahim? We subdue one attack, then there is the sound of trumpets from another wall."

"It is the way. You are the Emperor. It is what you were born for." How is it, Ibrahim asked himself, that I understand this so much better than he does himself?

"There is more to Empire than fighting wars, Ibrahim. We must build as well. We must create something that will endure after the dust of the armies has vanished over the horizon."

"There will always be armies, my Lord. Always." Thank God. What was a man, if he did not have a saddle under him and the smell of leather and dust in his nostrils? Süleyman was becoming too soft, too fond of his Harem.

No, too fond of Hürrem.

"I am tired of it, Ibrahim."

"My Lord, a man cannot be Sultan and live his life without conflict. He must subdue others or be subdued himself. It can never be otherwise."

"Then we are no better than the dogs in the street."

"It was Muhammad who urged us to the jihad, my Lord. When we go to the Lands of War, we carry the green banner of Islam with us."

Süleyman's face creased into a grin for the first time. "Muhammad! What do you care for Islam?"

"It is my religion, my Lord."

"Your religion is whatever pleases you. Don't you think I know that, old friend?"

Religion is for hypocrites and superstitious old women, Ibrahim thought. But if you know that about me, then why do you entrust me with so much? "I am a faithful soldier of Islam," Ibrahim said.

"You are a good soldier and a faithful Vizier. That is enough for me."

"You mock me, my Lord."

"You mock all of us."

No, Ibrahim thought. I do not mock you. You, I love like a brother. Perhaps because we are so different. I love you for your gentleness and your weakness. I love you perhaps because you need me. I love you because I have laid my dreams at your feet and you have allowed me to live them.

"In a few days we will ride together under the green banner, my Lord. The cool wind will blow away all these misgivings."

"No, Ibrahim, not this time. I did not wish to go Vienna three years ago, and I was persuaded. Time proved me right. For five months I watched our cannons sinking deeper into the mud under the walls of a fortress whose name I even now cannot remember. Frederick did not come, and Charles did not come, as I said they would not. This time I will not be swayed. You will take my army to Persia alone."

Ibrahim stared in stony silence at the floor.

"Is this such a terrible burden I have placed upon you, Ibrahim? Other men would weep at such an honor."

"A Sultan's place is with his army."

"Do not lecture me on my duty!" Süleyman barked, and then more gently: "Can you crush this Shah Tamasp, and rid me of this meddlesome mosquito?"

"Of course, my Lord."

"Then do it, Ibrahim. From now on, you will be the guardian at my gate."

"I wish you would not do this, my Lord."

"I have decided."

Ibrahim was silent a long time. It was time, he decided. It must be said. "My Lord, there is a matter that concerns me greatly."

"Speak freely, Ibrahim."

"A messenger came to me today from Manisa. There has been an attempt on the life of your son, Mustapha."

A sharp intake of breath. Süleyman's lips tightened into a grim line. "Who brought you this news?"

"It was one of Gülbehar's own couriers, my Lord. There is no mistake."

"What happened?"

"He sat down to dine with a captain of his personal bodyguard. The man drank some wine and fell ill abruptly. He died in agony an hour later."

"And Mustapha?"

"He had not yet drunk from his cup, praise be to God."

Süleyman slammed his fist on to the floor. "Who did this?"

"There is no proof," Ibrahim said, but in such a way as to suggest that he knew. Süleyman detected the nuance and looked up sharply.

"Who, Ibrahim?"

"My Lord, there is no proof. But we must consider the possibility."

"Who?"

Ibrahim did not answer. He avoided Süleyman's eyes. *Let us see if he is so blind that he cannot see what stares the rest of us in the face.*

Süleyman suddenly reached over and grabbed Ibrahim's wrist. Ibrahim winced. He had forgotten how strong he was. "You are wrong," Süleyman hissed.

"My Lord, who else?"

"It is another of Gülbehar's fantasies! Bring me proof, Ibrahim. Bring me one shred of proof!"

"My Lord, you have given her too much power! She rules you day and night! How often do I see you now? We no longer hunt, we eat together but rarely, you never send for me to play for you! She occupies your every waking minute!"

"I see," Süleyman murmured softly, "so you are jealous."

"I am afraid. I am afraid of what is happening to you. The Süleyman I knew would not let his army go to battle without him."

"The Süleyman you knew was a boy who simply did as his father did. I am my own man now."

Ibrahim knew he had already pushed too far, but he could not hold his tongue now. He felt the blood drumming in his ears. "She wants Mustapha dead so one of her sons can be Sultan!"

Süleyman stared at Ibrahim for a long time before he spoke. When he did his voice was empty of all emotion. It was as if a part of him had withdrawn from the room; had withdrawn from Ibrahim. "You have been my friend a long time, Ibrahim. Do not make me hate you."

"My Lord . . ."

". . . Go now. I must think."

Ibrahim rose to his feet and left the room. *Damn the little witch. Perhaps he had already left it too late. Now, with Hafise Sultan gone, who was there who would bring Süleyman back from the edge?*

THE *TIMARIOT* HAD heard what they called him. The Man Who Never Smiled.

He had expected to feel some sort of fear in his presence. But Rüstem Defterdar had no aura of evil, and his face had no scars, nor outward sign of malevolence. He was like any one of a hundred scribes in the great Palace. There was nothing in his expression to indicate that anything existed for him except the parchment in front of him. He did not look up when the timariot entered the room. He continued to stare at the document on the table between them.

"You are Muhammad Dürgün?"

"I am," the timariot replied.

"You are from Kirklareli?"

"Yes."

He still did not look up. "Your father served at Mohaçs and the siege of Buda-Pesth?"

"He did." The timariot hesitated, not knowing what to say or do next. What if the stories he had heard about The Man Who Never Smiled were not true? "He died last year. From the pestilence."

"If that is true, then by law the lands return to the Sultan." Rüstem Defterdar took the quill from the desk and made a notation on the document in front of him.

"Is there . . ." The timariot paused, wondering how to say it. He had ridden two days to come here, driven by the fear of losing the land Selim the Grim had given his father after the siege of Belgrade. "Is there not some way?"

Rüstem Defterdar paused. "Your father's name was Hakim Dürgün?"

"Yes."

"According to my records you are mistaken. He still lives. He should return to the Treasury the equivalent of one asper per sheep each year. Do you have any questions?"

"No, Defterdar."

"Then that is all."

The timariot left the Defterdar's office, stunned at the simplicity of what he had just done. The Fatih's kanuns strictly forbade any fiefdom from passing from father to son. Yet in a few simple words he had become the owner of his father's land—at a price. His father had been taxed at one asper per two head of sheep. For the privilege of allowing him to retain the land, Rüstem had just doubled the tax. He could imagine where the rest of the money would go.

Still, it was worth it.

He only wished he could have seen what color eyes belonged to The Man Who Never Smiled.

49

THE SIX-SIDED kiosk behind the Gate of Felicity dominated the *selamlik* gardens. The marble dazzled the eyes, the colored windows fretted with gold. The kiosk nestled among a grove of black cypress, the walls inlaid with a faïence of tiles in turquoise and blue, in *saz* patterns, an enchanted forest of feathery leaves inhabited by fearsome chillins, their eyes set with rubies and *majolica* stones. Thick rugs repeated the saz patterns in ruby and ivory. Cufic inscriptions in cerulean blue and white were interlaced with the cedar paneling above the doors. The floor had been so carefully crafted by Süleyman's artisans, that it appeared to be made from just one piece of rock crystal. It was a paradise within a paradise, a blazing sanctuary of marble.

Süleyman rested on a gold-embroidered mattress while Hürrem sat at his feet, playing a soft, repetitious melody on her viol, her voice rising and falling in cadence. He lay on his side watching the sunlight dance from the damascened lantern that hung from the cupola above his head, the coral and crystal glittering like jewels.

Now, once again, they wanted to call him from his silence and his happiness to the lonely mountains of Asia.

Duty, he heard his mother whisper. Duty.

But where was his duty now? Throwing more raw meat to his yeniçeris or building the foundations of the future for his Osmanli sons? To live on the smell of blood, like his father, in the Lands of War; or secure the peace, in parchment and stone?

He looked away, through the latticed window, through the garland of honeysuckle that dripped from the trellis, along the path of colored pebbles that wound through the dappled shadows of the plane trees. Why give this up, these hours with Hürrem, the chance to spend time with his sons, Selim and Mehmet and Bayezid and Çehangir? He had spent so little time with his boys. He hardly knew them. And who could foretell the future? One day one of them might be the shahzade.

Shahzade. In the end, it seemed, all that mattered was the shahzade.

Even from the moment he settled into the throne, all eyes turned to Mustapha to judge if he was capable. From the moment of becoming Sultan, they are prepared for your death.

Hürrem finished the song and laid the viol aside. She reached up and stroked his cheek.

"You are frowning. What are you thinking?" she whispered.

"About Mustapha," he said.

The smile flickered, like wind brushing a flame. "What is wrong, my Lord?"

"Ibrahim has brought me distressing news, little russelana. Someone has tried to poison my son."

He stared at her. She looked back, her eyes wide and candid. "He is all right?"

"Praise be to God, yes."

"Who did this?"

"We do not know." He watched her, looking for some clue. "Ibrahim accuses you."

Hürrem sat up, her face pale. "My Lord . . . but why?"

"He thinks you want one of your sons to be Sultan."

Her eyes searched his face, tried to divine what he was thinking. "My Lord, of course I do. Do you think Gülbehar will be gentle with me when her son is Sultan? Do you think I wish my sons all to be murdered in the Osmanli fashion? Of course not. I pray that God will spare me and my sons. But Ibrahim flatters me to think that I have the power, here in your Harem, to harm a great prince five days' ride from Stamboul. And that I would harm Mustapha. He is your son and I could not cause you that pain. I would rather die first."

Süleyman stared at her, saying nothing.

Hürrem leaned forward suddenly and snatched the ceremonial dagger from the scabbard at his waist. Before he could react she held it in her right hand, the blade pressed against the soft flesh of her wrist. The rubies and sapphires studded in the handle and guard glittered in the yellow afternoon sunlight.

"If you believe it, tell me to open my veins, and I will do it. I would rather die than have you suspect that of me. If there is even a grain of doubt, say the word and I will save your bostanji from blunting his sword."

Süleyman watched her. He wanted to believe her with every fiber of his body. He wanted to believe.

Suddenly Hürrem slashed down with the dagger and the crimson blood splashed on the pure white of her chemise and ran like a crimson river down her arm. Süleyman sprang forward and wrenched the dagger from her grasp and threw it on the floor.

"Hürrem!"

"No—I don't want to live now! Let me do it!"

He gripped the wound in his palm, ripped the rich brocade of his gown to bind it. Hürrem struggled, crying hysterically. He took her in his arms and rocked her, terrified he was going to lose her.

NIGHT.

By the flickering light of the candle Muomi carefully unbound the brocade that still bound Hürrem's wrist and examined the wound. Hürrem watched her. Her face shone with sweat.

"Is it bad?" Hürrem whispered.

"The blade missed the main vein, my Lady," she whispered. "If you had cut there, it might never have stopped bleeding." She began to dress the wound with a poultice of herbs and a fresh linen bandage. "You must have cut very carefully."

"Oh, but I did," Hürrem said, and she smiled weakly. "I was quick. But I was very, very careful."

50

HÜRREM WAS SMILING when the Kislar Aghasi was ushered into her presence. Abbas knew that could be a good or a bad thing. The fact that she was laughing might mean anything. He imagined she would probably be in excellent spirits the day she ordered his execution.

Since the death of Hafise Sultan, Hürrem had assumed the position of Sultan Valide. It meant that Abbas was no more than her chief servant, subject to a thousand caprices, and quite powerless. She had the ear of the Sultan while he was captain of three hundred increasingly restive odalisques, a harem in name only. Some of the girls had complained to him that they had cobwebs growing between their legs.

He executed the three ceremonial sala'ams that were required and allowed his two pages to help him back to his feet. Hürrem watched the performance with amusement.

"My Abbas," she murmured.

"Your servant, Veil of Crowned Heads."

Hürrem dismissed the pages with an almost imperceptible nod of her head. The fountains that bubbled from golden spigots on the four walls of the room would disguise their conversation from eavesdroppers. Abbas experienced a shiver of dread. He never enjoyed Hürrem's secrets.

"Do you enjoy your post, Abbas?"

"Yes, my Lady."

"You're trembling. Is something the matter?"

She was toying with him. *Ziadi!* Witch! "I am simply overcome by the presence of your beauty."

Hürrem threw back her head and laughed aloud. "Abbas, you are pathetic."

What is the point in being otherwise? he thought, since I am no longer a man and for some reason I do not wish to die. "Yes, my Lady."

"You suspect that the Palace executioner may be standing behind you with his cord."

Abbas felt the sweat erupt on his face. He did not dare turn around, yet simply by her suggestion she had forced him to imagine the cord biting into the flesh under his chin, the strong arms twisting the knot . . .

"Poor Abbas. There is no bostanji. Look for yourself."

Abbas continued to stare at her.

"Go on. Look."

He did as he was told. The chamber was empty, and the water bubbling in the fountains mocked him. He turned back to face Hürrem, hating her with such intensity that he felt a sharp pain in his chest. She is killing me, this witch, he thought. She wishes me never to have peace again.

"The information you gave me about Güzül was true. I compliment you."

"My Lady."

She leaned forward, resting her chin on her hand, studying him, as if for the first time. "While the Lord of Life seems to have little use for his Harem, you are largely redundant, are you not, Abbas?"

"As my Lady says," Abbas said. What was this leading up to?

"Since the death of Hafise Sultan, may God bless her and keep her in Paradise, it seems your main function has been as head of my household. Our fortunes are interwoven."

"I am much blessed."

The green eyes examined him with candor. "Yes, Abbas, but am I blessed with an obedient servant?"

"Veil of Crowned Heads, I live to serve you."

"Perhaps." She studied him for a long time, and Abbas felt the dread settle in his chest like cold lead. "Do you remember Julia Gonzaga?"

Abbas swayed slightly on his feet. "One of the Harem girls, perhaps?"

Hürrem laughed again. "Perhaps."

". . . Ah, I remember her now. She did not please the Lord of Life. She sleeps in the Bosphorus."

"She sleeps in Pera, with the Gaiours."

It was as if a taut cord had snapped inside him. Well, she knows, he thought. I am at her mercy now. Damn this little red witch. Damn her, damn her.

"Why did you do it, Abbas?"

You think I would tell you that, and allow you to mock the only thing of dignity I still cling to? "She paid me."

"You defied the Sultan for money?"

Abbas summoned his courage. "Wouldn't you?"

Hürrem clapped her hands with delight. "Ah, I like it so much better when you are honest with me, Abbas. You are a snake pretending to be a sheep. I feel so much better when you show me your fangs."

"Am I to die?"

"Do you want to die, Abbas?"

"A part of me wants to die."

"I would not try to stop you. Of course you know the punishment for disobeying the Sultan in this way. They will hang you on a sharpened spike and leave you to die in the sun. They say it can take three days, sometimes longer . . ."

"Please, my Lady . . ."

"I do not expect you to beg, Abbas. That is not what I called you here for."

"What is it you want?"

"Your obedience, Abbas. That is all. Your obedience until the day I die."

Abbas stared at the patterned rug at his feet. "I am already a slave. It does not matter who the master is."

"Then you will find me someone who can bring me Ibrahim's head?"

The very notion took his breath away. ". . . Ibrahim?"

"You think I would let you escape the Sultan's bright, pointed hook for nothing, Abbas? I will not trade your three days of mortal agony lightly, my eunuch."

Abbas raised his eyes to hers. Oh, I would like to wipe that smile of triumph from your eyes. Oh, I would like to take a whip to you, little Ziadi, and scourge you till you lie weeping and groveling at my feet. Oh, I would like to ravish you, hold you helpless under my thighs. But it is all beyond my power.

"I will help you," he said.

ABBAS SAT ON the sleeping mattress he had unrolled from its niche in the wall, a white cat curled on his lap. He stroked it gently. He now believed, as Muhammad had taught, that cats had souls like men, and he spoke to it as he would a man.

"What can I do, little Ziadi? She has held a mirror up to my face and I see nothing there. She has shown me my weakness. Once I thought I had courage. But it is one kind of courage to risk death, another to embrace it. Even after what they did to me, I could still be a man, if I chose to end my servitude with my own knife. But I cannot, I cannot. So what else is there for me?"

The cat purred gently, rhythmically, and the big green eyes blinked slowly in the half darkness.

"If she wishes to destroy Ibrahim, then I will show her. What does it matter to me now? I will give the Laughing One her perfect foil. The Man Who Never Smiles."

51

A WARM NIGHT, THE first of the spring. They lay on the divan, in the candlelight, the crescent moon that hung low over the minarets framed by the open window.

"Stay here for ever," Hürrem whispered.

Süleyman smiled. "And what would happen to the Osmanlis if I did?"

"The Empire would crumble into dust. I don't care."

"Sometimes . . ." He left the sentence unfinished. "There have never been enough hours, Hürrem."

"Will there be any hours this summer, my Lord? Will the Aga beat the great war drum again soon?"

"The Shah of Persia has become too impudent now. It is time to swat the mosquito."

Hürrem frowned petulantly. Sometimes, he thought with affection, she was like a little child. He picked up her hand and gazed at the linen bandage on her wrist. He shuddered at the memory it invoked.

"And you?" she whispered.

Süleyman smiled. "All the way to Persia for one troublesome insect? I shall leave that to Ibrahim."

Hürrem put her arms around his neck and hugged him. He felt the wet of her tears on his neck. "You really mean it, this time?"

"I have had enough of war, little russelana."

"What of the Roman Emperor, Charles?"

"The Pope demands an alliance against us. He wants Naples and Venice to join with him, to secure the Mediterranean. Ibrahim says such an alliance will not succeed."

"Ibrahim . . . ," she said, mocking him.

"I trust his judgment."

"Does he give you guarantees?"

"No one can guarantee what a Gaiour may do next. Five years ago Charles's own armies sacked Rome. Such men have no honor. Who can foresee what such barbarians might do?"

Hürrem looked away. "My Lord, forgive me my impudence, but last night I had a dream. I dreamed you treated with the King of Naples and the Doge of Venice for peace. You offered them sanctions and a treaty. You considered that if they agreed, you had then secured the sea against Charles. If they did not, you said it would give your admirals an excuse to raid their coasts all summer long. Do you think that a fine dream?"

Süleyman stared at her, then threw back his head and laughed. Such a calculating mind was wasted on a woman! he thought. She would have made a fine vizier. He was continually astonished by her facility for politics. But perhaps this mind is not wasted; not while it speaks only to me.

"One day I will make you my Grand Vizier," he laughed.

"One day perhaps you should," she laughed. "I will have Ibrahim as my scribe."

"Ibrahim would die first." He grew serious. "Do not mock him. Without Ibrahim we would not have this time together. It is Ibrahim who helps me shoulder the burden."

Hürrem stroked his beard, while he watched the play of her thoughts on her face. She began to chew on her bottom lip, a sure sign, he knew, that she had something on her mind.

"What is it, little russelana?"

"It is nothing."

"Tell me."

She looked up into his eyes. "It is Ibrahim. Sometimes . . . well, some-times . . . do you worry that he might . . . abuse . . . his power?"

"Ibrahim? Of course not."

"It is just that there are always such rumors in the Harem. Because I never know the truth, I worry for you."

Süleyman sat up, alarmed. "What rumors?"

Hürrem hesitated. "I do not wish to speak against Ibrahim. It was not my intention . . . I bear no malice to him . . ."

"What rumors?"

"That he mocks Islam and consorts with the Gaiours. That when he meets with ambassadors, he calls himself Sultan."

Süleyman stared at her for a long time, stunned. Then he threw back his head and laughed. "Women's fantasies!"

Hürrem hung her head. "I am sorry. I should not repeat the stories I hear. It is almost always vicious nonsense. But I hear so much, and when I do not see you for a long time, I do not know what to believe."

"Ibrahim is rash and boastful. But he would never betray me."

"Do you forgive me?"

"What is there to forgive?"

Hürrem smiled, like a small child who had been told she had been excused from a spanking. She rose slowly to her feet. Her hair, her hands, and her feet had been dyed with henna, and there were thick circles of kohl around her eyes. It was her role for that day, it seemed, to be exactly like any of the scores of houris in the Harem.

Unexpectedly she performed the three ceremonial sala'ams that he would have expected from any Harem girl brought to his bed for the first time. He watched fascinated as she stood up and began to unfasten the pearl buttons of the silk gömlek. Her nipples had been painted with hashish. It was a favorite trick of the Harem girls. As he suckled her breasts, he would swallow a tiny amount of the drug, and it would enhance his cli-max later.

Bare to the waist she dropped to her knees and approached the divan like a common slave. The white silk of her pantaloons was almost transparent, and the roundness of her hips and the white flesh of her thighs and buttocks were plainly visible through the sheer of the material.

His breath caught in his throat. Just when he thought he knew all her tricks, she dressed or behaved in some unexpected way. She seemed to possess a limitless imagination, always introducing some new game to keep him enthralled with her.

She is my Harem, he thought. She is like a thousand women.

She reached the foot of the divan, and kissed his feet in the traditional act of humility, and began to crawl toward him. But Hürrem introduced a new twist to the ritual and he felt her lips nuzzling his groin and he gasped as her fingers loosened his robes for her ministrations.

The black deaf-mutes who guarded the doorway could not hear his moans. A peacock, rustling among the tulips below the window looked up startled, and then continued with its feeding. And then the Sultan's sighs mingled with the murmuring of water from the fountains, until the moon edged below the branches of the planes, and the flames on the candles guttered and died.

THE CITY WAS a vast mosaic of color, below the long fingers of the minarets and the gleaming cupolas of the mosques. The Kanun of the Fatih proscribed that all houses should be painted for the religion of their inhabitants; there were clusters of gray houses where the Armenians lived, ghettos of yellow for the Jews, huddles of dark gray in the Greek quarter. The Turkish houses were painted either yellow or red, though members of the court were required to paint their houses black.

It made the Defterdar's house easier to find.

Abbas had ventured into the crowded alleys of Stamboul, his anonymity assured by the black ferijde cloak. Rüstem's house was surprisingly large, built of red stone, with its own courtyard at the rear. A page ushered him inside. Rüstem was seated in a kiosk at the rear of the courtyard. A marble fountain murmured nearby.

Rüstem executed a brief temennah and indicated that Abbas should sit opposite him on the crimson Damascan carpet. A black page brought them sherbets and laid a silver platter of pastries between them.

"For what reason am I honored by the presence of the Kislar Aghasi?" Rüstem asked.

"I have come at the request of the Lady Hürrem."

Not even a flicker of interest on his face, Abbas noticed. The man has a face like a statue. "Well?" Rüstem said at last.

"It seems you have a common interest."

"What might that be?"

"Yourselves."

Ah, a reaction, Abbas thought, satisfied. Not much, just a slight tremor in his cheek, the lifting of his eyes for a moment. But enough.

"I am sure you intend to explain yourself, Abbas."

Abbas had known of Rüstem's corruption for some time, but had kept his silence. He had learned quickly that in the Harem one did not spend a valuable currency like information too freely. It might be used at any time to lift the mortgage over one's head. Like the mortgage Hürrem held over him now.

As Defterdar, Rüstem was responsible for collecting the taxes from the timariots, the feudal cavalrymen given small fiefdoms in return for services in battle. The spahis then collected taxes in kind from the local farmers, converted them to cash, took expenses for keeping themselves and their horses, and forwarded the balance to the government.

But the land remained the Sultan's and on their death it was supposed to return to the state. It was one of the basic tenets of the Osmanli system. Only the Sultan could accrue hereditary wealth.

Abbas leaned forward. "The Veil of Crowned Heads has asked me to tell you about a man named Hakim Dürgün. It seems last year he died of the pestilence. Yet he still farms his *timar* near Adrianople. A remarkably diligent ghost, do you not agree, Rüstem?"

"Remarkable. I will look into it."

"There are other stories. There is a timariot in Rumelia who died four seasons ago. About the time you became treasurer. Since then he has taxed the farmers on his lands eight aspers per sheep. And yet you have done nothing about this dead man. Is it because you are afraid of ghosts or because you are receiving two aspers per sheep yourself?"

Rüstem made no attempt at denial, and Abbas did not anticipate that he would. It was not in the man's nature. "How did you find out these things?"

"Wherever there is a black man, I have a pair of ears, Rüstem. I have many other tales to tell."

"I see." Rüstem selected a pastry and chewed slowly. "What do you want? Money?"

"I have not come here for myself. The Lady Hürrem sent me."

"She does not need money."

"Of course."

"A favor, then?"

"Much more than that, Rüstem. Much more than that."

"Tell me."

"She wishes an alliance."

For the first time Rüstem raised his eyes and looked directly at Abbas. They were gray eyes, Abbas noticed. November eyes. Not cold. Just gray and empty.

"It would be an interesting arrangement. Does she realize that Ibrahim is my patron?"

"Of course. You do not think I would keep that from her?"

"I think you will tell her whatever you need to tell her and no more."

Abbas ignored the jibe. "I understood you were to accompany the Vizier on the campaign to the east."

"And what interest does the second kadin have in a military campaign to Persia?"

"No interest at all. Her only interest is Ibrahim."

Rüstem frowned, as if puzzling over some mathematical problem. "He is the most powerful man in the Empire, except for the Sultan himself."

"Yet that is his greatest weakness. If he were to become too convinced of his power, he may one day remove his own head. His boasting is already the scandal of the court and the bazaars."

"That much is obvious. What would the Lady Hürrem have me do about it?"

"She would have you hurry that day along, Rüstem. She wants evidence of his treachery."

"He relishes the power that has been given him. That is hardly treachery."

"He relishes it too much."

"It could be made to seem that way." Rüstem selected another pastry. "And if I cannot find a way?"

"Then one night, when the Sultan is wrapped in the embrace of Hürrem's thighs, she will whisper to him of how you have embezzled taxes from the timariots, and corrupted the fiefs."

Abbas studied the other man's face, but there was no fear there, just a rueful admission of surrender, as if he had been outmaneuvered at chess. He understood the mathematics of power. She had power over him, so he must submit.

"And what reward should I hope for, should I prove a powerful ally?"

Abbas was surprised by the question. "Your life?"

"I want more than that, Abbas. Tell her I may prove to be an invaluable servant. But I want much more than that."

"I will tell her," Abbas said.

Later, as Abbas made his way back through the streets, he passed a dead horse that had been left to die in the gutters. The dogs had been gnawing at it, and the entrails had been dragged out through a hole torn into its abdomen. It seemed to Abbas that the stench it made was more pleasant than all of Hürrem's rosewater perfumes and the sweet, acrid scent of Ibrahim's Defterdar.

52

Galata

GALATA LAY JUST across the Horn from Seraglio Point, dominated by the Galata Kulesi, the tall round tower that had been built by the Genoese as the highpoint in the town's fortifications. Tiny houses and shops clustered at the foot of the hill, next to the harbor, the homes of Jewish and Genoese commission agents. There were Berbers from Africa and Arabs from the Red Sea, their warehouses filled with imported spices, ivory, silks, glass, and pearls. There were even small shops where wine and *arak* were served. The smell of fish and salt from the Bosphorus overlaid the dank urban stink. The palaces of Pera overlooked the town from the hill above, as if the rich foreign merchants wished to raise themselves above the vulgar huddle of commerce on which they all depended.

Ludovici kept a house in the quarter, although no one ever lived there. Its purpose was as neutral ground where he could receive information and pay baksheesh to Palace officials. Endless visits to his palace at Pera by government pashas would have invited investigation.

The house was painted yellow, the color of the Jews. Inside, it was sparsely furnished. There was a low cedarwood table, and some cushions and carpets scattered about the floor, the rich Persian silk belying the humble surroundings.

Abbas sat cross-legged at the table. It had taken four pages to ease his enormous bulk to the floor. Now he sat silently, his attention focused on the pastries piled on the silver plate in front of him. When they were gone he dipped his fingers daintily into the silver bowl proferred by another of Ludovici's servants. He belched politely into a silk handkerchief he produced from the abundant folds of his robe.

He came once a month, disguised by his heavy black ferijde, for his meetings with Ludovici. For Ludovici, he had become an invaluable source to the inner world of the Topkapi, always willing to trade information or pass on a baksheesh. Ludovici had tried at first to speak to him as he would to a friend; but the Abbas he had known was gone. He had withdrawn into himself, either too ashamed or too bitter to reveal any of the old passions that had once dwelt inside him. He seemed to gain no pleasure from these visits, and Ludovici wondered why he still came; perhaps it was because Ludovici was his last link with Julia.

"How is Julia?" Abbas said, breaking the silence. It was always his first question.

"She is well, Abbas. She is well."

Abbas nodded, and for a moment there was an expression of desperate reproach on his face. He had never asked about Ludovici's relationship with her. "Business is good?"

"Thanks to your help."

Abbas shrugged. None of it really seemed to interest him. He quickly became bored talking of commerce.

"She cannot stay in Stamboul any longer," Abbas said, abruptly.

"Abbas?"

"You must get her out of the city. It is no longer safe for her here. Even in the Comunità Magnifica."

"What has happened?"

"Just politics, Ludovici. Trust that I know the extent of the danger."

Ludovici shook his head, stalling. I cannot do this, Abbas. "It won't be easy. Where can she go?"

"It does not matter. Please, Ludovici. I have done all I can to protect her. If you want to help her—if you want to help me—get her out of Stamboul as soon as you can."

"I shall do what I can."

Abbas leaned toward him, gripped his wrist in his huge fist. "No, Ludovici, one way or another, you must get her out!"

"All right," Ludovici said.

Abbas nodded, satisfied. "Good," he said. "Now then. Let us get down to business."

The Hippodrome

SÜLEYMAN SAT ON a pure-white Cappadocian horse, watching the army move through the Atmeydani, on its way to the ferries at Üsküdar. Behind him, Süleyman knew, veiled on the latticed platform, Hürrem would be watching too. The knowledge of her presence helped still his nagging doubts.

The Hippodrome shook to the rumble of the supply wagons and siege engines, the clatter of the hoofs from the squadrons of cavalry, the iron-spiked shoes of the yeniçeris, and the timbals, flutes, and drums of the bands. Choking clouds of dust swept across the square and spiraled into the air, like the tail of some terrible beast released to stalk the plains.

I should be at their head, Süleyman thought. That is my place. That is my duty after all.

He saw the flap of a white cloak through the dust. Ibrahim galloped toward him. The grim set of his face did nothing to still Süleyman's self-reproach. "Your blessing on our endeavor, my Lord. Would that you were with us!"

"You must defend Baghdad," Süleyman shouted back.

"I will crush the Shah as you have commanded me!" He reined in his horse to review the procession at Süleyman's side.

First came the azabs, the irregular infantry, criminals and ruffians who came to fight for booty or die in battle and go straight to Paradise. They had nothing to lose and would be sent in at the main charge of every battle. "Moat fillers," Ibrahim called them.

The regular cavalry—the Spahis of the Porte—thundered by, their horses caparisoned in cloth of gold and silver, the saddles studded with jewels, their conical helmets and the burnished steel of their chainmail gleaming in the sunlight. They were a spectacle in themselves, in robes of purple, royal blue, and scarlet, the silks and satins and velvets embroidered with gold, according to their rank or regiment. Each rider wore two sheaths, one for his bow, the other filled with arrows; each carried a spear in his right hand. A scimitar studded with gems and a steel club hung from his saddle.

Their scarlet banner fluttered above them.

Next came the yeniçeris, their enormous Bird of Paradise plumes waving in the wind like a moving forest, dark blue skirted cloaks swinging in stride, harquebus muskets slung over their shoulders. They all wore long dervish caps, in memory of the flowing white sleeves of Hadji Bektash, their founder, each sleeve thrust through with a copper spoon. The great copper cauldrons that served as the standard of each regiment were carried along with them. Above them fluttered a white banner emblazoned with the flaming sword of Muhammad, embroidered with gold text from the Qur'ān. Ahead of them marched their Aga, bearing his three-horsetail standard.

Each of the mustachioed faces was European. Our strength, Süleyman thought. Our most feared weapon, the elite yeniçeris, draws its blood from Christian babies. As the Faith commanded.

Then came the dervishes, naked except for green aprons fringed with ebony beads, wearing their towering hats of brown camelhair, chanting from the Qur'ān or playing their solemn, mournful music on horns and flutes.

Madcaps rode up and down the lines, long hair straggling from under their caps of leopard skin, dolmans of lion or bearskins slung across their shoulders, their horses festooned with fur and feathers. These were the crazy scouts, the religious fanatics who carried out the suicide raids no one else would attempt.

At the rear were members of the Divan, judges in their green turbans of dignity and fur-trimmed robes, the viziers and their horses glittering with jewels. With them came camels bearing the Qur'ān and a sacred fragment of the holy Ka'aba stone, lumbering under the brilliant green folds of the standard of Islam. A metal *sanchak* Qur'ān, a miniature Qur'ān inscribed in bronze, jangled at the top of the standard.

At the rear of the procession came the heavy supply wagons, loaded down with grain, camels bowed under the weight of powder and lead, and the rumbling siege cannon with their great bronze mouths.

I should be at their head, Süleyman thought again. This is wrong. I should be with them.

"I will bring you back the head of the Shah," Ibrahim shouted.

Süleyman felt a shudder of unease. What was it that Hürrem had said? "Are you worried he might abuse his power?"

He gripped the reins of Ibrahim's horse and pulled himself close. "We must regain Baghdad," he said. "As Defender of the Faith, I am sworn to defend it."

"You have put your faith in me, my Lord. I shall do all I can to serve you."

Süleyman glanced toward the platform, then back to Ibrahim. Yes, I have put all my faith in you, he thought. God grant that I have not trusted you too much.

Pera

JULIA WAS SITTING on the terrazza, in the sun. Ludovici stopped on the marble steps that led up from the garden and watched her. She is beautiful, he thought, so achingly beautiful. If only I could make her feel about me the way she must have once felt about Abbas. She is mine now; but then she has no choice. She is virtually a prisoner now. She cannot leave my protection for fear of her life; if she returned to Venice, having once been a concubine, she would be disowned by her father, and old Serena, her husband, would probably send her away to a convent. She would be regarded as little more than a prostitute. Their Christian charity is little better than the Muslims they despise so much; a woman's virtue is everything.

She looked up and saw him watching her. He ran up the steps to join her on the terrazza. He was wearing a rust-colored kaftan, and the silk rustled as he walked. He enjoyed playing the renegade among the Comunità. The Osmanli clothes and customs that he had adopted underlined his contempt for Venice.

"It is pleasant in the sun," he said.

She looked up from her book, but she did not smile. So remote, he thought. An angel carved by an artisan from ice. I know she possesses great passion. Yet it remains hidden from me.

He had pulled her from the Bosphorus himself that morning. The image still haunted him. She had been half naked, and he had gasped when he saw her. But when he reached for her, she was blue from chill and suffocation. His first touch of her had been cold. Ever since, she had remained as remote to him as a marble statue: beautiful, cold, lifeless.

She had been ill for weeks afterward. Later, when she had recovered sufficiently he had told her the truth; that it was Abbas, and not Providence, that had saved her. She had perhaps already suspected it, for she accepted the news calmly, as least to outward appearance. But she had sunk into a depression for months. She dressed and behaved as a widow. And Ludovici realized: she still loved him. Yet he might as well be dead to her now.

So what was he to do with her? Since his meeting with Abbas that morning he had thought of nothing else, and it had suddenly occurred to him that he had kept himself at a distance from her also. She was no more to him than an angel he had unconsciously preserved here among the gardens and terraces of his palace, a longing too sanctified to touch. He knew how much Abbas had loved her; to take her for himself would be a betrayal.

But now Abbas wanted him to send her away. He must do it or face the truth that he wanted her for himself. Abbas no longer had claim to her. Ludovici hated the cruelty that had been done to him; but he could no longer deny it.

He sat down. "We must talk."

Julia put down her book and looked up at him with her ice-blue eyes. A vision, Abbas had once described her, he remembered. Cold, when he pulled her from the water. Yes, he thought, it was as if she were not real at all.

"Julia, you have been here, under my protection, over two years."

"You know I will always be grateful to you for what you have done," she said.

"Are you happy here?"

"No, Ludovici. Of course I am not."

"Why?"

She seemed surprised by the question. "I am lonely."

Ludovici spread his hands. "What can I do? If you leave here you will be in danger. And Venice . . ." He shrugged, helplessly.

She said nothing. Without a male guardian, she was helpless.

What can I do? Ludovici thought. She is a married woman. Serena is still alive on Cyprus. I cannot send her back there. Yet I have to keep her presence here a secret, even from the rest of the Comunità Magnifica. *Corpo di Dio!* What am I thinking? I want her! Damn Abbas. My guilt will not give him back his balls!

Perhaps she read his mind. "Tell me," she asked suddenly. "Do you ever see him?"

"Yes. Sometimes."

"Does he ever ask after me?"

"No," Ludovici lied.

Her eyes glistened. "Poor Abbas," she whispered.

He reached across and took her hand. It was warm. "I will try to help you not to be lonely," he said. No, Abbas, I will not send her away. She is going to stay here. With me.

53

THE DOOR WAS slightly ajar and the flickering yellow of candlelight danced in the darkened hallway. Ludovici paused in the shadows, deafened by the sound of his own heartbeat. His mouth was dry.

He pushed open the door. Julia sat at her dressing table, combing out her hair. The silk of her nightgown shimmered in the light as she moved. She saw him in the reflection of the mirror, and stopped, startled.

Ludovici saw his own reflection, the gold of his beard and the hard unfocused look of his own eyes.

Julia set down the brush. "Ludovici?"

He stood behind her, his hands on her shoulders, and watched her eyes in the mirror. She did not seem frightened, or even surprised. "Stand up and turn around," he whispered, and his voice was hoarse.

He traced the lines of her shoulders with the palms of his hands. No, not marble, he thought. She was soft and round and full and warm. She was lonely. The nightgown followed the contours of her body, and clung to them. His chest felt tight. A small gold cross glinted between her breasts.

Enough of the loyal Christian gentleman, he thought.

He bunched the front of the gown between his fists and tore it open along its length, and pulled it over her shoulders. "You're perfect," he whispered.

He kissed her neck, her shoulders, her breast. He glimpsed the reflection in the mirror. She had not moved. He picked her up and laid her on the edge of the bed, pulled away the scraps of the nightgown. He had waited so long for this moment.

She watched him as he removed his clothes. Still, she did not move, or speak.

He lowered himself on top of her, groaning at the swollen ache in his groin. He kissed the soft curve of her neck, inhaled the soft fragrance of her hair, and started to push himself inside her. Julia lay still under him and watched him as he spent himself.

Afterward he lay on top of her, unable to speak or meet her eyes. He had clutched at his prize but the prize was gone. He had tasted perfection but the taste in his mouth was familiar, and he recognized the bitterness for what it was.

Disappointment.

Azerbaijan

Rüstem had already calculated that, provided he did not commit himself too soon, he could profit from the Kislar Aghasi's revelation, regardless of how the dice fell. It was apparent that there was to be a confrontation between the Harem and the Divan; it was politic not to be found in either camp during the conflict. Or rather, it was best to be in both.

He would therefore encourage Ibrahim in his ambition. If he succeeded, he would be at his side. If he failed, he would seek his reward from the ziadi, Hürrem.

It had been a long march through the lonely steppes of Anatolia. The huge army lumbered across the plateau, trailing a cloud of dust that spiraled a hundred feet into the air. The jackals fled in their wake; peasants, shepherding long-haired angoras and bleating fat-faced sheep, stood in the fields and stared.

The long column wound farther and farther into the wilderness. Mile after mile after mile, the akinji ranging and scouting ahead, the camel trains and the heavy guns rumbling across the rutted and dusty roads far behind, the column stretched across the horizon of the steppes. A summer passed as they threaded their way eastward, finally arriving at the feet of the great mountains of Asia, and gazed at their own bearded, dusty reflections in the cool, still waters of Lake Van.

They continued on into the mountains, halted in front of the blue-tiled domes of Tabriz. Ibrahim hurried on after the Shah Tamasp, but he refused to fight, unwilling to risk his cavalry against the yeniçeri artillery, and instead slipped away into the mountains of Sultania.

And the soldiers felt the first chill of autumn in the air and shivered and looked up at the sky in fear.

IBRAHIM'S STANDARD OF six horsetails—only the Sultan had more—was thrust into the hard, bleak earth. The tent flapped and whipped in the wind. The plain was surrounded by razor-backed mountains, gray and foreboding against a mottled sky.

Inside the pavilion Ibrahim sat brooding on a portable throne of ivory and ebony and mother-of-pearl. Copper braziers had been lit inside against the chill. And this was summer! Rüstem shuddered at the thought of what it might be like to spend a whole winter here.

Rüstem touched his forehead to the thick carpets in salute.

"Rüstem! Should you not be guarding the camel train and the silks?" Rüstem noted the hard edge to Ibrahim's voice. He was in a dangerous mood. The frustrations of the past weeks had begun to tell on him. The quick, decisive victory he had anticipated had not come.

"I thought I might be of service, my Lord."

"To help count my money? I can do that well enough on my own."

"It is the matter of the Shah, my Lord."

Ibrahim's face quickly flushed with rage. Rüstem had never seen him quite like this. He wants this victory too badly, Rüstem thought. It will disturb his judgment.

"The Shah! The Shah is no better than a jackal! He runs before us, then follows our spoor, to savage our kills . . ."

Your rhetoric is all very well, Rüstem thought. That will not solve the problem. "Our scouts have still not located his army?"

"He still hides somewhere in the mountains."

"Perhaps there might be a way to draw him out."

Ibrahim's eyes glittered with the hunger of his desperation. "How, Rüstem?"

"If you offer him a treaty . . ."

"Never! I have vowed to crush him!"

"You are not treating with a great European king, my Lord. The Shah is no more than a jackal, as you have said. Vermin, to be destroyed. There would be no dishonor in using the offer to treat, merely to draw him out of his lair."

Ibrahim stood up suddenly and began to pace the room. "How will we find him?"

"You can be sure the Sufavids are watching us. Any lone messenger traveling from the camp will be intercepted."

"Yes, and his ears and nose cut off and returned to us in a leather pouch!"

"Perhaps the Shah does not wish to spend every summer skulking in the mountains. He cannot make war on us forever. Like all heretics, he will grasp at any sanctuary where he can breed his lies."

Ibrahim went to the entrance of the tent, stared out at the wild mountains. The sky was turning lead gray with the late afternoon; the dark shadow of rain clouds swept toward them with the swiftness of charging cavalry.

"I have to draw him into the open," he murmured.

Rüstem took a deep breath. This was the moment. But he had assessed the risk, and he knew that the stake was worth the gamble. One act now would ensure his wealth and his fortune. He could not be the Vizier's clerk forever. "Let me take a message to him."

Ibrahim turned and his expression underwent a dramatic change. "You, Rüstem?" He threw back his head and laughed.

"I can coax the jackal from his hole, my Lord. I am sure of it."

"When does a Defterdar become an ambassador?"

"I cannot remain a Defterdar forever."

Ibrahim seemed to recognize an ambition like his own, and he nodded his understanding. He became suddenly serious again. "What is your plan?"

"A sealed message from you, my Lord, offering him Tabriz and Azerbaijan in return for the Holy City of Baghdad. We respect his borders to the east."

"He will never believe we would strike such a bargain."

"I can persuade him. You have a duplicate of Süleyman's *tugra,* his personal seal. If it is affixed to the offer, he must believe it genuine."

"And if you persuade him to treat?"

"We bring him and his soldiers to the plain. And we massacre them."

Ibrahim shook his head. The rainstorm was overhead now. It broke like the crash of artillery, thundering onto the hard ground and slapping like a thousand arrows against the sides of the tents. The flames in the brazier flared up in a sudden draft of wind.

"He will never believe it," Ibrahim said.

"Let me try."

He had promised Süleyman the Shah's head. After Vienna he could not afford another failure. Not with the witch Hürrem whispering against him. He needed this victory.

Ibrahim raised his hand to Rüstem, palm up. "I want him, Rüstem." He closed his fist. "If you can bring him to me, your reward will be beyond your wildest dreams!"

Rüstem bowed in acknowledgment of the offer, but his face betrayed neither pleasure not gratitude. He had already calculated the risks in his mind. He knew what they were worth. To Ibrahim.

Or to Hürrem.

54

SHAH TAMASP REGARDED the miserable creature in front of him. The man had been brought to the camp blindfolded and in chains, by two of his scouts. He had been lying face down in the pebbles and dirt at the entrance to the tent, with two scimitars pressed into the flesh of his neck, while the Shah read the contents of the missive he had brought with him.

The Shah showed the letter to the mullah and the generals who sat on either side of him. They shook their heads in solemn silence. What trickery had the Sultan's great Vizier devised now? When they had all seen it, he read it again, for the third time. He was a young man, with a thin cruel mouth and a dark, carefully groomed beard. He had long slender fingers that caressed the parchment as he read the letter, and the small brown wrists that extended from the sleeves of his robe were thin and brown as walnut.

When he spoke his voice had the high, sibilant quality of a girl's. "What is your name, messenger?"

The wretch raised his head a few inches from the ground and spoke in the direction of the voice. "Rüstem, my Lord." His iron-gray beard was covered with dirt and there was blood crusted to it. It had come from his lips, where his guards had been a little too enthusiastic in assuring his forehead remained humbly pressed to the ground.

"What is your rank, Rüstem?"

"Defterdar, my Lord."

"A treasurer? When do the Osmanlis send their treasurers as messengers?"

"The Grand Vizier trusts me, my Lord."

The Shah studied this man more exactly. He was pale with exhaustion but he did not seem frightened. From what he could see of his face behind the blindfold, an unremarkable man.

"So Ibrahim is persuaded to sue for peace. Does his Sultan want peace also?"

"Ibrahim has the confidence of the Lord of the Two Worlds. He has his tugra."

"Yes, I see that."

"He will uphold any treaty my Lord Ibrahim makes."

"Messenger Rüstem, can you tell me why your Lord of the Two Worlds does not lead his army against us himself, as his father did?"

"He has tired of war, my Lord. He wishes only peace."

The Shah shrugged. Perhaps. Perhaps.

The offer was a reasonable one. Too reasonable? he wondered. And yet if it were true, he could present his mullahs with a great political victory. They surely could not hope to hold Baghdad in the face of the Osmanli armies. When Ibrahim finally tired of chasing him through the mountains, and went back to Stamboul, he could retake Tabriz and the Holy City. But he would have to surrender it again the next season, when he returned.

Finally he would have to treat. This way he obtained peace now, and some valuable ground. More converts for his mullahs.

And yet.

"Such a treaty may be possible, messenger Rüstem. But we must meet at a place of my choosing, with no more than our own bodyguards in attendance."

"You doubt Ibrahim's honor?"

The Shah smiled. "I doubt his ability to resist such a temptation."

He nodded to the two guards, who dragged Rüstem roughly to his feet.

"If he agrees to my conditions, tell him I accept his offer. Go in peace, messenger Rüstem."

The guards dragged him away. The Shah watched them put him, still chained and blindfolded, on a horse and lead him through the rows of tents toward the south. He wondered again about Süleyman. An Osmanli who wanted peace? It was either a lie or the first sign of weakness. As God wants, he decided. We will soon see.

The wind was cool, but winter was still a long way off. He was already tired of hiding in the mountains.

"IF YOU FOLLOW the spur, it will lead you to the valley where your friends are camped," the Persian said, and he ripped the blindfold from Rüstem's face. The other rider unlocked the chains and dragged them from his wrists.

Rüstem blinked in the sunlight. One of the Persians, a bearded ruffian in a battered conical helmet, tugged at his beard. "Next time we meet, perhaps the Shah will let me wet my sword on your liver." He grinned.

Rüstem ignored him, and pulled at the reins of the horse. He had been right, the risk had been negligible after all. A simple thing now to conclude the business.

Poor Ibrahim. But he was much too fond of heroics to be a truly successful Vizier. True greatness required more careful thought. Someone with the ability to see opportunity in a crisis.

Someone like himself.

The two Persians galloped away, and he was left alone on the high steppe. Now he was alone, he allowed himself a small, chill smile. Then he rode back down the spur to the great camp.

55

BRAHIM'S EXPRESSION WAS curious. His features betrayed both amusement and wonder. One finger tapped the arm of the throne, in time with the flapping of the silk tent, as the cold evening wind buffeted and sighed.

"You found the Shah?" he said at last.

"Yes, my Lord."

"They took you there blindfolded, no doubt."

"Yes, my Lord."

"They treated you well?"

"Passably, my Lord."

Ibrahim studied him. Rüstem's robe was torn and filthy. There was matted dirt in his beard. Had his experience in the mountains affected him? The pale gray eyes betrayed nothing.

"Your lip is cut."

"It is nothing."

Ibrahim laughed unexpectedly. "And I thought we might never see you again. What a loss you would have been to the world of poetry and conversation!"

"I think not, my Lord," Rüstem said. The irony seemed to have been lost on him.

Well, I might have expected that, Ibrahim thought. He sometimes entertained a fantasy in which he scooped off the top of Rüstem's skull with his sword, like an egg. When he peered inside there was no brain. Just an abacus.

"So what does the Shah say to our offer of treaty?"

"He has refused it, my Lord."

Ibrahim's face darkened, but the smile stayed doggedly in place. "He does not trust us, Rüstem?"

"It was the authority of the letter he mistrusted."

"The authority . . . ?"

"He said he could not treat with you."

The smile had vanished now. "Why not?"

"He said you were only a soldier. He said that he could only accept such an offer if it were signed by the Sultan, not the Sultan's clerk."

Ibrahim stood up. He clenched his fists to try and stop the trembling in his hands but his body was overtaken by some terrible force beyond his control. He grabbed Rüstem by the shoulders and threw him on to the ground.

Rüstem did not resist. He lay at Ibrahim's feet, looking neither surprised nor angry.

Ibrahim turned away and drew the killiç from the jeweled sheath at his waist and raised it, double-handed, above his head. He brought it down, with all his strength, splintering the throne, splinters of ivory and mahogany spinning across the tent.

"The Sultan's clerk! Is it the Sultan's clerk who sits every day in the Divan and administers the Empire? Is it the Sultan's clerk who leads his armies into battle while the Sultan pleasures himself in his Harem? The Sultan? I AM THE SULTAN!"

"He spoke in ignorance, my Lord."

"Does he think that the Sultan would send his clerks into battle now? Eh, Rüstem?"

"My Lord, I only repeat what he said to me. He said he could not treat with any but the Sultan of the Osmanlis."

"The Sultan! How long must I endure this? The Sultan has entrusted his power to me, his kingdoms, his wealth, everything! The making of war or the granting of peace are in my hand. Does the Shah know it was I who called for the army to come here? It was I—not the Sultan! I take the burden and now I am to be called the Sultan's clerk!"

"But my Lord—"

Ibrahim held the killiç before Rüstem's eyes, turning it slowly so that the light pooled and shivered on the blade. "When we take him, we take him alive," Ibrahim growled.

"First we must lure him out, my Lord. If the Sultan were here, we could draw him out and finally put an end to his impertinence. If we could convey to the Lord of Life a message—"

"No! I swore I would bring him back the Shah's head! Should I now rush to him with entreaties for his aid?"

". . . Then perhaps there is another way."

"Another way, Rüstem?"

"All the Empire knows how greatly the Sultan has honored and trusted you. Perhaps you must impress this upon the Shah also. You must prove to him that you have the authority to make such a treaty."

"How?"

Rüstem blinked slowly. "You must extend the offer again, my Lord. Only this time you must sign as the Sultan."

Ibrahim stared at him. Did this lunatic realize what he was saying? But Rüstem was anything but a lunatic. He was an abacus. It was a logical solution to the problem.

"That is impossible."

"It will suit our purpose. What else may we do, my Lord? Except perhaps chase him through the mountains for the rest of the summer, then go home with no other prize but a few Persian silks."

"I may do many things, Rüstem, but I may not assume the title of Sultan."

"Who will know once we have lured him out of the mountains? You may bury the document with the Shah."

Perhaps he is right, Ibrahim thought. What do I have to fear? Süleyman has entrusted me with his Divan, and with his armies. I am Sultan in everything but name. If Süleyman did not wish me to invoke his power, then why would he entrust me with so much?

"I cannot," he said.

"There is no other way to lure him out, my Lord. He told me that if the Sultan would not come, then he would see us next spring in Tabriz."

Ibrahim closed his eyes. What could he say to Süleyman if he returned without victory once more? The Austrians had humiliated him at Güns; now the Shah taunted him from the mountains. He was powerless to crush him, as he had vowed. And until the Asian border was secure they could not take their armies to wage the great war against the Emperor Charles in Europe. His destiny was at Vienna, not here. It was Vienna that would finally carve his name alongside Alexander's in the books of history.

He looked at Rüstem, who was watching him with what appeared to be almost detached curiosity.

"Bring your quill and parchment," he said.

To the Shah Tamasp of Persia, greetings and health, may prosperity and glory signal your days. From sundry verbal communications we have cognizance of your desire for peace, and by the grace of the Most High, whose power be forever exalted! We ourselves have no desire to make war on our brothers in Islam. We therefore make it known that should you give up the Holy City of Baghdad and all territories you have conquered by force of arms, we shall cede to you Tabriz, and the lands known as Azerbaijan, should you pay tribute each year of one thousand gold ducats. Night and day our horse is saddled to ride and meet with you and conclude our peace.

Written in the year of the Hejira 941.

Ibrahim. Seraskier Sultan

56

SERASKIER SULTAN!
Rüstem reined in his horse on the ridge overlooking the Osmanli camp. The smoke from the morning campfires still drifted upward, throwing a gauze over the distant panorama of the mountains. From here,

Rüstem could see the great scarlet tent of the Grand Vizier, the standard
with the six horsetails limp in the breeze.

Seraskier Sultan!

Rüstem turned and rode away to the north. He spurred his horse
beyond the first ridge, then wheeled around and galloped west. When he
did not return Ibrahim would assume that the Shah's men had murdered
him. By the time he finally gave him up for lost he would be in Stamboul.

Ibrahim, you fool . . .

Seraskier Sultan!

Topkapi Saraya

SÜLEYMAN CRUMPLED THE letter in his fist, his face ugly with grief.

The pashas and mufti and generals who surrounded him in the Divan
were silent. Each of them felt a sense of triumph, to greater or lesser
degree, but none would allow it to show on his face. Ibrahim had finally
gone too far! The vain, boastful Greek had written his own death warrant!

Rüstem Pasha stood in the center of the great hall, and waited his turn
to speak. The immaculate, anonymous Rüstem, Süleyman thought. There
was no scent of perfume from him now. He stank of horse, and the creases
on his skin were thick with grime and dirt. He claimed to have ridden for
three weeks from the borderlands of Azerbaijan to bring his news.

I would rather the horse had fallen and broken your neck, Süleyman thought.

"You wrote this at his command?" Süleyman said finally.

"Yes, great Lord. He bid me take it to the Shah Tamasp."

Süleyman swallowed hard to retain his composure. Ibrahim, I could
have forgiven you anything, but not this! Even if Rüstem had come to me
privately, I could perhaps have found some way to excuse you. But now he
has come here in the midst of Divan and presented me with a treachery I
cannot be seen to tolerate. What have you done?

"Were you seen, Defterdar Rüstem?"

"No, my Lord. Ibrahim thinks I ride alone into the Shah's domains. But
I know my duty. I could not allow such treachery to go unpunished."

You pathetic little worm, Süleyman thought. How dare you speak to me
of treachery! Ibrahim has served me faithfully for more than a quarter of a
century, as friend, as seraskier of my army, and as my Vizier. How do you
know what motivated him to this? How can you be so certain?

"The Sultan owes you a great debt, Defterdar Rüstem," he forced himself to say. He stared again at the crumpled parchment in his hand. "How does the campaign against the Shah progress?"

"Badly, my Lord. Since Tabriz, Ibrahim Pasha trails the Shah's men through the mountains, but our only glimpse of them has been the tails of their horses as they retreat from minor skirmishes. His generals urge him to Baghdad, but he ignores their counsel. He says he is the only one capable of achieving victory. He says it has always been so."

There was a barely audible sigh in the great chamber. How dare Rüstem repeat such things? Süleyman wondered. He repeats such calumnies as if they were numbers from a balance sheet. What would Ibrahim say next? Would he lay claim to the glory of Rhodes and Buda-Pesth and Mohacs?

"And what of the morale of the army?"

"It is poor, my Lord. They all ask for your presence to lead them. The yeniçeris clamor for you to lead them to victory. They fear Ibrahim will lead them only deeper into the mountains, to disaster."

Süleyman looked upward, at the dust filtering down through the shafts of yellow sunlight from the high windows. The passage of dust. The passage of all reputations.

Behind him, he knew, was the great latticed window, the window of fear, that looked down on the Divan. There was no one behind the black taffeta curtain this morning to witness this, but Süleyman wished with all his heart that he was there now, that he could watch someone else make the terrible decision that he knew must finally be made.

57

The Eski Saraya

LIGHT FROM THE candles rippled on the tiled walls and shimmered on the brass censers that hung from the vaulted ceilings. Süleyman removed his turban, and ran a hand over the smooth skin of his scalp, to the single scalplock at the back of his skull, the legacy of his ghazi forefathers. He closed his eyes. He was feeling the burden more keenly today than any other time in the fifteen years since he had accepted the mantle of Osman.

He eased himself onto the divan and waited.

"My Lord."

She entered silently, through the velvet curtain, and knelt at his feet. For once, there was no smile to greet him. She bowed her head to kiss his hand and then rested it against her cheek.

"You knew?"

"Yes, my Lord."

"How?"

"Whispers, my Lord."

"There are always whispers."

"When I came through the curtain and saw your face, I knew this time the whispers were true."

He stroked her hair, and his face softened. "What am I to do?"

"May I see the letter, my Lord?" she whispered.

He held out his left hand, and opened it, palm upward. The letter had remained there, crumpled in his fist, ever since Rüstem had appeared at the Divan earlier that day.

Hürrem unfolded it. It was barely legible now. It was badly creased and the sweat from Süleyman's hand had blurred the ink. But she could understand it was a treaty for peace. And she could still read the signature.

"*Seraskier Sultan.*"

Oh, Rüstem! Hürrem thought. Abbas chose you well. You have a rare genius for intrigue!

"He sues for peace," she said.

"It is madness," Süleyman whispered, his voice hoarse. "What could have possessed him to do such a thing?"

"Is this Defterdar Rüstem to be trusted?"

"How could he profit by such a lie? Besides, there is no lie. It is there, written beneath my own seal. 'Seraskier Sultan.' Sultan! There is no circumstance, no provocation, under which any man may call himself Sultan other than me! To do so is rebellion. He knows it."

"He is your friend, Süleyman. So often you have spoken of him to me—"

"Yes, he is my friend. Much more than a friend! It only makes this the more unforgiveable!"

"Do not act too rashly, my Lord."

"Hürrem . . . you may be the only one today who speaks for him. Suddenly he has enemies I did not dream of. They have swarmed from every crevice in the Palace walls to denounce him!"

Yes, I will speak for him, Hürrem thought. And when his head is rotting on the Gate of Felicity you will remember that I was his friend. If I become the instrument of his death, you will hate me too. Time must take care of Ibrahim now.

"You must go to him," she whispered.

He nodded slowly. "The longer I delay, the more I am threatened. I cannot do nothing. Yet I cannot bring myself to harm him, little russelana. It will be like cutting out a piece of my own heart."

"It may not be necessary. My Lord, if he is indeed your friend, there must be some way you can excuse him."

He snatched the letter from her hand. "There is no way! What excuse can there be?" He jumped to his feet and went to the candle burning on its silver pedestal by the doorway. He held the letter to the flames, twisting it with his fingers, watching it burn.

"Will you confront him with the letter?" she said.

"And have him deny it? He will tell me of the letter with his own lips when I arrive. If he is truly my friend, he will not try to hide this from me." He let the burning parchment slip from his fingers onto the floor. He crushed the flames and ash with the sole of his leather boot.

He flung himself on the divan. "Ibrahim . . . !"

Hürrem got up and sat beside him. She pulled his head to her breast, and she felt him cry, softly, in her arms.

"Hürrem," he whispered, "what would I do without you?"

"Shhh," she murmured and stroked his temple with her fingers, despising his weakness more than she had ever done.

58

I T WAS THE last of the hot days of August, the time of year when only the poor were left behind to swelter in the furnace of the city. Süleyman had only recently returned with his Divan and Harem from Adrianople, where he had retired for the hunting and to escape the hot breath of the Sirocco. No time to start a campaign, so dangerously close to winter, he thought. The prospect of the long, crushing ride across Anatolia depressed him. But there was no choice. He had to join his army, and quickly.

He crossed the Bosphorus with three hundred solaks and a squadron of spahis and rode to Üsküdar, and then headed east across the great baked plains of Anatolia toward the mountains of Asia.

He knew there would be a full cycle of the moon before he reached his destination, a month of choking dust and aching muscles and riding, riding, riding.

Sultan Seraskier!

HE FOLLOWED THE trail of Alexander, through orchards of figs and olives, fields of cotton and wheat. They passed through Konia, where his forefathers, the Selçuks, had once dwelt and where he stopped to honor the Mevlana Türbesi, the tomb of Jalal ud-din Rumi, who had founded the Dervish order.

From Konia they rode on across the parched, rolling steppes, roasting under the desert sun. Their only companions on the high plateau were the lonely black tents of the nomads, flapping on the plains, and the baked stone walls of the caravansaries that offered sanctuary for the camel trains from Samarkand and Medina.

They passed through Edessa, the birthplace of Abraham, where old men sat in the shadow of the fortress and tossed chickpeas into a pool of sacred carp. From there they rode on into the vast and barren mountains, where the hot desert winds could not penetrate. The air turned suddenly cooler, and the brown steppe gave way to bare rock and streams so cold they seemed to cut into bare skin like a razor. The weather would change suddenly and rapidly, a wild storm appearing from a blue sky in just a few minutes, the wind savaging men and horses like a whip. It was a place only the goats and the sheep and the Kurds could survive.

And the Shah, Süleyman thought.

They rode twelve hours a day, stopping only when the horses were too tired to continue, foam spuming along their muzzles and flanks, their eyes pink and wide with exhaustion and thirst. But it was still not till late in August that they finally reached Azerbaijan.

The scouts rode ahead to locate the camp and warn Ibrahim to prepare to greet his Sultan. A week later they approached the crest of a ridge and saw skeins of smoke rising from the valley. The Osmanli camp stretched in panorama in front of them.

Süleyman wanted only to throw himself on the ground and weep with relief. Exhaustion had settled into his bones, almost a part of him now, like the dirt that grimed his skin. But he could not show his fatigue to his lieutenants, and least of all now, to the yeniçeris. He drew himself up in the saddle and spurred his horse down the slope.

AS WAS THE way, the tents had been erected in long crisp lines, according to division and regiment. Holes had been dug at regular intervals for excrement. Horses had been corralled, siege engines, supply wagons, and cannon drawn up in strict order.

The camp was silent, for no fighting or gambling or drinking was ever tolerated. But when the men of the *askeri* recognized the Sultan's standard of seven horsetails and saw the tall, bearded figure on the white horse, with his green robes and snow-white turban, they began to cheer.

Word spread quickly. Süleyman was returning to lead them once more! He would guide them out of the mountains and to victory!

He reined in his horse in front of the scarlet silk tent with the six-horsetail standard. Ibrahim emerged, and quickly executed a ceremonial sala'am on the ground in front of him.

"My Lord," he said.

Where was the boyish grin now? Süleyman wondered. Where was the young man who would rush to embrace him whenever they had been apart? Look at this scowl of petulance.

"Do you have the head of the Shah?" Süleyman said.

Ibrahim took a long time to reply. "Not yet, my Lord."

"Then we will remove to Baghdad. The Sultan shall lead his army now."

59

I T IS GOOD that you are here, my Lord."

"Is it, Ibrahim?"

"It is just the reason that you came that distresses me. Do you no longer trust me as your seraskier?"

"A Sultan's place is at the head of his army, as you have never ceased to remind me."

"Is that the only reason, my Lord?"

They were sitting cross-legged on the thick carpets in Süleyman's pavilion. The coals in the copper brazier glowed hot, fanned by a sudden draft of wind. Close by, a horse stamped its foot and snorted, frightened by the moan of the wind and the sudden cold.

Süleyman was tired. The journey had exhausted him. His eyes were gritty from lack of sleep; he could barely force himself to think. And he was cold. He had not experienced such cold in a long time. He pulled the fur-lined ermine robe closer about his shoulders.

"As Protector of the Faith I am obliged to defend Baghdad, not have my army chase phantoms through the wilderness."

"Once we defeat the Shah, Baghdad is ours anyway."

Süleyman searched Ibrahim's face for the truth. Any moment, he thought; any moment he will confess to me what he has done, he will explain why he did such a thing. There can be no secrets between us; he would never allow it.

He would give him his opportunity. "Perhaps we should treat with him," he said.

A flicker of fear showed in his eyes. It was unmistakeable. "And what would we offer him?"

"What do you think we should offer, Ibrahim?"

"Nothing. Except perhaps a rope for his neck."

Süleyman shook his head. "He is as elusive as the Roman Emperor. Perhaps we will never bring any of them to battle, Ibrahim. It is more important that we do our duty. We defend the Faith."

"The Faith!"

He could see that Ibrahim regretted the blasphemy the moment it was spoken. "It is the reason for my army, Ibrahim. There is no other. The jihad is for God. It is our duty." The horses were growing restless. He could hear them stamping their hoofs over the whistling of the wind. "Tomorrow we prepare for Baghdad. We will retake the holy city and if necessary we will winter there. The mountains are no place for an army of this size."

Süleyman could sense Ibrahim's humiliation. The Vizier stared at the glowing charcoals, his lips compressed in a thin line of fury. "Why did you do this to me?" he whispered.

Süleyman felt his hands clench into fists in his lap. After your treachery, you dare question my actions? he thought. "I am tired. I must sleep," he said. "Leave me now."

It was their tradition to sleep in the same pavilion when on campaign. But tonight Süleyman did not ask for his presence and Ibrahim did not protest his banishment. He rose to his feet, made his sala'am, and left.

During the night a blizzard erupted over their heads. Süleyman woke to the sounds of horses and camels screaming in the storm. Men were shouting in the darkness, and then another gust shook the pavilion so viciously he imagined it had torn a huge rent in the length of the gold silk. He threw on a fur-lined robe and rushed to the entrance.

Curtains of cutting sleet and snow obliterated everything. He covered his face to protect it from the stinging slap of the ice. He could hear the shrieks of animals and men but the night was hidden behind a veil of white. Torches flared for a moment and were extinguished by the wind.

The pages were trembling with terror. Even one of his own solaks fell to his knees. "May God protect us," he murmured. "It is the Persian magicians!"

"It is only a storm!" Süleyman roared, straining to make himself heard. "Get up, man!"

He hauled the soldier to his feet with his own hands. Damn Ibrahim, he thought. Damn him for his treachery and his stupidity! Damn him!

Ibrahim staggered through the drifts, stunned by the spectacle that the dawn had offered him. The valley was blanketed in white. Tents sagged under the weight of snow. The frozen leg of a camel protruded like a long branch from one of the drifts.

"God help me in my sorrow," he murmured.

An eerie gray light tried to force its way through the slow, black anvils of cloud. A terrible hush had fallen across the valley. Whole regiments had been buried by the drifts; tents had been torn away by the force of the wind. Pieces of canvas flapped on broken poles, like the tattered banners of a defeated army.

Ibrahim heard what he thought was the moan of the wind, but the wind was still now. He realized it was the cries of men trapped under the snow, mingled with the bellowing of dying camels and horses.

He had never looked on defeat before, but he recognized it now. Instead of blood, there was snow. It was not an enemy that had outflanked him, but the mountains.

Men staggered, dazed and snow-blind, through a landscape they did not recognize from the previous evening. Some clawed desperately at the snow to release a comrade, or hauled at the reins of a horse half buried under a snowbank.

Most turned their eyes to the jaws of the pass, dreading the silhouettes of Persian horsemen against the dawn. They were helpless. Utterly helpless. If they should come now . . .

"Ibrahim!"

He span around. Süleyman stood above him on the slope, the jeweled killiç buckled at his waist. He recognized on his face the same berserk fury he had seen only once before—at Rhodes, when he had called for the bostanji to rid him of his seraskier and Grand Vizier.

"What have you done?"

Ibrahim spread his hands helplessly. Who could have anticipated such a storm in September?

"If the Persians come now, we will all die here!" Süleyman roared.

Ibrahim stared at him. What was there to say?

Süleyman came closer, so the pages and solaks that surrounded them could not hear his next words. "I sometimes wondered if you and I were not born to the wrong families," he whispered. "It seems we were not."

Süleyman turned away and plunged through the thigh-deep snow toward the wreckage of the yeniçeri camp. They must reorganize quickly, Ibrahim realized, and make their retreat. But that was no longer his responsibility. The Sultan was in command again now, and he would issue the orders of the day.

60

Galata

THE LIGHT FROM the waxed candle shimmered on the glaze of the single row of blue tiles. Each time Abbas shifted his weight the silk of the kaftan rustled like dry leaves before a great wind. He sighed and stared at Ludovici. "These are dangerous days," he said.

"Every day is dangerous, Abbas."

"You have made sure she is safe. She is out of Stamboul?"

"Yes," Ludovici answered, and he met Abbas's gaze. "She is gone." Abbas grunted, satisfied.

"Do you still love her, Abbas?"

"Love?" The rustle of silk. "I don't know, Ludovici. How can I still love her the way I am?"

Ludovici did not know what to say to him.

"Do you still have eunuchs in your household, Ludovici?"

"I have a harem of my own," he said, as if this explained everything.

Abbas said nothing, but there was reproach in his silence.

"Do you ever think of the old days, Abbas? In Venice?"

"It seems like a hundred years ago. My memories of that time are like flicking through the pages of a stranger's diary."

"I wish you had listened to me then."

A suggestion of a smile, grim and sad. "Yes, you warned me, I remember. And time has proved you correct."

"It gave me no satisfaction."

"I know that, Ludovici. But a man's fate is written on his forehead by God at the time of his birth, and this was mine. I could not have acted differently, as a cloud cannot decide which way it will glide through the sky. Its direction is guided by God's wind, as my life has been."

"Then on the Day of Judgment, God will have no right to judge your sins. Instead it is He should ask your pardon."

"That is blasphemy, Ludovici, and I shall not listen to it." He clapped his hands in signal to his mutes and rose to leave. "One last question," he said. "Did you ever take Julia into your harem?"

Ludovici was startled by the question. "But she is no concubine. She is a Christian woman of high birth."

"Yes, but did you do it? Did you make her your houri?"

"No," he lied, "I did not."

"Good. I believe you," Abbas said, but something in his face suggested to Ludovici that he had lied also.

WHEN LUDOVICI RETURNED to his home at Pera, he went alone to his study, and stood at the window, looking over the Horn, thinking. He shouted his instructions to Hyacinth, who scampered away along the corridor. Ludovici sat at the great oak desk by the window and waited.

Julia entered silently, heralded by the soft rustling of her long skirts on the black and white marble. "You wanted to see me?" she asked him.

Ludovici stood up and offered her a chair. "Please. Sit down," he said. She sat and he pulled up a chair next to her.

"Is something wrong, Ludovici?"

He shook his head. "Do you hate me, Julia?"

"Why should I hate you?"

He did not answer her.

"You only did to me what the Sultan does to all his concubines, what you do to your own. Only you at least did not try to put me in a sack afterward and drown me in the Bosphorus."

"I am ashamed."

"Once I would have been ashamed too. But then the Turks made me into a whore and I have no shame left."

"You are not a whore!" He stood up suddenly, his chair crashing on to the marble tiles. He turned his back to her and stared at the twilight gathering over the Horn.

"I am grateful, Ludovici. You saved my life. You gave me sanctuary here. I think perhaps I prefer to be a concubine than a nun. Though perhaps the only difference is the evening entertainments."

He turned around. Was she mocking him? He folded his arms and leaned against the stone still. "Serena is dead," he said.

She took a deep breath. "When?"

"Three weeks ago, on Cyprus. I learned the news today."

She shrugged her shoulders. "It changes nothing for me."

"Perhaps it does." Ludovici turned away from the window. "Marry me."

Julia stared at him, surprised. "Why?"

"Because I love you."

"I am content to remain a concubine, my Lord. Marrying you will change nothing for me."

"I have told Hyacinth to sell my harem. I want only you, Julia."

Julia stood up and crossed the room. "You want me to love you, and I cannot."

"You can try," Ludovici said.

Julia shook her head. "I am in love with Venice and a few stolen afternoons on the canals." And Sirhane? she thought.

"I want you."

"You already possess me."

"Then let us say I do this out of shame. Marry me anyway."

She leaned forward and kissed him gently on the cheek. He reached for her and crushed her in his arms but when he kissed her there was no answering pressure and he knew what he really wanted from her was as unattainable as it was for Abbas.

Mesopotamia

BAGHDAD HAD BEEN built from the same brick and stone as the ancient city of Babylon. It straddled the Tigris and the Euphrates, the city of the caliph Harun Al-Rashid. Palm trees framed the domes and minarets, promising silks and gold and jewels and women.

Süleyman sat motionless on his white Arab stallion, watching the siege engines and cannon trundling into position, and breathed a prayer of thanks. The crisis was past.

The Persians had not come that morning. His presence alone had galvanized the army, and by the evening following the storm they had reorganized, and had begun the long, slow retreat from the mountains that might have buried them.

The Empire of Muhammad, the Army of Islam, would have been destroyed, thanks to my Seraskier Sultan! he thought bitterly. True Believer or not, he had a duty to me. His ambition blinded him to it.

Ibrahim rode toward him, the rubies and emeralds that had been embroidered into his saddle and arms glittering in the warm morning sun. He grinned, as if the horrors of the last week were just a bad dream to be dismissed with the dawn.

"Why so solemn, my Lord?"

"You should have stood at these gates two months ago."

Ibrahim shrugged, as if his was a minor offense. "The Aga of the yeniçeris was hungry for a long campaign," he grinned. "We have given it to him! The old bear is still melting the snow in his boots!"

"This was our objective, Ibrahim. Not to placate the Aga, not to find the Shah. We were here to chase away the dogs."

Ibrahim grew sullen. "You said you wanted the dog's head."

"No. You did." Süleyman squeezed the flanks of his horse with his knees, and trotted forward, leaving Ibrahim alone on the plain.

61

The Eski Saraya, 1535

IT WAS EARLY spring, but snow still clung to the roofs of the kiosks in the Topkapi Saraya, fell in minor avalanches from the dome of the Aya Sofia, and froze the fountains in the courtyards of the Eski Saraya. Only Hürrem and the Kislar Aghasi himself were allowed the fur-lined kaftans of rank. The other odalisques and servants froze in their thin kaftans on their way across the icy courtyards and the freezing cloisters. Inside the Palace, with all shutters and doors tightly closed against the cold, the stale aromas of incense and charcoal and hashish mingled with each other to create a suffocating fug. Hürrem had her servants spray her apartments with orange blossom and rosewater to relieve it.

"A courier has arrived at the Palace, my Lady. Süleyman will be back in Stamboul in the next few days."

"With Ibrahim?"

"Yes, my Lady," Abbas said. It was the scandal of the whole city, of course, how Ibrahim had defied Süleyman even to the point of assuming the title "Seraskier Sultan." The secret had been intended not to go beyond the Divan, but Rüstem had assured that within days the whole city knew of the treachery. The Defterdar had indeed been a revelation.

The fall of Baghdad and the passage of the long winter months had not stilled the gossip; if anything, it had stimulated it. News came infrequently, couriers riding day and night for twenty, even thirty days to bring news. And all Stamboul waited to see what the Sultan would do, how he would deal with his "Seraskier Sultan."

Merchants still spat and cursed the Greek in all the bazaars. The statues in front of his Palace in the Atmeydani had been defaced one night. All Stamboul hated him, resented his power over the Sultan, the way he flaunted his wealth before them. Only one man still tolerated his excesses, it seemed.

Many times Hürrem had wondered if Ibrahim was already dead, strangled in his tent by the bostanji, or hung on a gibbet in Baghdad square. She knew he could have been moldering in his grave for weeks by the time the *chaush* arrived with news. She had told herself, when Süleyman had left Stamboul at the end of the last summer, that she would never see Ibrahim alive again. But, like some terrible dark spirit, it seemed he could not die.

Hürrem chewed her bottom lip. For the first time Abbas wondered if she had miscalculated Süleyman's temperament. How far could Ibrahim goad the Sultan before he acted against him?

"There is other news," Abbas said.

"Tell me."

"The Shah attacked the rear guard of the army on its return through Azerbaijan. Four *sançak beys* were lost, eight hundred yeniçeris surrendered."

"Who was seraskier?"

"Ibrahim. The Sultan rode ahead with the solaks."

Hürrem seemed to relax. Her face softened into a broad smile. "It seems the golden touch has deserted him, Abbas."

"Yes, my Lady."

Abbas felt no personal triumph at the intrigue in which he had been engaged. He had been compelled by circumstance to play his role. The only real pleasure he could imagine in his life was to have Hürrem tied in a neatly weighted sack and then ferry her to the mid-point of the Bosphorus.

Perhaps one day . . .

"You have done well, Abbas."

"Thank you, my Lady."

"Rüstem too. He shows a great talent. I am sure we will find a use for it again in the near future. You can convey to him my thanks and assure him he will be amply rewarded."

"I will tell him."

Abbas executed a temennah, eager to be out of the room. It was not just the overpowering heat from the charcoal braziers and the cloying smell of perfume—it was so warm in the reception chamber, Hürrem wore nothing but a velvet jacket and silk drawers—but these days her very presence unsettled him. Süleyman had given her too much ease, too much power. She was becoming a monster.

"By the way, have you seen Julia?" Hürrem asked him, as he was about to take his leave.

"No, my Lady."

"I am curious, that is all. I have been wondering about what you told me. How much could a simple slave girl pay you that would be worth risking your neck?"

She knows. "I took pity on her also, my Lady."

"My good, brave Abbas."

"It is as you say, my Lady."

"She is married to Ludovici Gambetto, one of the Venetian merchants on Pera. Did you know?"

The room started to spin. Abbas hoped his confusion did not show on his face. "Yes, my Lady," he lied.

"I hope she pleases him more than she pleased the Sultan."

"I hope so too, my Lady."

"Thank you, Abbas."

He returned to his cell, a fire burning in his heart. *Ludovici, what have you done? You lied to me, you lied, you lied!*

Poor Julia.

I hope you are happy.

I did all I could.

62

Süleyman looked suddenly old. It was as if time had frozen like the fountains in the Eski Saraya, while outside on the mountains and the plains ten seasons had gone by. Yet it was not a physical change. There was no more gray in his beard, his back was still as straight, there was no limp, no scars.

Perhaps it was his skin, Hürrem thought. It had been burnished by a long winter in the desert and the mountains, pronouncing the lines on his face; or perhaps it was just his demeanor, as if the Persian desert had drained all the juice out of him. There was no fire left in him, no spirit. He looked defeated.

He sat in front of the low table, staring at some private vision, his hands clenched into fists on his lap. Hürrem laid the tray of food in front of him, and knelt at his side.

"What is wrong, my Lord?"

"Ibrahim . . . !" Süleyman murmured.

"My Lord . . . ?"

"What may I do, little russelana?"

"You confronted him about the letter?"

"I waited for his admission. It did not come. What should I now do? Bring Rüstem before him?"

"May he find excuse that way?"

Süleyman shook his head. "I wanted only his free admission. I could not bear to listen to his lies. The letter was signed under the duplicate of my seal. What could he say now that would pardon him?"

"And yet?"

"And yet I love him, Hürrem. Not as I love you, but yet I love him. What may I do?"

You must execute him, Hürrem thought. Any less than that and we are all in danger. How can you hesitate so long? "You might exile him, as you did Achmed Pasha."

"Achmed Pasha used his place of exile as a basis for revolt. Do I dare take the same risk with Ibrahim, who is far more powerful than he ever was?"

Of course not, Hürrem thought. "He has been your friend for so long, my Lord. I know you love him as a brother. Do not ask me for my counsel in this."

"Yet who else may I trust?"

She stroked his cheek, felt the answering pressure against her hand. "He has been your greatest Vizier."

"Yes, little russelana, but now his ambition and his greed have out-reached him. On our return from Baghdad he allowed the sançak beys of Cairo and Syria to camp carelessly in a valley, with no escape. As seraskier, he should have guarded our rear against attack. Instead he was more concerned with ensuring the safety of the bales of Persian silk he had looted from Persia. He allowed the Shah's cavalry to inflict the greatest defeat my army has ever suffered. Instead of celebrating our victory at Baghdad, we have returned to Stamboul in disarray, licking our wounds. All thanks to the 'Seraskier Sultan'!"

Hürrem held his hands in hers. "He has conspired against the Osmanli throne, in action, if not in his heart. He is, by your own words, guilty of negligence in his duties. My Lord, I feel your pain, but what else can you do?"

Beyond the window the sun was setting, turning the snow-covered roofs of the Old Palace the color of roses. "He comes tonight to dine with me alone at the Topkapi Saraya."

Hürrem put her head on his shoulder. Incredible! One would have to be a complete fool—like Ibrahim—to lose your loyalty. "What will you tell him, my Lord?"

"I never thought this day would ever come."

"We none of us suspect our real future. We only imagine what we dream."

"I cannot end his life, Hürrem. I cannot. I have given my word."

"My Lord?"

"I made a vow when I made him my Vizier—I swore to it in the sight of God!—that while I lived he need not fear me. He has my oath on that."

They sat for a long time in silence. Long shadows crept across the carpets. Pages crept silently into the room to light candles and oil lamps.

"Must he die?" Hürrem whispered.

"The law says he must."

"Then there is a way, though, my Lord, I hesitate to even whisper it. But if it ceases your torment . . ."

"Tell me."

"You have sworn not to put him to death while you are living. Then let the order be carried out while you sleep. The muftis say that while a man sleeps he does not truly live. It is like a small death. So you can fulfil the law, your duty to the throne and to Islam, and not violate your oath."

Süleyman did not answer her for a long time.

"So be it," he said at last.

63

Topkapi Saraya

THE FLICKERING LIGHT of the lamps reflected on the rubies inlaid in the censers. They reminded Ibrahim of the campfires in the valley of Sultania the night before the snowstorm. The memory was like a physical pain in his belly, and he tried to push it away.

He ran a finger around the rim of his jade cup, stared into the rich, dark Cyprian wine. Süleyman was sullen, his eyes hooded. It was not his usual somber broodings that troubled him, Ibrahim knew. This was very different.

"You have given a lashing to the Persian dogs," he said. "They will lick their wounds for a long time."

"Perhaps. But the campaign was not well advised. We were almost drawn into a trap. As it was, the final battle went to the Shah. He will be celebrating now, despite our victories at Tabriz and Baghdad."

"There will be other summers."

"To what purpose? You do not take a cannon to kill a mosquito, Ibrahim."

Ibrahim's anger was sudden. "We have an Empire that rivals that of Alexander the Great. Why should we engage in this moping, as if we had been defeated? We have Baghdad, the Sufavids have the snow and the rocks!"

"We lost many of our most talented young men. The Defterdar Rüstem, for example."

Ibrahim felt the blood drain from his face, and a cold, oily sweat saturated his whole body almost instantly. His spies had whispered to him that Rüstem was still alive, had been seen at Manisa. Rüstem!

He had tried to grapple with the enormity of the betrayal, his instinct finding the truth before his mind had seen it and grasped it. So clever. In other circumstances he might have applauded such sleight of hand. Was this what Süleyman was hinting at now?

"What do you know of Rüstem?" Ibrahim said, without looking up.

"Only that he was murdered by the Shah. Did he volunteer for his mission or did you order him to go?"

"He volunteered. He seemed very eager to go."

"And what was his mission?"

"I attempted to lure the Shah out of the mountains. That was my only intention." It sounds as if I am pleading, Ibrahim thought. Well, perhaps I am. He must know that I did not mean harm against him.

"It seems you failed."

Ibrahim tried to read Süleyman's eyes. God help me in my sorrow! he thought. He does not believe me.

"You must believe I tried everything to bring the Shah out of his hiding place. If I went too far, it was only enthusiasm that was my fault." There. It was said now. It was a plea for forgiveness, without admitting to any sin. What if Süleyman only suspected? What if Rüstem were dead, after all?

Unless Hürrem has had some hand in this, he thought, and he experienced the first cold thrill of fear.

"Well, it is done now."

"There will be other victories, my Lord. Like Rhodes and Mohacs. Do you remember how we stood on the precipice at Rhodes? If we can endure the black times, God is certain to reward us finally."

"It was your counsel that prevailed then, Ibrahim."

"I only wished to serve you."

"And you have served me well, many times. But victory in itself means nothing unless it serves Islam. Perhaps we have forgotten that."

"Every victory furthers Islam."

"You must know the mind of Muhammad before you can speak for him."

Ibrahim swallowed his anger. Even in his panic he bridled at Süleyman's attempt to lecture him. Did he really think he would have prevailed at Rhodes and at Mohacs without him? Or perhaps he did think that. What if Hürrem had been whispering against him?

"I was not born to Muhammad," he said carefully. "I still have much to learn."

"It is too late for that," Süleyman said. "I do not think anyone can teach you anything now."

If he had smiled as he said those words, Ibrahim might have been relieved. But he did not smile.

Ibrahim refused to believe that Süleyman would ever . . .

"Shall we go hunting to Adrianople again this summer?" he said.

"Only God knows the future."

"I could fly the falcons for you again. Like the old days."

Süleyman did not reply.

"Do you remember that time the boar rushed my horse from the thicket, on the Marantza River? You saved my life then."

"You stood and faced it, even though you were unarmed. You looked then as if you were not afraid of anything."

The boar only had razor-sharp tusks, Ibrahim thought. Not a palace full of mutes with bowstrings. "I was not afraid because you were there to protect me."

"I cannot always be there. We must all face death alone at some time."

No! *No!* He could not mean it! I am your Grand Vizier, your seraskier, your friend! I have eaten at your table, slept in your tents through endless campaigns. No, Süleyman, you cannot be contemplating this . . . "The only thing I fear is the way death comes. You swore to me once that you would never condemn me. I could not bear the dishonor of that kind of death."

"I remember my oath. I will never break it."

Ibrahim stared at him in confusion. What then? What is it he is planning? Why these veiled threats, these murmured ambiguities? "My Lord, I am just a man, I have made many mistakes. There is something I must confess—"

Süleyman put out a hand to still him. When Ibrahim looked up, he saw a strange expression on Süleyman's face. He realized with shock that it was pity.

And disgust.

"You do not have to plead your case with me, Ibrahim."

"My Lord—"

"There is no need to say more. I am tired. We will talk again tomorrow."

Süleyman rose to his feet, his head almost too heavy to hold up. The drugged wine had affected him more than it seemed to have affected Ibrahim. But then he wanted more than anything to sleep. He wanted it to be morning, for this ordeal to be over.

"The pages will prepare your bed. Sleep well, my friend."

Ibrahim rose. The end would not come like this, he was sure. Not with a simple goodnight. "Sleep well, my Lord."

Süleyman embraced him, suddenly. Then he pushed him away and disappeared into his private chamber, the door locking behind him.

Süleyman's face was a sickly gray.

Hürrem rose from the bed and hurried over to him. She was naked, except for rose-damask trousers. They rippled in the candlelight as she walked. There was a single pearl fastened around her waist, and her hair was braided with green silk ribbon.

I must not let him brood on what is happening, she reminded herself. I will make him drunk with the wine and with me and when he has had surfeit of both, he will sleep. When he wakes it will be over and there will be no reprieve.

"My Lord . . ." she whispered.

"He all but begged me for life."

She laid her head on his chest. There must be some way to still his doubts, she thought.

"Stop this now," she whispered. "Forget the law. Forget, for once, your duty."

"If I forget my duty, I may no longer call myself Sultan."

"Is there nothing I can do?"

"Hold me, Hürrem."

She led him to the bed.

"Drink this," she whispered, and offered him a goblet of wine.

"It will help me sleep?"

She nodded, and he swallowed it in one draft. He allowed her to undress him then, something he had never before allowed. He sat, with his head bowed, and when she had finished she laid him on the bed and rested her body above him on the bed, her thighs between his.

She raised herself on her arms so that her small breasts brushed his chest. She began to kiss his cheeks and eyes, wriggling her loins against him. He did not respond. She worked her lips along his smooth, shaven body to his groin . . .

Suddenly he twisted away from her and sat up. He started toward the door. "My Lord!"

He turned, his face horrible with grief. "I cannot . . ."

He sank to his haunches, his arms held across his stomach as if experiencing some great pain. Hürrem refilled the goblet with wine from the crystal jug and brought it to him. She held it to his lips, and he gulped it with the desperation of a dying man.

"It will help you sleep, my Lord," she murmured.

"Do not let it happen while I am awake . . ."

"My Lord—"

"Do not allow me break my oath! Let it not happen while I am awake!"

She cradled his head between her breasts, cooing to him as if he were a baby. "Sleep, my Lord. Sleep . . ."

After a while she felt his head growing heavy and he sagged against her. She lay on the floor beside him and held him, while he twitched and muttered in sleep. She stroked his head, and waited for the bostanji to do their work.

64

IBRAHIM PACED THE room, ignoring the bed the pages had made for him, fighting the heaviness of his limbs, and the numbing tiredness that seemed to have invaded his brain. Suddenly his body collided with the wall. He gasped and jerked himself upright. The wine! Süleyman had drugged him! No! *No!* He would never do that! *Never!*

He must stay awake! He would not let them find him sleeping, let them snuff him out like a candle. He was Ibrahim, the most powerful man in the Empire, Vizier to the Magnificent.

He could not die at the Sultan's hand. He had his word, his oath before God.

So why had the pages locked the door behind them?

He groped through the candlelit room like a blind man, fighting the nausea of fear and the dizzying effects of the wine. This is the workings of my imagination, he told himself. This is not happening.

He heard shuffling footsteps in the corridor and a noise that sounded like the yelp of a dog. The deaf-mutes! The bostanji! A key creaked in the lock and the handle began to turn.

God help me in my sorrow!

The door swung open.

There were five of them, all Nubians. The bostanji assassins were eunuchs, prepared for their unique Palace assignments by further mutilation; their eardrums had been pierced with needles, and their tongues had been cut out. This way they could not succumb to the pleas of their victims or reveal their orders in advance.

Ibrahim removed the dagger from his belt and staggered to the wooden door that separated his room from Süleyman's.

He hammered with his fists. "My Lord!"

He looked around. The bostanji were moving toward him.

"My Lord! Süleyman! Please! Stop this!"

SÜLEYMAN JERKED AWAKE. "What was that?"

There were fists hammering on the door. "My Lord! Please!"

Ibrahim! Ibrahim was dying.

Hürrem covered his ears with her hands and cradled his head against her breasts. She started to sing, to drown out the shouts from the next room.

Ibrahim is dying, Süleyman thought. There is no small death of sleep. While I yet live . . .

More hammering. He heard someone scream. It must be Ibrahim.

I have broken my oath. I have murdered my best friend.

But I have obeyed the law.

EACH OF THE bostanji held a silken bowstring, the ritual instrument of execution for those of high position or with royal blood. It was the silken bowstring that had dispatched Süleyman's uncles, cousins, and nephews.

Ibrahim held the dagger in front of him and faced them.

The first bostanji grinned at him and moved in, as if he had not even seen the knife; perhaps he is just confident in his ability to evade it, Ibrahim thought. He lunged toward him, but Ibrahim was ready and sidestepped him easily, the knife snaking upward and outward.

The bostanji stopped in the middle of the room, his eyes wide with surprise. He released the bowstring. Blood was spurting from his neck on to the wall. He put his hands to his throat in a vain attempt to staunch the flow of blood and slowly fell to his knees.

Ibrahim backed against the other wall, as the other bostanji fanned across the center of the room, more wary now. Their comrade fell on his face, thrashing with his legs, the gore still spurting from the gash in his throat.

He saw them signal to each other with deft, almost imperceptible movements of their hands, the language of the bostanji deaf-mutes. He tensed, ready.

They moved quickly, in unison; Ibrahim struck out in a broad arc in front of his body and they leaped back. One of them groaned, a deep, mournful sigh from deep within his chest. There was blood pouring from a gash on his arm.

Ibrahim became aware of the nauseating smell of excrement. The first bostanji had fouled himself in death.

The assassins moved in again, quicker this time. Ibrahim slashed again, and one of them fell, but Ibrahim's shout of defiance was cut off as a bowstring closed around his throat. The remaining two bostanji moved in, but Ibrahim slashed again, desperately, and he saw another of them fall back, clutching his face.

But then the other had his arm, and turned his body away, twisting, trying to break Ibrahim's grip on the knife. The bowstring tightened against his throat.

No, no! I cannot die! I am Ibrahim . . .

He kicked out in panic, between the man's legs, and some part of him immediately registered his mistake. He kicked again, his heel connecting with the man's kidneys this time, and the grip loosened just enough for him to twist his dagger arm free, the blade of the weapon slicing through his assailant's hands and arms as he pulled it away.

He turned it in his hand and stabbed behind him. He felt a rush of warmth on his back and the noose on his throat fell loose. Ibrahim fell back gasping.

Instantly, the dagger was torn from his grip. The bostanji still had the handle of the dagger protruding from his ribs. Ibrahim bent down and tugged at the handle. It would not come free.

Another bowstring closed round his throat. His attacker was one he had already wounded; he felt the blood dripping from the man's arm and down his neck. He kicked again, but the assassin jerked backward with the noose, pulling him off balance.

He put his hands to his throat, tried to slide his fingers under the bowstring, but it was drawn taut, biting deep into the flesh. He could not breathe. His chest spasmed and his arms and legs jerked involuntarily, in an agony of pain.

He kicked out in panic, his reason gone. Bright flashes of light exploded in front of his eyes.

He tried to scream Süleyman's name, but no sound came. He fought, but he could no longer control his limbs. Black shadows closed in from all sides.

Suddenly all memory ended.

The Hippodrome

GÜZÜL HURRIED ALONG the Atmeydani under the imposing red walls of Ibrahim's palace. A messenger had brought an urgent summons to her house in the Jewish quarter a few minutes earlier. Ibrahim wanted to see her.

Now.

She was ushered through the gate by the guards. She hurried across the courtyard to the great stairs that led to the pasha's Hall of Audience. She kept her head down, lifting the skirts of her ferijde, as she ran, taking care not to slip on the thin film of ice that coated the stone.

She was halfway up when she was aware of a figure watching her from the top of the stairs. He wore a fur-lined green pelisse, and great white sugarloaf turban. The Kislar Aghasi! She stared at him in surprise and confusion.

"Ibrahim is dead," Abbas said. There was no triumph in his voice. He sounded sad, if anything. Or reluctant.

Güzül turned and looked behind her. Two bostanji stood at the foot of the stairs, their killiç drawn.

"It is the orders of the Lady Hürrem," Abbas said by way of explanation, and turned away, with no appetite to witness the bostanji complete their work.

Topkapi Saraya

SÜLEYMAN WATCHED FROM a window high above the Third Court as the corpse was loaded onto the back of a horse. A blanket of black velvet had been laid on the horse's back, and a special ointment had been put in its eyes to make it weep. A bostanji led the horse away. Süleyman had ordered the body be taken to Galata, and buried in an unmarked grave.

The two dead bostanji had been dragged from the room. Of the others, Süleyman had been told, one had lost an eye, the other his nose. There were dark splashes on the wall.

"He fought well," Süleyman said.

"Please, my Lord," Hürrem said. "Do not torment yourself. Your orders were just. You could do nothing else."

But she could see that guilt had already begun to eat its way into his heart. His face was white. He was trembling.

"Little russelana . . ." he murmured. He clung to her. After all, she thought with relief, he can cling to no one else.

Not now.

PART 6

THIS WOMAN HÜRREM

65

Çamlica, 1541

ÜLEYMAN WATCHED MUSTAPHA spur his Arab to the crest of the hill. Its long, silky tail stood straight in pureblood fashion. The wind whipped at its red tasseled headgear and Mustapha's white robes. He has grown into a handsome young man, Süleyman thought. A fine prince. Already he has four sons of his own from his harem. Twenty-six years old already. The same age that he had ridden from Manisa to take the throne.

He urged his horse to the rise to join him, watched the archers and their dogs sweeping through the marsh below. The awkward, bowed figure of Çehangir followed, on horseback, the hooded gyrfalcon on his outstretched arm.

Süleyman had been surprised and gratified at the friendship that had developed between Mustapha and Çehangir in the past two weeks. Mustapha's compassionate nature had seen the same virtues that dwelt behind the boy's twisted, deformed frame, and he had taken him under his wing, showing him how to train and hunt with the falcons, spending hours with him in the Place of Arrows, or just riding in the hills beyond the city. Süleyman was gratified by the attention his young shahzade had shown for his least likely half-brother; it mirrored Süleyman's own feelings for the boy.

For his part, Çehangir was in awe of Mustapha and overwhelmed by the attention paid to him. During Mustapha's visit to the capital he had followed him around the saraya like a puppy, and spent hours watching Mustapha ride at the çerit.

"He is a good boy," Süleyman said. "He is a good scholar, and he tries hard to overcome what God has willed."

Mustapha turned in the saddle. "The ghazis need scholars as well as warriors."

Süleyman watched the gyrfalcon sweep into the air, after some prey still invisible to Süleyman. "Promise me you will never harm him," he said.

"Why would I harm him, my Lord?"

"When the throne is yours."

Mustapha seemed angered by the suggestion. "I am not my grandfather."

"It is your right, if you wish it."

"I give you my word, I will not harm him. Do you think I would make so fine a prince that my first act would be to murder my crippled brother?"

"I just want your word."

"You have it."

They stared at each other. I wish I could believe you, Süleyman thought. But I remember how easy it was for my father. His blood is in my veins, and in yours.

"What you do after I am gone to Paradise is with you and with God. But spare Çehangir."

"None of my brothers need have fear of me, my Lord. That bloody custom has ended with my grandfather."

"You may feel differently in time."

"If they do not raise their hands against me, I shall not harm them."

"Selim and Bayezid are almost grown now."

"The decision will be theirs. If they arm against me, then I shall act. That is the way of princes. The throne shall be mine, in time, and I intend to take it. But you may tell them, my Lord, that if they do not draw their swords, they shall live in peace. I want no blood on my throne by choice."

Fine words, Süleyman thought. But how can you be sure what you will do when the whispers begin. He thought of Ibrahim. When was there a day when he did not? "Just promise me you will not harm my Çehangir," he said.

The gyrfalcon swooped down on its quarry and the dogs bayed and sprang forward and the yeniçeri archers let out a whoop of triumph. Another life ended on a beautiful spring morning.

The Eski Saraya

THE SHADOWS RETREATED across Asia toward the cold dark of Europe. Sunlight inched through the cloisters and dark gardens, dissolving the wisps of white mist that curled among the roofs. A spider, clinging to its beaded web, was outlined against a lemon sky. An owl tolled the watchsong of the dawn among the cypress.

Hürrem was shrouded in a fur pelisse, her hair hanging loose about her shoulders, uncombed and unbraided. She shivered as she leaned against the lattice, staring across the waking city to the tower of the Kubbealti and the minarets of the Aya Sofia, flashing like the tips of lances as they broke through the morning mist.

All across the city the muezzins began to call the faithful to prayer. "*Allahu akbar! La ilaha illa' llah . . .*"

From here she could see the ancient Burned Column of Alexander, overlooking the marketplace where she had been sold. A slave then, and for all her power and wealth, a slave now.

And a heartbeat away from oblivion. If Mustapha should live, she thought, my sons will be murdered or imprisoned, I will be banished to some lonely palace in Anatolia, with only the jackals and goats for company.

A slave then, a slave now.

She called for Muomi to come and perform her toilet. She sat in front of the mirror and watched her comb out her hair, staring at her reflection. This morning she felt as if she were staring over the edge of a cliff. And there was only blackness beyond.

"Stop!" she ordered.

She leaned closer to the glass. She withdrew her hand from the pelisse and ran her fingers through the gold strands of her hair, saw the terrible truth confirmed. A gray hair.

You are getting older, the mirror said. You cannot deny me any longer. The tiny lines at the corner of my eyes will grow deeper until you can no longer hide them with kohl, and my first gray hair will be followed by others until you can no longer tell yourself it is all a trick of the light. You are helpless to watch your beauty crumble and fade in front of your eyes.

And what will happen then? Will the Lord of Life still be yours to command, for all your charms? Will he still forget that he has a paradise of willing, ambitious little houris eager to use their transient beauty to replace you in his bed? Is there another Julia priming her supple flesh in the hammam? Worse, is there another Hürrem scheming to exile you, as you did Gülbehar?

Hürrem snatched the ivory-handled brush from Muomi and smashed it into the mirror, splintering her reflection into shards.

"Get Abbas," she screamed. "Get him now!"

"How is Julia?"

Abbas felt himself once more falling toward a black pit. She would never let him be, this witch. She would torment him with this until death. Damn Ludovici. He had put him at her mercy. What did she want from him now?

"I trust she is well," Abbas said.

They were alone in Hürrem's audience chamber, their voices lost to the echoes of the high-vaulted ceilings and drowned by the murmuring of the marble fountains along the walls. It was in a room such as this that one might be called to account before God, Abbas thought. Then he looked into Hürrem's cold green eyes and he thought: No, not God. The Devil.

She sat on the divan, her legs tucked beneath her, her body curled into the fur of the long green pelisse. She was smiling.

"Oh, Abbas, you should not be frightened of me. I am your friend. If I intended to denounce you to the Lord of Life, I would have done it long ago."

"I live only to serve my Sultan and the Crown of Veiled Heads. I am thankful for your pardon, though I shall surely answer for all my sins before God."

Hürrem clapped her hands in delight. "What a fine speech! You have become the perfect diplomat, Abbas. You are a credit to all eunuchs everywhere!"

How I would like to rip out your evil tongue and keep it in a jar! "And you are a credit to all women everywhere, my Lady."

Hürrem cocked her head to one side, and her tongue traversed her upper lip. She got up slowly, letting the pelisse fall away from her shoulders. She was quite naked.

Abbas gritted his teeth and lowered his eyes to the floor.

"What is the matter, Abbas? Am I too ugly to look at?"

"No, my Lady, your loveliness dazzles me," Abbas said, trying to maintain control of his own voice. Nearly twenty years in the Harem have done you little harm, he thought. You know your body can still stir a man, even an incomplete one. You have taken care never to suckle any of your infants and you have not dedicated yourself to sweetbreads like some of the other fat old crows. But why are you doing this to me? Because it amuses you to see me suffer, no doubt.

"They tell me you were razored after puberty. How old were you, Abbas?"

"Seventeen years old, my Lady."

"Did you have knowledge of women before then?"

"Some, my Lady."

"Not many survive such an operation at that age, do they? You were lucky."

"I should hardly call it luck," he said, before he could check himself.

She reached up and stroked his cheek. He could smell her perfume. "Poor Abbas. Do you still sometimes feel desire, then?"

He lowered his eyes to her body. Oh great God, help me in my sorrow! She knew the answer to that, of course. Even in his hatred he wanted to caress the soft outline of her breast, tenderly, like a lover. The look in his eyes had already betrayed him, he knew.

"No, my Lady."

"Not even for Julia?" she asked, and her voice dripped honey.

He felt himself choking. "No, my Lady."

"I can have your unbiased opinion, then. Do you think I am still as lovely as the other girls in my Lord's Harem?"

She turned around slowly on the tips of her toes.

"Indeed you are," Abbas said.

She smiled, her eyes glittering like emeralds. "Isn't it strange. A naked woman is powerless before a real man. Yet with you I am quite safe. It creates a bond between us, doesn't it, Abbas?"

To the death, Abbas thought. Mine. Or yours. "We are tied by the bonds of service."

"Exactly. And you have to give your service to me, don't you? Because of Julia."

Just tell me what you want. Stop tormenting me. Tell me what you want, and leave me in peace.

"I want you to do something for me," Hürrem said.

"You have only to name your desire."

"My desire?" She watched for his reaction. "My desire is that you burn down the Harem. I want this place utterly destroyed. You can do that for me, can you not, Abbas. Yes?"

66

THE SIROCCO ORIGINATES in the Sahara, its hot, dry breath scalding the North African coast before moving north across the Mediterranean. By the time it reaches the far shores it is heavy with moisture. Thunderheads bank to the stars behind it. Everything wilts.

Tonight the Sirocco rushed through the narrow streets of Stamboul, bending the branches of the cypress and plane trees in the Palace gardens, whipping the red and green flags of the Palace into a frenzy, piling froth onto the far shores of the Bosphorus. The atmosphere became sodden and oppressive, but the rains had not yet come.

Perfect weather, Abbas thought.

He had delayed four nights before judging the time to execute Hürrem's latest caprice. The Palace was in darkness when he set off with two bostanji, through a little-used gate in the southern wall. The three eunuchs were gone for less than an hour but when they returned, an eerie orange-pink stain was already creeping up the horizon, and over the roofs of the cramped, wooden houses, a false dawn.

When they were safely back inside the saraya, Abbas found the bostanji-bashi and slipped an emerald ring into his palm. He used the bostanji's own sign language to indicate that the two men who had accompanied him on his errand should not live to see the morning.

Then he retired to his cell and waited, wondering what other sins he might yet commit in the name of survival.

THE BOOMING OF the wooden tambours echoed through the dark streets. The Palace woke to the cries of "*Yanghinvar! Fire!*"

Abbas ran from his cell. The cloisters were still empty, but he could hear women screaming from one of the upstairs dormitories. In the courtyard below, the two guards had drawn their yataghans in confusion—

idiots, Abbas thought impatiently—but remained at their posts, circling each other in bewilderment.

Abbas detected the acrid odor of smoke.

He did not hesitate; after all, he had had days to rehearse each move. And Hürrem had already made it quite clear what his first duty should be.

He rousted two of his pages from their beds and rattled off the list of instructions he had memorized by heart. Prepare the coaches. Get all the women downstairs to the courtyard. Send six other pages to the dressmaker and bring all of the Lady Hürrem's possessions down to safety.

Naturally, he thought, she could not leave anything of hers behind. Not even if the whole city roasted.

Then he lumbered up the stairs to her apartments.

HE WAS ASTONISHED at her appearance. She has been grooming herself all night, he thought. She was wearing a stunning emerald-green kaftan of alternating crescents and stars over a white chemise emblazoned with rumi scrollwork in gold thread. Her hair was plaited with tiny emeralds and pearls, and her yashmak was in place. Muomi stood beside her, holding a ferijde of violet silk.

She was wearing a perfume of jasmine and oranges. Of course, he thought. She will not present herself to Süleyman, freshly rescued from the fire, if she is reeking of smoke.

"What took you so long, my Aga?" Hürrem hissed. "Was it your intention that I should cook in my bed?"

"They have just sounded the alarm, my Lady," Abbas gasped. He was panting from the exertion of climbing the two flights of stairs.

"Why would you need to wait for the alarm? You already knew the city was alight!"

Abbas lurched to the latticed window, and groaned aloud. God help me in my sorrow, he thought. I had not meant for half the city to be swallowed by the conflagration! The wind had worked the flames into a frenzy and the wooden buildings on the hill below them were being gobbled up in moments. The fire was rolling toward them like a wave.

House after house crackled and splintered like a falling tree and caved in, sending another shower of sparks high into the night sky. In the alleys below, people rushed away, their backs loaded with their meager possessions, tripping over each other in their panic. The mass of terrified humanity looked like a river flooding through a chasm, a torrent of torches and baskets and staring-eyed oxen, blindfolded, rearing horses, and unveiled women.

God forgive me, Abbas thought. I never imagined this.

A red-hot cinder was hurled along on the wind and caught his cheek. He howled and jumped backward.

"We must hurry!" he shouted.

"I have been ready for hours," Hürrem said, as if she were late for a formal entertainment in the Hippodrome.

Muomi helped Hürrem slip into her cloak, drawing the *cazeta* over her face, preserving her anonymity and thus her dignity. Muomi put on her own black ferijde and Abbas led them out of the apartment and down the stairs.

He felt his heart barreling around inside his chest. Fear, exertion, excitement, pulsed through him. He had assumed they would have more time. In a real emergency, he thought, I could not cope. There would not be time to get everything ready. Even now, I might be too late.

The coaches were already waiting. "Get . . . inside!" Abbas shouted, gasping for breath.

The two small shrouded figures pushed past him and into the first coach. One of them—he knew it must be Hürrem—pulled aside the taffeta curtain and a hand snaked out of the ferijde and grasped his own. The hooded head leaned out toward him, and for one moment he thought she was about to whisper her thanks.

"Leave behind anything of mine," she hissed, her features invisible behind the violet gauze of the cazeta, "anything at all—and it will be your head!"

Topkapi Saraya

ABBAS SLUMPED GRATEFULLY to his knees to execute the required sala'am at the feet of the Lord of Life. He rested his forehead on the carpet a little longer than was necessary and was almost unable to rise to his feet once more. His pelisse reeked of woodsmoke and his face and sugarloaf turban were smeared with grime.

Süleyman watched him, his face creased with anguish.

"A thousand pardons, my Lord," Abbas gasped.

"Does my servant need the physician?" Süleyman asked.

"I am merely fatigued, my Lord." He staggered slightly on his feet.

"There has been a fire at the Eski Saraya?" Süleyman waited impatiently for the Kislar Aghasi to tell his story and leave. Where was Hürrem?

"The Palace was in flames when I left. However all the women are safe."

"Hürrem?"

"She awaits outside the door, my Lord. I guarded her life as I might that of your most . . ." Again, he staggered and recovered ". . . precious treasure."

"We are in your debt," Süleyman said. Depart and let me see Hürrem, he thought. He was aware that he himself was not the image of propriety. He had been awakened from his sleep and had barely had time to dress. He wore only a white silk kaftan, and fez. He was dressed to see his little russelana, not for formal audience. "There were no injuries at all?"

"I fear a number of my pages and guards were burned in the fire . . . as they were attempting to recover some of my Lady's clothes and jewels from her apartment."

"The Palace is destroyed?"

"My last vision of it . . . it was totally engulfed in flame."

"I commend you, Abbas, for your efforts. Send in the Lady Hürrem and then rest yourself. We shall speak again in the morning."

"My Lord," Abbas said, and slumped again to the ground to perform a final sala'am. For a moment Süleyman feared he was about to fall unconscious but with one final effort he raised his great bulk from the floor and staggered from the room.

A few moments later a figure swathed in violet silk appeared and almost immediately slumped to the ground. Süleyman leaped from the divan and rushed across the room.

"Hürrem? Are you all right?"

He threw back the cazeta. Hürrem's face was pale and cold as marble, her eyes red-rimmed and swollen from crying.

"My little russelana . . . are you hurt?"

She shook her head, and he felt her tremble in his arms like a small bird. "They should not have gone back into the flames," she whispered.

"Who?"

"Those poor servants . . . they were only a few trinkets, a few silks . . . not worth a life . . ."

He hugged her to him, felt her heartbeat against his side and thanked God for it. "When the messenger told me about the fire and I saw the glow above the saraya . . . I knew if you were hurt I could not go on. Thank God you were saved."

"It was terrible, my Lord. It was the smell of smoke that woke me . . . I thought I was going to die . . ."

He threw back the hood and tore open the ferijde. "Are you hurt anywhere?"

"I am not hurt, my Lord. I thank God for it."

He buried his face in her neck, clinging to her with relief, the woodsmoke mingling with the jasmine and orange scent of her. Gratitude swiftly transformed into desire. He hooked the first and second fingers of his right hand into the V of the chemise and tore downward, ripping the silk apart, tearing the gömlek and kaftan together down the full length of her.

"Until the coaches came I feared you were gone," he whispered, urgently.

"It was kismet," she whispered back.

His hands explored the soft, giving flesh, as if to satisfy himself that she was whole and alive, that she was really there. "My little russelana," he said, and felt his voice catch in his throat. He eased up his own gown and rolled between her legs, almost sobbing with relief.

His little russelana. Where would he be without her?

SÜLEYMAN DOES NOT look quite as well disposed to the mercies of the Great God this morning, Abbas thought. He looks, perhaps, even a little sour.

"You must accommodate Hürrem and the other women in the Palace here until other arrangements can be made," Süleyman said.

"It poses a problem, my Lord," Abbas said carefully.

"I do not wish to hear of problems."

"My Lord, I would not burden you with such trivialities, but it requires your special permission."

"To set aside one corner of the Palace as my *haremlik*? How difficult might it be to find rooms for a few women and their servants?"

Despite himself, Abbas felt a glow of pleasure. Could it be that the Lord of Life was really so ignorant of the true size of his Harem—and, in particular, Hürrem's private arrangements? "My Lord, my Lady Hürrem's retinue alone is a large one, as befitting the favored kadin of the Lord of Life."

Süleyman shifted irritably on his throne. "How large?"

"She has herself thirty pages and slaves . . ."

"Thirty!"

". . . and one hundred and three ladies in waiting . . ."

"What?"

". . . and of course her purveyor and dressmaker. It means a total of one hundred and thirty-seven people, including myself and, of course, the Lady Hürrem."

"Abbas!"

"Add to that number the one hundred and nine girls who still remain in my Lord's Harem, plus perhaps an equal number of black pages and hand-maidens . . ."

Süleyman tugged at the wispy beard on his chin, his other hand drum-ming on the arm of the throne. "My private quarters will be totally domi-nated by the Harem!"

"Until other arrangements are made, my Lord," Abbas said, and strug-gled to keep the note of satisfaction from his voice. Yes, she's a little witch, isn't she, Süleyman?

Süleyman sighed. "Very well."

"My Lord?"

"There is nothing that may be done. The Harem must be housed some-where. Take whatever rooms you need, I will authorize it. In the meantime I shall summon the architect, Sinan. We shall have to set to work on a new saraya for the Harem immediately."

67

THERE ARE LINES around her eyes, Selim thought. I never noticed them before. But then, how often have I seen her in the last twelve months? He kissed her hand and Bayezid did the same. Then they stood back, their arms crossed on their breasts as they had been taught in the Enderun. Hürrem examined them both critically. Muomi stood behind her, on her right.

Selim hated her. Black and sullen and malevolent. She's the witch, he thought, not mother.

Mother's just evil.

"You've grown into a fine boy, Bayezid. Your tutors tell me you are a fine horseman and athlete."

"Thank you, Mother."

"But you must study more. Even when you leave the Enderun, you should never stop learning. If you are ever to become Sultan you will need more than just a horse and a javelin to succeed."

"I will do my best, Mother."

He will ignore you completely, Selim thought. My brother's handsome head is as hollow as a drum.

"And you, Selim . . ." Hürrem sighed, and her face registered her displeasure. "They say you are too fond of sweetbreads."

"I study hard," he said.

"Your tutors have to pound every lesson into your head with their knuckles."

Yes, they do. And I will never, ever forget it. "I will do my best, Mother," Selim said, testing the defense Bayezid had used.

"Your best is not good enough. You are my firstborn. You are the one on whom the hopes of the Osmanlis rest if anything should ever happen to Mustapha."

He knew from the way she looked at Bayezid that her hopes resided elsewhere. It was never a secret who her favorite was.

She was not alone, of course. He was everyone's favorite. The tutors loved him. Everyone loved him except Süleyman. He doted on his other idiot brother, Çehangir, now Mehmet was dead. So unlike him to get sick. Until then he had been so perfect.

Selim tried to conceal his excitement. At last he had the chance to get away from the Palace, away from the shadow of Bayezid. As he took up his governorship in Konia, Bayezid would be on the other side of the Anatolian plateau, at Amasya. Perhaps he would fall off his horse one day, playing his beloved çerit.

One might always hope to the Great God for such miracles.

"You must write to me often," Hürrem said.

"We will, Mother," Bayezid said for both of them. I will curse you every dawn and evening in my prayers, Selim thought. You have always hated the sight of me.

"My hopes rest in you," Hürrem said. Then she turned to Selim with a beatific smile. "Oh, Selim! You are the shape of a watermelon!"

THE SHAPE OF a watermelon.

Selim often wondered who it was he hated the most: himself, for not being more like Süleyman, or Bayezid because he was. While he was olive and fat, Bayezid was lean and tall and handsome. It was one of life's cruel jokes: two brothers, born under the same roof, one with personality and strength and talent, the other without talents at all. He imagined God would have the same sense of humor as his mother.

Selim's only consolation was Çehangir.

Çehangir was seven years younger, born a hunchback and a cripple. If God had been cruel to Selim, he had been vicious to Çehangir, and it had become Selim's consolation in his earlier years to taunt him with his bad fortune. It won him a little attention and even some grudging laughter.

Çehangir had been sent to the Enderun when he was eight years old. Selim used to follow him across the courtyard every morning, trailing one leg stiffly behind him, his shoulders hunched, his head bowed, imitating his younger brother's curious lopsided walk.

It was an easy way to evince laughter from the others. And he had already discovered that finding another target was the best means of deflecting ridicule from himself. Besides, Çehangir never complained. How could he? He already knew he was an embarrassment. He would not have dared attract further attention to himself.

But one day Bayezid was there. Selim was not even aware of him. He was trailing Çehangir across the cobbled courtyard, savoring the muted echoes of his audience's laughter, when suddenly the laughter was cut short.

Something tripped him up and he found himself lying on his back. Bayezid was standing over him. He reached down and cuffed him smartly, twice, across the face.

"He's our brother!" Bayezid shouted at him. "What do you think you're doing?"

Selim rolled aside and scrambled to his feet, aware that every eye was on him. His cheeks burned with humiliation. Bayezid was two years younger. He could not let him best him.

He charged.

Bayezid easily stepped aside and tripped him again, throwing him headlong onto the hard cobbles. Selim gasped as pain coursed through his knee and his elbow. It paralyzed him. He was convinced he had broken a bone and he lay still, sobbing.

"If I see you mocking our brother again, I'll break your head!" he heard Bayezid hiss at him.

The other boys moved away, whispering. Several of them laughed out loud. After a while the pain subsided and he sat up. His head was bleeding and he could barely straighten his leg. He groaned aloud and wiped the bitter tears from his eyes.

The courtyard was almost empty now. Only Çehangir remained. He shuffled over and offered Selim his hand. But Selim could not bear the look of genuine anguish in his eyes and so he ignored him and staggered to his feet unaided. He turned his back and limped away.

THE ENDERUN WAS the inner school of the Palace, where the princes were groomed for leadership along with the cream of the devshirme. Aside from the princes, whose blood had been diluted by generations of concubines anyway, none of the other boys were Turks. The young Christian slaves were taught they no longer possessed any family, any country, any future, outside the Sultan.

They learned the Qur'ān in Turkish, Arabic, and Persian; they were trained in pike- and lance-throwing as well as music, embroidery, and the care and training of birds and dogs. They were taught good manners and honesty, falconry, leatherwork and weapon making, as well as manicuring, haircutting and turban dressing.

Their lives were strictly regulated: they had a bath daily, and a manicure and pedicure every week. They were given a fresh handkerchief each day, and a haircut once every month. Discipline was strict and included frequent beatings or even the bastinado from the white eunuchs who were charged with their education, men who looked for all the world to Selim like mummified old women.

Graduates of the Enderun learned not only how to become soldiers but were taught also all the principles of statecraft and courtly behavior. For six years they would not leave the Palace, undergoing a constant process of culling. The best would be inducted into the Palace system, as treasury clerks or masters of the wardrobe and might become pashas or governors in time. Others might become pashas and officers in the Spahis of the Porte, the Imperial Cavalry.

Only Selim and Bayezid and Çehangir attended the Enderun through hereditary right and not through merit, a distinction that was only painless for Bayezid, whose proficiency on horseback and easygoing charm soon earned him the respect of his classmates and his tutors.

For Selim, every day was a nightmare, and he longed for the day when power would disguise his shortcomings.

One of his tutors, Hakim, even beat him when he could not recite his

Qur'ān, although he would never beat Bayezid. Once he even put Selim to the bastinado. It was a simple device: stocks secured the feet, and the soles were beaten with long sticks. Even five years later Selim could still recall the pain. Each blow had made him shriek like a baby, and Hakim only finished when Selim had begged through his tears for him to stop. He had been unable to walk for a week and it was a month before the scars healed.

As soon as he could walk again he tried to kill Bayezid.

There was a playing field below the walls of the Second Court where the boys of the Enderun practiced the çerit; the tutors called it a game, though it was in fact more like a mock battle. They used horses with short necks and strong bodies, bred for their speed and ability to check quickly. Riders, armed with javelins three and a half feet long, would maneuver in two teams of twelve around an open field and hurl their weapons at each other's heads. The side with the most hits at the end of the "game" would be declared the winner.

There were frequent injuries and sometimes boys were killed. Selim dreaded it, but Bayezid threw himself into the game with typical recklessness, and excelled at it.

Although they were on opposite teams—Bayezid rode for the Blues, the Sultan's favored team (of course), and Selim for the Greens—he knew that any attempt to injure Bayezid himself was doomed to failure. He was just too good a rider. All that would happen was that Selim would expose himself to risk. His usual tactic was to hang back and try and preserve his own skin.

It was a simple enough matter to find Bayezid's horse and cut halfway through the saddle with a knife before the start of a game.

Tents had been pitched around the field, and crowds of yeniçeris clustered around to watch the sport, as they often did when not away on campaigns. Selim knew that the Sultan would probably be watching also, from the walls overlooking the field.

Well, they won't be able to cheer their young hero today, Selim thought. I'd like to see Hakim's face when Bayezid is trampled under the hoofs.

The two teams of riders circled each other, the thunder of the hoofs echoing from the Palace walls. Clouds of dust drifted across the field. The leading rider of the Blues—the proud hooked nose of Bayezid beneath the turban—wheeled his horse and charged. Two riders from Selim's own team split from the group and headed toward him, at full tilt. Selim pulled

at the reins, checking his own horse to the flank of the group so that he
might have a better view of what was about to happen.

As the riders closed, he heard a shout, and saw a body fall. The horses
thundered over the top of a figure in white, who lay facedown and still in
the dust.

Immediately the other two riders dropped their javelins and leaped
from their horses.

"It's Bayezid!" someone shouted. "He's hurt!"

Selim walked his mount through the settling clouds of dust and milling
horses. Bayezid had not moved. There was a satisfying smudge of blood on
his younger brother's turban. He tried to look concerned.

"Is he dead?" he asked, hopefully.

BUT BAYEZID DID not die. The lump on his head was impressive, and he
limped badly for many weeks and could not ride the çerit, but he did not
die. When it was discovered that the fault was with the saddle harness,
Hakim himself was put to the bastinado for negligence and exiled to Bitlis.
It was some compensation for Bayezid's survival.

But now, as he said his goodbyes to his mother, he realized the fragility
of his position. When his father died . . . tomorrow, in thirty years, but
someday . . . the fight for the succession would begin. It would begin with
Mustapha, and he guessed that even his noble soul would not hesitate to
have all Hürrem's spawn executed to protect his throne.

If, by some great fortune, he were already dead, the throne would be
Selim's. But he did not imagine for an instant that Bayezid would let him
have it. One of them would have to die. The Fatih's law allowed for a Sultan
to kill all his brothers and their children to protect his succession and the
stability of the Empire.

That was his own future, he knew. He would one day be Sultan, or he
would one day be dead.

"Go in peace," Hürrem said to Bayezid and Selim.

HÜRREM SAT WITH her eyes focused on the vaulted ceilings, unseeing,
long after they had gone. A germ of an idea had insinuated itself in her
mind. It nagged at her, like a mosquito in a darkened room. It was persis-
tent and threatening, but she could not quite grasp it whole.

Selim.

He was so obviously not a son of Süleyman, yet by the time he had grown, Çehangir had been born to cast doubt on everything. Who would have believed the Lord of Life could have sired a hunchback cripple? So why not a fat, pasty-faced, and surly youth with no real talent except for nursing slights?

Yet he did not look so much like the Kapi Aga either, Hürrem thought. Those dangerous days in the court of the Eski Saraya seemed so long ago, but in Selim they lived on. For a long time after the birth she had been unsure whether his father was Süleyman or the Chief White Eunuch. She still had her doubts. Yet he certainly did not behave like an Osmanli. She had heard what the Valide had said about him, and she reluctantly agreed with the assessment. He was no ghazi, and no Sultan.

Anyway, did it matter?

As it was, just one life stood between her and becoming the mother of the next Sultan. It was quite obvious to her which of the boys would succeed in any struggle for the throne, and which one should therefore have her blessing and her encouragement. Bayezid would make a fine Sultan, a magnificent one, almost as good as Mustapha.

And then the idea gelled in her mind in one panoramic and glorious image and she laughed aloud.

68

The Bosphorus, off Çamlica

THEY ESCAPED THE heat of the hot August night by seeking refuge on the slick, waveless waters of the Bosphorus. A black and gold caïque was always in readiness at the water's edge by Seraglio Point, and Süleyman took his ease there with Hürrem, accompanied only by three deaf-mute bostanji, at the tiller and the oars. The torches that burned at the prow and stern threw long shadows over the oily waters.

He sat beside her in the cabin at the stern of the rowing barge, anonymous behind the heavy black velvet curtains. Hürrem peered out once, saw the dark cedar-grown cemeteries of Çamlica sliding past in the darkness.

He was silent, preoccupied, Hürrem thought. He had changed since Ibrahim's death. At first she assumed that the passage of time would salve his conscience, but instead the iron of guilt had embedded itself into his soul. He seldom laughed anymore. He had dismissed all the singers of the seraglio, and had their musical instruments burned. He only rarely asked her to play for him now. He said the music of the viol reminded him too much of Ibrahim.

He had become almost ascetic and had learned to punish himself in small ways. He had had the fine green and white Chinese porcelain that had been his favorite sent back to the treasure house at Yedikule, and instead ate exclusively from earthenware. He had grown a wispy beard, and had not allowed one drop of wine to pass his lips since Ibrahim's death.

"I have consulted with Sinan," he said. "He has drawn some plans I would like you to see."

"You are going to build a great mosque in my honor, my Lord?"

"It is not holy to joke in such a way."

"I thought you liked me to be a little wicked sometimes."

"I have asked him to design a new Palace on the ruins of the old Eski Saraya. I believe he has surpassed himself this time."

"He always surpasses himself," Hürrem said. He is obsessed with the rebuilding of Stamboul, she thought. As if another mosque, another school, will somehow remove Ibrahim's blood from the Palace walls.

"I would like you to study his plans and give them your approval."

Hürrem pouted, folding her arms. "Is it so terrible having me in the Palace? Can you not abide my presence a moment longer?"

"You know that is not the case. But there is simply no room for the Harem at the Royal Palace. It is impossible."

"Of course it is possible. A man could gallop all day through the Fourth Court and still not reach Seraglio Point."

"A wild exaggeration, little russelana."

"There is more than enough room to build there."

"There are other considerations."

"Tell me them."

"Considerations of state."

"It sounds so pompous, my Lord."

"The Harem simply cannot be part of the Royal Palace." Süleyman said angrily. "It has always been that way, ever since the Fatih."

"It is still a large Harem, my Lord. Do you still hunger for the other girls?"

"Of course not."

"Then perhaps if you no longer require them, you could order the Kislar Aghasi to find them husbands. Then it would be just me and my household."

"What you are asking is unthinkable. Sinan has been commissioned. There is an end to it."

Hürrem realized she had perhaps gone too far. She nuzzled closer to him, resting her head on his chest. She had not expected that he would agree. There was one other way . . . "I am sorry, my Lord, if I gave you offense. It is just that I will hate so to be parted from you again."

"Hürrem, sometimes you forget yourself," he whispered, his voice sounding hoarse.

She nestled closer to him. "Do you love me, my Sultan?"

He smiled. "I love you more than my life."

"More than Gülbehar?"

Gülbehar! He had not thought about her for months. "You know I do."

"Yet she is first kadin."

"It is the law."

"But you love me more?"

What does she want from me? Süleyman thought. I have sent Gülbehar away. I do not visit my Harem unless it is to see her. What more could she want? "I love you more than I have loved any woman."

"And will you make me your queen one day?"

Süleyman said nothing for a long time, dazzled by the impertinence of the suggestion. Then he started to laugh.

"What are you laughing at?"

"Do not look so angry, little russelana."

"Why are you laughing at me?"

"It's impossible."

"Impossible to think of me as anything but a slave?"

Well, what did you expect of her? he asked himself. If she were a little mouse, like Gülbehar, you would not have chosen her. Of course she would always be looking for more.

"The Sultan may not marry."

"It is the Law? It is part of the Sheri'at?"

"There is nothing written."

"Then why not?"

Süleyman put out a hand to brush an errant strand of hair from her face but she twisted away. "No Sultan has married since Bayezid the First."

"You are greater than Bayezid. You are greater than any Sultan there has been."

"No, Hürrem. I am no greater. Certainly not greater than my father, Selim, nor my great grandfather, the Fatih."

"Dead men make the rules for you? You are the Kanuni, the Lawgiver. You are the Sultan. Not ghosts from the past."

He sighed. "I will tell you a story, about our history and the very first Bayezid of the Osmanlis. He was Sultan long before we came here to Stamboul, when we were still practically nomads. He had married a Serbian princess, a beautiful woman; her name was Despina. At the time we were struggling with the Mongols for control of Anatolia. Bayezid met Tamerlane in battle at Angora and was defeated. It was a terrible defeat; Bayezid was captured, and so was Despina. Tamerlane wanted to humiliate us, so he forced Despina to wait naked on Tamerlane and his generals at his table. It was the darkest moment in our history. The shame of it still burns with every ghazi. Our weakness, you see, is our women. Since then no Sultan has ever married. We can never be weak that way again."

"That was long ago. Your people were nomads then. Now you are Lord of the world's greatest Empire. Who will ever take me prisoner, my Lord?"

Süleyman sighed. It seemed the importance of the story had been lost on her. "What you ask is impossible."

"There are no more Tamerlanes. The whole world quakes at your feet . . ."

"Let us not talk more about it."

"But my Lor—"

"We talk no more about it!"

She slipped to her knees on the floor of the barge, and kissed his hand. "Forgive me, my Lord. My passion for you sometimes drowns the voice of my reason."

She felt him lift her from the floor, and onto his lap. His broad hands were on her shoulders, and his face had a look of weary forbearance, as if he were admonishing a small child. "I want you to give me your opinion

on Sinan's plans. Let that be an end to it. You are fortunate that I indulge
you so much, Hürrem."

"Yes, my Lord," she whispered, and lowered her eyes.

She allowed him to lay her on the divan beside him, her hands above her
head, surrendering to him as he slowly unfastened the pearl buttons of her
chemise. The night was warm. The moans of the Sultan's pleasures drifted
across the still, black waters, but the deaf-mutes were oblivious to all
sounds, and only the owls in the cemetery at Camlica added to the sym-
phony of the night.

69

Stamboul

THE AYA SOFIA had once been the greatest church in all Christendom,
until the Fatih had conquered Constantinople and claimed it as his
mosque. Every part of the great church, except the great wood and
iron Imperial Doors, was covered in millions of sapphire-blue and gold
tiles, blazing with mosaics of the Queen of Heaven and Christ Pantocrator.
A great dome soared overhead, seemingly unsupported, like the cupped
hand of God. It was said that when Justinian entered his great creation for
the first time, almost one thousand years before, he had exclaimed: "Glory
to God that I have been judged worthy of such a work. Oh Solomon! I have
outdone you!"

It was sunset, the hour of lamp lighting, but the flicker of the lamps
could not pierce the gloom of the vast mosque. Far below, the Reader
was illuminated by a sepia spotlight from the stained window above him,
the last light of the day. He stood on the prayer stand, a sword in one hand,
a Qur'ān in the other, his voice echoing around the walls from the great
blue dome.

Hürrem was concealed behind a latticed screen, kneeling on her *seccade,*
a ruby-red and ivory prayer rug of age-worn silk. Below her, thousands of
turbans bobbed in unison, whispers of supplication murmuring around the
walls like the sound of distant thunder. This ritual, though it still meant

nothing to her, always impressed her with its power. What a vast energy it was to tap! Here was the fountainhead of the Osmanli Empire.

Perhaps, she thought, a velvet fist I have overlooked in my contempt.

The droning baritone of the mufti and the repetition of movement focused her mind perfectly. She had achieved so much, she decided, but she had still not approached this mysterious vortex. She was still at the mercy of Süleyman's caprice. She had no control over her own fate. Or the future of her sons.

It seemed Süleyman was intent on building a new Harem Palace on the site of the old. Yet now, with the Eski Saraya in ashes, was perhaps her best opportunity to persuade him to relinquish it. If he made her his queen, she would be safe from another Julia, another Laughing One.

Whenever she thought of the injustice of it, it torched again the fury smoldering inside her. It was unbearable. Slave girls who had come to the Harem at the same time as she had long ago been married off to some pasha or spahi officer, and now had their own property, and status as a wife. She, the favorite of the Lord of Life, still remained a slave. She was Süleyman's constant companion and bedmate, but it was another woman's son who would inherit the throne after Süleyman's death.

She touched her forehead to the carpet, murmuring her prayers, aware of the gloom gathering through the great church, a thousand lamps glowing brighter around the walls. The answer was illuminated in her mind that same way, slowly and inexorably.

Yes, there was a way to persuade Süleyman to make her his queen. It lay here, with Islam. She would use the will of God to bend him to the will of his woman.

Manisa

THE GARDENS OF Mustapha's haremlik blazed with hundreds of tulips. Gülbehar sat alone in a kiosk below the turrets of the fortress wall, gazing at them, listening to the rhythm of the bees. She did not hear her son approach.

"Hello, Mother."

"Mustapha!"

"I find you well?"

She smiled with surprise and pleasure, and held out her hand. He raised it to his lips and sat down beside her. "Better for knowing you are returned!" she said to him. She clutched his hand in both of hers and would not let it go. "I have missed you! How was Stamboul?"

"Ripe with gossip, as always. Everyone, from the lowliest hawker to the Mixer of the Sultan's Cordials fancies himself as seraskier and plans the next campaign against the Holy Roman Empire."

"I am sure they will leave you some part of it to conquer when you are Sultan."

He grinned. "If God is merciful."

She searched his eyes. "You saw your father?"

"I saw him."

"Did he ask after me?"

"He sends his felicitations for your continued good health."

Her smile vanished. "I keep thinking one day he will ask for me again. But what would he want with an old woman? He still consorts with the ziadi?"

"Mother . . . she is not a witch. She is just a woman."

"You love him too much, Mustapha. He's not the saint you think."

Mustapha squeezed her hand. "I do not condone what he did to you. But he is my father and my Sultan. Never ask me to speak against him."

Gülbehar pouted. Bitterness has made you ugly, Mustapha thought, with genuine sadness. It has turned down the corners of your mouth, and put too much gray into your hair.

Gülbehar seemed to sense what he was thinking and turned her face away. She had promised herself that when he returned she would be gay and attentive and not speak of Süleyman. But as soon as she had seen him, there had been this urge to know. In truth, she had thought of nothing else since he had been gone. Süleyman, Süleyman . . . my Lord, my Life.

She forced a smile. "And what other news from the city?"

"There were great dramas while I was there. There was a fire at the Eski Saraya. The Old Palace was burned to ashes, and most of the surrounding quarter . . ."

"Hürrem?"

"She was not harmed. She sleeps now in the seraglio—"

"The seraglio!"

"What else might Süleyman do with her?"

"She actually sleeps in the Palace!"

Mustapha shrugged, amused by his mother's trepidation. "Sinan is to build a new Harem on the site of the old."

"It will never happen. She is inside the Palace now . . ."

". . . Mother!"

"She schemes, she spins her webs. Be careful, Mustapha, be careful."

"I am the shahzade, she cannot change that. You credit her with too much." He raised Gülbehar's hand to his lips once more. "He loves her more than you. I wish it were not so. But it is no more than that. Try to forget."

Forget!

He talked then about his family, asked first about his sons, and hoped she had not had trouble from his kadins. Gülbehar ruled the harem as his grandmother, Hafise Sultan, had done. She knew all that happened, spoiled his sons, and only barely tolerated his kadins.

Gülbehar took care not to mention Süleyman again, but her mind was distracted, and the pleasure of seeing her son once more was soured by old ghosts and new fears. When he had gone, Gülbehar crushed her fists into her lap. He did not see the danger, did not see it at all. But why should he? After all, he was only a man.

Topkapi Saraya

THERE WERE TWO codes of law in the Islamic Empire of the Osmanlis. There was the kanun—the laws formulated by the Sultan himself—and the Sheri'at, the sacred and immutable laws of Islam. While the Sultan ruled alone and with absolute power of his subjects, even he was subject to the sacred Muslim law, which was the written word of God.

The Sheri'at was interpreted by the ulema, the council of religious judges, who alone were able to issue *fetvas,* or opinions, on any question in accordance with Islamic jurisprudence. However, their power was held in check in that they could not issue a fetva unless invited, and could not speak unless their opinion was sought.

Each governor, each *bey,* each sançak, each *beylerbey* had their own mufti to guide them in matters of religious law. The foremost judge, the *sheyhülislam,* was assigned for the spiritual guidance of the Sultan himself; only he could declare a war holy, and therefore justified. As Defender of the Faith, the Sultan's sworn duty was to uphold the Sheri'at, so in effect the sheyhülislam was one of the most powerful men in the Ottoman Empire. His name was Abu Sa'ad.

This morning Abu Sa'ad was about to receive an important and unexpected visitor, and he was curious. The Lady Hürrem had recently shown an encouraging and passionate devotion to Islam, and had used a great deal of her personal wealth to build a hospital and a mosque. Now she had asked for an audience with him and the sheyhülislam wondered why.

His room was a simple chamber overlooking the gardens of the Second Court. There was little furniture, as befitted a man of ascetic taste. There were a few Persian silk rugs piled high on the floor, a low walnut table, and two tall silver candle holders. A brass censer, inlaid with turquoise, hung from the ceiling. The room was dominated by a Qur'ān stand of ivory and tortoiseshell. A Qur'ān lay open on it, the pages illuminated in gold and blue script.

The Lady Hürrem was preceded into the room by the Kislar Aghasi, two pages helping him ease his great bulk to the floor. Then Hürrem entered, completely hidden by her *chadoor,* a ferijde of violet silk that covered her entire body. The sheyhülislam clapped his hands together twice to indicate to his pages that they should fetch sherbets for his guests, although he knew only Abbas would drink. Hürrem would leave her cup untouched; to drink would expose her hand and her face to the sheyhülislam, and disgrace them both.

"I am honored by your presence, my Lady," Abu Sa'ad said. "God rejoices in the great zeal with which you have forsaken the pagan gods of your youth and embraced the one true faith."

"I still have much to learn," Hürrem said.

"We all have much to learn," the sheyhülislam said graciously.

He glanced at Abbas, looking for some clue as to the purpose of the meeting. But the Kislar Aghasi stared stonily out of the window, seemingly disinterested. The pages brought them iced sherbets, and retired from the room. Abu Sa'ad waited for Hürrem to speak.

"As you know I have been much honored by the Lord of Life," Hürrem said.

"As you say," Abu Sa'ad answered, bowing his head in recognition of the Sultan's generosity and Hürrem's mendacity.

"It has given me great pleasure to pass on some of my great bounty to the glory of Islam."

"The foundation of a mosque is the greatest glory we can demonstrate to God."

"Indeed. But there is a question that has been troubling me. Is this donation also pious for the giver?"

Abu Sa'ad blinked. So this was why she had come! "It is indeed a pious act," he answered carefully.

"And is it recorded in Paradise for the salvation of one's soul?"

Abu Sa'ad paused. The answer, of course, was quite plain, but he took care in how he phrased his reply. "It is gracious, yes, my Lady. But as . . .

a bondswoman . . . it may not be recorded against your own name in Paradise. Rather, it increases the sanctity of your Sultan, may God keep him and grant him increase."

"Then my good works are to no avail?"

"On the contrary. They are to the glory of God and the Sultan."

"But there will be no place for me in Paradise?"

Abu Sa'ad thought he heard a small sob catch in her throat, but without seeing the woman's face it was impossible to tell exactly how deeply his answer had wounded her.

He kept his silence.

"Thank you for seeing me," Hürrem said. Abbas was helped to his feet. He, in turn, helped her from the floor. As she left, she moved slowly, her shoulders hunched. Abu Sa'ad felt almost sorry for her. But then he reminded himself she was, after all, just a woman, and did not feel the pain of the spirit as acutely as a man.

70

THE ÇINILI KIOSK had been built by the Fatih himself. It lay up a sharp slope through the Gate of the Cool Fountain, facing the waters of the Horn and the palaces of the Venetians and Genoese at Pera. It had been built in the shape of a Greek cross, and was completely covered in Turkish faïence, a glittering refuge of emerald and turquoise ceramics, verses from the Qur'ān emblazoned along the walls in Arabic script, yellow against midnight blue.

Süleyman, Lord of Life, Possessor of Men's Necks, reclined on a divan piled with cushions of verdant silk, and watched in dismay as Hürrem distractedly plucked at the strings of her viol. What was the matter with her? he wondered. Was she sick? Was she pining for something?

Or was it, he thought angrily, part of her ploy to discredit Sinan's attempts to design a new Palace for the Harem?

She had been fretting like this for the duration of two moons. The

Laughing One rarely smiled anymore. She seemed preoccupied with some great sadness, and he was growing impatient with her.

"Hürrem, come and sit by me."

Hürrem laid the viol aside and crossed the room, settling meekly by his side on the divan. She nestled her head against his shoulder.

"What is wrong, little russelana?"

"My Lord, it is nothing. It will pass."

"The last time I saw you, you told me it was your time of the moon. Before that you said it was just a passing melancholy. I cannot remember the last time I saw you smile."

"My Lord, forgive me if I give you offense. Perhaps you should send me away."

"Perhaps I should," Süleyman growled.

He jumped to his feet. The sudden movement startled the two black guards standing at the door. Hürrem curled her knees up to her chest and avoided his eyes. He put his hands on his hips and glowered down at her. "You must tell me what is wrong!"

"My Lord, I cannot."

"You cannot? I am your Sultan, your Lord. Have you forgotten?"

"How can I forget? I love you more than life itself."

"Then tell me why it is you mope like this. I cannot tolerate such miserable spirits a moment longer!"

Hürrem covered her face with her hands. "Oh, my Lord . . ."

"Will you please stop this sniveling and tell me!" He snatched her hands away but the sight of her crumpled, wounded face softened him. He sat down beside her and placed her arms around his own neck. "Tell me! Please!"

"My Lord, I fear for my soul."

This abrupt confession caught him off balance. He almost laughed with relief. "We all fear for our souls."

"But you may find pardon in good works, my Lord."

"I do not understand."

"If you fear for your soul, my Lord, why should you think that I do not fear for mine?"

Süleyman stared into her eyes and realized she was quite serious. He had never thought about this, and it surprised him that it had occurred to her. After all, she was a woman, and women—so the sheyhülislam had taught him—did not have souls like a man. Rather, they were on the level of dogs and cats. Besides, although Hürrem had accepted Islam from necessity, he had never been under the illusion that she had embraced it with any zeal.

"What do you fear, little russelana?"

"My Lord, I have begged audience with the sheyhülislam. He has told me that despite my many bequests for mosques and hospitals, I receive no credit for this in God's eyes. I shall be ignored, even in Paradise."

"I cannot imagine that even the great God will ever be able to completely ignore you, little russelana."

Angry tears welled in her eyes. "Do not mock me, my Lord! I am trapped in this world and the next! I live in mortal terror for my soul! What am I to do?"

Her intensity staggered him. She meant it, he realized. "I did not know you thought so deeply about these things."

"It is so unfair! Other women from the Harem have been married off to pashas and governors and have their own property to bequest to *waqfs* and earn themselves credit before God. But I, lover of the most exalted man on earth and Defender of Islam, will be below all of them in Paradise!"

Süleyman tenderly brushed away an errant lock of hair from her face. "What exactly did Abu Sa'ad tell you?"

"He told me that no bondswoman can earn credit in Paradise, that as long as I remain a slave, I am just dust in Heaven." She fixed his eyes with hers, and her hands curled into fists on her lap. "I want so much to have a soul, my Lord. I want so much to be saved!"

"Little russelana," he murmured. He had never felt such a surge of affection for her as he did then. She was right, of course. Before God, what else was there to do?

"Then I shall make you free," he said. "From today you are a bondswoman no more. And God and all his prophets shall rejoice in another soul who has found the true path."

THE NEXT DAY Abu Sa'ad again granted audience to the Lady Hürrem, to counsel her on affairs of the spirit. What she asked him stunned him to silence. But finally he gave her his fetva, and gave it honestly, as he was obliged to do, according to the dictates of Islam and the teaching of the Qur'ān.

71

THE SULTAN'S PERSONAL quarters and rooms of audience—the selamlik—were separated from his haremlik by a single door. It led from his bedroom onto a cloister and then to the maze of courts and dormitories that had once belonged to the pages and eunuchs of his own retinue.

It had quickly become known inside the Palace as the Golden Road, and it was along this cloister that Abbas hurried now, to the apartments of the great kadin, Hürrem. His curious, waddling gait made him a comical figure, the sleeves and hem of his pelisse trailing the cobbles behind him, his cheeks puffing with the exertion of conveying his great bulk at such speed. He paused before alighting the steps to the first-floor apartment of the kadin, readying himself for the effort.

When finally Hürrem received him, he had to pause to catch his breath once more, dabbing at the oily slick of perspiration on his forehead with a silk handkerchief.

"Well?" Hürrem said, watching the performance from her divan with barely concealed impatience.

"The Lord of Life commands your presence in his bedchamber," Abbas said.

"I cannot come," Hürrem said, and said it so casually that it was some seconds before the import of her words registered on the Kislar Aghasi.

"My Lady?"

"Tell the Lord of Life I am unable to attend him," Hürrem said, and Abbas stared at her, certain now that her power had made her quite insane. It was the moment he dreaded, for his fortune was now inseparable from Hürrem's. He groaned aloud.

The silly little minx.

SÜLEYMAN LAY SPRAWLED across the divan, apparently at ease. It was only the pinpoints of his eyes and the cruel set of his mouth that betrayed his fury.

"She refuses me?" he growled.

Abbas wished at that moment that he was anywhere but in that room. He could barely breathe. He felt the sweat trickle oily and cold down the length of his spine and he was aware that his knees were actually trembling. The silk gown fluttered around his legs as if he were standing in a strong breeze. His mouth was so dry it was an effort to speak.

"She said, my Lord, that her life was at your command, but that she might not come now without offending God and His sacred laws." Yes, she had said that, Abbas thought. She had said it with a grin of absolute triumph that I shall make no attempt to duplicate.

"She dares lecture me on the Sheri'at?"

"I only repeat what she said, my Lord."

Süleyman was still for long minutes, so that when he finally leaped to his feet, Abbas was quite unprepared and involuntarily took a step backward. Süleyman stamped to the bed and tore off the silk coverlet, tearing it in half in his rage. "She cannot defy me!"

"She says she wishes no offense," Abbas said, pleading now, he knew, for his own life as well as Hürrem's. "She says she has heard it from the shey-hülislam's lips. He says that being free, she may not now yield before you what, as a bondswoman, she could give without offense to God."

"Abu Sa'ad told her this?"

"Yes, my Lord," Abbas replied, with some satisfaction. Let that pompous and self-righteous old fool feel the torch on his skin for a change. If Süleyman were persuaded to seek his fetva, he knew they were safe. He would not dare defy the Sheri'at.

Süleyman drew his killiç from the scabbard by his bed. The rubies in the hilt glittered like hot coals in the darkened room. Süleyman looked at the sword, then at Abbas, his features ugly with anger.

God help me in my sorrow, Abbas repeated under his breath. He is going to smite me. Abbas felt himself lose his bladder control. Lately he had found himself wetting himself like an old woman. It was the result of the castration, he knew, the damage that had been done long ago to the urethra. It was the final indignity in a life liberally laced with humiliation. He had taken to wearing a cotton diaper, like an infant.

Süleyman raised the sword and plunged it into the mattress. "Abu Sa'ad," he said.

"It was his fetva," Abbas said.

"We must consult him, then, since he knows God's mind better than I."

Süleyman stormed from the room. Abbas whispered a silent prayer to the Prophet for his intercession, and followed.

ANY OTHER MAN would have been terrified at being roused from his bed to face the Lord of Life, the King of Kings, the Possessor of Men's Necks, to stare into the cold, proud eyes and bear the brunt of his towering rage. But the sheyhülislam feared only God, and knew, with unwavering conviction, the heart and mind of the Infinite. He performed the ceremonial sala'am that was Süleyman's due as Sultan, and then looked calmly into the other man's eyes and was totally without fear.

There were only three figures in the huge audience chamber: Süleyman, Abbas, and Abu Sa'ad. The guards who had fetched the sheyhülislam to answer the summons now waited, yataghans drawn, beyond the door.

Süleyman glowered from his throne, his mouth drawn down into a tight bow of bitter wrath. "I need a fetva," he said.

Abu Sa'ad bowed his head and said nothing.

"It concerns the Hasseki Hürrem—the Favored Laughing One. You know that I have released her from my kullar, my slave family? She is now a free woman."

"As you say," Abu Sa'ad answered.

"As a free woman, may she still lie with me without giving offense to God?"

Abu Sa'ad had been prepared for this question from Süleyman ever since it had first been asked by Hürrem. The answer, however, remained immutable, even for the Lord of Life. "Even if you have lain with her a thousand nights as a bondswoman, now she is free it would be a sin before God. She would put her soul in mortal danger."

"How may she resolve this problem?"

"She may only lie with you, without stain, if she is your wife."

Süleyman clenched the arms of the throne but said nothing. He seemed, to Abbas, to have found something in his mouth that was to his distaste and was considering whether to spit it out.

What was going to happen to them now? he thought. Since Hürrem refused his bed, and Süleyman could not possibly give her marriage, there seemed no help for it. Hürrem would be banished. What would become of him then?

"Go. Both of you," Süleyman said.

SÜLEYMAN REMAINED ALONE in the great chamber long after they had gone. The cavernous vaulted cupola above his head, the opulence of the faïence around the walls, the rich crimsons and sky blues of the silk carpets on the floor, the murmurings of the marble fountains and the dull glow of the turquoise embedded in the censers and lamps, and the loneliness of the great, splendid chamber all conspired to mock him.

The King of Kings felt despair as keenly as the poorest wretch in his hovel. It came down to one simple choice. Give her marriage or give her up. There was no other answer for him. In all his kingdom there was no one who could help him now. Not even Hürrem.

He sat slumped on the throne long into the night, watching the shadows retreat along the walls, into the distant corners of the room. He sat there until dawn drained color into the windows, and milky light filtered in from the high ceilings. And still he did not move.

Tradition, duty, and fear sat beside him through his vigil, but never in his life had he felt so utterly alone.

72

THE FOURTH COURT of the Topkapi Saraya was in effect a miniature forest of old pines and twisted cypresses swarming up the slopes of Seraglio Point, surrounded by the ancient sea walls of the city. On one side it overlooked the training fields of the çerit and the crumbling Byzantine monasteries that served as stables, on the other the sparkling blue neck of water the Turks called the Golden Horn. It was here that the Sultan could come for seclusion, to pray and to meditate.

Süleyman walked, head down, oblivious to everything but the tumbling confusion of his mind.

Give her marriage or give her up.

Give her marriage or give her up.

How could he truly give her up? It was as if she were there with him now, walking beside him, her braided red-gold hair stirred by the wind; he could hear her laughing, and as he imagined, he felt the solace of her simple wisdom: "You are the Kanuni, the Legislator. You are not bound by history, only by the restraints you place on yourself. You are only bound by the Sheri'at. My Lord, don't look so solemn! Is it really so great a terror that you do in law what you have already done in your heart?"

"Yet there is reason for this," he said aloud, as if to her. "I cannot easily break with tradition. It is tradition that ties us to our ancestors and our heritage. Ever since Tamerlane—"

"Do you really fear such a fate for me?" he heard Hürrem laugh. "Shall any of your enemies ever see the walls of Stamboul? Who is there that shall defeat you in battle?"

Süleyman climbed The Path That Made The Camel Scream, to the highest point of the court. From here he could look south, through the violet haze to the islands of the Marmara; beyond lay the Mediterranean, and his colonies in Egypt, Barbary, and Algeria; across the wind-whitened Bosphorus were the cypresses of Camlica, and beyond, Asia and the caravan tracks leading east to Syria, Azerbaijan, and Armenia. They all belonged to him. The harbor to the north was fringed by the masts of the moored galleys of Dragut, who had conquered the Mediterranean and turned it into a Turkish lake; beyond them lay the warehouses and palaces of the Venetians, the Genoese, and the Greeks; all these great republics paid him tribute. Beyond the Galata Kulesi was Rumelia, Bosnia, Wallachia, Transylvania, all fiefdoms of the Osmanlis.

"Look," he heard Hürrem saying, "what king is there now that may conquer you and make me wait at his table? Your Empire spans Europe and Asia and Africa. Even the great Emperor Charles dares not face you in battle. Who is it you are afraid of? Frederick? The Shah Tamasp?"

"They are dust at my feet," Süleyman said aloud.

"Then what do you fear, my Lord? Which king is it that makes you tremble that he can make you give me up . . . one who loves you so?"

Hürrem's eyes filled with tears. The image was so real that Süleyman reached out to comfort her. But there was no one. Just the wind and the pain in his own mind. If he gave her up, that was all there would always be. He would be alone again, with only the terrible responsibility of the Empire, and the heavy burdens of God. She was all things to him now: his conscience, his consolation: his counsel, his advocate, his friend. She was the Vizier he could never have, for a Vizier whom he loved too much would betray him, as Ibrahim had done. She was his Harem too, a thousand women in one; a woman who could soothe his spirits, and not just his body.

"I cannot give her up," he said, and the decision was made. He would do the unthinkable because the only alternative was unbearable.

WHEN ABBAS WAS summoned once again into the presence of the second kadin, he braced himself for every possibility except the one that confronted him.

She was, he noted with relief, in high spirits this morning. She wasted no time with her usual pleasantries. "How would you like to be rid of your girls, Abbas?" she asked him.

"My Lady?"

"The Sultan no longer has need of his Harem. The girls are to be married off to his spahis and ministers. You are to start making the arrangements immediately."

Abbas nodded, trying to disguise his astonishment. A Sultan without a Harem! How had she accomplished it? "I compliment his judgment."

"You compliment mine," Hürrem laughed.

"I shall proceed straight away, as you command, my Lady."

"Do you not wish to know why, my Abbas?"

"It is not for me to question the decisions of the Mighty," Abbas said, satisfied that he had kept the contempt from his voice.

But Hürrem detected it anyway and laughed, delighted. "Abbas, you are indeed a treasure! I shall tell you anyway, since you shall learn of it soon enough. The Lord of Life no longer has need for his Harem because soon he is to take a queen!"

Abbas blinked at her. "Queen, my Lady?"

"You are looking at the future wife of the Sultan of the Osmanlis, Abbas." She laughed again. "Are you not indeed awed by the splendor of such a sight?"

"As you say, my Lady," Abbas agreed. Impossible, he thought secretly. Impossible! Süleyman would never go through with it!

ON THE OCCASION of the marriage of Süleyman to the Hasseki Hürrem—the Favored Laughing One, as she was known inside the court—Stamboul witnessed the greatest celebration it had ever seen.

Bread and olives were distributed to the poor; cheese, fruit, and rose-leaf jam to the middle classes. The main streets were festooned with flowers and banners—the scarlet flags of the Osmanli Empire, the green standards of Islam.

There was a public procession of wedding gifts, hundreds of camels, laden with carpets, furniture, gold and silver vases, and a hundred and sixty more eunuchs to enter the service of the Lady Hürrem. Wrestlers, archers, jugglers, and tumblers performed in the Hippodrome day and night; wild animals were paraded along the Atmeydani—lions, panthers and leopards, elephants tossing balls with their long trunks, the giraffes with their impossibly long necks eliciting gasps of astonishment from the crowds.

In another procession a huge loaf of bread, the size of a room, was dragged through the streets on a raft by ten oxen, while the city's master bakers threw little hot loaves covered with sesame and fennel to the crowd. Thousands of people lined the edge of the arena, climbing trees to glimpse the Sultan or receive a gift of money or silk or fruit that the Sultan's slaves showered among the crowd.

Meanwhile, in the seraglio, Hürrem became queen in a simple cere-mony witnessed only by herself, Süleyman, and Abu Sa'ad. Süleyman touched Hürrem's veiled hand and whispered: "This woman Hürrem I make my wife. All that belongs to her shall be her property."

Just one man threw his shadow over the ceremony. He dogged her all that day, as he had dogged her for the last seventeen years.

Mustapha.

Now twenty-six years old, he waited his moment in Manisa. Popular with the pashas and the yeniçeris, he was the chosen, the next Sultan. Yes, I am Queen, Hürrem thought. I am safe now from other women. Now there is only man that I must fear. And I will remove that danger too, in time.

A RAISED PLATFORM had been erected in the Hippodrome and from here Süleyman watched the entertainments on a throne of lapus lazuli, his sons on either side of him. Behind him, in a ferijde of violet silk and heavily veiled, Hürrem watched also, through a gilded lattice.

Selim fidgeted, cross-legged on the thick carpets at his father's feet. He was hungry. A feast had been prepared at the Palace: venison, guinea fowl, *imam biyalti,* fruit soup with real ice, sherbets of lemon juice and snow flavored with honey, amber, and musk. His stomach growled.

Below them, in the arena, a lioness was tearing the innards from a boar with casual sweeps of its front paws, while her partner yawned and watched without interest. Selim grinned, enjoying the spectacle, giggling at the boar's kicking and squealing. It was on its back now, writhing in the dirt, smearing the dust pink. The lioness circled, watchful of the tusks, its claws slashing again, drawing some of the beast's entrails with it.

Something made Selim turn his face. Through the screen behind Süleyman's throne he saw a pair of green eyes watching him, like tiny emeralds blazing in the darkness. Mother, he thought.

He turned away quickly, but he sensed her eyes still on him. How did she arrange all this? he wondered again. How did she ever get Süleyman to marry her? To have such a powerful mother was both consolation and terror. If she was capable of bending the Sultan to her will, she was capable of anything.

So what does she want with me? he wondered. What plans does she have for me?

The lioness had finished toying with the boar now. The boar was shuddering, lying on its flank, still alive, when the lioness bent her head to tear free the first chunk of meat. Normally such things excited his appetite. But suddenly Selim discovered that he was not hungry anymore.

He forced himself to turn around once more but the eyes were gone.

PART 7

PARADISE ON EARTH

73

Pera

JULIA WATCHED THE black-painted carriage clatter to a halt in the cobbled courtyard below her window. A black eunuch jumped down from
the coach to settle the horses, while another opened the door. The windows were covered with black taffeta, so she could not see their visitor.
Julia was only mildly interested. Ludovici often entertained visitors during
the day, usually other merchants from the Comunità Magnifica.

She saw a figure emerge from the coach, head and face invisible beneath
the hood of a cloak and black cadeza. She frowned. Not a finger or toe was
visible, but by the hurried quick steps she guessed it was a woman.

A few moments later Hyacinth tapped gently on her door to announce
her guest.

She gaped as the figure removed the hood of her ferijde and grinned
at her.

"Sirhane!"

SIRHANE HAD CHANGED hardly at all. She was perhaps a little thinner,
and there were the faint tracings of lines at the corners of her mouth and
eyes. Otherwise it was as if the last six years had not happened. They were
back in the seraglio again, the wicked monastery they could see across the
water from their balcony, outlined in ink against a lilac sky.

Sirhane wore an *entari* jacket of green Bursa brocade, wide open in
front and joined at the waist by three pearl buttons. The long sleeves were
draped over the edge of the divan and reached almost to the ground. Her
chemise was of rich snow-white silk, edged with lace, and hung loose over
her white woolen salwar, which fell in folds to her ankles. Rubies glinted
on her fingers and glowed like sparks in her coal-black hair. There were

pearls at her throat, and her waist, and small gold chainlets at her wrists and ankles.

Julia, in the Venetian vestura of somber black, felt drab and lifeless beside her. She stared at the lustrous skin of Sirhane's arms, and felt the guilty stirring of longing inside her.

Julia clung to her hand like a schoolgirl. "Tell me," she said, laughing. "Tell me everything!"

"You are looking at a respectable and virtuous married woman!" Sirhane said.

"How did you get out of the Harem?"

"Süleyman is disposing of all his girls . . ."

"It's not true!"

"They say Hürrem has persuaded him that he no longer needs his Harem! The Kislar Aghasi arranged for my marriage to an aga in the Spahis of the Porte. His name is Abdül Sahine Pasha. He is a big brute of man with a beard and his member is as thick as my wrist!"

Julia clapped her hand to her mouth. "Oh, Sirhane!"

Sirhane shrugged. "He treats me well enough. I think he prefers the boys. I don't know. He is not so bad. Perhaps I could love him. If he were not a man." She reached out and rested her head on Julia's shoulder. "I have missed you so. Perhaps it is wicked, but while you were there, I was happy in the Harem."

"So was I," Julia said. "How did you find me?"

Sirhane sniffed and pulled away. Her eyes were wet. "It was on the morning that I was to leave the Harem. The Kislar Aghasi came to me and told me you were still alive, married to the renegade Venetian merchant, Ludovici."

"Abbas!"

"I thought you were dead," Sirhane told her. "For six years I mourned you. I still cannot believe it!"

She threw her arms around Julia's neck and kissed her. Julia heard herself whispering Sirhane's name over and over again and she closed her eyes and felt Sirhane pulling off her vestura and she gave herself up to the soft, teasing pleasures of her lover.

Poor Ludovici, she thought. If only I could love him like this.

THE SUN DIPPED below the seven hills, the sweet voices of the muezzins rose from the dusky, dusty city calling the faithful to prayer. Light pooled like liquid gold on the waters of the Horn, and the outlines of the planes and cypresses dissolved into the chill shadows beneath the walls of the seraglio. They sat on the darkening terrazza, talking in whispers.

"So tell me what has been happening," Julia said. "Is it really true? Süleyman has really married off his entire Harem?"

"There is no more honey in the honeypot," Sirhane said. "All that remains is Hürrem and her household. The Laughing One has a hundred slaves in waiting now. She comes and goes whenever she likes, thirty eunuch guards in her wake."

"If a snake can survive so many years among so many other vipers, it deserves to grow long."

"The Kislar Aghasi told me she was the reason the Sultan ordered you drowned."

Abbas, Abbas . . . Julia thought. Even now, she did not want to think about what they had done to him. *Corpo di Dio*, how could he go on?

"I am alive, Sirhane. It does not matter now."

Sirhane looked disappointed. "You should try to be more hateful. It is not becoming for a woman not to be spiteful."

Julia laughed. "What Hürrem does cannot affect me now."

Sirhane continued anyway. "Foreign ambassadors include gifts for her, as well as the Sultan, now. They even send her letters to try and sway her opinion. The viziers, muftis, and agas pay her tribute through the Kislar Aghasi. Even my husband does this. He says she is more powerful than Ibrahim ever was."

Julia smiled. "Poor Süleyman."

Sirhane curled her legs beneath her, curling into the divan like a sleek and pampered kitten. "What was he like?"

Julia seemed reluctant. "Tell me!" Sirhane urged her.

"He hardly said a word. He took off my clothes and then he lay on top of me . . ."

"And it's not big?"

"No."

"They say it's really huge."

"Sirhane . . ." Julia spread her hands helplessly, amazed, as she always was, to find herself discussing such things so shamelessly. "He lay on top of me and he made some noises. Then he rolled off again. Nothing happened." She remembered how Ludovici made love to her the first time. Until then, she had not realized why Süleyman had been so angry.

"So he is impotent! The Sultan is impotent!"

Julia grabbed her friend's wrist, alarmed. "If you tell another soul, we will all be killed!"

"The best gossip I have ever had and I cannot tell anyone!" Sirhane pouted, playfully.

"It will mean all our heads!"

"All right," Sirhane said, and she pulled away. ". . . What is it like with Ludovici?"

Julia lowered her eyes. "Not the way it is with you."

Sirhane seemed satisfied with the answer. She looked across the Horn, at the lamps flickering to life along the hills of the old city. The calls of the muezzins had died away, the echoes fading into the gathering violet of the dusk. A stillness had settled over the city. "I must go."

Julia reached for her hand. "I don't want you to."

"I must."

A few minutes later Julia watched from her window as the hooded figure climbed back inside the anonymous black carriage in the court-yard. I did not escape the Harem, she thought. I have brought it here with me. It was my captivity, and my liberation. It plunged me into mortal sin. Now that Sirhane has returned to my life, I am baptized into it again.

It was not just a sexual passion she realized, though the desire she had reawakened was real enough. It was more; it was a longing for an intimacy she could not share with any other person, a physical comfort that was without complication. An adultery without consequence, perhaps. But not without sin, she thought.

Yet a sin I cannot live without.

God help me.

Then Sirhane had disappeared behind the black taffeta curtains of the carriage and moments later the horses clattered away through the gates and Julia felt the loneliness return once more.

74

FATE HAD BEEN kind to Ludovici Gambetto.

Almost.

It had brought him a powerful and influential friend at the Sublime Porte: as a consequence his business had prospered beyond his imaginings. Fortune had also brought him a beautiful wife from a noble Venetian family.

Yet within both these shining gifts were tiny silver caskets of pain. His good fortune was founded on Abbas's private agony; Julia belonged to him only because she could not belong to anyone else.

Even after eight years, he had still not become accustomed to the idea that the friend of his youth lived now in the Sultan's Palace as a eunuch and a slave. He still could not meet with Abbas without feeling the acid of disgust and revulsion rise to the back of his throat.

And then there was Julia.

She was worthless currency now to anyone but him. He had lied to Abbas, and kept her in Stamboul for himself. And though Abbas had not spoken one word of reproach, he could see it in his eyes every time they met. He had found out, somehow. And the guilt of his duplicity still gnawed at him.

If only it had been worth it, if only she could have loved him a little.

A part of him—the part of him that was still Venetian—said that it did not matter. She was his wife, she was beautiful, his to bed and enjoy whenever he chose. What else could he want?

But there was another part—the renegade in his soul, no doubt—that wanted her to feel the same for him as he felt for her. He wanted her devotion. And it was the one thing that was yet denied to him.

He had built a new palazzo on the heights of Pera, overlooking the Golden Horn. He dressed Julia in the finest velvets and lace from Venice; there were rubies and diamonds glinting on her fingers. He had wealth and ease and influence, all that was denied him in his own country. But what he wanted most of all was Julia, the certain look in her eyes and passion in her dark embrace that would tell him she loved him also. And that he could not have.

Corpo di Dio! Why was it so important?

He stood on the terrazza and watched Julia reading in the garden. The summer flowers were in full bloom, the air heavy with the scent of cypress and umbrella pines. He walked down the marble steps into the garden. She saw him and put the book aside. "You look pleased with yourself," she said.

"Not with myself. I cannot take the credit." He sat down beside her on the marble bench. It was cool here, in the shade of the cypress pine. Through the leaves he watched the caïques glide across the bright waters of the Horn, toward the violet silhouette of the domes and minarets of the Seraglio on the far shore.

"What has happened?"

"I have heard whispers from the Porte. They say Rüstem Pasha is to marry the Sultan's daughter."

"Miharmah?"

"It is the whisper I heard."

"Then he will almost certainly become Vizier."

"Yes."

"That pleases you?"

"If I were on the side of the angels, it would not. But I am only a humble merchant, and I cannot afford to be." He gave her a sardonic smile. "I have not been on the side of the angels since I left Venice. Perhaps not even there. It is perhaps why I have all this." He indicated the palazzo and its gardens.

"I still do not understand."

"Süleyman's Vizier, Lütfi Pasha, is too difficult to deal with. He is too honest."

"A fatal flaw in a Vizier."

He smiled. "Indeed. Rüstem on the other hand would sell his own mother for ten percent commission."

"He will be excellent, then."

"I am sure he will be a great success."

"And you will be able to send more caramusalis through the Dardanelles without inspection. But what made Süleyman choose Rüstem for such a wonderful match?"

"His charm and good looks?"

Then Julia realized. "Hürrem!"

"Well, that is what they are saying in the bazaars. Time will tell. Though what he has done to deserve her patronage I can only imagine." He studied her. She looked different today. There was a bloom in her cheeks he had not seen before. "You had a visitor yesterday," he said.

She avoided his eyes. "Is that wrong?"

"Who was it?"

"A girl. A friend from my days at the seraglio."

"How did she know . . . ?"

"Abbas."

"He told her?"

"She is a friend. It is safe."

"Nothing is ever safe."

The lightness in her mood evaporated suddenly. "You pin me to the wall like a butterfly, to be gazed at and never touched. Sometimes I would rather be dead!"

Ludovici did not answer. After a moment Julia seemed to regret her outburst. "I am sorry," she murmured. "I know you put yourself in danger also when you went . . . fishing for me . . . on your boat."

Ludovici hung his head. "No. What you say is correct. I have no right. I have put you in unnecessary danger by keeping you here. I wanted you all for myself." He took a deep breath. "I have a vineyard in Cyprus. You could go there. You would be safe. Your very existence would no longer need to be a secret. You will be among other Venetians, like ourselves . . ."

"I am no longer a Venetian. And neither are you."

"You will no longer have to live like a prisoner. I can visit you there."

Julia smiled to herself. Perhaps yesterday she would have begged him to leave. But now . . .

"I will stay," she said.

He looked at her, surprised. "I can guarantee your safety."

"I do not want to leave Stamboul."

He grinned, misunderstanding her reasons. "I prayed you would not."

She looked away. Ludovici was confused. What did she want? Was it still Abbas? Impossible. Why did she want to remain here in Stamboul?

They sat for a while in silence while Ludovici contemplated the best way to tell her his next piece of news. "There is a legation arriving soon from Venice," he said at last. "They have come to see the Sultan, to sue for peace."

Ever since the Battle of Prevezo two years before, when the Turkish Admiral Dragut had decimated the Venetians, there had existed an uneasy truce between the Turks and La Serenissima. The Osmanlis had won control of the Mediterranean and were choking the lifeblood of the republic—its trade. Even war had not affected the life of the Comunità Magnifica at Pera—except that it had increased the price of Ludovici's illegal grain.

Julia glanced up at him, frowning, wondering why he had made a special point of telling her this.

"Your father is to head the legation," he said.

Her face drained of color. She gripped her hands together in her lap, the knuckles turning white. "Will he come here?" she said at last.

"Not unless I invite him. I can scarcely see reason to do that."

Julia tried to smile. "You did not imagine I would wish to see him?"

"No. I did not think so."

She closed her eyes. "What about Abbas?"

He stared at her. "Yes, Abbas. That is why I had to talk to you. I am going to tell him."

"Good."

"You mean that?"

"Yes."

He was surprised by how quickly she had replied. "Abbas has become a powerful man here in Stamboul. Ambassadors to the Sublime Porte have been thrown in the dungeons at Yedikule before now. Or worse. Are you sure you want him to know?"

Julia's eyes glittered with venom. "After what my father did to him?" She breathed deeply, her nostrils flaring. "Yes, Abbas should know. In fact," she added, "I would like to tell him myself."

Ludovici had not expected that. But yes, it had to happen finally. He would be a fool to try and stop her.

"I will arrange it," he said.

75

Galata

THE CARRIAGE WAS an oblong box on wheels, painted with flowers and fruit, no different from a hundred others in the city. It clattered through the filthy alley and stopped at the anonymous wooden two-story house, painted yellow in the color of the Jews, like so many others in the quarter. A page opened the door and Julia stepped out.

No one would have recognized her. They would have known only that she was a woman. She wore a ferijde, the long-sleeved cloak worn by all Turkish women in the street. It was of black silk, which gave a clue to her station; poor women wore cloaks of black alpaca, while women of the Royal Harem had cloaks of lilac or rose silk. She wore two veils; the gauzy yashmak that covered her face, nose, and mouth was invisible behind the black cazeta that fell from her head to her waist, with just a square-cut hole for her eyes. Nothing of her was visible, not even her hands or feet. The only clue of her femininity was the scent of musk and jasmine that accompanied her, a sweet oasis among the fetid smells of the city.

The robe kept a Turkish woman prisoner, but it was also her liberation; for with the ferijde and the cazeta even the most highborn woman could venture into the streets without being recognized.

The black figure hurried out of the street and through the door of the house, leaving the black pages to wait by the coach outside.

Abbas saw her and his mouth fell open.

He had grown even more obese over the years, Julia noted. Through the rich flowered silk of his kaftan, she could see that the folds of fat clung in coils to his body, and were bunched in pillows under his chin. He was sweating, even though it was still only early morning, and not yet warm. The perspiration glistened on his face, and stained the edges of his huge white turban.

She tried to recall what he had once been like, then tried to relate the image of a boy with a face of smooth, burnished bronze, as she remembered him on the gondola, to this nightmarish creature with one white, staring eye and bloated, fleshy face.

It was impossible.

She only remembered him as the Kislar Aghasi, the ugly, falsetto eunuch who had grimaced with outrage at their first meeting, and whispered those strange endearments as she waited to die one dawn on the Bosphorus.

So this was Abbas now.

He tried to struggle to his feet. He clapped his hands for the pages to assist him.

"Who are you?" he grunted, but she could tell from the expression on his face that he already knew.

She waited, without moving. What if the two Palace pages he had brought with him should recognize her? But he had already guessed what she was thinking and after they had assisted him, he sent them outside.

"Julia?" he said.

She lifted the heavy cazeta, let it fall behind her, like a cape, almost to the ground. Then she removed the yashmak, unpinning it carefully, so that he could see her face.

"Hello, Abbas."

He covered his face with his hands and turned his back to her.

"What's wrong?"

"You should not have come," he moaned.

"I had to see you. Just once more."

"I told Ludovici I never wanted to see you again. Why do you want to torture me this way?"

"Please, Abbas . . ."

"If you knew the pain you cause me, you would not have done this!"

Julia did not know what to do. Suddenly she felt like a fool. Still he would not turn around.

"Abbas?"

"Why did you come here? What could have possessed you? Why did Ludovici allow this?"

"Turn around . . ."

"So you can gaze on my beauty?"

"Ludovici is a handsome man. But I do not love him. And I have always loved you."

"Stop it!"

"Turn around . . ."

When Abbas turned back to her his face was mottled with fury, his one good eye stared at her in pain and outrage. "Go away! What good can this do now? My love for you has cost me everything! Just let me forget you, for pity's sake! Now go away!"

Julia held out her hands to him, then let them drop again to her sides. "Abbas . . . I never had the chance . . . you saved my life . . ."

"Because I loved you. Will you return my love? How? With your kisses? Will you take me to your bed? Shall we become lovers?"

The anger on his face crumpled away. Julia took a step toward him, to comfort him, but he held out a hand to stop her. "Don't . . ." he said.

"Can you imagine what it must be like for me, Julia? To feel desire for a woman, and know there is no way I can ever fulfill it? To still have this passion in me and no means of release? A man cannot feel love for a woman and not need to consummate it with his body. So what am I to do? There is no release for me, not ever. Not ever. I ache and I burn every day, surrounded by women. They have cut away my manhood but it is still there. Every day I feel as if I am trapped in a cage in which I cannot sit upright or extend my arms or my legs. All natural movement is denied me, physically and emotionally. I want to love and be loved. But how can I? How could I ever consummate love with a woman? They have stripped me of every reason for being alive! There is no hell after death, Julia. It is here, now. And I inhabit it!"

His rage spent, his shoulders sagged and he slumped against the wall, his breathing ragged in his chest. Julia hung back. What was there to say?

"Please go," he whispered.

"All right. But first there is something I have to tell you. I did not come here to torment you, as you suggest."

"Tell me, then, and go."

"It is about my father."

At first, the import of what she was saying did not seem to register with him. "Gonzaga?" he said finally.

"He is coming here to Stamboul."

"You are sure?"

"Ludovici was told yesterday by the bailo. La Serenissima is despatching a peace legation to the Porte. My father will be ambassador."

Abbas slipped down the wall and sat on his haunches on the carpet. He put his head on his knees. "So the Devil approaches Paradise," he murmured.

There was nothing else to say. Julia knew from his silence that she should go but she wanted desperately to comfort him. She knelt beside him. He did not protest so she leaned forward and gingerly kissed his forehead.

He did not pull away from her so she removed his turban and placed it beside her on the carpet. He still did not look up.

She ran her hands over the smooth, shaven skull. His baldness both revolted and fascinated her. She could see the individual bones outlined against the shining scalp. She put both her hands on each side of his jaw and raised his face toward her.

"Abbas . . ."

The one eye stared back at her, empty, pleading.

She reached down and lifted his kaftan. Her heart pounded as she ran her fingers along the shaved thigh, fighting to keep her horror from showing itself on her face. When she reached his groin, there was nothing. Like Sirhane, she thought, except there was no welcoming wetness, no rose petal lips. Just the waxy feel of the scarred tissue, the curious tender feel of the urethra.

She heard him gasp. With pain, with shock, with horror? He gave her no clue.

She had heard tales in the Harem—mostly from Sirhane, whose capacity for nonsense as well as fact was inexhaustible—that some women had induced orgasm in eunuchs by a combination of strong aphrodisiacs and urethral massage.

Or perhaps it was all nonsense.

Kneeling between his legs she reached down and drew the ferijde over her head. Beneath the cloak she was quite naked. "There is hashish on my nipples," she whispered.

Abbas was as compliant as an infant now. Slowly he put his mouth to her breast and began to suckle her.

Julia began her ministrations once more, cradling his head with one hand, her other between his legs, massaging his groin. She heard him groan again, with pleasure, and his breathing became faster and heavier. She twisted her head away to disguise her revulsion at the alien feel of the mutilated flesh between her fingers.

"Julia," he groaned.

She continued to massage him and after long minutes he began to move with her, panting, his mouth still covering her breast. It's working, she thought. I've done it. Sirhane was right.

He began to squirm, pushing his groin against her. She worked her fingers faster and faster, ignoring the cramping of the muscles in her hand. He threw back his head and began to sob, the same small sounds that Sirhane sometimes made.

Then suddenly, without warning, he shuddered, a long quivering spasm that coursed right through his body. His arms crushed her in a suffocating embrace.

Then he released her, and fell back against the wall, his eyes closed, his mouth thrown open, dragging in the air.

She leaned against him, exhausted, feeling the sweat from her body trickling between her breasts, mingling with his. For a long time neither of them moved.

"Abbas," she whispered, finally.

"Leave me now."

She reached for the ferijde, and got slowly to her feet.

"Wait," he murmured. "Let me look at you once more."

He stared at her for a long time; when he finally turned away she knew it was her cue. She slipped the cloak over her head, replaced the veil and cazeta.

I am anonymous once more, she thought. A sack.

Abbas was still crouched against the wall, bloated, his one blind eye still half open, his kaftan skewed around his knees. Anyone else, she knew, would find such a spectacle obscene.

Instead, she felt a wave of tenderness sweep over her. "I love you," she whispered, and left.

FOR ALMOST AN hour, Abbas did not move. He heard the clatter of the carriage as it moved away down the alley, then watched the shadows slant across the room, the sun rising over the roofs and angling in through the slats in the windows.

It was not the physical sensation that had paralyzed him. That had all been a sham, a piece of theater he had devised when he had realized that her efforts were quite pointless; she might as well have tried to stimulate a climax from the palm of his hand. But he had not wanted to humiliate her, and so he had feigned his pleasure.

What had touched him was her compassion for him. He knew his face and his body repelled others; they disgusted even himself. Yet she had shown him a humanity he had forgotten. She had given him loving and love.

He drew up his knees into his chest, and curled on the floor. After a while he started to weep, first with pity, for himself, and for her.

And then with rage.

Pera

IT WAS A dirty-blue afternoon. Antonio Gonzaga stared across the Horn at the Palace on Seraglio Point, the Kubbealti Tower rising like a miniature campanile from the skyline. The cypresses and umbrella pines clustered in the black shadows below the battlement walls like spies.

"So that is the home of Il Signore Turco."

"We must treat warily with him," the bailo said.

Gonzaga made no attempt to disguise the expression of scorn that came instantly to his face. It was not that he resented the bailo's preoccupation with trade—after all, it was trade that had made the Lion of San Marco what it was—but the gnawing suspicion he had had ever since he arrived here that the bailo's loyalties to La Serenissima had become compromised.

They were rich, too rich for simple merchants. They lived in grand palaces; some of them dressed in the Turkish style, wearing flowing kaftans instead of somber *togati*. What was most disturbing, they spoke of the Sultan and the Divan as if they were somehow more important than the Doge and the Consiglio di Dieci.

Süleyman Magnifico, they called him. Süleyman the Magnificent.

"We will prevail," Gonzaga said.

"Of course, Excellency. But until then we must not provoke him. The Mediterranean is, after all, a Turkish lake."

It was the truth and because it was true Gonzaga felt himself incensed. The Lion of San Marco would chew them all one day.

"Do not disturb yourself, bailo. One day the Lion of Venice will consume all its enemies. Until then, I shall play the lamb."

76

THE AMBASSADOR OF the Illustrious Signory of Venice made the short trip across the Golden Horn in the royal caïque. When he reached Seraglio Point, two pashas and forty heralds were waiting to escort his delegation on horseback. They rode in state to the Ba'ab-i-Hümayun, the Gate of the Majestic One.

Gonzaga tried not to appear impressed with the great arch of white marble, or with the contents of its mitered niches. The decapitated heads that occupied each niche were ripening in the sun, and there were more heads piled like cannonballs by the main gate. A group of urchins were playing with them.

The Ambassador of the Illustrious Signory of Venice put a scented handkerchief to his nose.

The massive arch was a full fifteen paces long. From there they entered the First Court of the Palace of Topkapi, the courtyard of the yeniçeris.

Gonzaga was immediately struck by the utter silence that descended as he rode through the Porte and into the sunlight. Even though the court was full of people—servants carrying a tray of hot rolls, a page being carried on a litter to the Infirmary, menials hurrying in conical felt hats, a troop of blue-coated yeniçeris marching toward the Ortakapi, the plumes of the veterans cascading in Bird of Paradise feathers almost to their knees—no one spoke above a whisper. The only other sounds were the ringing of the horses' hoofs on the cobblestones.

The Ortakapi—the gateway to the Second Court—was flanked by two octagonal towers with conical tops, like candle snuffers. There was a great double iron door, and Süleyman's tugra—his personal seal—hung above the door on a great brass shield. More heads were blackening on spikes on the wall above.

Until they reached this point Gonzaga had been reasonably satisfied with the respect that had been accorded him. But now he was ordered to dismount.

"We must go on foot the rest of the way," the interpreter stammered.

The Ambassador of the Illustrious Signory of Venice reluctantly complied.

There was a waiting room along a dark passage that led off to the right from the gatehouse. While Gonzaga cooled his heels in the sparsely furnished cell, the interpreter took the time to explain to him that the executioner's apartments were on the other side of the gatehouse, as well as a beheading block and a cistern for drownings. The bostanji could process up to fifty heads a day and afix them to the gatehouse walls, he explained proudly.

Gonzaga thanked him for the information and settled down to wait.

Three hours later he was escorted through the gate to the Second Court.

❦

GONZAGA WAS FURIOUS, so furious that he barely glanced at the long avenues of giant cypress that traversed the entire court, the paths lined with fountains and box hedges, the gazelles that grazed on the lawns. White with anger, he stamped between the honor guard of unsmiling yeniçeris that lined the pathway to the Divan, motionless as statues, his retinue hurrying behind him.

The one detail that did impress him was the utter silence. No one spoke. The only thing to be heard was the sigh of the wind in the trees.

He was escorted into the Divan.

Gonzaga had never witnessed such a riot of color. As he entered, the rows of courtiers bowed, and despite himself Gonzaga stared in awe at the brilliance and variety of the costumes in front of him, at the silks and velvets, brocades and satins. There was the Grand Vizier in robes of light green, the muftis of religion in dark blue, the grand ulemas in violet, the court chamberlains in scarlet. Ostrich plumes waved like a forest, jewels flashed in turbans and from scimitars, and reflected in the shining helmets of the Imperial Guard.

A hundred dishes of food were set out on the long silver tables, plates of roast mutton, guinea fowl, pigeon, goose, lamb, and chicken. The Ambassador of the Illustrious Signory of Venice was forced to squat on the carpets with the rest of the company to eat his lunch.

"When may I see the Sultan?" he hissed at his interpreter, an unhappy-looking man who seemed to be sweating profusely, despite the relative cool of the weather.

"Very soon," the man whispered back. "But we must be silent for the meal!"

As the interpreter had suggested, the meal was eaten in complete silence. As they ate, black pages squirted rosewater into their goblets with unnerving accuracy from a goatskin that was slung over their backs. They were served by attendants in red silk robes who moved silently in long files to and from the kitchen or stood waiting for the command of a raised finger, like painted figurines. Pastries, figs, dates, watermelon, and rahat lokum were served as dessert.

Not a word was spoken.

The solemnity of the occasion was not broken until the meal was completed and the assembled dignitaries rose to their feet. At that point the black slaves descended on the plates and scrambled for the remains of the food.

It only confirmed what the Ambassador of the Illustrious Signory of Venice had suspected about the heathen all along.

The Ba'ab-i-Sa'adet, the Gate of Felicity, guarded the selamlik, the inner sanctum of the Sultan. The huge double gate was surmounted by a heavily ornamented canopy flanked by sixteen columns of porphyry, and guarded, by Gonzaga's calculation, by at least thirty eunuchs. They wore vests of gold brocade, and each of them had his curved yataghan drawn, the razor-edged blades flashing in the sunlight.

Gonzaga was given a gold cloth to put on over his clothes, so that he would be fit to present to the Sultan. The Chief of Standard then came to receive his gifts.

Four Parmesan cheeses.

The interpreter did not comment on this bounty, or the lack of it. They waited beyond the gate while the offerings were presented to the Lord of Life.

Suddenly two chamberlains grabbed the Ambassador of the Illustrious Signory of Venice by the neck and arms, pinioning him. They forced him on to his knees to kiss the portal of the Ba'ab-i-Sa'adet, and dragged him across a gloomy courtyard, between another double line of guards and into the Audience Hall, the Arzodasi.

The Arzodasi was actually a kiosk of immense proportions, the overhanging roof supported by a pillared marble colonnade that circumscribed the whole building. Once inside, Gonzaga was hurried through an anteroom, paneled with sheets of pure gold and silver, and into the main Audience Hall itself.

Even though he was almost inarticulate with rage and humiliation, it was not lost on Gonzaga that the room he was in was one of the most extravagantly furnished he had ever seen.

The walls were inlaid with fine ceramic, and inscribed in Arabic with quotations from the Qur'ān, in *sülü* script. There were sofas upholstered with Venetian brocade or heavy Russian velvet or gossamer Chinese muslin. The floors were piled thick with carpets: Persian, Syrian, Mameluke, all silk; Chinese vases, larger than a man, stood in all corners of the room. Gonzaga was even afforded a glimpse of his own august person on his knees, held down by two black slaves, in the reflection of a gilt Venetian mirror.

The throne stood in one corner of the hall like a low four-poster bed, surrounded by a carpet of green satin embroidered with silver and pearls. Sheets of pure silk formed a billowing canopy under a cupola of finely worked cedar. There was an ornate bronze fireplace on one side, a cascading marble fountain on the other.

The throne itself had been fashioned from beaten gold, encrusted with peridot from the Red Sea, set in gold petalmounts. Pearls and rubies hung from silk tassels on the canopy. It was so large that the Sultan's feet did not touch the ground. For one absurd moment Gonzaga had the feeling he was about to address a child.

His impression of the Lord of Life was a fleeting one. A bearded face beneath a white turban, adorned with a huge egret feather, three braided diamond tiaras and a ruby the size of a hazelnut, a gown of white satin ablaze with rubies and sapphires.

The Grand Vizier stood at his right shoulder.

Gonzaga began his protest to the interpreter, but the man was not listening. Lütfi Pasha, the Vizier, was addressing him. It was perhaps fortunate for the Ambassador's sense of position that he could not understand the import of what was being said.

"Has the dog been fed and clothed?" the Vizier demanded.

"The infidel is fed and clothed and now craves leave to lick the dust beneath His Majesty's throne," the interpreter answered.

"Bring him here, then."

Gonzaga was compelled into the act of sala'am by the chamberlains. He was then dragged to the middle of the chamber, where they forced his head to the floor once more. Approaching the throne they forced his forehead into the thick carpet a third time.

"The dog has brought tribute?" the Vizier asked the interpreter.

"Four cheeses, Great Lord."

"Store them in the treasury with the other gifts," he told him.

The Ambassador of the Illustrious Signory of Venice was dragged backward to the door. Again he was placed in the position of obeisance, and then propelled from the Arzodarsi and into the forecourt, where the chamberlains released him.

Gonzaga was shaking with rage. He could barely articulate his words. "What . . . what is the meaning . . . you humiliate me this way . . . I have not addressed the Sultan!"

"But you may not address the Lord of Life directly," the interpreter answered, clearly bewildered. "Now we go to the Divan. You may put your entreaties to the Grand Vizier and the Council."

Gonzaga stared at him as if he had gone mad. Then he turned his back on him and stamped away.

77

Pera

I T IS A humiliation! We come here in peace and they spit on us! How dare they treat us this way!"

It was two days since the Ambassador of the Illustrious Signory of Venice had been honored with an audience with the Sultan of the Osmanlis, and he was still shaken. Ludovici poured him wine from the crystal decanter to placate him.

"All ambassadors are treated the same way. Ever since Murad the First was assassinated by a Serbian noble."

"I did not even get the opportunity to speak in person to him! Who does he think he is? I am a member of the Consiglio di Dieci!"

"He is the Lord of Life, the Emperor of the Two Worlds, Maker of Kings, and Possessor of Men's Necks—that's who he thinks he is, your Excellency." Ludovici said, trying to conceal his pleasure at Gonzaga's humiliation. "Besides, all decisions on foreign policy are taken by the

Grand Vizier. Süleyman will ratify them or not as he sees fit. He never bargains directly. It would be too demeaning."

"Demeaning!"

They were in the drawing room of Ludovici's palazzo. It was suitably impressive, Ludovici thought. Impressive enough that he could deal with Gonzaga on more or less equal terms. It was furnished with a long table of polished chestnut, and carved chairs upholstered with crimson damask. Gilt Venetian mirrors hung on three walls, allowing Ludovici to study his guest's discomfiture from different angles.

You do not know the true meaning of humiliation, Ludovici thought. Can you even guess at what Abbas has suffered?

"You cannot understand the Turks by judging them from our viewpoint," Ludovici said. "Their whole system is built around a rigid hierarchy. To their mind the Sultan has no equal, in the whole world. Not even the Emperor of Rome . . . or the Doge."

Gonzaga snorted with derision and drank his wine.

"The Sultan is the only one who attains his position by virtue of birth," Ludovici continued. "All others rise by their own abilities. They do not even have to be born Muslim. The last Grand Vizier, Ibrahim, was the son of a Greek fisherman. They have a system called the devshirme. They take men and women from non-Muslim families and train them to be part of the kullar—the Sultan's slave family. Among the men, those with real ability can rise through the ranks to become a great pasha. Those with more brawn than brain are conscripted into the yeniçeris. These elite troops that we fear so much and that have won half of Europe for the Turk were all born Christians! As for the women, the mother of a Sultan might start life as the daughter of a Circassian peasant farmer. The system is eminently fair."

"I understand the point you are making," Gonzaga grunted. "But perhaps your admiration is tempered by personal bitterness."

Ludovici bowed his head to concede this. "However, you must admit, your Excellency, although the Turk fights the infidel—as he calls us—with all the means at his disposal, nowhere else in the world can a man practice his religion as freely as he may inside the Osmanli Empire itself. Even when they made war on you . . . on us . . . we in Pera were allowed to practice our Catholicism in peace. Down there in Galata you will find Jews, Muslims, Christians, all working side by side, while in Rome they still want to put the Lutherans to the stake."

"Is that why you asked me here, Ludovici? To list the virtues of the Sultan? Perhaps you intend to convert to Islam yourself?"

"I remain a loyal subject of La Serenissima. It is just that I have lived here a long time, your Excellency. I feel I have a little understanding of their ways."

"Thank you for the lecture," Gonzaga sneered. "It has been most instructive."

"That was not my purpose for inviting you here."

"Oh?" Gonzaga finished his wine and helped himself to more.

"I understand your negotiations with Lütfi Pasha did not go well."

Gonzaga's face flushed red once more. "The impertinent little man wants us to pay tribute and cede the island of Cyprus! He will want to use the San Marco as his Summer Palace next!"

"Can we refuse their demands?"

Gonzaga stared at him, his face drawn with venom. "Ever since Prevezo, the Turk has ruled the Mediterranean, as you well know. Without uninterrupted trading routes, our republic will sink into the Adriatic. Thanks to your enlightened Turk!"

"There might be another way to settle this, Excellency."

"I'm listening."

"As I think you know, my activities are not always strictly legal . . . by Osmanli law anyway."

"We suspected that."

"It has led me to make some unusual and influential allegiances. These allegiances might now be of some use to La Serenissima."

"How?"

"It is true, I do admire the Turks, but I love my country more. Perhaps if you abandoned your negotiations with the Sultan I might be able to arrange a meeting for you with the Turkish admiral, Dragut."

"Dragut!"

"He is no more than a pirate, as you know. He is for sale to the highest bidder. *Ecco*, if Venice must pay tribute for the use of the sea lanes, I am sure Dragut would not be as unreasonable in his demands as the Grand Vizier."

Gonzaga drained his glass and studied Ludovici thoughtfully. "Well, my renegade merchant, perhaps you are right. You might be of service to the republic after all."

"I am glad you think so," Ludovici said.

JULIA WATCHED THE conversation from the shadows at the top of the stairs. Her father! It was like looking at a total stranger. He looked grayer, smaller, than she remembered. Perhaps it was age. It was almost twelve years since she had seen him. His face seemed thinner and the lines around his mouth had deepened, so that the corners seemed permanently drawn down into a sneer.

But his voice still sent a chill to her stomach. It brought back memories of cold, marble corridors, of silent, gloomy meals in his presence, of black and dusty Bibles, of disapproval, of restraint.

She felt as a convict might feel when meeting a former jailor in the street.

She searched her soul for some ghost of affection, but found nothing there but the shadowy horror of her former life. She felt a sudden surge of gratitude for Ludovici, and what he had given her.

And she remembered Abbas.

Abbas!

78

Stamboul

FROM THE WINDOWS of the Palace of Abdül Sahine Pasha there were views of the great dome of the Aya Sofia and the Firuz Aga Camii. On the fine days of summer the dolphins could be seen playing in the Sea of Marmara.

Sirhane now had her own hammam, the marble walls set with a frieze of Iznik ceramic, emblazoned with a verse from the Qur'ān in blue and white sülü script, around the circumference of the whole room. Light from the vaulted ceiling was diffused through the spiraling vapors of steam.

Julia sat naked on the edge of the bath while Sirhane held a small stone jar of scented oil and splashed some on her hands. She began to massage the perfume into Julia's neck and shoulders.

"You are tense. What's wrong?"

Julia lifted her head. "Do you remember your father?"

"Of course I remember him."

"How old were you when you were taken by the devshirme?"

"Fifteen."

"Did you cry?"

"For a week. Why?"

"Just tell me."

"We were farmers. My father had sheep and a few goats. Also we grew sunflowers and a little grain. He was a kind man, but he was very old when I left. He is probably dead now. My mother too. I had ten brothers and sisters. I miss them all. But what good does it do to brood about it? If I were still with them, I would be in a field driving a plow or picking sunflowers, not living in a fine palace with my own servants."

"But did you love him?"

"My father?" Julia twisted her head around. Sirhane seemed perplexed by the question. "Of course." She squeezed hard with her fingers on Julia's neck muscles, as if she could squeeze the tension from her by physical force. "Julia, please, what is wrong?"

"Sirhane, Sirhane. I fear for my soul."

"What?"

"There is something evil in me. I feel it."

Sirhane laughed, then realized Julia was serious. She wrapped her arms around her shoulders and hugged her. "What is all this madness? First you ask me about my father, then you tell me you are evil . . ."

"There is so much about myself I do not understand. Why can't I love a man? Why is it I prefer your company to my husband's?"

Sirhane turned Julia around to face her. "It's not wrong."

"Of course it is."

"We harm no one. A woman cannot violate another woman."

"Is that what it is, then? Love is just a matter of seed?"

"Julia . . ."

"I know he loves me. I know he wants me to love him. I betray him every time I see you."

"We give each other comfort. It is not the same as making love with a man."

"Because you cannot own property, as a man can? We cannot possess each other, then?"

"Julia, what is all this about?"

Julia sighed and rested her head on the other woman's shoulder. The gauze wrap the other woman wore felt rough against her cheek. She allowed Sirhane to cradle her.

"If you knew something terrible was going to happen to someone, and you did nothing to prevent it . . . is that wrong?"

She felt Sirhane's body stiffen. "You must tell me what is happening, Julia."

"Answer my question."

". . . It depends." Sirhane answered carefully. "Has this person done anything wrong?"

"Yes . . . oh, yes."

"And is his punishment ratified by law?"

Julia did not reply, and Sirhane did not press her again for an answer. Instead she said: "What will happen if you keep your silence?"

"Someone will die."

"And if you do not?"

"A guilty person will go unpunished."

Sirhane hugged her closer. "Do you love this person?" Who is it? Sirhane wondered. Is it Ludovici? . . . Is it me?

"I should love him. But I cannot. There is something bad in me."

"No, Julia," Sirhane whispered. "There is nothing wrong. You are kind, and you are gentle. No true Paradise would shut its doors to you."

No, Julia thought. I am not kind, I am not good. I have shamed myself with another woman, and with a *castrato*. I have disavowed my own father. My Confessor taught me that the true Christian virtues were chastity and forgiveness. I have immersed myself in flesh and vengeance. And I no longer even try to fight it.

My father.

Abbas!

Damn Antonio Gonzaga. She would see him in Hell.

She lay her head on Sirhane's lap, and put her arms above her head, arching her body in surrender. "Love me, Sirhane. Tell me it is all right. I need you to tell me everything will be all right."

Pera

IT HAD SEEMED natural to Gonzaga that as few people as possible should know of his meeting with Dragut, and so he informed only the bailo of his intentions in advance, omitting Ludovici's role in the arrangements. The merchant had most to lose should the negotiations fail, and Gonzaga was prepared to protect him—while he was still of some use.

A messenger had been sent that afternoon to the bailo's residence with a sealed missive for Gonzaga. It informed him that Dragut would be on the galleot *Barbarossa*, now moored in the harbor at Galata. Gonzaga was to meet him there, soon after midnight, and he was to come alone.

That night he left the bailo's residence in Pera in a wooden coach. It clattered out of the courtyard and down the hill into the inky bowels of Galata.

The bailo wished him luck and waved him farewell.

79

Galata

A PINK GLOW LIT the sky from the foundries and threw a roseate glow across the deserted docks. Suddenly a carriage clattered down one of the *yokush,* a violently steep alley that ended right on the waterfront itself. Abbas watched from the shadows as a man stepped out. The driver of the coach handed him a lighted lamp and the man—Abbas recognized the robes and bareta of a togato—walked away toward the wharf.

He passed within five yards of the doorway where Abbas stood, and he saw the features of his face quite clearly in the glow of the lamp. A decade rolled back and he was back in the hold of the stinking galleot, and the nauseating stench of his own blood was in his nose, and he could not stop the images he had dammed for so long from rolling over him again.

THERE HAD BEEN three of them, a knifer and two assistants. Abbas could remember them clearly, their faces, their voices, every finest detail, even twelve years later. He remembered the large raised birthmark on the knifer's temple, at the hairline; it had looked like a large raisin in the lamplight. He remembered too the man who held his shoulders, the cluster of blackheads in the folds of his nostrils. The one who held his legs had thinning hair, the dome of his skull gleaming like a mirror in the lamplight. In his fever and panic he imagined it would blind him.

The one with the knife had an unusually high-pitched voice, like a choirboy. He had laughed the whole time. As if it were a joke.

They had tied a white bandage round his lower belly and his thighs to prevent the bleeding. It had taken a long time because he had kicked and struggled. The knifer had sworn at him but he had not struck him and Abbas realized later that he had wanted him to exhaust himself. Next they had bathed his penis and testicles with hot pepper water. He had screamed at the scalding pain and the knifer had laughed again and said he would put them in cold water as soon as they were off and cool them for him.

Abbas had struggled and writhed and fought them with all the strength he possessed. He had begged and cried. He remembered with humiliation, even now, sobbing like a baby and pleading with them to name their price.

The knifer had laughed harder than ever and taken the sickle knife from his belt.

It was impossible to remember the pain, the actual physical effect; but he could summon those same feelings of despair and fear and helplessness at will. The remembrance filled him with such a terrible ache that sometimes lying awake at night he groaned aloud and thrashed on his bed.

He remembered he screamed so loudly that he could not speak for weeks afterward. When they cauterized the wound with boiling pitch he vomited and passed out.

When he recovered consciousness they were still binding the wound, using paper that had been saturated in cold water. They placed a spigot in an opening in the bandages to restrict the flow of urine and blood.

He remembered he was physically unable to stop screaming, but the screams seemed to come from outside of himself. Some other voice inside him was quite calm, and told him that soon he would bleed to death and it would be over.

The knifer's assistants dragged him to his feet and began to walk him round the hold. One circuit of the room took in Signora Cavalcanti's blue lolling head, Bartolomeo's staring eyes, a pool of lapping blood-stained bilge, a coil of tarred rope, some sacking, and a broken winch cable. Then it began again.

Signora Cavalcanti's blue lolling head . . . Bartolomeo's staring eyes . . . the pink-stained pool of bilge . . .

They walked the room for what seemed like days, and was probably just a few hours. What truly horrified him was the way the two men talked to him continually, encouraging him, recalling other operations they had seen and how everything would be all right, he must not despair. It was as if they were his friends, his physicians. They seemed to have quite divorced themselves from the reality of what they had just done.

What was worse, he found his hatred of them slipping away. He sobbed and thanked them when they finally allowed him to slip to the floor, half crazed with pain and only semiconscious.

He had no idea how long he lay there. Someone lit a fire inside his body and he started to burn with fever. But they would not let him drink and his tongue swelled in his mouth until it almost choked him and his lips cracked and he could not speak. Time no longer had meaning. He slipped without effort from consciousness to blackness, as if he were dozing in his bed before rising, reality and dream melting into a montage of nightmare images. And each time he woke he prayed only for darkness to envelop him again.

One day the two men came back into the hold and bent down to examine the wound. They removed the bandages and nodded to each other in satisfaction. When they released the spigot a flow of urine spurted across the room like a fountain.

"Well done." One of the men grinned at him and patted him on the shoulder. "You're going to be all right."

All right? he thought later. All right? What was "all right"? A few weeks later they sold him in the marketplace in Algiers. From there he was brought to the seraglio, to suffer in glorious splendor, to live the rest of his days as a freak, tormented by his disability. There was no consolation in the knowledge that he was surrounded by other freaks.

Most of the other eunuchs had at least never known sexual maturity. In a way, he envied them. Indeed, there were few days when he did not envy everyone.

And not one day when he had not cursed the name of Antonio Gonzaga.

THE MEMORY OF those days passed in just a few seconds, and then Gonzaga was gone; the only thing visible on the deserted wharf was the glow of his lamp, as he moved toward the *Barbarossa*. The galleot's outline was silhouetted in fire by the glow from the arsenal at Top Hane. Other shadows moved in other doorways. Their footsteps were swallowed by the clang of hammers and the roaring of the foundries.

Abbas moved out of the doorway and followed the bobbing lamp.

He had waited too long for this moment.

Pera

JULIA KNELT IN her private chapel and stared at the wooden crucifix that hung above the altar. She had come here to ask forgiveness, to pray for absolution and the strength to fight her weakness. Instead she felt only anger.

What sort of God could allow such misery? What sort of God would allow Abbas to suffer and Gonzaga to prosper this way?

Her father's God. Her father's vengeful, somber, male God.

She rose from her knees. She would find her solace elsewhere.

80

Galata

GONZAGA SENSED THE movement behind him before he heard the footsteps. Anticipating no danger, he felt no alarm. He turned and peered into the shadows.

"*Chi Xiè?*"

No answer.

But there was someone there, he was sure of it. If it was one of Dragut's men, surely he would have shown himself? He turned and hurried toward the gangway of the *Barbarossa*.

The galleot was deserted. The lamps that burned on the fore and main masts threw long shadows across an empty deck. There was no night watch, no sound from below.

Gonzaga felt the first prickling of fear.

He heard another sound from the darkened wharf, and he spun around.

"Who is there?"

He drew his sword, cursing himself now for being persuaded to come alone. Yes, there was definitely someone there.

He started to run.

Suddenly four shapes melted out of the shadows, blocking his way. He turned and ran in the other direction.

Four more silhouettes appeared from the shadows of the warehouses. *Corpo di Dio!* Who were they? What did they want?

He tried to compose himself. They must be Dragut's men. After all, he was expected. He had nothing to fear.

"Which one of you is Dragut?" His voice sounded shrill, even to himself.

"Dragut is not here," a falsetto voice replied, in faultless Venetian dialect. By the Lion of San Marco, what was happening?

"Where is he, then? I demand to see him!"

"He is getting drunk at Üsküdar, I shouldn't wonder," the voice said again. "Now drop your sword or we will be forced to take it from you."

Gonzaga heard the rasping of steel as swords were drawn from their scabbards. He uttered a sob of fear and let his own blade clatter onto the cobbles at his feet. He dropped the oil lamp and ran.

Instantly, two shadows loomed from nowhere and grabbed him by the arms. He kicked and shrieked in panic. One of the men laughed.

"Tie him up," the falsetto voice said.

There were at least half a dozen of them. Rough hands pushed him into the stinking mud, pinioning his arms behind his back, tying them with thick rope. He started to scream for help but a foul rag was stuffed in his mouth, cutting short his protests. One of the men lashed out with his boot, kicking him over onto his back.

Someone picked up the oil lamp he had abandoned and came to stand over him. Gonzaga found himself staring at one of the ugliest men he had ever seen, a fat Moor with one eye, and half his face mutilated by some ancient injury. In the half glow of the lamp, he looked like a devil from Hell.

"Antonio Gonzaga," the man said. So this was the falsetto! "Don't you remember me?"

Remember him? Gonzaga's mind reeled. What does he mean?

He squinted up at this apparition in the gloom, trying to get a better view of his tormentor. Yes, he was definitely a Moor, but no wharfside scum, like the others. He was wearing a sable-lined pelisse, embroidered with pearls and silver, and yellow leather boots. There was a large round pearl in his right ear.

Who was he? What did he want?

The man crouched down next to him, holding the lamp closer to the horribly disfigured face. He removed the sodden rag from Gonzaga's mouth.

"You really don't remember, do you?"

"Of course I don't remember you! I've never met you!"

"No, we never met. You're right. But you did know me. And I knew your daughter."

"My daughter's dead! She was murdered by pirates!"

"Perhaps."

"Who are you? *Corpo di Dio*, tell me what you want!"

"What do I want? I want you to remember. I want you to remember your daughter, the most beautiful creature I have ever seen, ever will see. I want you to remember back twelve years, to the son of the Captain General of the Troops . . ."

Gonzaga's eyes widened in sudden recognition—of the name, if not the face—and he moaned, open mouthed.

"Ah, yes, I see you do remember now. For myself, I have never forgotten. How could I? After what you ordered your bully boys to do to me!" He stood up. "Take him aboard!"

Gonzaga screamed but one of the men quickly shoved the rag back in his mouth. They lifted him easily—by the wrists and feet, like a stuck pig—and carried him aboard the *Barbarossa* and into one of the holds.

Perfect justice, Abbas thought.

This was how it began for me.

81

ABBAS HUNG THE lamp on a hook fixed to one of the beams, and leaned against the bulwark, while the men deposited their whimpering cargo in a lapping pool of tar and seawater at his feet. He seemed to be trying to plead with them, but the gag muffled every sound he made. His eyes were huge, almost starting from their sockets in his terror.

Abbas waited until they were alone. Then he said: "I will remove the gag. But if you scream I shall replace it. Is that clear?"

Gonzaga nodded his head desperately.

"There."

He tore the rag from Gonzaga's mouth and the words bubbled out in a torrent, as if he had pulled a bung from a barrel of wine. "I do not know what was done to you, I swear, I only ordered them to beat you, to discourage you, that was all. If I have wronged you, I swear I can make it up. I am a rich man, I have much to offer you, I am a Consig—"

Abbas stuffed the gag back in his mouth. The snuffling sounds he made in an attempt to plead for himself continued. Like a dog vomiting up its breakfast, Abbas thought.

Still, I understand. I pleaded like that once.

"I might have known," Abbas said. "I might have known that all I would hear from you is lies and vanities. What can you offer me, Consigliatore? Money? I have more than I shall ever need. The Sultan and his lady pay all my expenses. I have fine clothes, and more diamonds than I could fit even in your long pockets. No, what I desire more than anything is granted to every man at birth. And you took it away. You cannot give it back."

Abbas drew a short killiç from the sash at his waist. He held it close to Gonzaga's face, turning it in his fist so that the blade caught the reflection of the lamp. "Look at this, your Excellency. A simple instrument. You can cut bread with it or you can ruin a man's life. It depends on the intention. What is my intention, your Excellency? Can you guess?"

With surprising speed he pulled up Gonzaga's robe, exposing his thighs and lower belly. He grasped Gonzaga's testicles and held them in his fist, squeezing.

Gonzaga stiffened, and a shrill scream somehow escaped the gag. His face suffused with blood, the capillaries in his cheeks and nose livid against the death-white of his skin.

"Can you imagine what it is like, your Excellency? Can you for a moment imagine what it would be like?"

Gonzaga sobbed, his eyes squeezed shut, shaking his head violently as if he were trying to free it from a noose. Abbas watched him, remembering. Suddenly he stood up, and slumped against the bulwark. He replaced the knife in the belt at his waist.

"No, Consigliatore, I would not wish such a horror on even my worst enemy. Not even you, Consigliatore. Not even you. I could never stain my soul with such a sin."

All the strength seemed to drain from Gonzaga's body. He rolled on his side, curling his knees into his chest. He started to cry.

"I will show you mercy, your Excellency. I will even give you your life, such as it is worth. Every second that remains of it is yours to savor. In the morning Dragut sails this vessel for Algiers. I have instructed him to sell you in the marketplace as a galley slave. You have many years before you, Consigliatore. Many happy years, chained to a bench, awash in your own filth, straining eighteen hours a day at the oars. Some men survive five, even ten years of this torment before their strength gives out."

Abbas opened the door to the hold. "If only you had shown me such consideration—I would have thought it the greatest kindness, compared to the future you chose for me! Go with God, your Excellency!"

He looked for the last time on the Ambassador of the Illustrious Signory of Venice, then took the lamp from its hook, and left Antonio Gonzaga to the darkness and his dreams.

Pera

THE MOON HAD fallen below the seven hills when Ludovici returned. Julia was still awake. She sat by the window, looking over the Horn toward the city.

He stood behind her, placing a hand on her shoulder.

"It is done," he whispered.

He felt the answering pressure of her fingers on his hand but she did not reply. After a while he left her there and went to bed, knowing he would not sleep.

The Eski Saraya

ABBAS SELECTED HIS own key from the hundreds on the great key ring that was stuffed in his sash. The last Kapi Aga was the last of the white eunuchs ever to be given the responsibility of the keys. At least, he supposed, the Sultan could be sure that a rasé could be completely trusted with the responsibility.

He slumped on his tiny cot. The cat jumped on his lap, purring, and he stroked her distractedly, his attention focused on some shadow play deep in his own mind. He removed the turban and put his head in his hands.

Revenge did not taste sweet, he thought. It merely replaced one emotion with another: hatred with bitterness, anger with longing. He no longer had a dream of vengeance to cling to, only the pain of remembrance. The scores had been settled; he had to live the rest of his days grappling with the price he had been forced to pay.

Nothing could change what had been done.

Nothing.

THE CRESCENT MOONLIGHT shimmered on the cupolas and minarets of the Harem like frost, lending an aura of ghostliness to the plane and cypress trees standing sentinel in the courtyards.

The eunuchs guarding the iron-studded doors stood like statues carved from mahogany. Far above them two pairs of eyes watched from the windows high above the cramped and grim streets of the city.

One stared across the impenetrable black horizons to the waving grass of the Georgian steppes; the other pair of eyes was turned toward the sun-dappled canals of La Serenissima. They both invoked brothers or lovers, gondolas or wild white horses, and agonies of loss that still seared the soul like a brand, and banished sleep. Abbas and Hürrem, enslaved by mutilation and beauty, paced the night, their souls eroded by bitterness and frustration, each a tiny outpost of Hell in one man's Paradise on earth.

PART 8

THE DANGEROUS WINDOW

82

Topkapi Saraya, 1553

FOR OVER A decade the executioner's sword had hung over his children. There was nothing that even the King of Kings could do to protect his own children after his death, because his own great-grandfather, the Fatih, conqueror of Stamboul, had made this bloody kanun:

> The ulema have declared it allowable that whoever among my illustrious children and grandchildren may come to the throne should, for securing the peace of the world, order his brothers to be executed. Let them hereafter act accordingly.

As the years of his reign lengthened, and Süleyman felt the first gnawing of age and doubt, the consequences of his own mortality haunted him more and more. It is our weakness, he had decided. We will never be a great people unless such bloodshed among brothers and sons is put aside.

It had begun years before. One night she placed the problem before him, giving voice to the unease for the first time. "I am afraid," she had whispered to Süleyman as she lay in his arms.

"Afraid? Of what, little russelana?"

"Not for me. For my sons."

"You have nothing to fear."

She laid her head on his bare, smooth chest. "My Lord, when you die—may that day never dawn!—my life shall no longer be worth living, so I fear nothing. But when Mustapha attains the throne, the Kanun of the Fatih says that he may rid himself of all his brothers to secure his throne . . ."

"We have stepped beyond such barbarity. It will never happen again."

"Ah, my Lord, it is not Mustapha I fear. He has a good heart, and has shown only goodwill toward all my sons, even poor Çehangir."

"What then?"

"My Lord, I fear those who may surround him when he is green to the throne, before he discovers his own authority. We know Mustapha shall be Sultan, but who will be his Vizier? Would some dried-up eunuch like Achmed Pasha show compassion for poor Çehangir? Could even the astrologers of the House of Time foretell what plans the Aga of the yeniçeris might hatch against Selim, because he cannot ride? What traps might a jealous pasha lay for Bayezid, because he is so able? Already the yeniçeris and the Divan hang on Mustapha's every word and every deed like dogs hungry for every scrap. It makes me afraid."

Süleyman held her tighter. Poor Hürrem. She was right. After his death, there was nothing he could do to protect her, or her sons. Selim and Bayezid, of course, would have to take their own chances, as he had done. But what of a poor cripple, like Çehangir? Mustapha had given Süleyman his word and yet . . .

For all his power now, he was helpless beyond the grave.

He must rely on Mustapha's nobility. The boy was no butcher, like Selim the Grim. Süleyman had watched him grow from an infant. He was as loyal as he was brave, and he was just. There was no cunning or malice there. His was the good hand, the just hand, into which to pass the banner of Muhammad.

"He is a just man, little russelana."

"His mother still lives. And she hates me."

Yes, Gülbehar! She had had ten years to brood on her slights in Manisa. When he died, she would be Valide Sultan. Would she press Mustapha to invoke the Fatih's law?

"What would you have me do?"

"Never die."

He smiled in the darkness at the flattery of her reply. Ah, little russelana! "We all die. It is God's path for us."

"Then I shall pray I have a voice in the Divan to protect me. Rüstem perhaps . . ."

Süleyman smiled at the wisdom of it. Rüstem Pasha, his son-in-law! Yes, he would surely protect his wife and her brothers. He was still young, and he had proved his loyalty with Ibrahim.

"Mustapha will not harm you, little russelana. The Osmanlis will no longer butcher each other. You have my word on it."

But when Süleyman's Grand Vizier, Achmed Pasha, died of the pestilence, Süleyman ignored the laws of succession and proclaimed his own son-in-law the new Vizier.

The Man Who Never Smiled became the second most powerful man in the Osmanli Empire.

ABBAS WAS USHERED into the presence of the Vizier, executed his temennah, and allowed his pages to lower his bulk to the carpet. Rüstem reminded himself that this grotesque eunuch was not his master; he just spoke the words of the one who was. The purple silk of his robe is like the royal tent, he thought. When he moves it's like a squadron of yeniçeris buggering each other under a blanket.

He did not allow his amusement to display itself on his face. Abbas did not matter. Abbas was just an instrument, his channel to the voice and ears and heart of the Sultan's selamlik.

"May I extend my congratulations on your great fortune," Abbas greeted him. "God indeed smiles on you. To be the Vizier of the greatest of all Osmanli Sultans is indeed a blessing almost too great to comprehend."

The Infinite had no hand in this, Rüstem thought. It is just that I possess more cunning than those other fools in the Divan. But he said: "All thanks and praise to Him."

"Indeed. However, my mistress asks me to remind you that though God is great, there are times when His bounty—as His vengeance—may need prompting by more earthly agents."

What a pretty tongue you have, Rüstem thought. "Tell your mistress I shall not forget."

"Indeed," Abbas said, "that is why I am here. To discuss the many ways you can display your remembrance."

Rüstem clapped his hands and his black pages scurried away to fetch sherbets and halva while they settled to their discussion.

"YOU HAVE HEARD the whispers in the bazaars, pasha?" Abbas asked.

"The *bazaaris* do more than whisper, Abbas, as you know. They shout to each other in their bedestens how our Sultan has lost his appetite for war."

"Such talk is dangerous."

"Indeed. But what is there to be done, Abbas? He finds glory now only in the great task of rebuilding the city. He spends more time with his architect, Sinan, than with his generals."

"He ignores his avowed duty to God. As Protector of the Faith he is pledged to carry the banner of Muhammad to the Lands of War."

I wonder where this conversation is leading, Rüstem thought. You and your mistress care as much for the banner of Muhammad as you do for the price of melons in the fruit market. What concerns you, of course, is Mustapha. We must all be careful, with such a shahzade as he waiting, his horse saddled to ride.

"You have heard these other rumors, from the barracks?" he said.

"Everyone in all Stamboul has heard them. So many whispers that together they are like the rumbling of a distant army at night."

"None of us are unaware of the risk." But one must not act rashly, Rüstem thought. The gamble must be carefully weighed before any decision is taken. I hope your mistress realizes this.

The trouble had started, as always, in Persia. Shah Tamasp was once again raiding their eastern border, torturing and killing the muftis and flaunting his Sufavid heresies, growing all the time bolder while Süleyman wrote poetry and dictated laws and planned mosques in his summer *yalis* in Adrianople and Çamlica. Meanwhile his yeniçeris waited behind the Palace walls, hungry for action, increasingly impatient with the former conqueror of Rhodes. They talked more and more openly about their adored Mustapha, the charismatic Heir Apparent who waited in the wings, with the first wisps of gray sprouting in his beard. He would not hesitate to lead them against the heretic Persians, they said. He would give them fresh victories to savor. He would give them blood and plunder and the action they craved.

But his dawn would herald the twilight of other lives, Rüstem thought. Hürrem's, for example. And mine.

From somewhere along the colonnaded gardens, a bell sounded the hour.

"What would the Lady Hürrem have me do?" he said.

"Just remember where your loyalty lies."

I remember, Rüstem thought. It lies with myself. "I understand," Rüstem said.

83

ÜLEYMAN HAD LIVED nearly fifty-nine years and suddenly he found his age had begun to gnaw at his bones. He sensed his own mortality and began to spend more and more time in consultation with the shey-hülislam and reading his Qur'ān.

He had contracted gout, his elbows and knees occasionally becoming swollen and tender, attacks lasting sometimes as long as a week. He had also developed edema, his face and ankles had swollen, and he had taken to using rouge to disguise the sickly pallor of his skin. He ate little now, usually only some baby goat, washed down with iced sherbet.

Hürrem watched him, and was afraid. These outward manifestations of Süleyman's mortality reminded her of her own fragile tenure on life.

Particularly if Mustapha was allowed to live much longer.

She had been patient so long, waiting for the moment. Now she was afraid that time was no longer on her side. She stood at the windows of the saraya and stared at the night and the black waters of the Horn and knew that she would have to find a way to remove this threat and she knew she must do it soon.

SÜLEYMAN LAY WITH his head on her lap, his eyes closed. Insects murmured in the garden but in the Harem it was cool, almost chill. Even though it was almost midday, the sun had not penetrated the plane trees and the high walls and only a little weak, yellow light filtered through the barred windows.

"You look tired, my Lord," Hürrem said.

"There is so much to do, little russelana, so much to do before I am finished."

"You must not work so hard."

But that is my duty, Süleyman thought. Already I have abrogated the responsibility of the day-to-day running of the Empire to Rüstem and his Divan, so that I can devote myself to the rebuilding of the city. Stamboul will be a far worthier testimony to my reign than Rhodes, or Mohacs, or Buda-Pesth. When my grandfather conquered the city that was once Justinian's Byzantium, much of it was already abandoned and derelict. Before I die the city will have surpassed all its former glory; I shall be able to shout: "Justinian, I have outdone thee!"

The focus of much of the rebuilding was the construction of imperial mosques, for each mosque also included a *külliye,* a cluster of charitable institutions such as a hospital, a religious school, baths, a cemetery, a library, sometimes even a hospice and soup kitchen. New quarters with new populations quickly built up around them.

Already completed were the Sehzade Camii, housing the tomb of Mehmet, and the Selimiye Camii at Fener, honoring his father. Now he had commissioned Sinan to start work on the Süleymaniye, on the site of the Eski Saraya. It was to be his masterpiece; the great stone cupolas and minarets would dominate the Horn and the City of the Seven Hills for a thousand years.

He had also set himself the herculean task of drafting a complete legislature that would be the foundation of all future government. The thousands of kanuns that he was in the process of devising would regulate the judgments and decrees of the Divan, and give the Osmanlis, for the first time, a complete code of law. It had earned him his nickname "El Kanuni"—the Lawgiver.

It had also earned him the contempt of the yeniçeris, he knew. One day, he dreamed, there would be no need for them either. But that work would have to be undertaken by another.

He stared at the shadowed ceiling and the dusty gilt lantern above his head, and it was almost as if he could hear the time slipping away from him. He prayed to God for strength and the hours to finish the task he had set himself.

Hürrem stroked his cheek. "So deep in thought, my Lord?"

"I was thinking how quickly time slips by."

"Perhaps then you should not spend so much of it closeted with your scribes."

"I cannot rest till the work is finished. I dare not entrust it to Mustapha to continue. He is a great soldier and governor, but he cannot apply himself to studying matters of law. Besides, other matters press on me. I must go to Persia this summer. I cannot ignore the Shah any longer."

Hürrem frowned, pouting like a spoiled houri.

He smiled. "What is the matter, little russelana?"

"Why send a great professor to spank an errant child? Is Tamasp so great a king that he should occupy your individual attention?"

"He grows too bold. I have no choice but to move against him."

"Send Mustapha. The yeniçeris adore him; they will follow him anywhere, even into the deserts and mountains of Persia."

A nerve in Süleyman's cheek jerked of its own accord. He stared at her. "Why did you say that?"

"Have I offended you, my Lord?"

"What whispers have you heard concerning Mustapha?"

"Nothing sinister, my Lord. Indeed, I hear only good reports. They say he is a just, good man, as indeed you have always said. A great horseman, a great commander."

"Too great perhaps," Süleyman murmured.

"Can a man be too great?"

"Do you fear him still?"

"My Lord has assured me I have nothing to fear from his son."

"Perhaps," Süleyman said.

"My Lord?"

"I do not fear him as Sultan when I am dead. Yet I sometimes fear him when I am still alive. I fear the yeniçeris."

"They will never love him as they love you," Hürrem assured him. "You gave them Belgrade, you gave them Rhodes, you gave them Buda-Pesth."

"Their memories are short. Many of the young recruits were not even alive then."

"But you are their Sultan."

"So was my grandfather."

"You told me yourself, my Lord, that Mustapha is a just man, a good man. Do you think he would intrigue against you?"

Süleyman sat up, his eyes tormented with fear and doubt. It had been so long since he had seen Mustapha, he no longer remembered the lively, bright-eyed boy. His mind conjured only images of an embittered Gülbehar, and an ambitious, capable young man, growing older, and more impatient.

But his father's shadow, and the Kanun of the Fatih, still haunted him. For there was an antithesis to his vision of civilization; its name was the yeniçeris. They were the bedrock on which the Empire had been built; they were now its greatest threat.

The yeniçeris were the elite of the Osmanli army. They were full-time professional soldiers in an age when most armies were made up of groups of noblemen who each brought their feudal peasants along with them as infantry. The yeniçeris owed their allegiance to just one man. It was the Sultan who fed them each day, and food had become their most important symbol. Their aga was called the Chorbaji Bashi—the Head Soup Ladler; his second in command was called the Ashçi Bashi, or Head Cook. Each man had a spoon in a brass socket sewn in the front of his cap. Their battle color was the *kazan,* or soup kettle, which was emblazoned on all their standards. Each regiment would carry their own cauldron with them on every campaign, and these would be piled in front of the tent of the aga when they were in camp. The loss of a regimental cauldron to the enemy in battle was the greatest disgrace imaginable.

The yeniçeris replenished their ranks from the devshirme, young Christian youths chosen for their brawn, not their brains. They were toughened further with manual labor in the Palace gardens, in the shipyards, or on building projects. Afterward they received their military training, and were taught unquestioning obedience to their agas. They lived harsh, celibate lives in spartan barracks on poor pay; the only way they could hope to fill their own pockets was by the plunder they took in battle. It was the reason they loved Süleyman's father so much; they were never starved of action or plunder when they followed Selim the Grim.

It was the yeniçeris who had forced Süleyman's grandfather, Bayezid II, to abdicate; and Süleyman had never forgotten that once, early in his own reign, they had overturned their kettles under the great plane tree outside their barracks in the First Court as a symbol of revolt. Even though the rebellion had been quashed, he had been forced to increase their wages. Even twenty years later he still glanced at the soup kettles with a feeling of apprehension each time he rode through the First Court on the way to the mosque. In theory at least, they were his slaves; but with their constant demands for war and booty, the continuing threat they posed to the security of the throne, he wondered sometimes if he was not theirs.

"There must be no more blood spilled over the throne," he said, as if reminding himself.

"Do not look so troubled, my Lord," Hürrem said, and wrapped her arms around him.

"You understand many things, little russelana, but you do not understand the yeniçeris. There have been times when they have ruled my actions, when I have gone to the Lands of War purely to satisfy their lust for battle, even though I wished otherwise. If they can rule me, perhaps they can rule him."

"How far is Manisa from Stamboul?"

"When my father died, I rode here in five days to claim the throne. Just five days . . ."

"Then if you truly fear him, my Lord, give Bayezid the province of Saroukhan. Send Mustapha east to Amasya or Karamania."

"Manisa is the traditional seat of the shahzade, the chosen. He will think I have abandoned him, in favor of your sons."

"He knows that you cannot give him guarantees."

"I cannot do it to him."

"Then let us speak no more of it. If Mustapha is a good and just man, what is there to fear?"

Yes, Süleyman thought. What is there to fear?

I fear I will lose everything I have labored so long to build.

He had always wanted to give his Empire a future, outside of tents and war. The nomad people of the Anatolian steppes who were his ancestors would soon have a capital that would boast some of the finest architecture in the Orient, and a formal system of government. Literature, music, and painting were flourishing. They had left behind the barbarity that marked his father's accession; his own death and the peaceful succession of Mustapha would be proof of it.

Or so he prayed.

But the next day Süleyman spoke to Rüstem in private audience. Later he set his seal on a letter commanding Mustapha to leave Manisa and take his family and court to Amasya, far to the east, twenty-six days' ride from Stamboul.

Pera

BEHIND THE DRAWN curtains of one of the palaces on the other side of the Horn, Ludovici Gambetto knocked softly and entered his wife's bedchamber. She was waiting for him; the white silk of her nightdress shimmered in the flickering candlelight. He sat down on the edge of the bed and took her hand.

She sat up and took a lock of his hair between her fingers. "Gray hair!"
He twisted away from her. "Nonsense!"

She was laughing. "At last! I thought you would never grow old!"

"I was in the kitchen. The cook threw flour at me."

"It is a gray hair. There must be others. Do you want me to look?"

"It is just a trick of the light."

"I have them, look!" She draped a long braid of her hair over her palm
and pointed with the finger of her other hand. "With my black hair you
cannot mistake them."

"You still look beautiful to me," he whispered.

He took her face in his hands and kissed her. "I want you," he whispered.

She held out her arms to him and smiled, but he only wished that he
saw need in her eyes, and not just surrender.

AFTERWARD HE LAY beside her in the darkness while she slept, watching
the gentle rise and fall of her breast by the candlelight. He traced the contours of her cheek with his fingers. There might be gray in her hair but she
was still beautiful to him; still beautiful, and still as firmly locked away as
she had been in her father's palazzo.

It was not that she was incapable of great emotion, he knew. Her
friendship with Sirhane had demonstrated that. Two years ago she had
left for Amasya with her husband, who had been appointed to the shahzade Mustapha's bodyguard. Julia had been almost destroyed by grief.
She would not eat and would not leave her room. Her door had been
locked to him for the first time, and for a long time afterward she had
refused him.

He tried to understand; Sirhane had been the only real friend she had
had. Yet her desolation seemed magnified beyond proportion. Still, he had
not tried to force himself on her; he had sensed that had he done so, her
mood might never break.

After some months she had left her door open again and she had
allowed him back into her bed. He tried not to let it matter to him that
she never really responded to him; he understood she could not make
herself love him.

But the envy tormented him. First Abbas, then Sirhane. Why was it
that she could give him her companionship, and reserved her passions for
others? Why was she able to give so much to them and yet for him, who
had dedicated so much of his life to her, there was nothing?

Amasya

CLUMPS OF COBALT-blue forget-me-nots were pushing through the patches of hard snow and between the crevices of the rocks. Wild ducks rose from the grass, their wings whirring as they flapped away, panicked by the sudden thunder of hoofs.

Mustapha turned his Turkoman mount away from his escort and waited for Çehangir. Here in the mountains, with only the wind for company, they could not be overheard.

"A fine day's hunting," he said.

Çehangir looked flushed and tired. But he enjoyed these expeditions although they exhausted him physically.

"Indeed it was," he said. He was always flattered by Mustapha's attention. His stepbrother was everything he was not; strong, handsome, a good rider. Everything his own father admired.

They rode for a short while in silence while Mustapha decided how to best broach the subject that had been on his mind. "How is our father?" he said, finally.

"He suffers with the gout," Çehangir said. "His temper is sometimes foul."

"And you have to endure him in Stamboul!" Mustapha laughed.

"I stay out of his way if I can."

"Does he seem troubled?"

Çehangir realized that the enquiry was not just a polite one, and he felt suddenly nervous. Mustapha was actually seeking his opinion! "Perhaps . . . but I see him only rarely."

Mustapha turned to watch a mountain hawk circling high above their heads. "Does he speak to you of me?"

"Is something wrong between you?"

"I do not know," Mustapha said. Çehangir was startled. It was unlike Mustapha to be so somber.

"You are the shahzade," Çehangir said, as if that were a talisman against all troubles.

"One can be a shahzade too long," Mustapha said. The sun had retreated behind the purple mountains and there was ice in the air. Mustapha shook himself from his musings. "We must hurry. The mountains are cold here at night, even in spring."

Çehangir spurred his horse after him, troubled. If even Mustapha was afraid, then the world was no longer a safe place to be.

IN THE COURTYARD below, the yeniçeri guards stood motionless in their huge leather cloaks. Torches around the walls set long shadows dancing over the cobbles, glazed with a film of ice. It was cold at nights here, even in spring, for the fortress was perched high in the mountains overlooking the Green River.

The kiaya entered in a turban of apricot-colored silk and set a gilded silver jug of steaming black coffee on the low table beside the divan. Gülbehar sat down, warming herself by the charcoal brazier, and waited for Mustapha.

When he finally arrived, his face was bronzed from the cold wind. He has been hunting, Gülbehar thought. That is why he is late. He has ridden home in the darkness, though he knows the dangers of ice and swollen rivers at this time of year.

He bowed and kissed her hand, and settled himself on the divan beside her, grinning like a boy. Nearly forty years old, she thought, and he still possesses the energy of a raw youth; which is just as well. He will be an old man by the time he is Sultan.

"How are you, Mother?"

"I am well. Here, I have had the kiaya fetch us some coffee." She clapped her hands, and one of her black gediçli stepped forward and poured the steaming black liquid into two silver cups.

Gülbehar sipped at the drink, scalding and sweet, laced with honey. She disliked the bitter taste, but she had heard it was the fashion in Stamboul to drink it. She sometimes liked to pretend she had never left the heartbeat of civilization.

"So, now Rüstem has reduced your allowance," she said.

Mustapha grinned again. "Does the shahzade have no secrets?"

"Not from his mother."

"Do not upset yourself. It is nothing."

"Nothing! It is an insult!"

"He is trying to goad me into some action that would benefit him more than me. He is a fool, but he has cause to be afraid when I become Sultan."

"If."

"Mother . . ."

"You trust your father too much. Look what happened to me." She immediately regretted those words. It makes me sound like a bitter old woman, she thought. Perhaps that is what I am. But I know I am also right in what I say.

"I am sure my father knew nothing of this."

Gülbehar found her hands were trembling. She put down the tiny silver cup. "How many more insults will you bear? He marries the witch, makes her queen, then exiles you here to the mountains, and gives Bayezid the shahzade's seat at Manisa. Now he turns his back while Rüstem reduces your allowance! It is unheard of! If it is a goad, then why don't you accept it?"

"That would be foolish."

"Would it, son?" She felt her eyes fill with tears. A fine boy, the finest prince the Osmanlis would ever see, and they were conspiring to ruin him. And so handsome. There was a little gray in his beard, a few lines now on the wind-beaten face, but they only accentuated the authority of his features. You deserve to sit on that throne, she thought. And the ziadi will do all she can to stop you.

"I will not raise my hand against my father. I do not condone what he has done to you, as I have said many times. But he is my father, and he is my Sultan. Any action against him would be a sin against Heaven and against Islam."

"I am sure no such noble thoughts have ever crossed the mind of the ziadi."

"Hürrem may be kadin but she is only—" He stopped himself, he was about to say: "only a woman." "She is not Sultan. In the matter of succession, Süleyman is judge."

"How naïve you are!"

Mustapha did not take offense at this; instead, he grinned at her. "Jealousy."

"More than jealousy, son." Much more than jealousy. I hate her with every aching beat of my heart. More than you could ever know.

"I have only to wait. In time, the throne is mine, and then we can balance all injustice, if there is any. I do not fear Bayezid, and certainly not his fat sot of a brother. Even twenty-six days' ride from Stamboul, the yeniçeris will not accept either of them over me."

"Yes, the yeniçeris want you, Mustapha, but unlike you, they are not prepared to wait."

Mustapha's grin fell away. "No. I will not raise my sword against my father's."

"Süleyman's father did it."

"He has been judged in Heaven."

"Mustapha . . ."

"No! I will not do it! There is no need. One day the throne will come to me by right. I will wait. I will not offend my father, and I will not offend God!"

Sultanahmet, Stamboul

"HE HAS TO die," Rüstem said.

Mihrmah blanched, and lowered her gaze, as if looking at something too shameful for a woman's eyes. "But Mustapha is the shahzade . . ."

"Yes, Mihrmah. And if he is ever Sultan, what do you think will happen to us? I will tell you. Mustapha's first act will to place my head on a spike in the Ba'ab-i-Sa'adet, and send you into exile. And do you think he will show any greater mercy for your brothers?" His voice was calm, almost somnolent. She had never known anyone discuss death with such dispassion as her husband.

Mihrmah turned her head away. Such a pretty day to be discussing murder. The Palace looked out over a maze of gardens, and had been designed to catch the breeze from the Bosphorus and Marmara. It was spring, and a warm breeze was blowing from the south. In the aviary, a nightingale had begun to sing, its sweet voice at variance with the visions of blood conjured here on the shaded terrace.

"Is it not dangerous?"

"I have calculated the risk. There is more danger if we do nothing."

"What does my father say? Does he know what you plan?"

"Your father will say whatever he is led to believe. Should he ask you, you will say that you live in mortal fear of the shahzade. Make up any story you please to add credibility to your claim. Providing it is plausible, of course."

Mihrmah watched her husband eat. Mechanically, it seemed to her, and without relish, as if he was calculating the cost of each mouthful.

"Whose idea was this, my husband? Yours—or did it come from the Hasseki Hürrem?"

He grinned at her, and the effect was chilling. She knew what they called him in the Divan—The Man Who Never Smiled. It was not true, of course. She had seen his smile, and she also knew his secret; his two eye teeth were larger than their fellows and when he smiled they betrayed him, for they gave him the appearance of a wolf.

"Does anything happen in Stamboul that Süleyman's queen does not instigate, by her desire or by her actions?"

"And if we fail?"

"If we fail, then we have lost nothing, for Mustapha is already our enemy. If we succeed, we have power over this Sultan and perhaps the next!"

84

T HE SULTAN'S APARTMENTS, as the rest of the Palace, served two functions, which were fundamental: to display the wealth of the Osmanlis, and to preserve their secrecy.

And so it was with the Sultan's bedchamber. The wealth was quickly apparent. The walls were ablaze with ceramic; verses from the Qur'ān, in sülü script, circled the room, white on blue, and the stained-glass windows were masterpieces of azure and emerald and crimson. Gilt Vicenzan mirrors hung on every wall; the bed itself was raised on a canopied platform, strewn with coverlets of gold brocade and pillows of crimson velvet. By the side of the bed was a ewer of gold set with turquoise and rubies for washing hands.

But it was a silent show, for no one saw the Sultan's bedchamber except his eunuch slaves and Hürrem, his favored kadin.

The compulsion for secrecy was demonstrated by the fountains that were cut into the walls, golden spigots murmuring perfumed water into marble urns; and the *sacnissi,* little gazebos that jutted out from the walls, where the Sultan could sit and observe the gardens without being seen himself.

Soon after Hürrem became queen there had been a further refinement. A concealed doorway had been carved into the stone behind one of the gilt mirrors, and a stairway cut from the bedroom directly to the apartments of the Lady Hürrem herself, so that she could leave or enter without being seen.

It was from this doorway that Hürrem emerged now. She found Süleyman not at his ease on the bed, but pacing the room like a caged beast, though his right knee was still swollen from another bout of gout, drawing his features taut with pain.

"My Lord," Hürrem murmured, and performed the ceremonial sala'am that even she had never dared ignore.

Süleyman barely acknowledged her. He was holding a document in his right hand, and now he waved it in her direction. "What am I to do? What do you make of this?"

"I cannot tell, my Lord, from this distance. But if you were to ask me, I should say that it was a piece of parchment."

He remembered himself then, and he sighed, mocking himself. "I am sorry, I forget myself." He hobbled toward her, and helped her to her feet. "I can scarcely believe the evidence of my own eyes."

"My Lord, none of this makes any sense to me. I am only a poor, uneducated Tartar girl."

"You are nothing of the sort," he muttered, and he handed her the parchment he had in his hand. "Read it."

Hürrem read it quickly. It was addressed to the Shah Tamasp, the heretic Persian, and after a long soliloquy of greeting, made an offer of marriage for one of his daughters. It then went on to outline the benefits to both parties of such a match.

It was signed under the tugra of the shahzade Mustapha.

"It is a forgery," Hürrem said, but admitted to herself that it was a very good one. Rüstem was to be commended. "It must be."

"You think so?"

"How can it be otherwise?"

Süleyman collapsed in despair on a divan. "Why would someone do this? Why?"

"Enemies of the Empire are everywhere. It would serve Charles well were you to fight with your own son. It would even not be beyond the Shah himself to arrange such a forgery."

"I would you were right!" He gasped and held his knee. The gout had aggravated his temper.

Hürrem sat on the divan beside him, and stroked his temple with her long fingers until his fists unclenched and his chin collapsed onto his chest. "What am I to do? What am I to believe?"

"Why would Mustapha do such a thing? It would serve him nothing. The Shah is the sworn enemy of the Osmanlis."

"There is a saying, Hürrem: 'The enemy of my enemy is my friend.' If Mustapha sees me as his enemy, perhaps an allegiance with Tamasp would suit him well."

"I cannot believe it!"

Süleyman shook his head. "Yet it frightens me."

"Where did you get this?"

"One of Rüstem's spies at Amasya. Rüstem has spies everywhere."

"Duping one of Rüstem's spies would be easy to arrange."

"Perhaps." Süleyman looked down at her, and his lips curled into a sad smile. "You are such a comfort to me. I live my life among snakes and vipers. Yours is the only voice of reason and moderation." He winced again.

"Shall I send the doctor for your knee?"

"No, fetch the viol. That is greater medicine than any potion the physician can give me."

Hürrem sat down and played for him. After a while he closed his eyes and she thought he had gone to sleep. But when she put the instrument aside, he opened his eyes again and said: "I must ride east again with the army."

"My Lord, you are unwell. You must not!"

"We must finish with the Shah and his heresies. There can be no peace while he is still conspiring against us in Asia. The yeniçeris, the agas, even the ulema are clamoring for me to act. As Defender of the Faith, I have no choice."

"Send Rüstem in your place."

"The army expects me with them."

Hürrem lowered her eyes. "Please, my Lord. I am afraid. For myself I do not doubt Mustapha's loyalty, but doubt there is. If I am wrong, I and my sons, even Çehangir and Mihrmah, are in terrible danger. You are unwell, and the mountains of the east are cold even in summer. You yourself have told me that a week in Azerbaijan is like a month in the mud of Hungary. I beg you, do not expose yourself to risk before this question is settled."

"I must go."

Hürrem stared at him, and she felt herself trembling. You could really die there, she thought. Do not turn your back on this truth when you have believed so many of my lies!

"I know you do not fear any danger or any hardship, my Lord," she forced herself to say, "but by choosing another course you might also serve a double purpose here, my Lord."

He smiled, slowly. "Ah, my wise little russelana. I knew there must be some plan in that pretty little head."

"I am no longer pretty, my Lord."

"You still enchant me. Now tell me what it is you are thinking."

"Let Rüstem advance to Persia through Amasya. Sign orders telling Mustapha to accompany Rüstem on the campaign, with his own troops. This way Rüstem may soon satisfy himself of Mustapha's loyalty. I am sure he will find all these rumors and forgeries unfounded."

"That is the most devout wish of my heart. But I might divine Mustapha's loyalties just as well myself."

"Yet not as wisely, my Lord. If Mustapha plans treason, do you risk discovering his true ambitions with the yeniçeris in attendance?"

Süleyman stared at her for a long time. "Do you really think it will come to that?"

"I only counsel caution, my Lord."

Süleyman thought for a long time. "Perhaps you are right," he murmured at last.

Hürrem knelt at his feet. "I love you with my life, my Lord. I wish there was some way I could spare you this pain."

"Only my sons can do that, Hürrem. Though why they are so eager to sit on my throne, I can only wonder. If I could ever give it up, and still do my duty to God, I would willingly exchange my lot with any blacksmith in this city. Aside from you, the sultanate has only brought me care beyond belief."

She rested her head in his lap. He allowed the letter to slip from his fingers onto the floor.

85

L UDOVICI MET ABBAS every month in the yellow house in the Jewish quarter. He never relished these encounters. They never spoke of the past, by a tacit and unspoken agreement; and the sight of his old friend's gross and mutilated body depressed him. The fat made Abbas sweat. He perspired freely even in winter, and in summer it dripped steadily from his fingers like rain dripping from the eaves of a roof.

Now, as they sat behind the shuttered windows, Abbas said: "How is Julia?"

They were always his first words: "How is Julia?" And always Ludovici would answer, as he did now: "She is well, my friend. She asks for your prayers and hopes you are well also."

Abbas made no comment. He lowered his head and concentrated on the business at hand: black-market wheat.

The black market for wheat was the worst-kept secret in the Osmanli Empire. There was active complicity from every Turkish nobleman with arable land; eighteen months previously even Rüstem himself had sailed his own roundships to Venice by way of Alexandria and made a huge profit on just one shipment.

Ever since the summer of 1548 Turkey had enjoyed five excellent wheat harvests, while Venice was starved for grain. The profits for the black-market wheat traders grew in proportion. Ludovici was the most success-ful; his caramusalis sailed regularly through the Bosphorus to Rodosto on the Black Sea, ostensibly to load hides or wool. On the way they made secret calls to the port at Volos to pick up the black-market grain. On the return trip through the Bosphorus and the Dardanelles, they were ignored by the Turkish galleots who were supposed to enforce Turkish trade regu-lations; but the privilege was expensive.

"Rüstem Pasha wants another one thousand ducats a month," Abbas said.

"I can't afford that!"

Abbas shrugged. "I am sorry, old friend. But there is much baksheesh to pay. If it were just Rüstem . . ."

"If it were just Rüstem I suspect the price would still be a thousand. Is there no limit to his greed?"

"Apparently not."

"Tell him I refuse."

"Don't be rash, Ludovici. Even after the extra baksheesh, you will still make a twofold profit on every kilo of grain unloaded in the lagoon at La Serenissima. What do you pay here? Twelve aspers the kilo? Rüstem knows you are getting thirty-five in Venice."

"I have to make a profit."

"Those were his words also."

Ludovici sighed. There was nothing to be done. If you wanted to do business in the Empire, you must pay whatever the Vizier demanded. Everyone knew that.

They continued their business: agreeing on routes for his ships, payments to minor officials in the provinces, and the counting of the silver ducats that Ludovici brought with him to the meetings in a leather pouch. Finally it was done, and Abbas relaxed. He helped himself to a little perfumed water—he never drank wine—and, as usual, began to gossip about activities inside the haremlik like an old woman at the market.

Abbas was Ludovici's prime source of information on the moods and internal politics of the Sublime Porte. After Abbas had finished his regular tirade against the iniquities of the ziadi, as he referred to the Lady Hürrem, and the extent of the corruptions introduced by Rüstem Pasha—of which he was now an integral part—he lowered his voice and whispered: "It is said that the shahzade is planning revolt."

"Mustapha?" Ludovici was suddenly attentive. Abbas's tirade against the Court Within was a regular feature of their meetings; this was something new.

"It is said he has arranged marriage with one of the daughters of the Shah Tamasp. He solicits his support in a rebellion against Süleyman."

"This is true, Abbas? You are sure of it?"

"You Venetians had best make a delegation to treat with him. If he comes to the throne he may not be as well disposed to your black marketeering as Süleyman's ministers."

"You think he might succeed?"

Abbas shrugged his shoulders and the great dewlaps beneath his chin trembled. "He has the support of the yeniçeris."

Ludovici was stunned. Mustapha's popularity with the army had never been a secret but he had heard no word of sedition until now. But then, he reminded himself, all rebellion must have a beginning. He tried to assess how such a violent wind change might affect his own life. Süleyman had been on the throne ever since he had arrived in Stamboul; Abbas was right, what would Mustapha's attitude be toward the traders who had helped line Rüstem's pockets? The enmity between the two men was well known.

"What about you, Abbas?" he said, thinking aloud. "What will you do?"

"I will accept the will of God," Abbas said, as if this were obvious.

"You think Mustapha will really court the Sufavids? You think this rebellion is inevitable?"

"Only the outcome is uncertain," Abbas said.

"Süleyman knows of this?"

Abbas seemed astonished. "You think you and I should know something that was hidden from the Lord of Life?" He clapped his hands—it was the movement of his hands that was the signal, not the sound—and the two deaf-mutes who accompanied him hurried to assist him to his feet. It was not easily achieved.

Finally Abbas was ready to take his leave. "Go with God," he said.

"Go with God," Ludovici repeated, and watched Abbas clamber into the anonymous black-painted coach that waited outside the door.

Mustapha! he thought. It must be true. Abbas had never wagged his tongue too loosely before. If he was correct now, he should place his gamble on both cards, the king and the knave.

Topkapi Saraya

"IT IS DONE?" Hürrem asked.

Abbas bowed his head. "I have done as you asked me."

"Good. You are a faithful servant." She smiled, the coy, knowing smile of the professional courtesan. "How is Julia?"

"Julia is well," Abbas said, refusing the bait. "She asks for my prayers."

"I am sure you will remit them to Heaven. You may go, Abbas."

Abbas left, disgusted with her, disgusted with life. Disgusted with himself.

I am sorry, Ludovici, for using you this way. But it will not harm you, I promise you that. It is just one more ploy. But it will not harm you or my beloved Julia.

Or I would not have let the minx persuade me do it.

POOR ÇEHANGIR, SÜLEYMAN thought.

He could never look at the boy without feeling a physical pain in his chest. Çehangir's deformity made it impossible for him to stand erect; he always appeared to have an invisible, crushing weight on his shoulders. He could not ride a horse above a canter, could not aim a bow and arrow, could not lift a sword.

A fine son for a ghazi. Yet he felt compassion for him also; of all Hürrem's sons, Süleyman loved him best.

"You have seen Mustapha?" he asked him.

Çehangir did not raise his eyes. He never does, Süleyman thought. He cowers before me like the most humble *raya*.

"He is well, my Lord," Çehangir said. "He sends his greetings."

"His mother is well also?"

"Indeed, my Lord."

Oh Çehangir, Süleyman thought. You look as if you fear I am about to send for the executioner. "You look tired," he said.

"It is a rigorous journey, my Lord."

"The hunting was good?"

"We hunted every day."

Süleyman frowned. "Mustapha shows you much friendship." Why? he asked himself. Because he loves you? Or does he use you to spy on me perhaps? What companionship could such a man find in a cripple?

"I think he feels sorry for me," Çehangir said, as if he knew his thoughts. Süleyman was startled by this candid admission. Çehangir was always more acute than he sometimes credited.

"I am sure that is not the case," Süleyman said, but he brooded on this possibility for a moment and then said: "Did he speak of me?"

"He asked after your health many times."

Because he loves me, or because he wants me dead? Süleyman thought, and immediately he realized how the Divan had poisoned him. When did this happen? When did this cancer find its way into my blood?

"I am happy to see you safely returned," he said.

Çehangir seemed eager to leave. It occurred to Süleyman that his youngest son was as terrified of him as he had been of his own father. It seemed that this, not the Empire, was the true legacy of the Osmanlis: to destroy their own children.

If they did not first destroy themselves.

86

Stamboul

AS THE SUN rose over the city, the steam began to rise from the damp cobbles and the twitching flanks of the donkeys and horses that trudged in files through the narrow, twisting streets and alleys around the fruit market. It was melon season and the hawkers had piled their produce in tiers and pyramids on their stalls and on the ground, a mass of variety and color and pattern, flecked and striped, green and yellow and golden. The smells assaulted the senses, ripe and heavy with fruit, overlaying the more usual taints of urine and damp and woodsmoke.

Süleyman forced his aching joints up the steep cobbled street. He followed one of the *hamals,* the porters of the bazaars, bent double, his hands almost to his ankles, boxes of figs roped in a huge tower on his back. I feel my burden is almost as great, he thought. It was still cool and damp, the morning sun unable to penetrate here because of the ancient wooden houses that overhung the street. He stopped at one of the stalls and pretended to examine the peaches while he listened in on the hawker's conversation with his neighbor.

"They say the Sultan will ride east again, against the Shah," the man was saying.

"He should have gone years ago," the other man was saying. "The Persian has mocked us long enough. We have the greatest army in the world and he lets them grow old in their barracks!"

"Mustapha would not have let the Shah goad us like this," Süleyman said.

The merchants regarded Süleyman with suspicion. But the merchant could not resist giving voice to his frustration. "Mustapha is a great warrior. He would have had the Shah's head moldering on the Ba'ab-i'-Hümayun years ago."

"Perhaps it is time for Mustapha to be our padishah," Süleyman said.

The men looked at him as if he had gone mad. "Keep your voice down!" the man hissed. "The Sultan has spies everywhere!"

"I am not afraid of the Sultan," Süleyman said, frankly.

"He only says what everybody already knows," the merchant's neighbor said. "Süleyman is an old man. I was still drinking mother's milk when he last won a great victory."

"Still, he has done many great things," the merchant said. "He has built many fine mosques, to the glory of God, and given us our laws and his navies rule the Mediterranean."

"The yeniçeris want meat," Süleyman said.

"It is only a matter of time before Mustapha rouses them and sweeps Süleyman from his throne," the other man said, "and everybody knows it!"

"Be still!" the merchant said to him, and then turned to Süleyman. The man's eyes were hostile. He obviously suspected Süleyman for what he was: a spy. "If you want to buy some peaches, let me see your money. If not, go away and talk someone else's head off their shoulders!"

Süleyman followed a donkey, the wicker panniers on its flanks piled high with cherries, down the alley and out of the fruit markets. The man's words still rang in his ears: "It is only a matter of time before Mustapha rouses the yeniçeris and sweeps Süleyman from his throne—and everybody knows it!"

So everybody knew it, then. Lost in thought he did not see the donkey lift its tail to defecate on the cobbles. Suddenly the Sultan of the Osmanlis, King of Kings, Lord of Life, found himself with shit on his boots. Well, perhaps it is about time, he thought.

87

Amasya

A MONTH LATER RÜSTEM arrived below the cliffs on the Green River with a squadron of Spahis of the Porte and an *oda* of the yeniçeris. He camped under the somber walls of the citadel and the ancient Pontic tombs, planted his four-horsetail standard outside his tent, and waited.

Rüstem knew Mustapha was coming long before he heard the beat of his horse's hoofs. Unlike the camps of the Christian armies, the Turks maintained order and an iron silence. There was no drinking and no gambling; and except when in battle, prayers were observed five times each day.

So it was the breaking of the silence that warned Rüstem. It came on like a wave, a distant susurration, a rolling thunder that accompanied his approach. It was as if a skirmish of cavalry had broken through their lines, the shouts and alarms sweeping along with them. Rüstem jumped to his feet and hurried through the vast pavilion to meet him.

There were no more than two dozen riders, all except one wearing the scarlet silk jackets of spahi cavalry. Only the leader was dressed in white, and there were heron's feathers in his turban. A diamond clasp flashed in the sun, so that Rüstem had to raise his hand to protect his eyes.

The yeniçeris were following the riders, surging around the flanks and tails of the horses, their blue coats flapping as they ran, happy to eat the dust thrown up by the hoofs of the Chosen. They were cheering as they ran, a great army of throats sending up a chilling ululation that echoed from the cliffs until the noise seemed to surround them on all sides. Mustapha did not answer their shouts; he turned neither to the left or right. He kept his eyes fixed on the royal tent.

Rüstem waited, the solak bodyguards drawn up on either side. God help me in my sorrow! Rüstem thought. You are a dangerous man!

Mustapha reined in his horse in front of Rüstem, his dust drifting in an orange cloud over the waiting group. Rüstem tasted the grit in his mouth. Enjoy your glory, he thought. Soon you will have your own taste of dust. An eternity of it.

Mustapha dismounted with one fluid movement, and the cheers of the yeniçeris faded away. They waited, a great, savage, shuffling mass.

Mustapha executed a swift temennah. "Where is my father?"

"He is unwell. I am seraskier for this campaign."

Rüstem could see the play of emotion on Mustapha's face. First disappointment, then excitement. Was his day drawing near? "How ill is he?"

"His physicians say it is not mortal. But he could not bear the rigors of a long campaign." Rüstem looked beyond Mustapha to the crowd of faces now ringed behind the little troop of horses. A thousand yeniçeris, he thought, and every one of them is now standing within a hundred yards of us. "I have never heard such loud cheers. Not even for the Sultan."

"They cheer me because I am his son," Mustapha said, carefully.

"Perhaps," Rüstem said. "Let us withdraw inside. The dust has parched my throat."

Rüstem led the way inside the great silk pavilion. Pages brought halva and rosewater and then Rüstem produced a letter from the folds of his robe. He handed it, without comment, to Mustapha.

It was the letter offering marriage to the Shah's daughter, under Mustapha's tugra. "This is monstrous," Mustapha murmured.

Rüstem's eyes were fixed on the carpet between them. "You deny it?"

"Deny that I would offer an alliance to one of our Empire's sworn enemies? Of course I deny it!"

"It bears your seal."

"It is a forgery! Has my father seen this?"

"Of course."

"And what does he say?"

"I am not privy to his deliberations. He awaits your reply."

"I smell your stink on this!" Mustapha said, and threw the letter in Rüstem's lap.

The Vizier lifted his gray eyes for the first time. "I am not your enemy, Mustapha. Those yeniçeris outside are your enemy. They cheer too loudly."

"I have never and will never say or do anything against my father. I have sworn it. He must know that!"

"He awaits your reply," Rüstem repeated.

"He shall have it."

"First I have orders for you from the Sultan himself. You are to assemble your troops and accompany me on the campaign against the Persian heretics. Under my command, of course."

"I shall do as I am commanded," Mustapha said with disgust, and got to his feet. He left without speaking another word.

Rüstem listened to the beat of hoofs thunder across the plain, then sent for the Aga of the yeniçeris. He was a fair-haired, wiry man, a Slav, the left side of his jaw deformed where he had taken grapeshot during the siege of Rhodes. The great Bird of Paradise plumes on his cap bobbed and rustled as he performed his sala'am. He stood to receive his orders.

"You should prepare a squadron of your best men," Rüstem said. "Mustapha is to be taken from the Palace tonight and returned to Stamboul in chains."

The Aga hesitated. For a soldier trained from the age of eight years old to unquestioning obedience, it was a telling reaction. "As you command," he said.

"The men should be ready at dawn. That is all."

"As you command," the Aga repeated, but his eyes blazed with sudden venom. You are so plain to read, Rüstem thought. Your emotions light your face like our best scholars illuminate a Qur'ān with their vermilion and sapphire inks.

It was so simple. As simple as Hürrem said it would be.

Topkapi Saraya

THE GOLDEN ROAD led from the Harem mosque, past the Sultan's apartments, and through the haremlik to the Divan and the small, dark tower of

the Dangerous Window. A darkened staircase led to the latticed and curtained window from which the Sultan could listen to the deliberations of
his pashas and viziers in the Divan.

An opportunity that was now available to Hürrem also.

The Golden Road was the shimmering highway of power, glittering
with tiles of royal blue and gold and tomato red, of flawless glaze. As
Hürrem hurried along, her silk kaftan rustling on the cobbles, she was
aware of its sanctity, its potency. She now knew the heart of the Divan; the
Divan did not know her.

When she reached the top of the darkened stair, her heart was hammering so hard against her ribs that she clutched her chest in pain. She
moved closer to the taffeta curtain and watched.

The golden canopy of the Divan rested upon ten marble pillars. The
taffeta screen across the window turned the mirror surfaces of marble and
gilt and the brilliant silk and brocade costumes into a shadowplay of jet
and gray. The splendor of Divan was lost to her. But it was the voices that
were important, and she could identify each word with crystal clarity.

". . . you are sure of this?" she heard a man say. It was Süleyman. He
had returned to his duties in the Divan, in the absence of Rüstem.

"My information is very reliable." She did not recognize this other
man's voice. One of Rüstem's army of bureaucrats, no doubt.

"There is no chance your spy is mistaken?"

She heard the man cough with embarrassment. The word *spy* was obviously repugnant to him. "I have gleaned my information from several
sources, my Lord. They all confirm that the Venetians are convinced
Mustapha has made an alliance with the Shah Tamasp. The bailo himself has
sent a chaush in secret to Amasya with a letter. The contents of the letter
we do not know."

How satisfying, Hürrem thought, to hear one's own rumor repeated
back in the Hall of the Divan! Abbas had done his work well. For years
he had given Ludovici little morsels of truth with which to establish credibility. Now the foreign community at Galata had swallowed the big lie
whole.

Wonderful, too, that not one word of the ugliness that constantly
swept the bazaars about Hürrem or Rüstem ever reached the ears of the
Lord of Life. True power involved the control of whispers. When even the
spies feared you, no one dared repeat a word against you in the court, even
if it were only secondhand.

Süleyman had still not pronounced his judgment, but Hürrem could imagine his expression. It would be as if he were straining to break wind. She almost giggled aloud and put her knuckles to her mouth to restrain herself.

"I still cannot believe this," she heard him say.

"My Lord, my inform—"

"Enough! I do not want to hear any more!" Süleyman shouted, and she heard him stamp from the hall.

Hürrem hurried away at once. Her Sultan would no doubt summon her soon for solace for this latest blow. It would not do if he discovered she already knew the reason for his misery.

88

Amasya

A N ANGRY MURMUR broke the stillness of the night, like the drone of bees disturbed by a foraging bear. The two solaks standing guard outside Rüstem's tent shuffled nervously at their posts. It was the second time that day that the silence of the camp had been disturbed by the shouts of the yeniçeris. If they were to rebel . . .

The discharge of the harquebus sounded like cannonfire, and the echo still resounded from the cliffs long after the first solak had fallen, screaming, clutching his chest. The second drew his sword, in a futile effort to defend himself. There were more flashes away to his right, like sheet lightning, and two more shots rang out. He did not see the man who killed him. The ball entered his left eye and minced his brain before he even had time to cry out.

Dark figures raced out of the shadows into the pool of light thrown by the torches, torches that had illuminated the targets so perfectly for the harquebuses. Swords flashed, as two of the dark-coated figures paused to deliver finishing blows to the two solaks who lay on the ground.

Then they hurried inside the tent. In the torchlight, Rüstem recognized only one of the men, the Aga of the yeniçeris; though it was plain from the long gray caps that they were all his men.

He settled himself on his horse and turned to one of the spahis alongside him. "It seems we are faced with rebellion."

"You read the mood of the troops correctly, my Lord," the man said.

"Yes. It is fortunate I am not in my tent at this moment. I daresay the butchers are even now firing their harquebus into my mattress."

The spahi nodded, still stunned by what he had seen.

"We must ride back to Stamboul and report what has happened to the Sultan. I fear Mustapha has lost patience with waiting for the throne."

He turned his horse away from the cliff and rode into the darkness with his escort. They encircled the encampment, and headed west.

IT WAS LATE. Gülbehar had been awakened from her sleep with the news of the rebellion in Rüstem's camp. Now she sat shivering in an ermine robe, warming her bones around the glowing coals of the brazier. But the cold of dread would not leave her.

Sirhane entered and performed her sala'am in front of her. She looked dazed from sleep, and her hair had not been combed. The kaftan, thrown on hurriedly, was crumpled. She was pale, and trembling. Her husband was Mustapha's equerry. She thinks she is a widow, Gülbehar thought. She thinks that is why I have summoned her.

"Your husband is safe," she said.

Sirhane's shoulders sagged with relief. "My Lady . . ."

"But there is danger. For all of us."

Sirhane looked at her, confused. "We must leave Amasya?"

"There is nowhere to run."

"My Lady?"

Gülbehar pulled the robe tighter round her shoulders. "There has been a rebellion at the royal camp tonight. The yeniçeris tried to murder Rüstem Pasha."

"Did my Lord . . . ?"

"Mustapha did not incite them. If he would, there would be no danger. When Süleyman hears of this, he will certainly blame my son. I need your help, Sirhane."

"My help, my Lady?"

Gülbehar stared at her. "If Süleyman moves against my son, he will move against all his household too. Your husband will be executed, his property confiscated, and you will be exiled. You will end your days as a beggar. Do you want that, Sirhane?"

Sirhane lowered her eyes. "No, my Lady."

"I did not think that you did. Nor do I want my son's life wasted for one man's blindness! You remember the Kislar Aghasi, do you not?"

"Yes, my Lady."

"I want you to go to Stamboul and find him. Offer him anything. Anything!" She leaned forward. "I want Hürrem dead. If he can do this for me, my son will become Sultan and Abbas can have anything he desires. Persuade him, Sirhane. For my sake—and for yours!"

89

Topkapi Saraya

SÜLEYMAN SAT HUNCHED on the throne, as if his chest had collapsed inward and his shoulders and chin had no support beneath them. His mouth was drawn down at the edges, a crescent scimitar of disapproval and disgust. He regarded Rüstem steadily through thick gray furrowed eyebrows. His only movement was the flaring of his nostrils as he breathed.

Rüstem performed his sala'am and waited his invitation to speak.

"Well?" Süleyman growled.

He must have heard this already, Rüstem thought. The rumors are sweeping the corridors, there was a grassfire of whispering around the Palace even before I arrived.

"I bring news that grieves my heart," Rüstem said.

"Just tell it. Why have you abandoned my army to come here?"

"My Lord, I rode here in fear of my life. Yet it was not my life that I held so dear, but yours."

A low growl escaped Süleyman's lips. It seemed to come from deep within him, hung in the room for long seconds, like the rumbling of an earthquake.

"Mustapha?"

"I do not know, my Lord. The yeniçeris came in the middle of the night and killed my guards and entered my tent. I was forewarned and was able to escape."

"How many?"

"Too many to count, my Lord. The Aga led them."

"And Mustapha?"

"When he rode into camp the yeniçeris cheered him till they were hoarse. They shouted openly that he could lead their standards to the House of War more swiftly than their Sultan. They shouted you were now too old to lead them, and that I was a Defterdar with no knowledge of fighting."

"You showed him the letter?"

"He said he was not answerable before any save the Sultan. And since I was not the Sultan, he had nothing to tell me. He also said . . . that I should write my final letters to my family. He said that as soon as he claimed the throne he would hang my head on the Ba'ab-i-Sa'adet . . . He also told me to inform the carrion crows they would not have long to wait for their dinner."

"These were his words?"

"On my head, my Lord," Rüstem said. How snugly lies nestled among the truth!

The cry of anguish startled Rüstem, as no simple act of violence ever could. The Sultan threw back his head and wept.

He waved a hand, dismissing his Vizier. Rüstem eagerly obliged. He performed his sala'am, and backed out of the door, astonished and delighted that his lie had worked so well.

THE SUNLIGHT REFLECTED from the gilt censers of the kiosk, the summer garden was heavy with the scent of herbs and fruit and roses, the rhythm of the cicadas was hypnotic. It was so easy to lie here in Hürrem's arms and forget that the tapestry of the future was unraveling in his hands.

He had depended on Mustapha. Every kanun he had decreed, every foundation stone he had laid, every campaign he had fought, had been ensured with the knowledge that Mustapha would one day take the banner from his hand, consolidate every progress he had made. Sedition would undo everything. The Osmanlis would return to the regular feasts of blood and barbarity that had eclipsed the ascension of his father, his grandfather, and the Fatih himself.

Perhaps the yeniçeris were right, he was too old. But the burden was his till death, that was the law of the Osmanlis and the Sheri'at, and to allow Mustapha to usurp would be to open the floodgates for the blood of the Osmanlis for centuries to come.

"Do not listen to them," Hürrem whispered. "Be proud you have a son who gains so much admiration, and the love of the yeniçeris. You are his father. His sense of duty to you will prevent him from making wrong use of this uncanny power he has."

"I thought you feared him," Süleyman said.

"I fear the Kanun of the Fatih. But I do not fear him with you by my side. You are Süleyman, the greatest of all our Sultans. No one can replace you with the people."

"It is not the people who clamor against me. It is the yeniçeris."

They heard a great sigh above them and looked up, through the open shutters of the kiosk. Each spring the storks built their nests from loose faggots on the flat stone on the edge of the mosque domes and the cupolas of the *medressi*. But on this hot day of August thousands of them had taken to the air over Stamboul, flying south for their first reconnaissance ahead of the winter migration. Even in the buzzing warmth of summer, it was a reminder that winter was not far away.

"I must ride east to the army, or I will lose the throne," Süleyman said.

"What will you do?" Hürrem whispered.

"I do not know. Who can guide me in this?"

"Abu Sa'ad perhaps?"

Süleyman considered this for a long time. "Perhaps," he said.

Abu Sa'ad sat in silence and watched the Kislar Aghasi devour almost the entire tray of halva his pages had set before him. It was a delicate process; he placed each pastry into his mouth, with the tips of his index finger and thumb, consumed it, then chose another. He had on his face a look of ecstasy the sheyhülislam had seen before only on the faces of the dervish when they entered the trance. But then, eating might be a religious experience for some men, he conceded. Especially those with unrestrained passions, and no means of expressing them.

Finally Abbas was satisfied, and he washed down the honeyed cakes with a little iced sherbet. "I have a message from the Lady Hürrem," he said finally.

"May God preserve her," Abu Sa'ad murmured.

"Indeed. It seems she has found great comfort in our faith."

"She has indeed been most diligent in her studies of the Qur'ān."

"As you say," Abbas answered. "It now seems she wishes to glorify God in some way that will endure beyond our own mortal clay, and preserve the faith through the centuries."

"God shall smile upon her."

"Indeed, she intends to shortly make over a great part of her personal fortune in the form of a waqf—that is, she will place it in trust, so that more mosques may be built and maintained in the city."

Abu Sa'ad bowed his head in acknowledgment. "Her generosity becomes such a great lady."

"She asks me to convey to you that it has been your great inspiration that has persuaded her to do this. She has been most satisfied with the service you have performed to her, in leading her to the one true faith, and also to the Sultan, in his hours of trouble. She asks only that you will continue to do your work diligently."

It was some moments before the mullah understood what was required of him. He stroked his beard in contemplation. "The troubles in the east weigh heavily on the Lord of Life at the moment," he said.

"Were his troubles resolved!" Abbas said. "The Lady Hürrem says she has prayed night and day to God to help him in his sorrow. She would give anything to have these burdens lifted from her Lord."

"I shall give him what guidance I can," Abu Sa'ad said.

"As you say," Abbas said.

After he had left, the sheyhülislam produced his tespi beads and murmured prayers of thanks and supplication. God was good, God was great. But to bring His teaching to the people and build great mosques to His greater glory a man must sometimes bend his soul a little to the winds of the time.

90

Stamboul

ABBAS THREW BACK the hood of the ferijde and regarded Sirhane from one cold eye set with suspicion. "I received your message," he said. "What is it you want with me?"

"I need your help," Sirhane said.

Abbas sighed. Just as he had feared. "It seems I am useful to everyone except to myself."

"Gülbehar sent me."

"I had anticipated that," Abbas said. He looked around the room, the gilded ceilings, the glazed floral tiles on the walls, the pink shadow of the Aya Sofia looming over them through the fretted wooden grills that covered the windows. "So this is the Palace of Abdül Sahine Pasha."

"He is equerry to the shahzade now."

"So I have heard. He grows in wealth and good fortune."

"Is it good fortune to belong to the house of a condemned man, Abbas?"

Abbas shook his head. "There is nothing I can do."

"Gülbehar said that I may offer you anything—anything."

"She is generous. In that case, will she offer to return my manhood?"

"Abbas . . ."

"My mistress dresses me in the finest clothes, feeds me, and pays all my expenses. Because of my power and influence I have amassed wealth beyond the dreams of most men. And it is useless to me. If she wishes to tempt me and put me in mortal danger let her offer to return my manhood to me for just one night that I might once again truly feel a woman's touch!"

Sirhane lowered her eyes. She had hoped somehow to avoid this, but she had already made up her mind what she would do if Abbas refused her. She knew that Gülbehar was right. If her husband died with Mustapha, she would be shown no mercy. She would end her days in rags, starving and exiled, a pariah.

There was still one thing, she knew, that Abbas wanted. "And does Süleyman know of Julia?" she said, suddenly.

She did not look up, but she could hear the sharp intake of breath from Abbas. His hatred was suddenly almost a physical presence in the room. "You little harlot," he hissed.

He must assume that Gülbehar knows also or he would kill me now, Sirhane thought. She could not look into his face. "Very soon, a woman will die. Perhaps Hürrem, perhaps Julia. You decide."

"You said you loved her . . ."

"We all love ourselves more, Abbas."

"They have cut off my manhood, but they have not cut out my heart. For the first time in many years there is someone else who I feel sorry for. You make me want to vomit."

Sirhane took hold of her resolve. She looked into the cold, unblinking eye. "Do it or she dies, Abbas. Spare me your speech."

Abbas slapped her hard across the face. He signaled his pages to help him rise. He stormed from the room. Sirhane touched her cheek, tenderly, hating herself then as she had never hated anything.

Topkapi Saraya

"I HAVE A problem I need your help with. A certain case was brought before me in the Divan that has perplexed me greatly. I have decided to come to you for your ruling under the holy laws of the Qur'ān."

Süleyman paused, to collect his thoughts.

"A merchant of good position has been ill for a short time," he continued. "While he was ill, he gave over the running of his affairs to his servant, whom he had always trusted with good salary and good position. However, no sooner had he taken to his sick bed than the servant embezzled him and plotted against his family and even planned to kill his master. When the merchant was well again, he discovered all these things, beyond doubt. What should that merchant do, and what sentence should lawfully be pronounced under the Sheri'at?"

Abu Sa'ad did not blink. "The Qur'ān is quite explicit in such matters. The servant must die."

Süleyman's shoulders sagged beneath the folds of his kaftan.

After a while he remembered himself and drew himself up. He locked his gaze on to the sheyhülislam's. "And if that servant's name was Mustapha, the shahzade?"

"Death," Abu Sa'ad said.

Two days later Süleyman mounted his horse once again by the fountain in the Third Court and left the Palace with his household regiments for the east. Orders had already been sent to the agas at Amasya to bring their troops south for the march on Erzerum. A chaush was sent on horseback with further orders for Bayezid to come from Manisa and administer government at the Topkapi.

Süleyman knew he must hurry to reassert his authority over the agas. But first he must talk to Selim.

SHE LOOKS RADIANT, Abbas thought. She never looks as young and lovely as she does when she is planning an execution. It rejuvenates her. The green velvet taplock had been pinned at a jaunty angle on her head, and she wore a kaftan of pistachio velvet bordered with ermine. Rosettes of pearls gleamed on the insteps of her *ship-ship*. She toyed with long strands of her golden hair as she regarded him.

So it is my day to die, Abbas thought. Well, I have delayed it long enough. Now that it is decided I feel curiously free, even light-headed. It is delightful that you are in a happy mood also. I would have hated to have cut out your black little heart when you were as sick of the world as I.

"Have you done as I asked?" Hürrem asked him.

"I have spoken to the mufti, as you commanded. He has come to realize what is required of him."

"My good, faithful Abbas."

"As you say, my Lady."

"And what shall be your reward?"

Oh, so you are going to try and torment me! Abbas thought. I had hoped you would. I have had twenty-five years of impotence. Tonight I shall have power over you.

"What reward would you like to honor me with, my Lady?"

"Your pick of the Harem, perhaps?"

Abbas smiled at her mordant wit. He bowed. "My Lady is too kind."

Perhaps she divined the difference in his manner then, for her eyes were suddenly hard. "You look pleased with yourself, Abbas. Perhaps you would like to share the joke with your mistress?"

Abbas took a step toward her and his hand moved to the jeweled dagger in the sash at his waist. His fingers rested on the ivory handle. Hürrem lowered her eyes, and he realized she knew instantly what he intended. But the black guards positioned around the room were too far away, too somnolent at this routine audience, to stop him. He smiled at her. As soon as she screams, he decided, I will do it.

But Hürrem did not scream. "Ah, my Abbas. So you have become a man at last," she said. She seemed almost . . . excited.

"I have waited for this for so long," he whispered.

"And what has stopped you?"

Abbas stared at her. What has stopped me? The answer is simple, he thought. I am afraid to die. Not afraid of pain—God knows I have known enough of pain—and not in love with life, for there is nothing in this life I am fond of. Just afraid of what is after this. I could not do it before. But I will do it now, for Julia.

The guards had noticed nothing. Abbas still stood, one hand at his waist. Hürrem relaxed, almost lounging, in the divan.

"Are you not afraid?" Hürrem whispered.

"This time it will not stop me."

"Not for yourself, dear Abbas. Are you not afraid for Julia?"

Abbas felt his fist tighten on the warm ivory. Do it now! something screamed inside him. Do it now! Before the witch finds some way to weaken your resolve!

"Julia?" he heard himself saying.

"On my death there is a letter I have placed in safe keeping, to be delivered to my Sultan. He will be most disconcerted to find she still lives in Pera and perhaps is still the source of many of the rumors about his failings in his Harem."

Abbas felt the Palace crashing about his shoulders. He felt frozen. There was absolutely nothing he could do. He could not kill her, he could not withdraw. He was dead.

He waited for her to call the bostanji to drag him away. I should kill myself now, he thought. Spare yourself the death of this witch's bright imagination.

Hürrem laughed. "I would almost swear that your black face has gone quite pale!"

Abbas swayed on his feet. An oily sweat erupted on his skin. Use the dagger on yourself! a voice shouted. Do it now!

"You think I am going to punish you," Hürrem said.

He looked into her face. Her eyes were aglow with pleasure. "I shall kill myself first," he said.

"My dear Abbas, why would you do that?"

"You have tormented me for the last time."

She leaned closer. "Take your fingers away from that crude instrument. Do you think I should want revenge because you thought to murder me? Half of Stamboul wants me dead! Instead you have just proved to me that no matter how much you hate me, you could never harm me. It makes you the most trusted and obedient servant I could ever have. I have never trusted loyalty for its own sake. It is too unreliable!"

Do it anyway! The voice inside Abbas screamed. Do it!

Abbas slumped to his knees. "I am weak," he mumbled.

"Yes," Hürrem said, laughing. "But very useful!"

91

Konia

THE CITY STOOD alone in a vast, dusty wheat bowl on the Anatolian steppe, the mecca of the Osmanlis, the home of the monastery that contained the bones of Jalal ud-din Rumi, the founder of the Dervish order. It was also the governmental seat of Karamania, where Selim was apprenticed as second prince in succession to the throne. It was here that Süleyman came, looking for hope, before his confrontation with his errant shahzade.

He had heard the rumors, whispered in the corridors of Topkapi and the bedesten of the city. Hürrem's oldest son was a drunkard. Selim the Sot they called him. The short, awkward youth, always overshadowed by his younger brother at the çerit and the archery field, had now become a buffoon, a figure of fun. He was certainly no threat to the throne, as Mustapha was. But neither was he the future that Süleyman had envisaged for the Osmanlis.

Now, as he gazed into his son's face, inflamed with the effects of too much wine, the broken capillaries on his cheeks and nose spreading like some spider's web of crimson, he closed his eyes in disgust and thought: Can I do this?

Selim's attention was already engaged by his own personal diatribe. "Of course Mustapha hates me. Should he come to the throne I have no doubt his first act will be to send the bostanji to murder me. Can you imagine what it is like to live like this? I have no friend in all the world but you; without you there would be no one to protect me."

You whine like a peasant, Süleyman thought. And here we sit in your fine palace, while you sip your sherbet and pretend that it is nectar, and you think I do not see your hand shaking when you pick up the chalice.

"You have heard the calumny against Mustapha?"

"I do not doubt a word of it."

Of course not, Süleyman thought. But then, yours is scarcely an objective point of view. "We shall settle this at Aktepe. If I were to hand Mustapha to the bostanji, you would be next to bear the yoke of the Osmanlis. Do you think you can bear such a heavy burden, my Selim?"

Selim avoided his eyes, but Süleyman sensed the dawn of anticipation in his son. "I am your son. I was born to it. But if I am next, why then did you give Saroukhan to Bayezid?"

"It was expedient to do so."

"If I am to be shahzade, I should be at Manisa."

Süleyman sighed. He was like a recalcitrant child. "It is not settled yet. We are talking of Mustapha's life, my Selim. It is not a matter to be dismissed lightly. I only ask whether you think you can carry my burdens. I have not promised them to you."

Selim grew sulky. "Yes, Father."

Süleyman could scarcely believe this was his own son, named after the rampaging warrior who was his own father. Yes, he decided, the rumors were all true. He could see for himself the degradation of body and spirit that excess had wrought on Selim; his nature was only too plain. Yet, why should he be surprised? He himself was not the butcher his own father had been. Why should he expect Selim to be in his own image?

Or perhaps it was his fault for ignoring his sons; he had dedicated the future to Mustapha; he had forgotten that Selim might one day step forward for the banner also. Now it was too late. Selim had grown without direction, and he was lost to him.

All his hopes were in Mustapha, and they had foundered.

"What will you do about Mustapha?" Selim asked him.

"I don't know," Süleyman told him. "I don't know."

Pera

JULIA COULD SCARCELY contain her impatience. She watched from the window as the coach clattered to a halt on the cobblestones and a figure in a purple ferijde stepped out and hurried inside. Too long since she had seen her. Much too long. Her hands were trembling like a girl's.

Hyacinth escorted Sirhane into the room and bowing, made his exit. As soon as they were alone, Julia threw her arms around her neck and hugged her until Sirhane protested and pulled away to catch her breath.

Julia tore the cazeta from her face. "Take this away. I have to see you," she said.

Sirhane removed the ferijde. She was dressed in a kaftan of rose-pink silk with a waist shawl of bright blue calico. Julia took her hand and led her to a divan.

"I have missed you," she whispered.

"You still defy the years, Julia," Sirhane whispered.

Julia looked at her. If only I could tell you the same, she thought. You look gaunt, and tired. There are dark circles under your eyes and shadows behind them. Something is wrong.

"Are you well?" she asked her.

"A little tired from the journey, that is all," Sirhane said, and she put her head on Julia's shoulder in case she should see the lie written on her face.

"It's been so long. When your messenger came, I could not believe you were really here in Stamboul."

Sirhane seemed nervous. Not the confident, sophisticated woman Julia remembered. Not at all.

"Tell me all your news," Julia said. "What brings you here?"

"Abdül sent me away. There has been trouble."

"Trouble?" Julia squeezed her hand. "Abdül is all right?"

"Yes, but . . . he feels it is dangerous." Sirhane would not meet her eyes.

"Are things really that bad?"

"You have not heard?"

"Only rumors. They say Mustapha wants to make an alliance with Shah Tamasp."

"That is Rüstem's doing. But there is much worse. The yeniçeris tried to murder the Vizier while he was camped on the Green River. He blames Mustapha."

"Is it true?"

"Of course not . . . but what can we do? My husband is loyal to the shahzade. If there should be war . . ."

Julia tried to comfort her, but Sirhane squirmed away.

"I'm all right. I should not panic about these things."

"War?" Julia stared at her. "Is there anything we can do? Ludovici has influence inside the Porte. Perhaps if he—"

"No, there's nothing you can do," Sirhane said, too quickly.

"If you need to hide . . ."

"Hide from the Sultan? When he is king of half the world?" Sirhane looked up and suddenly threw her arms around Julia's neck and wept. "I am sorry."

"Sorry. What for?"

But Sirhane wept and did not answer her. Julia felt the trembling of her body and the wetness of her tears through the gauze of her smock. Her crying seemed to go on for hours.

Finally Sirhane pulled away. "I would never hurt you," she said.

"I don't understand . . . what are you saying?"

Sirhane caressed Julia's cheek. "Just remember I would never hurt you."

"I know that. But I still don't understand. There's something else. What is it? What's wrong?"

Sirhane shook her head. "Just hold me," she said. "I'll tell you later. Not now."

BUT SIRHANE DID not tell her what was wrong. Instead they went together to the hammam and bathed. Julia massaged her shoulders, felt the bowstring tautness of the muscles, and could not soothe it away.

"You are so tense," she whispered.

"Of course I am tense. Do you wonder at it?"

Julia did not answer her, startled by the abruptness of the reply. She poured a little more sandalwood oil onto her hands and rubbed it into the muscles of Sirhane's neck.

"How is Ludovici?" Sirhane asked her.

"He prospers."

"Is he an attentive husband?"

"Yes. Yes, I suppose he is. Does Abdül still treat you well?"

"He has another wife now. An Armenian. She is eighteen and very beautiful. She was selected at the last devshirme."

Julia did not know what to say.

"He still comes to me once a week. But of course he spends most of his nights with her. I miss him then. Do you ever miss Ludovici when he is away?"

"I miss you," Julia said.

"Perhaps you should learn to love him more." Sirhane twisted around. "You are right, I am too tense. Here, I will attend you."

Julia ached for Sirhane's physical touch, but when she oiled her she did it with the reserve of a gediçli. Finally Julia took her hand and brought it to her breast, but Sirhane pushed her away and whispered, "Not yet."

Instead she lounged in the water and talked, gossiped like any silly concubine in the hararet, idle chatter about life in the citadel in Amasya and inconsequential memories of their life in the Harem at Seraglio Point. Their former intimacy was gone. Suddenly they were strangers and Julia had no idea what obstacle had been placed between them or why.

Finally they simply ran out of things to say to each other and then Sirhane said she must go.

As she was leaving, Julia took her arm. "You have still not told me the real reason you came to Stamboul," she said.

"Next time," Sirhane said. She pulled away and pulled on her ferijde.

"Will there be another time, my Sirhane?"

"I will send a message." She kissed her lightly on the lips, and then replaced the cazeta to hide her face. "Goodbye Julia," she said, and there was a dreadful finality in her voice.

Anatolia

SÜLEYMAN REJOINED THE army on the plains of Aktepe.

The yeniçeris were silent as he rode among them, their faces either averted, or sullenly respectful. He posted the seven-horsetails standard outside the royal tent and summoned his chaush. He sent him to Amasya, with a document carrying the royal tugra, summoning Mustapha urgently to his presence.

Then he waited.

92

Amasya

F OR PITY'S SAKE, you must not go!"
Mustapha patted his mother's hand. She withdrew it, angry at his con-
descension to her, but he only grinned. "The Sultan commands it. If I
refuse, I will be accused of disloyalty."

"And if you go, he may accuse you anyway and who will protect you
then?"

"They already rumor against me in the Palace. It is my chance to answer
their lies."

"If he wanted your answers, why did he not come here? Why did he go
to Konia?"

"Perhaps he is afraid to come here."

Gülbehar stood up and turned her back to hide the tears of anguish that
had welled in her eyes. "Let them accuse you of what they will! They can
prove nothing!"

Mustapha wondered whether to tell her about the letter, and his conversation with Rüstem. He decided against it. "The yeniçeris already laud
me as leader. Where can I be safer than in their midst?"

"Here! You will be safer here, in your fortress, far away from Süleyman
and Rüstem!"

"I must above all things obey my father. He has summoned me. I will go."

"And what if the bostanji are waiting?"

"He gave me my life. He has the right to take it back."

Gülbehar turned, her eyes bright with hatred and fear. "No! He has no
right! I gave you life also! I suckled you at my breast and I raised you from
an infant! He has no right to take you from me!" Suddenly Gülbehar felt as
if she had received a blow to the stomach. She doubled over, sobbing and
gasping for breath. Mustapha reached for her, cradling her in his arms, and
led her to the divan.

He held her for a long time. Finally he whispered: "I have to go."

"Take the throne. You have waited long enough. You have only to say the word and the yeniçeris will rise with you. There is no need for bloodshed. Your own grandfather removed Bayezid from the throne, and exiled him. It is within the law."

"It is against the law of Heaven. Süleyman taught me that."

"Of course he would!"

"I cannot do it. It is impossible. I would rather die than dishonor my name before the other princes of the world, and stain my soul before God."

"Mustapha . . ." Nothing would move him, she knew. The minx had won. She had an image of her now, sprawled across her divan, her head thrown back, laughing. Life was so simple if you believed in nothing but your own preservation.

"My honor is worth more than any empire this world may give me. What sort of king shall I be if I give up my soul to attain it? I shall rule without shame or I shall not rule at all."

"You are a fool," Gülbehar muttered.

"You know you do not mean that," Mustapha grinned. "If I were to relent, you would be ashamed. And so would I."

"You let her win so easily," Gülbehar murmured, but Mustapha did not hear her.

"Anyway," he added, "if I do not go, it is an admission of guilt. He will not harm me, Mother. He has given his word. He is a man of honor, as I am."

No, Gülbehar thought. He is a man of duty. They may seem the same to you, but they are spurs of quite different metal.

"I will leave at dawn," he said.

"Go with God," Gülbehar whispered and she let him kiss her hand and leave her. When he had gone there were no more tears to weep; she sat instead by the window, watching the stars wheel across the face of the earth, consumed with rage, helpless in her prison.

Aktepe

THE SMOKE OF damp fir wood clung to the air. The camp was in silence. Water carts creaked between the rows of tents, sheep scurried in choking clouds of dust to the butchers' tents. A group of blue-jacketed yeniçeris played fortune dice by a glowing charcoal brazier, huddled around it against the chill of the evening.

When they saw Mustapha, they jumped to their feet and crowded around his horse, as they had done at Amasya. Word quickly spread through the camp; the shahzade had come to lead them against the Persians! A few even called him Padishah, and their cries carried through the camp to where Süleyman sat on the throne, in consultation with Rüstem. They fell silent and listened to the voices, and Rüstem saw the old man's features harden with resolve.

Padishah! *Emperor!*

"Here comes the ghost of my father," Süleyman murmured.

The cheering continued for a long time, long after Mustapha had erected his pavilion close to Süleyman's, waiting for the summons to appear and speak against his accusers.

But that night his accusers spoke for him. The ghost of Selim appeared at the foot of Süleyman's bed; he held out his hands to his son and in them he held cupped the head of his own father.

"Grandfather," Süleyman murmured in his sleep, "you should have killed him. You were too weak."

He thought of Çehangir and his Mihrmah, and he knew what he had to do.

93

DAWN.

All the previous afternoon and evening Mustapha had received the salutes of the viziers and agas in his tent, but now the camp was once again in silence. The muezzin called the army to prayers; thousands of turbans were drawn up in rows, bobbing like silken hedgerows against a mauve sky.

When Mustapha finished his supplications to God, he made himself ready. He dressed all in white, as a token of innocence, and put his letters of farewell inside his robe close to his bosom, as was customary for any Turkish man when facing danger.

He mounted his Arab stallion, and prepared to ride the few yards that separated his tent from his father's pavilion, as demanded by tradition. His Aga, and Sahine, his equerry, mounted their horses beside him.

Mustapha felt every eye in that great plain turn toward him, expectant. Every man knew what was to take place that morning, why Mustapha had been summoned. Would they reconcile or would Mustapha issue a challenge to his aging father?

The yeniçeris set about their duties, but not one of them had a mind for it. Some of them prepared to hail a new Sultan before the sun crossed the sky.

At the entrance to the Sultan's pavilion, Mustapha slid down from his horse and removed the dagger at his waist and handed it to Abdül Sahine. He went unarmed to meet his father.

MUSTAPHA SALUTED THE solak guards who stood outside, and signaled to his Aga and his equerry to remain where they were. The entrance flap fluttered closed behind him.

Abdül Sahine clung to the reins of the horses, and glanced apprehensively at the Aga. He heard footsteps behind him and saw a squadron of solaks wheel to attention between them and the rest of the camp. Without hesitating they drew their killiç and came toward them.

THE PAVILION WAS enormous, divided into sections by great walls of billowing golden silk. The entrance was covered with rich ruby-red and peacock-blue carpets, and there were divans of *seraser* brocade at each wall. A small silver-topped table stood in the center.

"Father?"

Mustapha stepped through the entrance hall and into the audience chamber. The tent whipped in the wind, with a sound like a pistol crack, and he whirled around.

A black bostanji stepped from the shadows in the corner. And another. He turned around. Three more came from behind the curtain in front of him. One of them held a silken bowstring.

He saw a shadow move behind the silk. "Father?"

The bostanji moved silently toward him, on great padded feet, their arms held loosely at their sides. Mustapha realized he had been expecting this. But there was no fear, just anger. He stepped into the center of the room.

"Father, listen to me first! Let me answer my accusers! This is not just!"

This was not the way his father had taught him; there was no honor in this.

He heard the rasping of steel, followed by shouts, and the screams of a wounded man. He realized his Aga and Abdül Sahine were being attacked. If he could get past the bostanji and into the open, the solaks could not harm him. A prince could only be dispatched with the bowstring. Once he reached the yeniçeris he would be safe.

But he did not want that. He wanted to speak to his father. "Father, listen to me!"

One of the bostanji tried to throw a noose around his head but Mustapha read his intention and ducked away. He barreled into the first negro and wrestled him to the ground, throwing him easily. Another came for him, but he eluded him, and the man's impetus sent him sprawling across a silver table, winding him.

"Father! I have never once betrayed you! Why do you betray me now? Come out and speak to me!"

"Will you never dispatch that which I bid you?" he heard Süleyman moan, his voice muffled by the silken curtain. "Will you never make an end to this traitor from whom I have not rested one night these ten years in quiet?"

But the deaf-mutes could not hear him. Mustapha was his only audience. "Call off your idiot assassins! I am innocent! You stain your honor more than you stain mine!"

"Get it done!" he heard Süleyman moan.

"Father, please!"

Süleyman placed his hands over his ears and closed his eyes, willing it to be over. No, no, *no!* There could be no excuse for treason! The evidence against Mustapha was clear. He might try to mesmerize him with his prettied words, but he had seen and heard reason enough. He would play the ghost of Selim the Grim now and forever.

If he let Mustapha speak, he would sway him. He would coax his weakness from him, and the yeniçeris would remove him, as they had removed his grandfather.

Oh, Mustapha, all of my hopes lay with you.

You were my first son. You were the hopes of my youth.

He thought of his remaining sons. Çehangir, the scholarly cripple. Selim the Sot.

It would have to be Bayezid. There was only Bayezid now.

Oh God, help me in my sorrow! He never thought it would be as painful as this. He never dreamed the agony would rip into him like this, like a knife tearing open his stomach, cause such physical pain.

No, no, no!

He threw aside the curtain.

"NO!"

Too late.

Mustapha lay at his feet on the rug, his eyes bulging open, the bowstring sunk into the flesh of his neck. Blood welled around a thin necklace of vermilion.

Süleyman signaled to the mutes: "Wrap him in the carpet and throw him outside the tent."

He slumped into the pearl-and-tortoiseshell throne, and waited. A soft moan like the sighing of the wind spread through the camp. It rose to a keening of despair, as the yeniçeris, approached the tent to mourn their champion. The sounds of their grief convinced Süleyman that he was right. Thanks be to God, for he had almost weakened! Now it was done. He had curbed the power of the yeniçeris, and saved the Osmanlis from a tyrant. He wanted to weep for Mustapha but found he could not.

In fact, he discovered that he no longer felt anything at all.

94

G IVE US RÜSTEM's head or we'll come and take it!"
Strange how even now he shows no fear, Süleyman thought. The man's veins run with ice. Even now he is calculating the odds, and he is convinced that I will save him. The yeniçeris swarm round my tent baying for his blood, like a pack of slavering wolves, and he looks as if there were stone walls three feet thick between him and them, not just a few strips of gold and purple silk.

"They blame you, Rüstem," Süleyman said.

"My Lord, Mustapha was his own undoing."

The tumult outside the tent had swollen to a crescendo. There were thousands of them, led by the Aga, milling at the entrance, their killiç drawn, their voices baying for the one sacrifice that would appease them: Rüstem. All that held them back was two solaks and the sanctity of the Osmanlis. None of them dared cross the threshold of the royal pavilion unbidden.

Yet it would take only one man to challenge the authority of the royal blood and the rest would follow him. The pavilion would be swallowed up, like a mound of sand under a raging tide. Despite this knowledge, Süleyman, too, felt calm, as if all natural fear had been shriven from him.

"The yeniçeris want a scapegoat," he told Rüstem. "Since they dare not touch an Osmanli, they have decided on you."

For the first time Süleyman noticed the uncertainty in Rüstem's gray, unblinking eyes. I might do it too, Süleyman mused, and he wondered at his own thinking. I have done the worst thing I could imagine. Now I might do anything.

"Have you dispatched a chaush for Amasya, my Lord?"

Süleyman was impressed. Even now, facing death, Rüstem's mind had returned to practical considerations. "Yes, his wife and sons will not leave him lonely long in Paradise."

"Then we have nothing further to fear from him."

"Not from Mustapha." Süleyman was shouting now, to raise his voice above the screams of the soldiers outside. "Do you not fear the yeniçeris, Rüstem?"

"They will do as you command them."

"They were ready to put Mustapha on the throne an hour ago."

"He is dead. The yeniçeris are like dogs. They need a master."

"They also need raw meat."

Süleyman rose slowly from the throne to the silken curtain, imagined it still warm from Mustapha's touch. He crossed the partitioned antechamber, and tore aside the curtain, to face the sea of eyes and jaws surging and screaming around the pavilion.

At once they fell silent.

Süleyman stared at them, and saw the hatred unmasked in their faces, felt the sharp, acid pain of venom in his own heart. He would have had all their heads on the Ba'ab-i-Hümayun if he could. These men were the reason for Mustapha's death. They had built the Empire; now, unchecked, they would destroy it.

The Aga broke the crackling silence. "We want Rüstem."

"Rüstem is to be replaced. The gold seal of the Grand Vizier will go to Ahmed, the second vizier. But Rüstem will not be harmed."

"He took our Mustapha from us!"

"I took your Mustapha from you."

The Aga stared at him, his eyes glittering with hatred. But he did not reply. Any answer would have cost him his neck.

"We march on the Sufavids," Süleyman said, "to take our *gaza* against the heretic, Tamasp. There will be booty and women. If your men want blood, let it be Persian."

"We want Rüstem," the Aga said, stubbornly.

"If you want him, you must kill me first," Süleyman said, and he drew the jeweled killiç from the scabbard at his waist.

And he watched as one by one the yeniçeris turned their backs and returned to the camp. It took long minutes, for there were thousands, but Süleyman did not move and finally he stood alone with the Aga. The old general finally turned his back and left.

So it is done, Süleyman thought. The future belongs to Bayezid now.

Amasya

THE MISSIVE WAS written in white ink on black paper. Gülbehar did not need to read it to know its contents. She had known when she had seen the Sultan's chaush dismount in the courtyard. No, she had known before then. Mustapha's fate had been sealed the moment he rode out of the gates.

She refused to take the letter from him. She spat in the chaush's face, cursing him and his sons for eternity, and tried to rake his face with her nails. Her Kislar Aghasi and her maidservants restrained her, and the man fled, his face pale, his hands shaking, the kadin's wails of grief ringing in his ears.

Stamboul

SHE KNEW MUSTAPHA and her husband were dead as soon as she saw him. He was a heavy, blank-faced Sudanese negro, castrato, and deaf-mute. He could not speak, he could not hear. There was nothing she could do to reason with him. All sentiment and mercy had been burned out of him by pain and mutilation and savage discipline.

His tongueless mouth made a strange yelping noise as he came toward her, his breath sawing in his chest. He held the bowstring in front of him, his eyes fixed on her intently. She knew who he was: the Kislar Aghasi's chaush.

Sirhane backed away from him, instinctively, though she knew there was no escape. He would leave only when she was dead, with her head in the leather pouch that hung from a sash at his waist for precisely this purpose.

"Now Mustapha is dead, it is safe for Abbas to act," she said to him. "He thinks I am still a threat to Julia." She felt the tears course down her face. "I would never have done it. I would never have betrayed her," she whispered to the deaf man. "It was just a bluff. I would never have hurt her. Never. But then she will never know that now. I do not mind dying, but I do not want her to hate me." She closed her eyes and put her arms to her sides. She would not fight him. She could not escape. "Julia, I would never—"

The bostanji looped the cord around her neck, choking off her words. He lifted her effortlessly from the floor, the corded muscles in his arms bulging, and quickly and efficiently strangled her to death.

95

Pera

J ULIA LOCKED HER door and stayed in her bedchamber for three days. Sometimes, in the evenings, Ludovici heard her crying through the door. He knocked and shouted to her but she would not answer him. He ate alone in the great hall, the soft echo of silverware on porcelain echoing in the vaulted dining hall. He stared at her empty chair and pushed the dark shadow of suspicion from his mind, and refused to look at it.

On the fourth morning, when Julia finally appeared, her face was the color of a linen shroud and there were dark circles under her eyes. Her face was empty.

He stood up and watched her slump into the high-backed mahogany chair at the end of the table.

"Are you all right?"

She did not answer straight away. Finally, she murmured: "Do you love me, Ludovici?"

"You know I do."

"Then find out who gave the order for this."

"What good would that do?"

"Just find out."

"What you ask is impossible."

"Abbas will find out. Abbas will know."

"And if it was the Sultan?"

"Just find out for me. Please."

He felt angry and he felt helpless. Would she go seeking revenge inside the Porte itself? Impossible. What did she really hope to achieve? In the Empire, execution was just the way. The arrival of a death chaush was like fate; it could not be foreseen or prevented. You accepted it as you would accept any natural misfortune, like lightning or earthquake.

He sighed. "I will find out," he said at last. Yes, he would ask Abbas. And then he would decide what he was going to tell Julia.

After all, Sirhane was just a friend. Julia had already spent more grief than was her due. She behaved as if she had lost her husband.

Ridiculous, he thought, and quickly pushed the idea from his mind.

Galata

ABBAS SHOOK HIS head. "There is nothing she can do, Ludovici."

"I have to know, Abbas. I have given my word."

Abbas selected another piece of halva from the plate in front of them and chewed it thoughtfully. "You have given your word before and broken it. Why not do it again?"

Ludovici's eyes flashed with the sudden, bitter anger of the guilty. But he said nothing. What was there to say?

"Once you promised me you would send her away from the Osmanlis."

"I love her," Ludovici said softly.

"Then you are a fool as well as a liar."

Ludovici jumped to his feet. He stood over Abbas, his fists clenched at his sides. "If any other man said that to me—"

"You have placed my life in danger countless times through the years by what you did. And now you are angry because I confront you with it. Did you think it was a trifle, Ludovici? Did you think I could ever forget it?" He selected another piece of halva.

"Love made a fool of you once."

"No, it made me a eunuch. But it did not make me a liar." He looked up at Ludovici. "If you are going to leave me or attack me, then do it. Otherwise, sit down. We have known each other too long for these histrionics."

"I will not give her up," Ludovici hissed.

"You do not have anything to give up!"

"What are you talking about?"

"Sit down."

Ludovici sat, his whole body tense as a bowstring. Some other sense told him he should not stay. Abbas had become a monster. What casket of maggots was he about to open now?

"How does she look these days?" Abbas said, softly.

"She ages with grace," Ludovici answered him.

"She is still beautiful?"

"She is no longer sixteen, Abbas. There is a little silver in her hair. But she is still as slim as she was when you saw her in Venice. Yes, she is still beautiful."

"It was I that picked the fruit. And you tasted it. Do you know how much I hated you for that?"

"I have always suspected it."

Abbas hung his head and for a moment Ludovici felt the familiar stab of his pity. But when he raised his head again Abbas had put away his pain. His face was hard. "You ask me if I can find out who sent the chaush for Sirhane. It is not necessary. I already know."

"Was it the Sultan or his witch?"

"It was neither the Grand Seigneur or his Lady. It was me."

Ludovici just stared at him.

"She was going to betray Julia's identity to the Lord of Life and name her as the instigator of the many rumors in the bailo. Süleyman is not a man who forgives or forgets easily, as you know. I did as you would have done to protect her."

Ludovici sagged. "Oh, Abbas."

"You may tell her this, or keep it from her, as you see fit."

"Sirhane was the only real friend she had. This will go hard with her, Abbas."

"She was much more than a friend, Ludovici. Did you never suspect?"

"Suspect?"

"They were lovers, Ludovici. They were lovers. They had been lovers in the Harem. They had been lovers ever since."

Ludovici closed his eyes. Well, of course. Of course. All these years he had thought it was Abbas that had stood between them. What did it matter? He had long ago settled on the compromise. A little was always better than nothing. She had never pretended to love him. It is just your pride that is hurting now, he reminded himself. Just your pride.

"Did you not know?" Abbas said.

"Yes, I knew," Ludovici lied. But in his heart he wanted to kill her.

Outside Tabriz

THE CHAUSH REINED his horse to a halt outside the silken tent with the seven-horsetail standard, the Sultan's pavilion. He had ridden day and night from Stamboul. He jumped from the horse and threw the reins at the Sultan's equerry. He was ushered into the presence of the Lord of Life by the solaks and prostrated himself on the ground.

The message he carried was handed to Rüstem Pasha who read it aloud to the Lord of Life. Çehangir had been found dead at the Topkapi Saraya. He had hanged himself.

Süleyman threw back his head and uttered a cry of anguish that could be heard around the entire camp and echoed from the surrounding mountains, sending a shiver along the spine of the most seasoned yeniçeri, a cry of pain and grief for the future of the Osmanlis.

Pera

THEY SAT TOGETHER in the gathering gloom; the renegade, in the silk robe, the slave girl in the black vestura. They watched the sun until it had disappeared below the rim of the earth and the world turned gray. Lights flickered on around the harbor, the masts of the Turkish galleots and Greek caramusalis were outlined against the pearly waters of the Horn like bones protruding from the mud. But still they did not move.

"I do not believe a word of it," Julia said finally. "He is only trying to protect me."

"I only tell you what he said," Ludovici told her.

Julia shook her head. "Sirhane would not put me in danger."

Ludovici kept his silence.

"I do not believe a word of it," Julia repeated. "Not a word."

"You must have loved her very much," Ludovici said.

Julia turned to him, tried to fathom his expression in the darkness. Did he know? Yes, he must know. The pain was etched into his features. She had never wanted to hurt him this way. What was it that Sirhane had said to her?

Perhaps you should learn to love him more.

For now, there was nothing to be done. She hurt too much. She just hurt too much.

"Abbas was lying," she said. But in her heart she knew it was true and she bled.

PART 9

DEATH OF
A NIGHTINGALE

96

Topkapi Saraya, 1558

By the grace of the Most High, whose power be forever exalted! By the sacred miracles of Muhammad, may the blessing of God be upon him! To thee who art Sultan of Sultans, the sovereign of sovereigns, the shadow of God on earth, Lord of the White Sea and the Black Sea, of Rumelia and Anatolia, of Karamania, of the Land of Rum, of Diabekir, of Kurdistan, of Azerbaijan, of Persia, of Damascus, of Aleppo, of Cairo, of Mecca, of Medina, of Jerusalem, of all Arabia, of Yemen, and of many other lands that my noble forefathers and my glorious ancestors (may God light upon their tombs!) conquered by the force of their arms, and which my august majesty has made subject to my flaming sword, and my victorious blade, Sultan Süleyman Kahn, son of Sultan Selim Khan. Father.

In sundry verbal and written communications I have appealed to my Lord for intercession against those who have sought to spread calumny against me. God knows I have never sought favor for myself, unlike others, who curry popularity with the ulema and the soldiery, to raise themselves in esteem and rival our own blessed father. I am powerless against their conspiracy, I, who have never sought but to serve you. All I have is your love, and that of my gracious Mother. My fate is totally in your hands. Yet because I do not try to sway the yeniçeris and swagger on my horse, I am at the mercy of those who conspire against me. I know I could never outshine the great light that you have thrown across the world.

I worry greatly for your safety, my Lord. Reports reach me daily that my own brother has been seen in the Porte, heavily disguised, talking with the yeniçeris in their barracks and spreading sedition and revolt. I pray that these reports are untrue for there is no rest for me knowing that my great Lord is in peril . . .

Süleyman tossed the letter aside and groaned with despair. He looked gray and shrunken on the throne of beaten gold, crouched between the two golden lions, almost as if he were their prey and not their master. Rüstem waited, silently, without expression.

"He pleads with me like a woman!" Süleyman said.

"He fears Bayezid."

"As he should. Bayezid is a lion. A true ghazi."

"As you say, my Lord."

"And what do your spies tell you of Selim? He still drinks too much wine?"

"He spends all his time at table or at the chase."

Süleyman made an impatient gesture with his hands. "And he wants me to protect him from Bayezid!"

"When the time comes, my Lord, Bayezid will take the throne from him."

"When I am dead, let God be the judge."

Süleyman closed his eyes. He had hoped to somehow end the bloodshed that accompanied succession of the Osmanli line, but in executing Mustapha he had only made it more certain. There was an old ghazi saying: *what has been, will be.* His father had murdered for the throne. It seemed his sons would do the same, despite all his efforts.

He did not understand why these young men sought power so ardently. For himself, he never had. His greatest regret had been that his father had not lived longer. These last years the mantle of the ghazis had rested on his shoulders like a burning yoke.

The throne had not only cost him Mustapha; a few weeks later Çehangir had hanged himself. Why? Grief for his stepbrother? Or because of his terror of his own father?

He tried to turn the thought aside. Rüstem was watching him, patiently. Süleyman indicated the letter that lay on the carpets between them.

"Is there truth in anything Selim claims? Has Bayezid been to Stamboul?"

"My spies have told me nothing of this," Rüstem said.

Süleyman nodded gravely. If Rüstem did not know of it, then it had not happened. Yet there was a seed of truth in what Selim had said; Bayezid had indeed inherited Mustapha's role as champion of the yeniçeris. Of course, that was as it should be; a Sultan could not take the throne without their support. Yet there was danger there, too, if Bayezid should become impatient.

"Who should it be, Rüstem? Selim is the oldest. The throne should be his. He is the shahzade."

"Bayezid is the only choice, my Lord," Rüstem said.

Süleyman nodded. It was in Rüstem's nature to be as dispassionate on such a subject as he was with finance and regulation. Dropsy had afflicted him cruelly these last few years, and the edema had swollen his limbs and his face, but the eyes were still the same, cool and gray. There was no room in his ledger for smudging decision with sentiment.

"Bayezid has no love for you, Rüstem."

"I shall not be here to fear him, my Lord."

Typical of him to speak of his own death with that same lack of intensity. "Should that not be the case, Rüstem, then I charge you with your last mission. When I am dead you must send a chaush on a speedy horse to Manisa to advise the shahzade, Selim, and tell him to make haste to the city." He paused, wincing at the gout in his knee. "Then you are to send another chaush to Bayezid, on an even faster horse, and tell him the throne belongs to the better man. In return Bayezid will no doubt spare you his displeasure when he is padishah."

"It will be done as you command, my Lord."

It was decided, then, Süleyman thought. Let God choose. He had done all he could. He had written the laws that would safeguard the future conduct of the Empire. Perhaps the Empire could survive another warrior or even a sot, if it should come to that.

Yet this would be his true legacy, he realized, his two sons squabbling over the Empire like vultures picking at the eyes of a body not yet dead. Perhaps it would always be that way.

God help me in my sorrow!

97

Pera

HE WAS SITTING alone in the great hall, staring at the logs burning in the grate. Julia came to stand behind him, and rested her hand on his shoulder.

"You look troubled."

"I was thinking . . . I was thinking what will happen when Süleyman is no longer Sultan."

"You have heard rumors?"

"He is old and sick. He has ruled at the Grande Porte for thirty-eight years. No man lives forever. Even the Shadow of God Upon the Earth has to die."

Julia smiled. "I suppose you will miss him."

Ludovici smiled too. "I am just a humble merchant. They could make one of their camels Sultan for all I care. But change and uncertainty make me nervous. I like always to know who to bribe and how much."

"Who will succeed him, Ludovici?"

"I imagine the Lady Hürrem will have a say in the matter."

"Perhaps she will proclaim herself Sultan."

Ludovici grinned. "I doubt that even she could manipulate that. No, it must be Bayezid. How could it ever be Selim? The man is a complete debauchee. He would make an excellent Bey of Algiers—but Sultan? Even I would not wish that upon the Turks." A log broke and tumbled in the grate. "I would wish it upon the Venetians, perhaps, but not the Turks."

"And Rüstem Pasha?"

"Bayezid would rather drown in boiling pitch than have him as his Vizier. Besides, he is growing old too. Soon everything will change. A new Sultan, a new Vizier. For a while they may even enforce the law and my business will be seriously disrupted."

The wind howled and rattled the windows and a draught flared the coals in the grate. "I am sure you will continue to prosper, Ludovici."

"Perhaps. But this uncertainty upsets my stomach. You can never be sure what these Osmanlis will do next. The Divan is a nest of vipers, Julia, and you can never be sure which hatchling is going to thrive."

Topkapi Saraya

A FROSTING OF ice glittered on the domes and semidomes of the Palace. The sun shone in a clear blue sky, without warmth. Hürrem sniffed the north wind for scent of the steppe, but it was as frigid as the black waters of the Bosphorus. She shivered and drew the ermine robe closer about her shoulders, but nothing kept the cold from her bones these days. She was getting old.

She nestled her feet farther beneath the *tandir,* the pan of lighted charcoal that sat under the square tin-topped table in front of her. But it was as if she could no longer feel heat. Everything was so cold.

She stared out of the latticed window, looking north again, beyond the Black Sea to the steppe, hidden somewhere beyond the violet horizon. She closed her eyes and her spirit drifted from the old woman dozing at the window, floated free across the waters and above the caravansary at Üsküdar. Üsküdar! Yes, she remembered it. The stone *han* with the central fountain where she had come thirty-five years before. She saw herself, a copper-haired girl with venom on her tongue, and defiance flashing in her eyes. She laughed. Look at her! She should have been bait for the fish in the Bosphorus! How did such a willful minx ever become kadin?

But the girl was far behind her now, lost on the horizon. Her spirit was still floating, and below her was the Kara Deniz, the Black Sea, the surface like a steel blade, dotted with the tiny specks of the caramusalis. And then she was soaring over the land again, like a carrion bird, and below her she saw a tribe of Krim Tartar, the hides of their *kabitkas,* the tent wagons, bulging black on the grass, the women milking the sheep and goats, their men galloping toward them from the steppe. She waved, and her mother looked up from the goat she was milking and waved back.

Hürrem started to run toward her, laughing.

Her father laughed too, and lifted her up in his strong arms on to the saddle of his Turkoman, and he took her splashing through the reed-grown islands of the Father Dnieper, past the towering fingers and domes of the mosques and the *catafalques,* and ahead of them she saw a great city of tents and horses, and heard the gypsy flutes . . .

"My Lady!"

Hürrem woke suddenly, her body jerking as if her flesh had been scorched with a white-hot knife. Her heart was hammering, there was oily sweat on her face. Muomi was staring at her, shaking her arm.

"What is it?" Hürrem said.

"You were shouting, my Lady. Is everything all right?"

". . . Shouting?"

"Were you asleep?"

"I was asleep," Hürrem repeated, and the disappointment made her feel as if she might choke.

"Are you all right, my Lady?" Muomi asked her, without concern.

"Go away."

Muomi sala'amed, and left the room.

Hürrem let her shoulders sag in weariness and she started to weep, softly at first. She had not wanted to come back. She had been happy, she realized, the first real happiness she could remember since she came here. And she had felt warm.

It had served her nothing, this struggle for eminence over other women. Oh, there had been relief when Süleyman had first chosen her, and a certain cold satisfaction later on in outwitting Gülbehar—though that was small achievement, God knows. But there had been no real happiness. Perhaps it was because women were not her real enemy. Men were.

And Süleyman. She hated him as much now as she had the day he had chosen her, thirty-five years before. No, before then. She had hated him from the very first day of her enslavement in the devshirme, when she had been led from the village with a shackle on her wrist. The hatred had not been made more benign by power or by his affection: it still resided there, deep in her soul, a bitter green poison, its potency undiminished by time.

But it was not the cold or her memories that had brought on this black mood. It was the nightingale.

It had been a present from Süleyman. He had given it to her on the day of her wedding, in a cage crafted from cedar and studded with onyx and pearl, and it had sung to her every day since. She had found it that morning lying on the bottom of its cage, stiff and cold. She removed it gently, cupping it in the palm of both her hands, and looked into its unblinking eye.

Her first reaction was not grief, but panic. As she stared at it, the bird sang to her for the final time. My life is yours, it sang. You have lived out your days like me, in this beautiful onyx and pearl palace, and the Sultan has admired you and enjoyed you and marveled at your singing and your beauty. But one day soon, just like me, your cold eye will stare at the dawn and you will not feel its warmth. It will be over. Your life will have passed. The cage door will never open. Your song will be gone and you will be forgotten.

She had thought that one day she might be the Valide, the mother of a Sultan, and then there would have been true power. Selim would have been easy to manipulate. After Mustapha had been destroyed, there had never been a moment when she thought she might not live to see one of her sons on the throne. Until now.

Now.

And now it did not matter to her anymore. All the power she had gained for herself had crumbled away in her fingers like clay. She was, finally, just a slave.

Süleyman's slave.

Yet there was still time to bring down her curse on the House of the Osmanlis and their arrogant male seed. She would yet have her revenge; a sweet justice she could savor from her grave for decades, perhaps centuries, to come.

Yes, yes. Of course. They wanted Bayezid. Left to their own devices, Bayezid would surely overcome poor little fat Selim in the race for the throne. He was the strong one, the leader, the ghazi.

Selim, for all she knew, was the son of a white eunuch.

So she would give them Selim.

Muomi rushed into the room, and seeing Hürrem awake, fell reluctantly to her knees. "My Lady, I thought I heard you shouting again."

"I was laughing, Muomi."

"Laughing, my Lady?"

"Yes, laughing, little Muomi. I feel suddenly warm again. Take the tandir and put it by the door. I think there is spring in the air."

THE DOMES AND spires of the Süleymaniye mosque rose from the city like a mountain of gray marble, one man's prayer for God's mercy, fashioned in stone. Other buildings swarmed around its feet—soup kitchens, hospitals, public baths, a caravansary, a library, a *medresse,* schools, and gardens; there were four universities also, with the best professors of theology and law in all the Empire. It had cost seven hundred thousand ducats, the ransom of a king, and it had absolved a Sultan's guilt for the murder of his son.

Perhaps.

Süleyman gazed at it from the latticed windows of Hürrem's apartment, his hands on her shoulders. "It is magnificent, my Lord. In a thousand years men will look at it and regret they were not born in an age such as ours."

"Perhaps, little russelana," Süleyman murmured. He held her tighter. She felt frail. He could feel the shape of her bones through the silk and seraser brocade, and it frightened him. He knew she had been sickening, but he had tried to ignore the signs. The realization that she might be truly ill suddenly brought him to the edge of a black chasm of terror.

He studied her more closely. She was wearing a little green taplock like the one she had worn the first day he had seen her, but it was a mocking echo of her youth. Beneath the kohl and henna and powder her skin was like parchment, thin and dry, it seemed that it might crack and powder away in his fingers if he touched it too roughly. Her cheeks had sunken beneath the bones and the outline of her skull was plainly visible in the piercing clarity of the early morning sunlight. Her hair had lost much of its gold; it was milky white at the roots like that morning's winter sky; only the green eyes were still as vivid, still as intense.

He hugged her to him as if he could protect her from death itself with his will and physical force. He realized he loved her more now than he had ever done. Physical passion had been replaced in these later years by spiritual comfort, a feeling of ease and intimacy in her presence that he shared with no one else. How could he live without her now? The very thought was intolerable.

"It is a great achievement, my Lord," Hürrem whispered. She had not guessed the direction of his thoughts. Her attention was still focused on the Süleymaniye.

"One day our bones will lie there, side by side," Süleyman said, and he thought: Let that day not come for many years!

"So I shall never escape the Eski Saraya, then? One day I shall return to the hill overlooking the slave market where you bought me?"

"Where fate brought you to me," he said. He was alarmed by the strange note of bitterness in her voice. "Are you well, little russelana?" he asked her.

"I have lost a little appetite."

"Shall I have my physician send you an elixir?"

"Muomi tends to me, my Lord. I shall soon recover. When spring comes."

The north wind, the *tramontana,* howled like a djinn through the stone walls, and Süleyman shivered inside his sable-lined robe. "You must take better care."

"Do not concern yourself, my Lord. A few aches are to be expected as we grow older."

Süleyman could not bear to dwell any longer on her mortality. "I have spoken to Rüstem," he said abruptly. "About the succession."

"What did you decide, my Lord?"

"When the day comes, they shall both be told. Let God decide it."

"If they are both told, there will be nothing for God to decide. Bayezid will claim the throne." She turned from the window and gripped his shoulders. "Will you help me to the divan, my Lord?"

Süleyman waved away her gediçli and helped her across the room, shocked at how light she felt against his arm, as if she had been hollowed out inside and only her shell remained. How long had she been like this? he wondered. How long since he had last seen her? No more than a week. How could she have sickened so quickly?

He helped her position her feet beneath the tandir, supporting her back gently with cushions.

"Thank you, my Lord."

"I should send for the physician."

"It is nothing. Just a slight chill." One of the gediçli threw a quilt over her knees. When she had settled herself, Hürrem said: "My Lord, I would talk with you further about this matter. They are my sons; I know their hearts."

Süleyman sat beside her on the divan and took her hand. "Little russelana, Selim is a loving son, but he could never be a great Sultan. Bayezid is the ghazi."

"So he is a warrior. He will be popular with the yeniçeris, at least."

"Without the yeneçeris, a Sultan cannot rule."

"The yeniçeris! For whom you have nothing but contempt."

"There are times when a Sultan is compelled to use his sword, even if he despises war."

"Bayezid knows nothing else. He would spend his whole life in the saddle if he could. My Lord, I say this not to condemn him, but only to give you pause. Selim is the shahzade. He may not be a warrior like his brother, but he may be a true knight in the Divan. You yourself have said that it is the law that will ensure the future of the Osmanlis, not the sword."

"Little russelana, we must face the truth. Selim is a debauchee and a drunkard. He rarely attends his own Divan in Manisa. Should we hope that will change if he becomes padishah?"

"If Bayezid takes the throne, Selim will die."

"Let God decide. Rüstem has his orders. When the time comes, a chaush will be sent to them both. In this you will not sway me."

Hürrem bowed her head, and squeezed his hand in response. "It is as you say, my Lord. I do not argue with your wisdom. I shall pray for both my sons."

He embraced her, a terrible dull ache in his chest. Please do not leave me, little russelana. I cannot live without you now! It is the only thing that has given my life any meaning. I have murdered my best friend and executed my son to preserve the sultanate of the Osmanlis. Yet I have never betrayed my love for you. It is the one thing I know in my heart has been true and good. Let me keep that for a little longer. I cannot rest without it.

Do not leave me, little russelana. Do not leave me.

98

Topkapi Saraya

MUOMI WAS WITH her when she fell.

Hürrem had ventured on to the balcony of her apartment to listen to her nightingales and gaze across the Bosphorus, as she did every morning. Suddenly she cried out and Muomi caught her in her arms. Hürrem's handmaidens ran to assist her, but by the time they had lain her on her divan she was already unconscious, her breathing ragged and shallow in her breast.

Galata

LUDOVICI RECEIVED AN urgent summons to meet Abbas at the Jewish house. Abbas was late.

When he finally arrived, there was no trace of the urgency that Ludovici had expected. After the usual pleasantries, his four pages helped him ease his enormous bulk to the floor. He sat down silently, his attention focused on the pastries piled on the silver plate in front of him. When they were gone he dipped his fingers daintily into the silver bowl proffered by another of Ludovici's servants. He belched politely into a silk handkerchief he produced from the abundant folds of his robe.

"I received your message," Ludovici said.

"You are impatient," Abbas said. "You have lived with these Muslims all these years and still you have not learned the simple art of patience."

"The message said it was urgent."

Abbas sighed. "Yes, the matter is urgent. Urgent in hours, not minutes. I hoped to savor our meeting. It will probably be our last."

"What has happened?"

Abbas leaned forward, his elbows resting on his knees. "The Lady Hürrem, the Laughing One, is dying."

"You are sure?"

"She has been suffering her malady for many months. Now she lies in her bed, with the smell of death about her. That smell cannot be mistaken. I have known it many times."

"But how does this affect me? Why this urgency?"

"It is Julia, Ludovici! You must send her away from Stamboul. Now!"

"I will never send her away."

"In the sight of God, Ludovici, I swear she lives under the sword in this city!"

"I will not give her up."

"You do not have to! I know you have land in Cyprus. Take her there with you!"

"Her offense was twenty years ago. Despite what you say, Süleyman will have forgotten her now. I will not give up everything I have built here to run from shadows!"

"He may have forgotten but once he knows she is still alive he will be bound by duty and pride before the Divan to punish me and her! Do you think he will hesitate to give the order—especially now! He will send his chaush for her even into the Comunità Magnifica! Do you think he fears the bailo of Venice?"

"I will not give up all I have built here."

"For pity's sake, get her out of Stamboul! Hürrem has put everything down in her own hand. She swears that it will be delivered to the Grand Vizier on her death."

"For what purpose?"

"She has her reasons!"

"I will not send her away."

"Then go with her, if you must!"

Ludovici leaned forward, and shook his head. "Leave everything I have built, to run from shadows! Look at me, Abbas. Your friend, the bastardo. My father's poor orphan bastard. I was not good enough for the togati, for polite Venetian society. So I came here and ever since I have enjoyed shoving my revenge down their throats with gold coins! Here, they have to bow to me!"

"They are not shadows you are running from, Ludovici. But if these things matter so much to you, then you choose . . . your precious empire of warehouses and ships, or Julia!" Abbas coughed. It made a wet, hacking sound in his chest. He brought the handkerchief to his lips and when he removed it Ludovici noticed a watery red stain. "I beg your pardon. Some days this cough troubles me more than others."

Ludovici was silent for a long time. Abbas waited, and did not attempt to interrupt his thoughts. "All right," Ludovici said, "I will do as you ask. Now you do one favor for me."

"If it is within my power."

"My caramusalis may enter and leave the Dardanelles as they wish. They are never searched. My baksheesh to Rüstem is handsome payment for the privilege. If I wished to take passengers on board, they would be guaranteed safe passage." He gripped Abbas's wrist. "You come too. If Hürrem betrays Julia to Süleyman, she betrays you also. Get away from here, now! At least you can live out your last few years in peace!"

Abbas looked away. Peace? Did such a thing exist? "Where?"

"Tomorrow at dawn, at Galata. One of my caramusalis will be there. It will be flying the Venetian lion from its stern, but it will be upside down. The captain will have his orders. Just get on board and hurry below."

Abbas wondered: what would it be like to be free again? "Where would you send us? To Cyprus?"

"There are no palace walls there, Abbas. Just vineyards and olive groves. Please. As much as you wish for Julia's safety, I wish for Julia's safety, I wish for yours."

Abbas nodded. "Thank you," he murmured. He coughed again, grimacing at the pain in his chest. He clapped his hands and immediately the deaf-mutes were at his side, lifting him to his feet. When it was done, Abbas clung to them still, wheezing from the effort.

"Goodbye, Ludovici." He executed a delicate temennah.

"Tomorrow at dawn."

"Yes. The start of a new day, perhaps." He stopped at the door and turned to Ludovici. "If I am not there, say goodbye to Julia for me."

And then he was gone.

Topkapi Saraya

"Muomi."

Hürrem's voice was no more than a whisper. Muomi put her ear close to Hürrem's lips to catch the words.

"Yes, my Lady."

". . . Revenge."

"Yes, my Lady."

"I am . . . dying now . . . but afterward . . . Süleyman . . . will come . . . to you."

"What am I to tell him?"

"Whatever . . . hurts him . . . the most."

Muomi smiled. "Yes, my Lady."

Pera

JULIA HAD NEVER seen Ludovici like this. He sagged in the oak chair in his study, his shoulders slumped. He stroked the gold and silver of his beard, his mind fixed on some private torment.

She waited patiently for him to speak. What could be wrong? she wondered. And then she decided: it was Abbas. And it was bad news.

"I am sending you away," he said, suddenly.

"My Lord?"

"I should have done this years ago. It is for your own safety."

She was overcome by a sudden wave of indignation. Again, she was just another pawn, to be pushed around the Mediterranean at another man's pleasure. "How can I be in danger?"

"The Sultan may know you are here."

"But surely, this was all years ago—"

"Abbas is certain of it. It is not forgotten. Soon the Grand Vizier will know and Süleyman will be forced to act."

Ludovici was sitting with his back toward the fretted windows. Beyond him, the Kubbealti on Seraglio Point was outlined against the sky. It is a poignant sketch of his dilemma, Julia thought. The power of the Divan intrudes on him always.

"Where do you want me to go?"

"I have estates at Cyprus. You will be well looked after."

Julia tried to imagine it. Another lonely villa, some vines, a few servants, perhaps a few books and her embroidery to occupy her. A monastery for all purposes. The prospect was intolerable.

She looked up at Ludovici and realized she would miss him. When had it happened? With Abbas there had been the rush of youth, the danger of romance; with Sirhane, it had been the release of pleasure, and yes, she thought, a way of ridding herself of the need for men, a sweet, ripe vengeance. It had not been until Sirhane's death that she had begun to see Ludovici for what he was, a mortal man who loved her perhaps beyond his capacity to show. Though he had become her husband, she had never given herself to him as she had to Sirhane, even as she did that once to Abbas; but he had become her companion, and her shelter, and might even yet become her friend. She would miss his warmth beside her in the bed, his wit, his strength.

No, she decided. I cannot be without him now.

"You wish me to go?" she asked him.

"No," Ludovici said. "That is the last thing I wish."

"Then I shall not go."

"You do not understand, Julia—"

"I understand perfectly. I just do not wish to leave you."

He stared at her, bewildered. "Why?"

"Perhaps I have grown fond of you."

"What?"

Julia's lips creased to a tight, sad smile. "Is that so hard to believe?"

"Yes. Yes, it is. I never expected to hear it."

"If you will come with me, I will go. If you cannot, then I will stay here. I am decided."

Ludovici stood up, and went to the window, his back turned toward her. *Corpo di Dio!* He had waited so long for one moment of passion with her that her calm acceptance had taken him completely by surprise. He did not know what to say or do. He had been resigned to finally giving up something he knew he had never really possessed; now this.

"I do not know what to say."

He heard the rustling of her skirts as she came to stand behind him. He felt her hand on his arm. "What will you do?"

"I cannot risk allowing you to stay here."

"Then you will come?"

"Yes. Perhaps I will like Cyprus. Perhaps I shall grow grapes and grow brown and wrinkled in the sun."

"It does not sound like you."

"I will leave the running of the business in the hands of my undermerchant. If Abbas is wrong about this, then after a few months we can return to the Palace. If he is not—then . . ." He shrugged his shoulders. "Perhaps the Venetian renegade bastardo has proved his point anyway." He turned around. She was smiling at him.

He remembered her as he had first seen her, with Abbas, in the church of Santa Maria dei Miracoli. The vision in velvet, as Abbas had once described her, was no longer the angel she once had been. She was flawed by age and by sin and by mortal weakness.

But he loved her still, as he had always done. And finally she wanted him. And in the end, that was enough.

99

ABDULLAH ALI OSMAN, Süleyman's private physician, was an unhappy man. Süleyman surveyed him from the divan, his face ferocious with despair.

"You must prescribe for her. If she dies, I shall make you responsible. You will enjoy an uninterrupted view of the next sunrise from a niche in the wall of the Ba'ab-i-Hümayun."

Ali Osman touched his forehead to the silken rug. "As you say, my Lord." *God help me in my sorrow!*

A guard of eunuchs, their yataghans drawn, escorted him through the great oak and iron gate into the silent sanctuary of the Harem. They passed a hushed and cloistered courtyard and climbed a flight of narrow stone steps to the apartment of the Hasseki Hürrem.

As they passed through the great domed audience chamber, he did not even spare a glance at the great blue and white Ming vases or the Vicenzan gilt mirrors or the jeweled censers that hung from the vaulted dome like fruit. Fear had turned his eyes inward. O that God had spared him to be alive in another time, when the Sultan did not love his women so much!

A double line of eunuchs lined the pathway into the bedroom so that he could see nothing beyond them, but he knew she was there; her presence, the hush that surrounded her, filled the room. The guards who had accompanied him from the audience hall stopped suddenly, allowing him to walk ahead.

Nothing was said, and he wondered what he should do.

Suddenly a hand appeared between the double line of eunuchs, pale and limp, the wrist held by the plump ebony fingers of an anonymous black eunuch. Probably the Kislar Aghasi, he decided. Her hand, he knew, would be all he would be allowed to examine. Ali Osman stepped forward.

He took the proffered hand almost reverently, for he knew he was the only other whole man, besides the Sultan himself, who had ever been allowed to touch her since she had entered the walls of the Harem. It was an old woman's hand now, of course, with blotches on the skin the color of spilled coffee, the skin flaccid on the bones. He felt for the pulsing of the blood, gauged the temperature of the skin that would tell him the heat of the internal organs. He pinched the quick of the nails, gently, testing for the quickness of the blood.

"Her heart beats very slowly," he said to himself. "Her body cools, in readiness for death."

He must hurry. He must prepare an elixir that might revive her organs, and quicken the blood. He had no wish to see the sunrise from the Ba'ab-i-Hümayun, no matter how splendid the view.

"HAS THE . . . OLD fool . . . gone?"

"Yes," Abbas told her. The guards filed out of the room. They were alone. Strange how he had hated her, Abbas thought, yet now admired the courage with which she faced her death. If only he had the same strength. "Yes, he has gone."

"I would not . . . trust him . . . to pare my toenails."

"No, my Lady."

The whites of her eyes were no longer white; they were stained with yellow, and had sunken deep into her head. It was almost as if the flesh were wasting off her as he watched. No elixir or potion in the world was going to save her, Abbas decided. She reeked of death.

Her lips cracked into a smile. "So you are . . . going to . . . see me . . . dead . . . after all, my . . . Abbas. That . . . must please . . . you."

"Yes, my Lady," Abbas said.

"Your candor . . . is so refreshing . . . they all . . . tell me . . . I am going to . . . live."

"I should say they are greatly mistaken, my Lady," Abbas whispered.

Hürrem turned her eyes on him, slowly, painfully. "I have . . . one more . . . errand for . . . you."

"I hardly think you are in a position to command me any longer, my Lady."

"You . . . want . . . the letter?"

Abbas controlled himself with difficulty. "Make your peace with God, my Lady. The affairs of the world will soon no longer concern you!"

Somehow, she laughed. The laughter cracked into a fit of coughing that left her desperately weak for several minutes. Finally, when she recovered, she whispered. "You are . . . right, my Abbas. Muomi has . . . the letter. She . . . has my command . . . to deliver it . . . to you."

"Then there really was such a letter?"

"Of . . . course. I never make . . . empty threats. But . . . I am not . . . a vindictive woman. Go in . . . peace . . . my Abbas."

Rot in hell, Abbas thought.

He rose to leave her. Tonight, he was sure, the witch would die. And at dawn he would be on a caramusali, gliding across the Marmara Deniz, and finally, finally free.

But as he stood up, he heard her whisper: "Do you not . . . hate them . . . these Turks?"

Had she really said that? Abbas leaned closer to her, his nose twitching at the stench of corruption. "My Lady?"

"What they have done . . . to me . . . to you. Do you not . . . hate them?"

"My bones ache with it."

Hürrem closed her eyes. The effort of speaking was tiring her. "They have made . . . me a . . . slave . . . and you a . . . joke." Well, Abbas thought, even in death she did not choose delicacy over candor. "Do you not . . . want . . . some measure . . . of vengeance?"

"What did my Lady foresee?"

"I foresee . . . Selim . . . as the next . . . Sultan."

"It can never happen!"

"Who knows . . . what will happen . . . my Abbas? Abbas? . . . Perhaps you may . . . still . . . yet be useful . . ." She tried to moisten her lips. They were cracked, and a little watery blood seeped from them. "I have . . . bequeathed you . . . to my son's service. Perhaps . . . you can help me . . . in this last . . . endeavor."

She closed her eyes again, and in moments she was asleep. Abbas left the room. He looked back at her once. She looked such a fragile and pathetic creature now, he thought. Like a child's rag doll lying on the pillow. How could he have dreaded her so much?

And how could he now find himself suddenly in such sympathy with her, at this late hour? "I will help you," he murmured. "This time you do not have to threaten. I will gladly do all I can."

He went out, closing the door softly behind him.

100

Marmara Sea

"WHY DIDN'T HE come?" Julia said.

Ludovici leaned at the rail of the caramusali, watching the domes and spires of the great city fading into the violet haze of the morning. "I don't know. I never understood Abbas's reasons for doing anything."

"But he said he would come."

"He also implied that he might not."

"Do you think he is still alive?"

Ludovici shook his head. "My sources inside the Porte will find out for me in time. If they have killed him, then we were right not to delay any longer. And if he is well, and chose not to come . . . well, nothing will change his mind once it is made up."

The water shimmered with pools of gold as the sun rose in the sky. The caramusali reached into the morning breeze, gliding past the islands bound for the Dardanelles and the Mediterranean. Julia remembered that other morning when she had first seen the city that had imprisoned and liberated her. A lifetime ago. Impossible to comprehend she might never see this skyline of minarets and domes again.

"I shall pray for him," Julia said. She put her hand on his. The breeze was salt and clean. She said a silent farewell to Abbas and Sirhane and felt the past slough off her soul, like an old and withered skin.

Topkapi Saraya

HÜRREM WAS DYING.

It was obvious to him, even as he entered the room. She was propped up on pillows; Muomi had braided her hair with pearls, the little green taplock had been pinned to her hair, and she had been dressed in a kaftan of purest-white silk, like a concubine readied for her first night with her

Sultan. It was an absurd parody of her youth, and he wanted to cry aloud when he saw her. What were they doing to her? Had they no respect? Was it some sort of cruel joke?

He barely recognized her now. Her flesh had fallen away from her bones so that the features that had made her face individual had gone. She seemed no more than a skull with a tight covering of translucent skin, her body shrunken and tiny, like a child's doll.

Muomi and Abbas crouched at her bedside, their faces dark with dread. For their own skins, no doubt, Süleyman thought.

Dear God, she was really dying.

"Little russelana . . ." he whispered.

Her eyes flickered open. "Süleyman."

The others moved back from the bedside. Süleyman sat on the edge of the mattress and picked up her hand. It was cold as marble. "Don't leave me," he whispered.

"I am free, Süleyman." Her voice had lost all gentleness; it had a hoarse, metallic quality, like metal on a rasp.

"Don't leave me."

Her mouth creased into a bow. "You fool."

He brought her fingers to his lips and kissed them, gently. "I love you, little russelana."

"I do believe . . . you do. Life has been . . . cruel to you, Süleyman. But then . . . you have deserved it."

Something deep in his stomach turned to ice. He wondered if he had heard her correctly, if he understood what she was saying. "What are you telling me?"

"I am telling you . . . to go and stew . . . in Hell."

Süleyman stared at her, appalled. He dropped her hand suddenly, as if she had just admitted to the pestilence, and stood up. He turned to the circle of faces around the bed. "Get out! Get out all of you!"

Muomi and the other gediçli hurried out. Only Abbas hesitated, his large black features twisted in surprise and confusion.

"Get out!" Süleyman repeated.

The door creaked shut behind him.

When he turned back to her Hürrem was grinning; yes, grinning, he thought, for it could not be called a smile. Her lips were drawn back from her teeth in a death's head vision of triumph.

"Little russelana . . ."

"I am not . . . your little russelana. I have never . . . loved you. Every day . . . of my life . . . I have hated you . . . until my teeth have ached . . . with the force of . . . my hatred."

Süleyman clutched at the fluted golden column of the canopy for support. "You are sick. I shall pay no attention to this," he said aloud.

"I was your prisoner . . . I could do nothing else . . . but submit to you. But oh . . . how I have hated you!"

Süleyman covered his ears in despair. "I shall not listen further to this!"

"Have you ever wondered . . . why Bayezid is such . . . a great warrior? It is because . . . he belongs to . . . Ibrahim!"

"No! That is impossible!"

"You trusted him . . . so much . . . fool . . . you never knew . . . what he did . . . after he returned . . . from Egypt."

"No!"

"So you see . . . this is my waqf . . . my bequest . . . to the Osmanlis. Choose, Süleyman! Selim . . . or the son . . . of the Greek! I curse you, and I curse . . . every Sultan who follows you . . . until your Empire crumbles away . . . into memory and ruin."

"Stop it! PLEASE!"

"How I . . . hate you!"

"NOOOOOOO!" He took her by the shoulders and shook her. "You love me! Say it! You love me!"

He looked into her eyes and watched the light die. A flicker of brightness, like a candle in a breeze, then darkness. He threw back his head and screamed. Then he threw her back onto the bed with all his force. She slumped onto her side.

"NOOOOOOO! IT IS NOT TRUE!"

He ripped the taplock from her head, and the pearls that were braided into her whitened hair scattered onto the marble floor, and her hair tore from the roots, and tangled between his fingers.

"Nooooooooo!"

He picked up a stool, and flung it at the Vicenzan mirror, watching the image of himself splinter into a thousand pieces.

Then he ran from the room.

When Abbas found him later he was curled up on his own bed, crying like a baby. His servants left him then, terrified, none of them knowing what to do. He lay that way for three days, crying and talking to the phantoms that surrounded his bed, and when he finally summoned Abbas once more it was to order that her rooms be locked and sealed, so that he would never again be forced to enter any room where he had once heard her laughter or felt her embrace.

PART 10

GOD'S WIND

101

Amasya, 1559

THE RIDERS GALLOPED toward at each other at full tilt, the horses' hoofs drumming on the soft earth, the mud tossed into the air behind them in thick brown clumps. The first rider threw his spear, and his opponent tried to slide out of the way on the lee side of his horse, but the pole struck him a glancing blow on the back. The mounted horsemen on one side of the arena cheered. The music of the drums and *zounas* became more urgent.

"Sssssss," Bayezid hissed at his Arab, who was prancing and kicking with his forelegs, agitated by the music and the shouting of the riders around them.

"Another three points," Murad grinned. "A good day for the Blues."

"Soon we may be throwing real spears," Bayezid said. He grinned like a lunatic and took off toward the center of the arena, toward two riders from the Greens. As they closed, Murad saw the first javelin, thrown too soon, pass harmlessly over his prince's shoulders as he ducked beneath the horse's head. Bayezid veered his Arab suddenly to the right, and the other rider had to pull up sharply to avoid crashing into him.

Bayezid reined in his horse, which responded immediately. Before the other rider had realized what was happening, he was behind him, and the spear struck the Green between the shoulder blades. The man cried out with pain and slumped over his horse.

The men around Murad stood in their stirrups and cheered.

Bayezid charged in, calling for another javelin from the pages who were darting between the legs of the horses. His face was flushed with triumph. He grinned through his thick black beard at Murad.

"Well, what do you say, Murad?"

"I say we march and cut ourselves a slice of Barley Pudding!"

Bayezid laughed. There was another whoop from the riders around them as another of their team scored a direct hit with his wooden spear and sent a Green tumbling onto the soft ground with blood spurting from his head.

They were invincible that day. They could not lose. It just did not seem possible.

SHE WAS AN old lady now. Bayezid found her in the gardens of the Harem, in the rose kiosk. The wooden pavilion was surrounded by a colonnade of fretted columns and was painted with gold leaf. The fretted windows and arched doorways looked out into a rose garden alive now with blooms of rose and gold and pink.

She sat alone in the pavilion, the silence broken only by the steady *click-click-click* of the pearl *tespi* as she ran them through her fingers, her lips moving softly as she recited the prayers of Muhammad. She wore a kaftan of ruby-red seraser embroidered with gold thread, and a pure-white cloth jacket trimmed with swansdown. Her face was hidden by a yashmak of muslin, but Bayezid could see the deep lines around her eyes that betrayed her age. The years had not been kind to the Rose of Spring. All that remained were her thorns.

"What are you going to do, Bayezid?"

"What can I do, my Lady? Süleyman has left me no choice. Yet my quarrel remains with Selim, not my father."

"You are wrong."

Bayezid lowered his eyes and did not answer her. It was beautiful here in the garden, the air redolent with the scent of the rosebushes that surrounded the pavilion. Too perfect a day to be talking about bloodshed.

A gediçli poured Gülbehar a perfumed sherbet into a crystal glass and she sipped from it.

"Whatever I do there will be war," Bayezid said.

"Because of Selim?"

"The troubles of the Osmanlis do not begin and end with Selim. The great-grandsons of the men who followed the Fatih to Stamboul now sit on their timars in Anatolia and watch their ghazi tribe ruled by the people their fathers conquered. The devshirme has burdened us with an army of bureaucrats. They are being driven off their land by their own Christian slaves. My father has forgotten the sheepskins of his ancestors. They grow mold in his treasure house while a Bulgarian vizier imposes taxes on even herbs and roses and forces the timariots off their lands while he fills his own pockets! Everything is baksheesh, baksheesh! What happened to Süleyman's own kanuns, that all promotions should be on merit alone? He has made his fine laws and then he has forgotten us! The true Osmanlis lived in tents and took their empire from the saddles of their horses, not by reclining on silk divans and counting their jewels!"

Gülbehar ran the tespi through her fingers, *click-click-click*. "Do you remember when Mustapha was murdered, Bayezid? Do you remember what the yeniçeris said? 'Our hope is lost in Mustapha.'"

"I remember."

"We need another Mustapha." She put aside the tespi and stared at him. "You, Bayezid. You are so much like him. You can ride, you can fight, you can lead. You are a true ghazi."

"If only my father thought so."

"Süleyman was my lord for many years, but truly, I do not recognize the man he has become. He has forgotten he is a ghazi. Even now the witch is dead. Look what he has done to you! He has shamed you, exiled you here to Amasya, as he did to my son. He has all but handed the throne to your fat sot of a brother!"

"It is his right. Somehow Selim has duped him into this. It is Selim I must settle with."

"No, it is Süleyman. Be careful!"

"Truly I do not love him, my Lady. But he is my father and my Sultan."

"Those were my son's words also." Gülbehar returned to her tespi and her silent prayers.

"He knows what kind of man my brother is. It makes no sense."

"It made no sense to kill my son. But he did it anyway. Be careful, Bayezid. Go with God."

She held out her hand. Bayezid kissed it and took his leave.

Ride against Süleyman? No, that was unthinkable. She was just a bitter old woman. Süleyman was testing his mettle, that was all. He must know that he could not allow Selim to remain at Manisa, just five days' ride from the capital, while he lived in virtual exile almost a month's ride from Stamboul. Selim had sworn to kill him if he ever took the throne. What else could he do? He had to move against him. It was the way, the Osmanli way. Surely his father could understand that.

Topkapi Saraya

SÜLEYMAN BROODILY CONTEMPLATED his Grand Vizier, and sat motionless but for the steady tapping of his index finger on the golden arm of the throne. Süleyman wore a sleeveless kaftan of crimson with gold tiger stripes and a lining of black sable, over a robe of green seraser brocade. Emeralds glittered in his turban, and on his fingers. But for all his magnificence he looked shrunken, Rüstem thought; as if there were no more than a wizened gray head on top of a bundle of empty, fine clothes. His cheeks had been heavily rouged to disguise his pallor.

"It was the illness," Süleyman murmured.

Rüstem frowned. "My Lord?"

Süleyman jerked his head up, as if suddenly aware of his Vizier's presence. "Ah, Rüstem . . ."

"I have come from the Divan, my Lord."

"The Divan," Süleyman repeated, as if trying to remember what manner of thing that might be.

"I have bad news, my Lord."

"Bayezid?"

"Yes, my Lord." Rüstem found himself off balance once more; Süleyman seemed one moment on the edge of madness; the next, he was lucid and alert. He had been this way ever since Hürrem had died.

"Has he answered the Sultan's chaush?"

"He has, my Lord."

"And what does he say?"

"His reply was short, my Lord." He produced the letter from the folds of his robes. He read the formal salutation. "He goes on to say just this, my Lord: 'In everything I will obey the command of the Sultan, my father, except in all that lies between Selim and me.'"

Süleyman uttered a small cry, like an animal caught in a trap. "She was very ill. She did not mean what she said."

"My Lord?"

Süleyman brought his fist down on to the arm of the throne. "Why does he defy me?"

What else can he do? Rüstem thought. You virtually exiled him to Amasya after Hürrem's death. "He raises an army at Angora," Rüstem said. "They say the timariots and the Turcomans are flocking to him."

"With what intent?"

"His intent seems clear. Selim has complained that he has received a woman's bonnet and apron from his brother as a gift. The message appears plain enough."

"We must stop this, Rüstem. While I live, they must obey me!"

"There may yet be a way, my Lord."

"Tell me."

"Restore Bayezid to Kütahya. If not there, then Konia. But by assigning him to Amasya you give the succession to Selim. If he goes he must accept certain death."

"He must obey me!"

"If you insist on this, we cannot avert a civil war."

"They are my sons. I am not in my grave yet! They must do as I say!"

"I fear we cannot persuade Bayezid to stay his hand, my Lord." He hesitated. "It was always my understanding that you wanted Bayezid as your successor."

"Then your understanding was at fault, Rüstem. You are getting old. Perhaps the dropsy has addled your brain."

Rüstem touched his forehead to the carpet. "As you say, my Lord." He would not allow Süleyman to see how painful it was to perform such a basic function. He must never allow anyone to perceive any weakness.

"Tell Selim he is to proceed to Konia, to guard our southern route to Syria and Egypt. Send Muhammad Sokolli to protect him, with a regiment of yeniçeris and thirty cannon. Meanwhile you may command Pertew Pasha to Bayezid to try and persuade him to return without delay to the governorship of Amasya and extract from him a promise of loyalty and fealty. They must not be allowed to drag the Empire into war, while I still sit on this throne."

"As you say, my Lord," Rüstem said. He rose slowly to his feet and hobbled from the room. Süleyman is mad! he thought. Hürrem's death had unhinged his mind. But he would do as the Sultan commanded. Let his sons worry about Süleyman's successor. He would be dead before then.

"You were ill," Süleyman said, to the echoing silence. "You did not mean what you were saying."

"There was a fever in my brain," Hürrem said. "It was the Devil who spoke."

"Bayezid is my son," Süleyman said.

"Of course he is your son. I loved you with all my heart. Besides, I was close guarded in the Harem. Ibrahim could not have reached me there. It was the Devil's lie."

"You love me. Tell me you love me."

"You were my Lord, the Lord of my life. I loved you with all my heart, always."

Süleyman reached out a hand to touch her but she was not there.

He closed his eyes, felt the tears, white hot, spill onto his cheeks. Tears of grief, and of pity for his own heart. For thirty-five years he had loved her, loved her more than any other living thing. He had given up his Harem for her, and made her his queen. Yet with her last words she had damned him to this purgatory.

It was the illness, of course. It must have been the illness.

But he could not rid himself of the memory. The words had been seared into his brain, and whenever he thought his weeping and fasting had finally driven them from his mind he would suddenly hear her voice, as if she were in the same room, or even see her, lying on the bed, her face a ghastly alabaster white, her voice as jagged as metal: "I hate you," she would whisper, "I have always despised you."

"My little russelana, please . . ."

He opened his eyes, expecting to see her. But there were only the Palace guards, deaf-mutes, dumb to his grief, their faces blank as stone.

Little russelana.

He closed his eyes again and remembered when he had first seen her, in the courtyard below the apartments of the Valide in the old Eski Saraya; the little green taplock pinned to her hair, a childlike frown on her face as she worked the needle and thread. An innocent child. She was incapable of so much hate. It was Satan speaking through her lips, he told himself; she was already in Paradise when he heard those words.

Yet he could not be sure. He could feel the doubt eating away at his innards like a festering ulcer, every day a little worse. It was the reason he had exiled Bayezid east to Amasya. It would assure Selim of the throne, of course, but better to have a drunken Osmanli prince, than break the line forever with the son of a traitor.

Even a traitor he had loved.

He threw back his head, sudden rage bulging the veins in his neck and his temples. "Curse you, Ibrahim!" he screamed into the vaulted silence. "Curse you!"

And curse you, Hürrem. But he could not bring himself to speak those words aloud, even now. It would have meant his whole life was worth nothing.

102

Angora

I N SPRING CAPPADOCIA is ablaze with wildflowers, the rains drawing a riot of color from the sun-baked steppes. Bayezid rode with his equerry, Murad, along a stream between ranks of tall, spindly poplars, fields of brilliant yellow rapeseed on either side, the distant hills wreathed in blue daisies.

They reached the crest of the spur and looked down over the plain. Bayezid's army was camped outside the village, under the great towers of the Hisar fortress. Bayezid felt the warm flesh of his Arab stallion quiver underneath him, as if it sensed his excitement. The camp was at prayer; men were lined in rows like hedges, on their knees. The turbans bobbed in unison, thousands, no tens of thousands, row upon row upon row.

In the past weeks they had arrived from all over the plains. There were Kurds in baggy trousers, broad scarlet sashes at their waists, wearing woollen skullcaps instead of turbans; Turkoman bandits in fur hats with sheep-wool ringlets hanging in curls about their flat Asian features; black-plumed spahis who had deserted the Porte in small bands to look for the new Mustapha; the dispossessed timariots, their motley selection of armor and conical helmets silhouetted against the mauve sky.

Now there were twenty thousand camped on the plain, a traditional ghazi army, the timariots and nomad warriors whose fathers had conquered the steppes in the name of the Osmanlis, gathered again to reconquer the new Christian armies of their masters. They were ready to go against Selim, and if necessary, against the yeniçeris and the spahis who supported him.

Murad turned to Bayezid and grinned. "You have lit a flame under the Empire. They are all flocking to you now. You are their future now."

"We will not let them down," Bayezid said. "Let their hope rest in Bayezid now!"

They spurred their horses down the slope and into the camp.

Manisa

THE SHAHZADE SELIM was in a black mood. Bayezid was massing an army against him, and still his father refused to move against him. Instead he had sent Sokolli and his cannon and a royal command to move on to Konia, to stand against him. Was he not the chosen? Then why did Süleyman still sit in his Palace watching the sun move the shadows round the walls while "the new Mustapha" gathered strength at Angora, ready to murder him? It was obvious to him now: he had been abandoned.

He emptied the crystal cup at his side and clapped his hands for the page to refill it from the ewer of Chian wine.

Damn them. Damn Bayezid. And damn Süleyman.

Perhaps it was all a plot against him. Süleyman might even be at Amasya now, plotting with Bayezid on how best to remove him. His brother would be feasting with him in his seraglio, or displaying to his father his prowess at the çerit. Even worse, Bayezid might be intriguing instead with the Aga of the yeniçeris to usurp the throne, as Selim the Grim had done.

He gulped down another draft of wine, and sobbed aloud. Life was so unfair. Hürrem had never shown him any affection, and Süleyman had ignored him in favor of Mustapha and Çehangir. Perhaps he should have been born with a spine like a camel's hump; then perhaps someone might have given him a little time, a little affection.

Damn them all.

He closed his eyes, assailed by a sudden wave of vertigo, as if he were on the edge of a great black cliff, and he clutched at the edges of the divan for support. He was going to die. They were all intriguing against him, and he was helpless.

He started to weep, hot tears streaking down his cheeks into his beard. Life was so unfair.

Even the wine would not help him tonight. He needed a distraction. "Abbas!"

His Kislar Aghasi stepped forward, bowing low in sala'am. Ugly brute, Selim thought. Why would Hürrem have insisted he be transferred to his service on her death? Perhaps he was a spy. Perhaps he should have the old eunuch's head decorating a sharpened spike. He would think about it.

"My Lord," Abbas murmured.

"I need some distractions, Kislar Aghasi."

"What does my Lord wish?"

"Bring on the herd," Selim said. "The bull is pawing the ground."

"As you wish, my Lord," the Kislar Aghasi answered. "As you wish."

Angora

THE OIL LAMPS had been lit in the prince's campaign tent, and his officers crowded in side by side with Turkoman and Kurdish bandits to stare at the scrolls of paper he had unfolded on the carpet at their boots.

"Süleyman has ordered Prince Barley Pudding . . ." a grunt of derisive laughter from the others for this, the nickname they had all given shahzade Selim ". . . to take his army and his household to Konia, to protect the land route to Aleppo and Syria. From us, I assume. Be that as it may, we have no quarrel with Süleyman." Bayezid looked around the hard, bearded faces in the tent. "Our quarrel is with Selim. We will ride south to confront him at Konia."

"He will run," someone suggested.

"Yes, my brother would like to run. But my father has sent him a back-bone, in the form of a yeniçeri regiment and thirty cannon. It may be a harder fight than we expected."

"Thirty cannon will not stop us," a voice said.

"The cannon are not important, nor the yeniçeris. It is not they who must be defeated." Bayezid looked at every face in the room, and when they looked back into his eyes, none of them doubted. "Selim is impor-tant. With Selim dead, the battle is won." He pointed to the map at his feet. "We will draw up our army here, on the plain and wait. Sokolli will be our adversary in battle, not Selim. He has orders to keep us apart, not to attack. So he will draw up his cannon in a defensive posture. We will give him the charge he expects, and keep him occupied. Meanwhile we will leave a cavalry squadron here in the hills to the west. It will be small enough to pass unnoticed; a tiny dart just big enough to cut the vein in Prince Barley Pudding's neck. When he is dead we can break off the attack. Our work will be done. There will be no other successor to the Kanuni."

His eyes flamed with conviction, and every face in the tent reflected his belief.

Manisa

THERE WERE FOUR dozen girls, all naked. They were the most beautiful girls in the Empire, none older than twenty, some as young as twelve, purchased by the sançak beys of the outlying provinces or by Selim's special procurators attending the market at the Place of the Burned Pillar. Since the Sultan no longer required new flesh for the royal Harem, the most select were provided for his sons.

Selim reeled into the hall, staggering from the effects of the wine, and grinned.

They were all on all fours, their long braided hair falling around their faces to the ground, their breasts swaying beneath them as they moved about the thick rugs, a moving herd of skins, coffee, alabaster, and olive. Abbas, the Kislar Aghasi, snapped a short oxhide whip in the air above their heads, like a cattle master, to keep them moving.

The faces of the eunuch pages shone in the torchlight, their eyes averted to a point high on the walls.

Selim roared like a bull and started to strip off his clothes.

The Kislar Aghasi stepped back, clutching the thong of the whip as Selim plunged in among the girls. Selim caught the back of the nearest girl, and tried to mount her. The eunuch saw her grimace in pain.

Selim roared again, and laughed. Finally he was inside her. He began to thrust against her violently. Then he pushed her away and crawled away, on all fours, after another girl, his belly sagging on to the ground. He caught another girl, a fair-haired Armenian, by the hips and she wriggled in sudden distress.

No, don't do that, the eunuch thought. He'll have you killed if you resist.

But Selim was too drunk to notice. He mounted her, his thick fingers cupping her breasts and squeezing viciously. The girl screamed and Selim laughed, excited. He roared again and with a final thrust of his hips, he released her.

He clapped his hands and one of the pages threaded his way through the girls with a cup of wine. Selim drained it in one draft and returned to his work.

He mounted another of the girls, gripping her braided hair as if they were the reins of a horse. "Damn you, Bayezid! See, I shall impregnate a whole herd of women and my sons shall swarm over the throne like ants over a corpse!"

He released the girl and scuttled after another, but now the wine had begun to slow him and he slumped forward onto his face. Laughing, he struggled to his knees once more. The girls had begun to cower away from him along the walls, but Abbas cracked his whip above their heads to force them back into the center of the room.

Selim grunted and made after the nearest one. He caught her leg, but she wriggled free and he toppled over and lay on his back, breathing hard, his chest heaving, his belly white and obscene, dwarfing his genitals. He had already lost his erection, Abbas noted with grim satisfaction.

Selim made an attempt to rise, but his head fell back onto the carpets. He laughed again, then his eyes closed. "Damn you, Bayezid!" Within seconds he was snoring.

Abbas clapped his hands and the girls immediately fled from the room. He clapped his hands again and four pages lifted the sleeping shahzade from the floor and carried him into his bedchamber. They grunted with relief when the job was done.

The prince of the Osmanlis, first son of the Magnificent, the pretender to the throne of the greatest Empire on earth, son of God's Shadow Upon the Earth, turned over and vomited copiously upon the crimson silken sheets.

103

Konia

THE DERVISHES HAD been fasting and praying for a month. Now, drunk with opium, faces ghost-white with talcum, they filed into the courtyard. The musicians had already formed a circle, seated cross-legged on the hard stone. The flutes began to play, their soft wailing drifting upward as a sliver of moon rose behind the dome of the türbesi. The torchlight threw long shadows on the walls of the monastery.

The flutes began to play faster, and the drummers joined in, quickening the rhythm of the heart as the dancers began to spin, their long skirts fanning out around their legs. The drummers started their chant, saying prayers for the great ones.

The rhythm of the drums and cymbals increased, and the dancers' pleated skirts mushroomed outward. They inclined their heads to their right shoulders, their heavy, inflated garments giving off a low whistling moan, like the north wind in the mountains. Faster. Faster.

Bayezid felt his own heartbeat increase in rhythm with the quickening of the drums and the chanting of the mendicants and the wailing of the flutes. Still they whirled, faster and faster, until the faces of the dancers began to blur. But none of them staggered, none of them fell.

The music ended without warning. The dancers fell prostrate to the floor, their heads rolling on their shoulders, flecks of foam bubbling from their lips. They were in the trance.

Bayezid stepped into the circle and approached one of the dancers, a tall, thin monk with a white beard and a brown face as wrinkled and hard as a walnut. He was reputed to be one hundred and eleven years old.

"Holy Man, can you see?" he whispered.

His eyes were open, but the pupils were cold and glazed, like a dead fish. "I can see," the old man answered.

"You can see for the Osmanlis?"

"I can see."

"Tell me what you see for the sons of Süleyman."

"If the one who is not the son of Süleyman becomes king, I see only misery and corruption and stink."

Bayezid bent lower over the old man, trying to make out his words more clearly. The one who was not his son?

"What of Bayezid?"

"I do not see him."

"Who do you see?"

"I see a wind. A great wind that blows a curtain over everything. God's wind."

"What else?"

"There is nothing else. I see only the wind."

Bayezid rose to his feet, frowning with disgust. All these holy men only ever spoke in riddles. There was no answer for him here.

He went into the mosque and fell on his knees, and sought some resolution from God.

Topkapi Saraya

SÜLEYMAN STARED AT the black woman who knelt at the floor of the throne. The tight black curls were grizzled with gray but her eyes, he noticed, had lost none of their malevolence. For thirty-five years she had been no more than Hürrem's slave, hardly worthy of his attention. Now she had been summoned to his presence by his express command, and he was terrified of her. For Muomi alone might possess the opiate for his grief.

He leaned forward. "How long were you the Lady Hürrem's handmaiden?" he asked her.

"Ever since she became gözde, my Lord."

"You knew her intimately?"

"Yes, my Lord."

"I wish then, to speak of intimate matters," Süleyman said. "There is no reason to fear," he added, indicating the eunuchs who stood guard around the room. "They are all deaf-mutes. They can understand nothing. Now you must answer me truthfully, for I am your Sultan, and your allegiance is to me, not the Lady Hürrem. She rests now, and is beyond mortal retribution."

"Yes, my Lord."

"I want you to think back, to your first years of service. Do you remember a man called Ibrahim, who was my Vizier for many years?"

"I remember, my Lord."

Süleyman hesitated, and leaned even closer to the kneeling figure, so that he was perched on the very edge of the throne. "Was it possible . . . that the Lady Hürrem ever received him in the Eski Saraya?"

For the first time since she had entered the audience chamber, Muomi raised her eyes. She stared back at Süleyman, but not in fear, as he had expected. There was something else there, something he could not divine.

"She received him once, my Lord."

He could not breathe.

"How?" he said finally.

"A bribe to the Kislar Aghasi, my Lord, the Captain of the Girls, before Abbas. The Lady Hürrem swore me to secrecy. She said I would die if I ever whispered a word of it."

She is lying, Süleyman thought. It is plainly written on her face that she is lying.

She must be lying.

She must be.

A lie, a lie, a lie.

"NO!" he screamed at her. He leaped from the throne and his hand whipped out from his side and smashed into her cheek. Muomi fell back, dazed, her hand at the smudge of crimson at her lip.

"Bostanji!" Süleyman screamed and he signaled to the deaf-mute who stood in attendance, waiting. The man stepped forward and drew the yataghan from his belt. With one savage movement he scythed Muomi's head from her shoulders. A fine pattern of blood sprayed over Süleyman's yellow leather boots.

It was a lie.

It had to be.

104

Konia

WIND.

The pennons ripped back from the leveled lances, and tore at the robes of the waiting horsemen. Bayezid sat immobile on his horse, his face partially hidden behind the nasal of the conical silver helmet. When he drew the damascened sword from the scabbard at his saddle, thousands of other horsemen along the line behind him echoed his movement, the sound of steel rasping on the sharpened blades audible even over the howling of the hot desert wind.

Bayezid spurred his horse forward into a walk. The line of horsemen behind him followed.

Even at this distance Bayezid could see the black mouths of the cannon waiting for them on the other side of the plain. He did not fear them. They would remain mute. He was convinced of it.

"*Vvvvvt!*" Bayezid whispered to his horse, and it broke from its march into a canter.

The dust rose from thousands of hoofs, a long purple tail that rose from the plain like a banner, and followed them on. Bayezid heard the ululation of voices behind him as they gathered speed. It was always an exhilirating moment, Bayezid thought, this first moment of the charge, when the thunder of the horses drowned out every other sound, when the ground flashed by in a blur and it seemed that nothing could stand against the wall of charging steel lances and the muscle of the great Arab stallions.

He brought his sword over his head and held it in front of his body, the sliver of steel pointing to the still-silent mouths of the cannon. The line of horses broke into a charge.

And as he rode Bayezid wondered for the first time if the yeniçeris could really be made to fire on their favorite son.

SELIM HEARD THE drumming of the hoofs where he sat, even over the moan of the wind, and he felt the vibrations through the thick carpets strewn on the floor of his tent. He gripped the arms of the tortoiseshell throne as if a chasm had opened in the ground all around him.

He clapped his hands and Abbas hurried to his side with the jug of wine to refill his glass.

"Abbas? Where is Sokolli?"

"He is with the yeniçeris, my Lord," Abbas said.

Selim drained the glass, but his hand was shaking, and the wine spilled on his beard and down the front of his golden robe. Abbas quickly refilled it. The last servant who had been too slow to refill the shahzade's goblet had lost his hands at the wrist.

"What is happening?"

"Bayezid attacks with his cavalry, my Lord."

"Sokolli should be here, with me."

"With respect, it is better he is with the gunners, my Lord. Someone must direct them."

Selim would have punished him for his insolence but he was too frightened to trust his voice. He needed badly to defecate. He drained his glass and rushed out of the tent.

THE HORSES HAD sensed the coming storm, and now they were restless. They shook their tasseled heads, and stamped their hoofs. "Sssssss," Murad said, stroking his horse's mane. "Sssssss!"

He rode to the crest of the gully, and anxiously scanned the sky to the south. The line between the ground and the sky had disappeared. A purple curtain had descended across the earth, and some unseen hand was dragging it across the dusty steppe toward them. He watched it sweep across the Mevlevi monastery on the crown of the hill that overlooked Konia, as if the dervishes themselves had summoned it by their will.

"Dust storm!"

"God's wind," Murad said. "It is heading straight for our cavalry. In a few minutes they will be blind." He drew his killiç from his belt. It was time. There were two dozen riders waiting in the gully below. He wheeled his horse to face them.

"Now!" he barked.

MUHAMMAD SOKOLLI HAD expected trouble.

He had brought with him from Stamboul a hand-picked squadron of yeniçeris and solak guardsmen. They were veterans of the campaigns in Persia with Süleyman; a handful of them had served as young men at Mohaçs. They were loyal to the Sultan, and they would not disobey. He had taken the precaution of deploying them in a line behind the artillery.

Now as he watched Bayezid's hordes charging toward them, he thanked God for the gift of wisdom.

There were two banners of cloud drifting toward their position: the cavalry from the front, the desert storm behind. He wondered which would arrive first.

"When I give the order, you will fire!" he screamed over the rushing of the wind.

The yeniçeris at the guns looked at each other, then at the advancing cavalry, and waited for a voice. Finally one of them found his courage. "We cannot fire on the shahzade," he said.

The horses came on.

"He is not the shahzade," Sokolli shouted at the trooper. "Selim is the rightful and chosen son of Süleyman! Prepare to fire!"

They hesitated. None of them bent to the pyramid of musket balls that stood at the feet of their cannon pieces. "Long live Bayezid!" someone shouted.

Sokolli could see Bayezid now, his green kaftan—a clever choice, Sokolli thought, the color of Muhammad—flapping around his knees. The ground began to shake beneath his feet, with the pounding of the hoofs.

Sokolli drew his sword, and turned to the squadron of yeniçeris now waiting in line behind the artillery pieces. "Prepare to fire," he barked. They rested their harquebuses on the forked sticks in their left hands, and aimed at the gunners in front of them.

Sokolli turned back to the artillerymen. "Fire, or I will give the order to shoot you," Sokolli said.

Still, they hesitated.

"Aim . . ." Sokolli said. Their nerve is going to hold, he thought. They will force me to fire on them.

The cavalry were close now, very close.

Suddenly one of the men picked up a cannon ball and heaved it into the mouth of his cannon. One by one, the others grudgingly followed.

"Light the fuses," Sokolli said.

The mouths of the cannon were lowered, gaping hungrily at the onrushing feast.

AT THE MOMENT when Bayezid had convinced himself that the guns would not fire, he saw the first tiny orange blossoms of flame flower along the line of the artillery, a pretty sight if you did not know what they were. Then he heard the howl of the shot in the air, and the earth erupted all around him. It was as if God himself had taken a scythe and hurled it with all his force along their ranks. Suddenly Bayezid was alone.

They were gone! Almost every man who had ridden with him in the first wave was gone. He rushed past a horse, wide-eyed with terror and agony, trying to rise to its feet, dripping blood from its severed foreleg. Its rider lay in a dusty heap beside it.

He turned around in the saddle. The plain was littered with little mounds, horses and men, some writhing, others still where they lay. The second wave came on. The ground erupted again, and for a moment they were lost behind a wall of flame and dirt.

Just a handful rode out of the cloud.

A third wave, a fourth.

They had to keep coming. He turned back and urged them on.

He heard the clang of crossbow bolts and musket balls on armor, the hiss and rattle of arrows. The ground erupted again, more horses were scythed away from beneath their riders.

Bayezid raised his sword and rose from the saddle so they could see him. "On, on!"

Another wave came on, and another. His ragged army of bandits and horsemen did not waver. He realized that while the new Mustapha sat in his saddle, they were ready to die.

They would do it! Bayezid decided. Despite Sokolli's cannon, they would do it!

BY THE TIME they reached Selim's camp, the storm had already rolled over it, obscuring the horsetails standard outside the shahzade's tent. Murad urged them on. They galloped through the camp, scything down the few guards who opposed them.

Then God's wind obliterated everything.

Murad could barely make out the ground a few yards ahead of him, as his horse twisted between the rows of tents. Suddenly he reined in his horse, confused. He twisted in the saddle, searching desperately for a glimpse of the standard.

"Where is he?" he screamed.

He could hear the rest of the raiding party, hear the hammering of the horses' hoofs, but all sight of them was lost in the stinging barrage of sand. He raised his arm to protect his face, and did not see the man who ran from one of the tents and swung his sword in a scything arc that severed the hamstrings in his mount's right foreleg. The horse bucked and screamed in agony and crashed onto its flank.

The horse fell heavily, trapping him, jarring the killiç from his fist and winding him. He gasped, and looked around desperately for his attacker. He glimpsed the blue jacket and gray cap of a yeniçeri, his sword raised. Murad fumbled for the spear at its sheath on the horse's saddle. He aimed, instinctively.

The practice in the çerit had served him well. The spear took the trooper through the center of the chest. He fell back, choking and kicking.

The crippled Arab was scrabbling at the dust, trying to regain its feet. For a moment his leg was free and he scrambled clear. He crawled to the dying yeniçeri and pulled the killiç from his fist. Gasping at the agony in his ankle, he pulled himself to his feet and limped away, lost now, blinded by the storm.

MURAD HEARD WOMEN's screams. The dust cleared for a moment, and away to his left he saw veiled figures running from a silken pavilion, darting in between the prancing horses and the silhouettes of fighting men. The rest of the squadron must have found Selim's harem, he thought. That meant Prince Barley Pudding could not be far away. He limped toward them, but then the dust closed around him again, and the running figures melted away into the purple shadows and were gone.

He suddenly found himself standing in front of a silken pavilion. He recognized the horsetail standard: Selim! But where were the guards? He realized they must have been lured away by the battle he had witnessed taking place before the tent of the women. With a shout of triumph he tore open the flaps of the pavilion and went inside, dragging his injured leg behind him.

I will not fail you, Bayezid, my Lord, he thought. You will be Sultan. I shall make sure of that in these next few moments.

He came face to face with an enormous black man. He wore a kaftan of flowered silk, fawn and pistachio and bright blue, and over the top, a pelisse lined with sable. There were pointed ship-ship on his feet, decorated with rosettes of emeralds, and a ruby glinted in the lobe of his right ear. But for all the beauty of his dress, Murad decided he was the most ugly creature he had ever seen in his life. His face had been scarred so badly by a sword blow that only one good eye remained, and he was obscenely fat, even for a eunuch. He gaped at Murad in surprise, then he fell prostrate on the floor in front of him.

"Please don't hurt me," he howled. "I am just a harmless page."

Murad snorted in disgust and burst through the silk curtain to the inner sanctum. Selim lay sprawled horribly on his belly, his arms and legs spread-eagled. Murad leaned his weight on his sword and rolled him over with his uninjured foot, expecting to see him split open, like the over ripe peach that he was.

He heard the rustle of silk as the eunuch followed him. "Is he dead?" Murad said.

"No, he is not dead, my Lord, only drunk. He fainted as soon as he heard the first cannon discharge."

"Then he is fortunate. He will not feel my sword tickle his ribs."

Murad raised his killiç for the death blow. Suddenly he felt as if every muscle, every nerve in his whole body had been numbed. He could not breathe. He heard the killiç drop onto the carpet, though he could not feel it slip from his fingers. He did not understand what was happening. He felt himself falling.

He lay on his back and stared at the eunuch. Abbas stared back at him. There was a jewel-handled dagger in his right hand and blood smeared on the blade.

"I am sorry," Abbas said to him, "but I am going to see that these Turks live to regret what they did to me."

But Murad could not hear him. And if he had, he could not have understood.

BAYEZID TURNED HIS horse away from the whipping blast of sand and rode back across the plain, his stallion picking its way through the humps of bleeding, moaning flesh, horses and men together. He had no idea how many they had lost, where the rest of his army had gone. The charge had been blown away by the wind and the cannon.

Even Sokolli's artillery was silent now. There was only the howling of the wind and the groans of the dying. A horse nuzzled a fallen rider; a fallen Kurd tried to crawl toward it, both his legs shot away, leaving a trail of gore in the dust. Bayezid jumped from his horse and with one movement administered the merciful blow, sending the man to peace and to Paradise.

They were defeated. Their charge had been halted by a barrage of sand and grapeshot. It was God's wind, and God's Will.

105

Topkapi Saraya

SÜLEYMAN WAS PROPPED on a divan in the Çinili Kösk, gazing out over the gardens. The Judas trees were in blossom along the Bosphorus, and the bay of Yenikapi bobbed with caïques piled high with eggplants, cucumbers, and melons ferried over from the Asian shore.

Summer. A time of plenty, a time of war.

"There is no answer to my letter?"

"No, my Lord," Rüstem said. "Yet it means nothing, it itself. Selim may have intercepted his chaush."

"Or there may have been no chaush. Perhaps he still defies me." Süleyman studied his Vizier. He looked desperately ill. His face and body were bloated beyond recognition and there were red streaks through the cool, gray eyes. He is in pain, Süleyman thought.

"What other news, Rüstem?"

"He gathers his troops again at Amasya."

"Then it is decided. The ambassadors from the Shah and Ferdinand are at court. Treat with them. We must not be diverted while there is business in our own house to be completed."

"Why do we draw our sword against him, my Lord? Is it wise?"

Süleyman leaned forward, his forehead creased into a frown. "Rüstem, you surprise me. Suddenly at this stage of your life you embrace a cause? I have trusted you all these years because your heart knew no emotion. Now you plead Bayezid's case for him? Are you in his employ now?"

"My Lord, I mean no offense. I am merely curious."

"Speak then."

"It is just that I do not understand," Rüstem said, and he heard a voice in his head screaming: Shut up! Why do you speak for Bayezid? He is no friend of yours! If he ever came to the throne his first act would be to exile you to Diyarbakir!

Be still!

"What is it you do not understand?" Süleyman said.

"The logic of it. Why must we destroy Bayezid? Mustapha, of course, went too far. He was a threat. But if we crush Bayezid, then the throne falls to Selim. And Selim . . ." He spread his hands in a gesture of despair.

"You are my Vizier, and yet one of my kullar. You are to do my bidding."

"And yet," Rüstem persisted, "what is his offense? Your own father, the Yavuz Sultan, was not shahzade, yet by his own strength of arms he secured the throne for himself, and for you. Would you wish this great Empire to be entrusted to a weakling? Did Selim gain the victory at Konia? No, by the ninety-nine holy names, he did not! It was the wind of the dervishes and the cannon of Muhammad Sokolli. Selim is not worthy. It makes no sense."

What djinn possessed me to speak so freely? Rüstem thought, as he looked up into his Sultan's face and saw the dark flush of anger there. Is it because you have had your way without intriguing for it yourself? You know he will not change his mind. He never does, once it is set. Why provoke him like this? A lifetime you have kept your thoughts to yourself. Why expose yourself to risk now?

For one blind, panicked moment he thought Süleyman was about to summon his bostanji and have him executed. But instead, he said softly: "I have decided that Bayezid is not worthy. Selim is my firstborn. Enough."

Rüstem bowed his head in defeat. He struggled to his feet and limped out of the chamber, cursing himself for a fool. What madness had urged him to say such things, with victory in his grasp.

In his mind he turned the pages of his personal inventory; eight hundred and fifteen farms, seventeen hundred slaves, eight thousand turbans, six hundred illuminated copies of the Qur'ān, two million ducats . . .

He had clearly won the game. He had played with cunning and determination all his life and now he had become the richest man in the Empire, save the Sultan. Richer and more powerful than even Ibrahim had been. By law it would all return to the Sultan on his death, but with the practical reforms he had instigated, he expected that his wealth would be handed down to his own sons, in the manner of a Sultan.

Yes, he had proved himself master of the game, the finest of the kullar and the foremost of all the viziers. The final bookkeeping of his life vindicated everything and demonstrated his worth.

He waited for the sense of elation to overtake him but now, with death beckoning him with one crooked finger, he struggled with the lingering sensation that perhaps there was something he had missed.

THE GREAT DRUM in the court of the yeniçeris had not sounded for many years. It sounded now, its echoes reverberating from the walls of the Palace, its rhythm hastening the last-minute preparations of the soldiers. Süleyman mounted his horse by the fountain in the Third Court, wincing against the gout in his knees, and led his army out.

The silent runners jogged beside his stirrup; the plumes of his solak guardsmen bobbed behind him. The army crossed the Bosphorus at Üsküdar, wound through the cypress groves at Çamlica, past the heavily laden wheat carts, the dry wind eddying across the dusty roads.

He tried to shut his mind to the rigors of the journey that lay ahead of him. At least twenty-five days of hard riding to reach the fortress at Amasya. A long campaign in the dust and heat of Anatolia, hunting down his own son like a wild boar. Civil war, he thought. I wanted to build, and instead I must help my children tear it apart.

I am too old for this. Truly, my old flesh already protests at the thought of these endless days in this saddle of creaking leather, each bone-jarring step of my horse, and the burning of the hot sun on my skin. I am too old for this now. Yet there is no choice.

As they rode, Süleyman wondered what had happened to his dream to abolish the army as an instrument of peace. It seemed now that that was all it was, a dream. The yeniçeris, the Spahis of the Porte, the cannon: these were the only symbols men understood.

He would not allow the Osmanli line to be broken; if Bayezid would not bend to his will, then he must be made to submit.

106

Armenia

FROM ERZERUM THE Anatolian plateau crumpled into a volcanic upheaval of soaring snow-capped peaks and plunging valleys. The villages here were made from red mud, the women uncovered and wearing skirts and baggy trousers, their headscarves threaded with glitter.

As they reached the high passes, the gray clouds enveloped them. The paths snaked along the sides of the gorges, the scree crumbling beneath the horses' hoofs, the rock walls polished by centuries of animals hugging them to keep away from the vertical drops.

The wind tore at their hair, a living force that sometimes threatened to dislodge men from the saddle. The black rocks rose in sharp teeth, eroded by centuries of wind and rain and ice, deserted except for the occasional lumbering figure of a brown bear.

They were more a part of the sky than the land. Bayezid felt that he only had to reach from his saddle to touch the scudding gray clouds above his head. The trickle of a stream dribbled over a few stones, then dropped over a sheer cliff toward a valley panorama of ocher and straw that seemed so far below them that it was as if they were perched on the edge of a chasm. Above the mountain, rock paled to white, like exposed bone.

A falcon wheeled and hovered above their heads. Its cry pierced the rushing of the wind, lonely and sad.

The surface of the tarn was black and crusted with ice. Bayezid slid from his horse and knelt beside the stream that trickled from the lip of the pool and refilled the water bottles. They had been riding all day, up the high passes from Lake Wan, now a steel-gray mirror far behind them; they were deep inside Armenia now.

Ranged along the slope were the shuffling remnants of the great army that had once stood on the plain at Konia. Now there were just a few thousand left, most of them bleeding, their horses lame and saddle-sore. Men sat hunched beside their horses nursing their wounds and the shame of defeat. He knew there would be countless other groups like theirs scattered through the mountains. Many of the Turkomans and Kurds had already melted away, back to their villages and hamlets, to tend their sheep and angoras and horses.

They had known the campaign was lost, ever since Amasya. It was there that Bayezid had said farewell to his wives, bringing his four young sons with him first aboard the heavy wagons, then on horseback, guarded day and night by his personal guards. The past months were a jumbled memory of battles and skirmishes, fought on the run. They were no match for Süleyman's army. As soon as his father had taken the field against him, he had known the immediate cause was lost.

But he had never uttered words of surrender or defeat; with him, on the camels and horses, he carried the treasure he would need to equip a fresh army. His sons would one day be the seed of a new sultanate. While he and they still lived, Selim could never rest. While they still lived he was not truly beaten.

If they could find some way to survive. Whatever happened, he vowed he would not throw himself on his father's mercy now; in the past he had displayed precious little of that particular emotion. Especially to those he had purported to love.

He wondered what had happened to the chaush he had sent to Stamboul after the battle at Konia, reaffirming his case, and his loyalty to Süleyman. Perhaps Selim's soldiers had intercepted him and killed him; perhaps his father had chosen to ignore his entreaties. He would never know, and it did not matter now. Too late for that.

The shepherd's hut had been built on the edge of the ridge, overlooking the valley; a trick of the eye made it appear as if it were floating among the mountains, the red stone stark against the moss green of the mountainside beyond.

Bayezid turned to his lieutenant.

"We will camp here for tonight. We will make our headquarters in the hut there."

"Yes, my Lord," the man said and hurried away to relay the order. Bayezid stepped inside the hut.

It had been abandoned for the imminent winter. It was simple and spartan, four stone walls with no shutters on the windows and no door. The floor was bare earth and the smell of animals was strong. A long way from the Palace at the Topkapi, Bayezid thought. Perhaps this time so far that I may never get back.

A rainbow arced across the valley, a bolt of sunlight tracing the oncoming shower of rain through a rent in the clouds. The light had turned a sulphurous green, and a chill wind stirred the grasses, bringing with it sudden, stinging rain.

Thunder echoed around the high passes, and a black anvil of cloud massed over the mountains, gathering its force, preparing to sweep down on the valley.

The gathering gloom mirrored his spirits. He would not surrender to his father, but he knew his band of rebels and timariots and horsemen could not continue the fight against Süleyman's cannon and the iron discipline of his yeniçeris much longer. The sense of desperation had settled upon all of them. It seemed just a question of time now.

THE TENTS WERE sodden, freezing rain dripping from the canvas, soaking into clothes and boots, seeping into everything, even after the storm had passed. The mist clung to the sides of the valley and drifted through the ragged camp like the malevolent ghosts of the mountains. Horses stamped and snorted against the dawn chill, the only other sound the cries of the wounded. Men moved through the camp silent and slow as wraiths.

Bayezid ate without appetite. They subsisted now on campaign provisions, yoghurt, laced with raw onions and salt, diluted with cold water, eaten with a little pita bread. His lieutenant built a small fire inside the hut to warm them. A jackal coughed and cried somewhere higher up the mountain.

Suddenly Bayezid heard shouts from the camp below and he jumped to his feet, thinking that Süleyman's akinji had found them. But the rider who had appeared suddenly on the ridge overlooking the camp had come alone, from the east, dressed in Persian armor. Bayezid's battered army rose from the ground and stood and glared back at him as he rode past them. They would not let an enemy see them with their heads bowed, especially not a Sufavid.

He was disarmed by two of Bayezid's personal guards and led through the scowling ranks of Turks to Bayezid's tent. Bayezid was waiting for him, sitting cross-legged on a silken carpet that had been spread on the floor of the hut.

The rider executed a formal sala'am. "I bring a message from the Shah Tamasp," the man said.

Bayezid nodded and his lieutenant took the letter from the courier and brought it to him. He read it quickly.

"So he offers us sanctuary?"

"Süleyman has never been a friend to Persia," the courier said. "When Sultan Bayezid ascends the throne, the Shah hopes to find an ally at the Sublime Porte at last."

The wind gusted through the valley, and gave an eerie moan as it gusted through the open windows of the yali. Ascend the throne! Bayezid thought. For now, survival would be enough. A chance to draw breath without my father's cavalry constantly sniping at my heels. Look at us. Cold and dispirited and defeated at every fight since Konia. What choice do I have?

"You will wait while I consider my reply," Bayezid said, but as the man was led away he already knew what that reply would be.

SÜLEYMAN LOOKED UP at the mountains, the green turf giving way to the purple and slate-blue of the scree slopes, and the patchy snow around the high crags. A gray, heavy band of cloud hung over the peaks and the passes, weeping rain.

"He has gone," Sokolli murmured. "He has crossed the border into Persia."

"The Shah?"

"He offered him sanctuary. My spies say he has taken a hundred of his men with him. The rest have dispersed into small bands through the mountains, back to their villages. They will not trouble us again."

"Let the army know," Süleyman said.

Bayezid, you fool! Süleyman thought. While you remained here in the Empire you yet had a chance. Did you not realize that my army was on the verge of revolt? Whole regiments of yeniçeris are refusing to march against you, squadrons of spahis trot off into the mountains and return three days later with their horses fresh and not a drop of blood on their lances. Only the akinji still fight, eager for any blood, they never care whose. If you had defied me one more month I could not have induced them to come back after this winter. They loved you. They loved the way you charged into the face of their guns at Konia, though none of them would have aimed his weapon at you. They loved the way you continued to fight even when I brought my army against you. They love you because they detest Selim and they think I am too old.

But now you have crossed the border and nothing can save you now. You ceased to be an Osmanli when you accepted the sanctuary of the Persian. When you left Turkish soil you turned your back on your heritage.

Yet you almost won.

Even I doubted. For these last days I had begun to suspect that Hürrem had lied. You fought so well, and so long. But now you have raised your true colors; no true Osmanli would have accepted sanctuary from a Sufavid.

You fool. Even your beloved yeniçeris will curse you now.

107

Amasya, 1561

SHE DID NOT perform her sala'am as he entered the room; she did not even look up. But then she is an old woman now; she is perhaps not as frightened of the consequences of offending me as she once was. I loved her so much for so long in my life, he thought. And now it is like meeting a stranger.

"My Lord," she said.

"It has been a long time."

"As you say, my Lord."

He sat down beside her on the divan. "Are you well, my Lady?"

Gülbehar stared at him for a long time, burning with the kind of hatred that only love and rejection can inspire. "As well as one can expect at this great age," she said. "And you, my Lord?"

"My legs swell and ache and I grow weary," Süleyman said.

"So what has brought you here, so far from the Porte?"

"You know what has brought me."

Gülbehar studied him, looking for some clue to his purpose. She fingered the pearl tespi in her lap. "Yes, I think I know," she said.

"I am to fetch my son from Persia."

"May he go with God."

"As you say, my Lady."

Time can be cruel, Süleyman thought. Look what it has done to you, my Gülbehar! Look what it has done to both of us. It has robbed you of your beauty and me of my dreams. In the end we had no more control of our destinies than leaves on the trees.

"I advised him to march against you," Gülbehar said. "He would not listen to me."

Süleyman was so surprised by her admission that he just stared at her.

"You do not believe me?"

Süleyman shook his head.

"After what you did to me? After what you did to my son? You still dare to come here?"

"I am still your Lord. You are still one of my kullar."

"Once I would have done anything you bid me, willingly. Later, I obeyed you because I was afraid. Now I do not care."

This was not what he had expected. He had come here—why? For reconciliation? For forgiveness? "I could order your execution at this very moment if I choose."

"Then do it."

Süleyman rose to his feet. There was a great blue and white Ming porcelain vase standing in the corner of the room. Süleyman drew the gold-handled killiç from its scabbard and smashed it with one blow. "I am your Lord!" he screamed at her.

"You are my son's murderer!"

"I gave him life! He turned against me! What did he expect that I should do?"

"He was innocent! You are a butcher just like your father!"

Süleyman screamed and raised the sword above his head. Gülbehar did not flinch. She looked him in the eyes and waited. The pearl tespi clicked through her fingers.

Just like your father.

The sword hung in the air for long seconds. Be done with it, a voice whispered to him. You are the Sultan. How dare she speak against you? She is only a slave, a concubine. How dare she question you, the Lord of Life, the King of Kings, the Possessor of Men's Necks? Do it. Do it.

He lowered the sword.

"Enough," he muttered. He threw the sword away, sent it spinning and clattering across the marble floor. He stormed out of the room. Gülbehar returned to her tespi as if he had never been there.

Shiraz, Persia

THERE WAS A nimbus around the moon.

Bayezid heard the clatter of hoofs on the cobblestones and hurried to the window. The rider jumped from his horse, leaving it in the care of one of the pages, steam rising from its breath and its heaving flanks. He shouted his password to the guard in the courtyard below and disappeared from sight through the gate below. Perhaps this was the news he had been waiting for. Perhaps . . .

He shivered in the fur pelisse and stared across the walls to the distant snow-capped Zagros Mountains, glinting in the moonlight, stark and alien and ice white. As if I had been exiled to the moon itself, he thought. Perhaps it would have been better I had died in my own country than to endure this estrangement any longer. So few of us left from that great army I led to Konia, and most of us scattered in citadels and palaces across Persia. Here I must spend my restless days with my sons, separated from my throne and my people by a rampart of mountains and the thousands of miles of distance between my father's heart and my own.

He remembered again what Gülbehar had said to him once: "It made no sense to kill my son. But he did it anyway. Be careful, Bayezid . . ."

That had been his mistake. He had expected that he would understand Süleyman's reasons, and he did not. But what else could he have done? Mustapha did nothing, and Süleyman had him killed. He acted like a true ghazi, and instead Süleyman had thrown the force of his arms behind his fat sot of a brother. How was it possible to understand such a man?

Yet he still could not believe his father would entrust the Empire to a drunkard and a debauchee such as his brother. That simply was not possible. This was a testing. He had had time now for more sober reflection, and he would see. He must.

He stared at the gardens below the walls. The apple and pear and cherry trees were bare and skeletal, the branches heavy with snow. The moon threw long shadows on the white garden.

A log crackled and broke in the grate. Perhaps the messenger would bring news of the winter's thaw . . .

Footsteps on the stone flags in the corridor outside, and the door was thrown open. Shah Tamasp . . .

The Shah entered, smiling. I don't like that smile, Bayezid thought; it is like the grinning of a jackal, and the corners of your beard are always wet, as if you are wetting your jaws. No, I don't want to trust you, but what choice do I have? Besides, you have shown me and my sons and my followers boundless generosity. Perhaps I should not judge you too harshly.

"I have good news for the young shahzade of the Osmanlis," the Shah announced.

"Your chaush has returned from Stamboul?" There had been so many messengers in the last few months—perhaps even more, he thought, than the Shah has told me. Perhaps now—at last—his father had relented on his terms. He felt a surge of hope.

"The chaush has indeed returned. A time and place has finally been agreed." He nodded. "Yes, Bayezid, he wants to meet with you."

Bayezid wanted to sink to the floor in relief. He had almost despaired of any reconciliation. He had begun to wonder if he and his sons must live the rest of their lives in exile.

"Where?"

"Tabriz," the Shah said. "He is coming there in secret. Everything is arranged."

"And Selim?"

"Selim knows nothing of the arrangement. Perhaps your father has reassessed his relationship with his sons. The Shadow of God Upon the Earth has perhaps discovered he is a mortal like the rest of us."

Bayezid wondered: has Selim finally stepped beyond even the generous limits that Süleyman had allowed him, or has he had a change of heart? He is my only hope. I cannot hope to go against Selim now, not without the support of the yeniçeris. If they did not help me at Konia, they will not help me now.

"May I see the letter?"

The Shah seemed to hesitate. "There was no letter. The message was entrusted to my chaush's memory."

You're lying, Bayezid thought. "It is unlike my father."

The Shah said nothing.

"Did he also commit to your chaush any intent of his purpose?"

"What else could it be but he wants a reconciliation with his ghazi?"

Unlike my father not to put his words under his tugra. The Shah is keeping something from me. But what choice do I have? If a meeting has been arranged, I must go.

"When?" Bayezid said.

"We leave tonight. We will wait for his arrival in the citadel at Tabriz."

Konia

THE SHAHZADE SELIM was just thirty-four years old, Abbas reminded himself. But he already looks like an old man. The great golden gown of silk that he wore did not disguise the grossness of his body. His face was bloated and florid so that his eyes peered from his head like two small black currants. No wonder he feared Bayezid so much. The yeniçeris would never follow this one into battle. Not Prince Barley Pudding.

Selim was slumped on a divan, picking desultorily at a large tray of halva on a silver table beside him. He selected three of the pastries from the tray and popped them into his mouth.

He regarded Abbas with a sulky expression. "You have news, Kislar Aghasi?"

"I do, my Lord," Abbas said. He wondered how he would react when he heard it. Even Abbas himself wondered what to make of it.

"From my father?"

"He has left Amasya and rides east."

Selim grunted and chose two more pieces of halva. The negotiations had dragged on for more than a year. It seemed the shahzade had proved to be worth much less than the Shah Tamasp had hoped. It had been whispered that he wanted Süleyman to return Mesopotamia in exchange for the young prince. Süleyman had refused.

"He looks sick, I hope?" Selim laughed, and a fine spray of saliva and half-chewed pastry glistened like frost on the carpet in front of Abbas's knees.

"The Lord of Life cannot spend as long in the saddle as he once did."

"Does he have his army with him?"

"No, my Lord," Abbas said. "My spies say he has a squadron each of solaks and spahis, and an oda of yeniçeris."

Selim clapped his hands. A page appeared instantly at his side, holding a pitcher of wine and a jeweled cup. Selim snatched the cup from him and held it out to be filled. He swallowed it in one draft and ran a sleeve across his mouth, the blood-red wine and golden halva matting into his beard.

The page refilled the cup and withdrew.

"For what purpose?"

"They say he goes to meet Bayezid at Tabriz. There are whispers of reconciliation."

Suddenly Selim was on his feet and the cup had spilled across the carpet. He stood with his fists clenched tight at his sides and uttered a piercing wail like a small animal impaled on a stick. Saliva leaked from the corners of his mouth and ran in tiny rivulets through his beard. He began to shake.

No one moved, not the pages, or the guards, or the pashas. Finally Selim fell back onto the divan.

Selim had bunched the corner of his robe into his fist. He stared at Abbas for a long time, his eyes seeming to be slightly out of focus.

"I have been betrayed," he said. Suddenly he jerked upright. "Wine! Where is my wine! You!" He pointed to the bostanji standing at attention beside his throne. The man sprang forward. Selim indicated the page holding the silver ewer of wine. "Chop off his head!"

The man did as he was bidden. Abbas silently withdrew, drawing no attention to himself. He had no interest in the spectacle. He had lived too long under the tyranny of princes.

108

Tabriz

MOONLIGHT RIPPLED LIKE burnished silver on the tiled domes of the Blue Mosque, burned like phosphorus on the chill waters of the Aji Chai River. Yellow light filtered from behind the shuttered windows of the citadel and the sound of flutes and drums carried on the still, cold air.

The music drowned out the ring of the horses' hoofs on the cobblestones in the courtyard below, and the strange and sibilant voices of the latecomers. They slipped from their horses and disappeared into the shadows, the guards' eyes glittering with fear and contempt.

In the great hall torchlight reflected from the brass censers that hung on long chains from the ceiling. Slave girls in gaudy silk and gossamer danced while the guests selected morsels from the silver plates arranged on the carpets in front of them, spiced lamb and kid, scented rice, and roasted fowls. In the center of the room sat the Shah and his guest of honor, Bayezid.

Bayezid ate without appetite, his mind occupied with the future.

Süleyman had finally agreed to come here and talk of reconciliation. What else can he do? Bayezid thought. Without me, the only survivor of the Osmanli line is Selim, and he is no choice at all. He has to negotiate. "Süleyman regrets what he has done to you," the Shah had told him. "Perhaps I can mediate between you. It is not too late. I will help you now, and when you are Sultan, Persia and the Osmanlis will be allies." I will agree to stay my hand, stay in the east until his death and risk Selim arriving in Stamboul before me. It will not matter. The yeniçeris will never support him over me.

The delegation was due early tomorrow. Bayezid was anxious to have the meeting done, to end his exile. Each day away from the Empire threatened his position with the yeniçeris. He had been impulsive, he could see that now. He must learn patience, and cunning. Time enough to see Selim's head on a pole.

Bayezid was aware of a cold draft on his back, realized that someone had entered the great doors at his back. Latecomers. He felt the short hairs on the back of his neck prickle with alarm.

The Shah had seated himself opposite Bayezid, facing the doors. He looked up for a moment, then returned to his meal.

"Who are our guests?" Bayezid asked him.

"They are expected," he said.

Then Bayezid heard it; it was a familiar sound, he had heard it many times in the palace at Topkapi and at Amasya, a panting, barking cough, like a dog trying to swallow a lump of gristle. The sound of a mute.

The sound of a bostanji.

The Shah smiled, with regret. "I am sorry," he said. "Your father insisted."

It was a poor bargain but the Shah had been forced, finally, to agree. Süleyman had offered him four hundred thousand gold pieces. The Shah's *mullahs* had urged intransigence. They still wanted Baghdad. Very well for them. They would have quickly disappeared into the mountains when Süleyman had marched his great armies on Shiraz.

Bayezid turned to him, his face twisted into a sneer of contempt. "You pledged me protection."

"It is what they call diplomacy in the Sublime Porte. You say what it is best to say at the time. I am truly sorry. It is a poor example of our hospitality. I wish it could have been another way."

Bayezid spun around. There were five of them. He recognized one of them. They said it was the man who had murdered Mustapha, the bostanji-bashi, the head gardener, a huge, ugly Sudanese. Each of them held in his great hands a loop of razor-thin silk.

Bayezid had brought just a dozen men with him from Shiraz; they had been posted in the courtyard. They must have been overpowered. The rest were still in the Shah's capital.

"What about the others?"

"I am afraid they are all dead."

Bayezid felt a flush of rage and his hand moved to the killiç at his belt, but the Shah already held his own jeweled dagger, and his bodyguards had moved in close behind him. Bayezid knew he was trapped. The armed guards at every entrance had seemed no more than token formality when he entered the hall. Now he realized they had also a very practical function. There was to be no reprieve this time.

He looked at his sons. They were watching him, expectantly. They were still too young to understand, too young to be afraid. God, help me in my sorrow! "Could you not have spared my boys?"

"Süleyman was quite specific in his demands," the Shah said.

"Then let Selim be his epitaph," Bayezid said. Suddenly the silken bowstring was around his neck and he was jerked backward over the eunuch's knee, choking. His hands clawed instinctively at his throat, but once the bostanji had the noose in place, there was no escape.

The children screamed. The oldest boy ran to help his father, shouting at the others to run, but the eunuchs caught them and bent to their work.

The Shah watched with a frown of disgust. He selected another sliver of lamb from the plate before him and proceeded to chew. Statesmanship was sometimes an indelicate business, but it had to be borne.

Bursa

A WOMAN WAS screaming in the courtyard below the window, her shrieks echoing around the walls like the wails of a djinn. The eunuch wished the guards would do something to keep her quiet.

Bayezid's youngest son was still only nine months old. He had been conceived before the battle of Konia, and his father had never seen him. He had been left behind here with his mother.

As the eunuch bent over the cot the child smiled up at him, put an arm around his neck and kissed him. The man's hands began to shake. He dropped the bowstring.

He went outside and gave the porter who had led the way up the steps two gold pieces and the silk bowstring. He waited. A few minutes later the man reappeared, and fled down the steps. The silk string fluttered onto the stones.

He went back inside. The child grinned at him.

"God help me in my sorrow," he murmured. He felt for the leather pouch at his waist. If he did not return with it filled, Süleyman would have him executed immediately.

He picked up the string and shut the door behind him. As he approached, the child giggled and held out his arms.

109

Konia

I T IS A long journey from Venice to Konia, in the middle of the Anatolian steppe, a long way from the Campanile and San Marco to the lonely Asian city, surrounded on the wide dusty plain by a few stone caravansaries and the black yurts of the nomads and a few wandering jackal. A long way from Venice and a lonely place to die.

They found Abbas in his cell.

He was slumped face down on the rug. A white cat was licking at the bloodstained handkerchief clutched in his left hand.

"Consumption," the physician muttered. Or perhaps poison, he thought. Perhaps death was infinitely preferable to being the Kislar Aghasi of the shahzade Selim. Or perhaps there were other reasons. Who could know? The less you knew, the better. Knowledge could be dangerous.

It took six pages to lift him and carry him out of the iron-studded door of the Harem and lift him onto the waiting cart. The physician remained behind to examine the room.

Abbas had been writing a letter. Quill and parchment lay on the low table beside the body. He glanced at it; the letter was unfinished. In fact he had only written the salutation.

"Dear Julia."

The Chief Eunuch writing to a girl? Perhaps it was his pet name for another of the black boys, he thought. Well, it did not matter now. He screwed it up and threw it in the fire.

Topkapi Saraya

AFTER THE WARDROBE page bowed and left him, after his final offering up of prayers, Süleyman was alone. He lay on his quilt listening to the sound of his own labored breathing, but sleep would not come. After a while, he got up and went to the latticed window, and watched the stars through the dark shadows of the cypress trees.

So it was decided. Selim would be next. If what Hürrem had told him was true, he had done his duty to the Osmanlis.

"But please tell me you lied," he said aloud.

"I was ill, I was dying," Hürrem said behind him. "How could you have believed it?"

"How could I be sure?"

"You loved me. How could you have doubted me?"

He stared at her. So beautiful, with her burnished-copper hair braided with glittering pearls, the green taplock pinned rakishly to her head.

"You said the child belonged to Ibrahim."

"My Lord, how can you believe that? Can you truly believe I deceived you for thirty-five years?"

Süleyman could not answer her.

"I would not have betrayed you that way," Ibrahim said. Süleyman turned toward him. Ibrahim, grinning in that arrogant, shout-at-the-Devil way of his. Ibrahim, swaggering with his thumbs in the sash at his waist, a livid raw wound around his throat.

"You had the opportunity," Süleyman said. "I loved you. I gave you my trust. I allowed you into the heart of my seraglio. You alone would have had the opportunity."

"She lied to you."

"Tell him!" he screamed at Hürrem. "Tell him what you told me!"

"I was sick," Hürrem said. "It was the Devil who spoke, not me."

Süleyman cried aloud and covered his ears. But it was Mustapha who spoke next. "I was the shahzade, Father. I did not betray you."

"The evidence against you was plain!"

Mustapha, as he remembered him the morning he came to his tent, the flowing white kaftan and silk turban, his beard neatly combed, proud, brave, his head held high in defiance. Mustapha, who had never lied to him. "It was *you* who betrayed *me!* You gave our Empire to Selim, a lecher and a drunkard. Is this your duty by the Osmanlis?"

"He is of my blood at least!"

"I loved you, my Lord," Hürrem said. "How could you have ever doubted that? Did you really believe Bayezid was not your son? I loved you!"

"Of course you loved me! I gave up my Harem for you! I made you queen! Of course you loved me! You must have loved me!"

"Then why did you murder our son?"

"Because I can never be sure!" Süleyman groaned, and he sunk to his knees. The black pages, deaf to his screams, watched him, terrified, but did not move from their posts at the door.

"Because I can never, ever be sure . . ." Süleyman sobbed.

And there could never, ever be any peace. Night closed around the place of silence, the paradise of marble and gardens and glittering stones, leaving the King of Kings, the Lord of Life, the Shadow of God on Earth to rail at the phantoms that had returned to taunt and torment him, and to writhe for five more years in Hell.

What men call empire is worldwide strife and ceaseless war
In all the world the only joy lies in a hermit's rest.

FROM A POEM WRITTEN BY
SULTAN SÜLEYMAN,
THE ONE THEY CALLED THE MAGNIFICENT,
DISCOVERED AFTER HIS DEATH IN 1566

EPILOGUE

Istanbul, 1990

THE SÜLEYMANIYE MOSQUE dominates the city of Istanbul, its minarets and massive dome towering over the harbor of the Golden Horn, dwarfing the mosque of Rüstem Pasha on the slopes below it. It is supported on massive columns of porphyry, granite, and white marble, its windows stained yellow and red, so that shafts of gold and blood angle across the rich crimson and cobalt carpets in the heat of the day. A mosque servant sometimes stands at the pulpit and recites the Qur'ān; he has dedicated his life to committing the whole book to memory. His mind is useless for anything else.

It is a memorial in stone to the man whom the Turkish people remember as the greatest of all the Ottoman Sultans. In the first three hundred years of the Empire, ten Sultans, culminating with Süleyman, built an Empire of thirty million people, encompassing twenty different languages, all of it won in battle from the saddle of a horse.

After Süleyman there were twenty-five more Sultans, an unbroken line of weaklings or degenerates who debauched themselves in their Harems, bled the Empire's finances with extravagance, or satiated their lusts with acts of unbridled cruelty to those unfortunate enough to fall under their power. The Osmanli tradition of soldiers and statesmen ceased with Selim II, the one they called the Sot.

Scholars have speculated that the line was broken. It can never be proved. It may simply have been the natural result of an excess of power, riches, and ease.

The answer perhaps lies buried in a quiet garden beside the great dome of the Süleymaniye mosque.

On this gray day a humid wind stirs the high branches of the plane trees. Doves fuss and warble on the high marble porticoes and in the wide courtyards. A mist of rain has started to fall.

The cemetery is at the southeast wall of the mosque. The gray headstones are fashioned in the shape of turbans, signifying the burial places of those who once held rank. They are overgrown with weeds. But inside the *türbeler,* the tomb of Süleyman, the air is sanctified with quiet. His tomb lies between two others. Turbans of rich crimson velvet have been placed over the draped mausoleums to identify the sarcophagi as belonging to men who were once Sultans of the Empire.

For five thousand Turkish lire, the *bekçi* will tell you about these men. "This is the tomb of Süleyman. In the West they call him the Magnificent; here he is known as the Kanuni Sultan, for the many kanuns, or laws, that he passed during his reign. He is recognized as the greatest of all the Sultans, for his great military victories, the magnificent buildings he created with his architect Sinan, for the great poetry and music of the age . . ." He recites the history lesson he gives to all the tourists, as if he were speaking of a member of his own family.

There is a smaller türbeler in a corner of the cemetery, with iron gates barring the entrance. The smell of the gentle rain mingles with the draft of must that seems to drift like vapor from inside.

A sign identifies it as the tomb of the Hasseki Hürrem, Süleyman's queen. I try the gates, but they are locked. I fetch the bekçi but he confesses to knowing little about her. It seems that now she sleeps alone. Her secrets remain with her inside her mausoleum.

A poster stuck on a board on the railing advertises the forthcoming festival at Konia. There will be performances by the dervishes and a çerit tournament. It is raining harder so I turn and make my way out of the cemetery.

It is getting late and there are few tourists today so the bekçi leaves also, locking the gate behind him. We leave the Sultan and his queen to their silence.

About the Author

COLIN FALCONER is the author of several historical novels, including *When We Were Gods,* a novel of Cleopatra, and *Feathered Serpent,* which have been published in many languages throughout the world. A former journalist and native of London, he now lives in Perth, Australia.